Never is not forever!

The One That Got Away

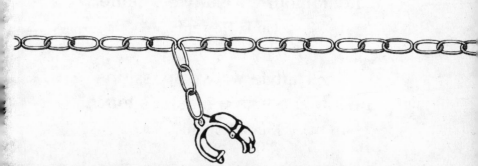

ELOISA
JAMES

"Her style is exquisite,
her prose pure magic."
Julia Quinn

"Romance writing
does not get much better."
People

CATHY
MAXWELL

"Her characters come alive on the page."
Columbus Dispatch

"Cathy Maxwell can't be beat."
Jill Barnett

VICTORIA
ALEXANDER
LIZ
CARLYLE
ELOISA
JAMES
CATHY
MAXWELL

*The One That
Got Away*

AVON BOOKS
An Imprint of HarperCollinsPublishers

AVON BOOKS
An Imprint of HarperCollins*Publishers*
10 East 53rd Street
New York, New York 10022-5299

ISBN: 0-7394-4722-x

CONTENTS

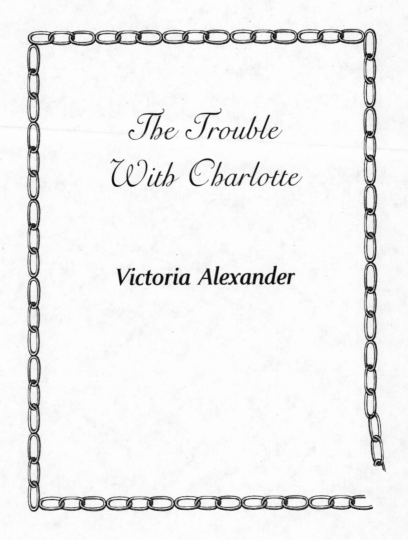

The Trouble
With Charlotte

Victoria Alexander

Prologue

Spring 1817

"And then, of course"—Reginald, Viscount Berkley slumped deeper in his favorite chair in the library at Pennington House, gazed morosely at his oldest friend in the world over the rim of his brandy glass, and heaved a heartfelt sigh—"she broke my heart."

"As all of your stories tend to end that way," Marcus, the Earl of Pennington said coolly, "do forgive me if I'm not surprised by the outcome of this one."

"I didn't expect you to be, although one does tend to hope. However." Reggie grinned. "That wasn't the point of it."

"I see. Then am I to assume there was a point?"

"There is always a point. At this particular moment I was attempting to help you feel better. Bloody decent of me, too, I'd say," Reggie added under his breath.

"Indeed it was, although somewhat unnecessary, as I do not feel especially distressed." Marcus sipped his brandy thoughtfully. "No, I rescind that. There was the potential for distress. Indeed, another day or two, perhaps a week, and I might well have been irrevocably involved."

Reggie raised a skeptical brow. "Love, Marcus?"

"I don't really know. Certainly there was affection, a genuine fondness, but as for love . . ." Marcus blew a resigned breath. "I admit, there might well have been the potential for that as well."

"How very interesting," Reggie murmured. "You have never, to my knowledge, been in love."

"Nor was I in love this time," Marcus said with a firm note in his voice.

"Yet."

Marcus paused. It was pointless to deny it. He had indeed been close to falling in love, saved only by the unforeseen circumstances of fate and misadventure. And remarkably poor timing. "Yet."

"It's been more than a month now and you have been annoyingly silent about it all." Reggie settled back in his chair and studied his friend. "It's past time you told me all the fascinating details."

"I did tell you."

"No, Marcus." Reggie shook his head. "You told me the barest bones of the story, which I allowed, as I was certain you were consumed by the throes of unrequited love."

Marcus snorted. "You thought that, did you?"

"No. I simply hoped." Reggie studied his friend. "The problem with men who never fall in love, old man, is that when they do, and inevitably they do, it may well be devastating."

"I am not devastated."

"But you could be."

"But I'm not."

"Then why haven't you told me all about it?"

"Blast it all, Reggie." Marcus glared at his friend. "I haven't told you because I feel like a complete and utter fool."

Reggie scoffed. "Nonsense. This was not precisely something that could have been predicted. Indeed the very thought would never have crossed anyone's mind."

"I suppose not." Marcus blew a long breath. "Still, somehow, I should have known."

"Don't be ridiculous. Now, tell me everything."

"Everything?" Marcus raised a brow.

"The pertinent points and any interesting details will do."

"You do realize that I don't know all the details of what occurred after my involvement ended."

"I suspect you can draw some conclusions with a fair amount of accuracy."

"I probably know most of it." In truth, Marcus knew far more than he really wished to know. Damn it all, he and the lady had become friends of a sort, and she'd felt compelled to tell him a great deal under the auspices of confession or atonement.

"We began seeing one another several months a—"

"Not that." Reggie waved off his words impatiently. "I know all that. I wish to know about the rest of it."

Marcus knew full well exactly what "the rest of it" meant.

"Very well then. It all began, or rather I should say it all ended, on the very afternoon I had planned on introducing the possibility, the subject as it were, to the woman known then as the widowed Charlotte Robb, of, well"—he winced in anticipation of the effect of this heretofore unknown information on his closest friend in the world—"marriage . . ."

Chapter 1

One month earlier . . .

It was past time she wed again. Everyone said so. Worse, she knew it herself.

Charlotte Robb, the widow of Captain Hugh Robb, who'd met his demise at the battle of Albuera six years ago this spring but who had, in truth, left her life long before his death, smiled with feigned interest at the gathering of friends in her salon and pretended to follow the ongoing debate over whether or not Keats was as brilliant as Shelley and if indeed Lord Byron should even be included in their company. The women were firmly in support of Lord Byron, as women generally tended to be. Still, it was a frivolous discussion, and Charlotte was rather grateful for that at the moment. She did love these gatherings, but today she was simply not in the mood for talk of a more serious nature than quibbling over the talents of poets. She had far too much on her mind.

It was an especially small group today, her guests only six in number. Her two dearest friends were in attendance, of course: Eunice, Lady Blackwell, and Isobel, Lady Hazelwood. All three women had been friends since their first season eight years ago, and all three now shared their respective widowhood. Eunice's state was not unexpected, as she'd wed a man more than twice her age. Indeed, the real surprise was that Lord Blackwell had lasted as long as he had, expiring a mere four years ago. While Eunice still swore she'd had genuine affection for him, her recovery from her grief at his passing had been relatively swift, helped, as she freely admitted, by the tidy fortune he'd left in her grateful hands.

Isobel was an entirely different story. She'd known her husband since childhood and had loved him nearly that long. When his death came three years ago, the result of a swift and unexpected illness, she was devastated. Without the support and love of her friends and family, the dear creature never would have survived at all. Fortunately, Isobel had a great number of relations and an equally large number of friends. Still, it was only in the past few months that Isobel had begun to show any interest at all in resuming her own life.

As for Charlotte, her own marriage had been a tempestuous mix of high passion and heady emotions and a disastrous error in judgment, on Hugh's part as well as her own. They'd been married, or rather had done battle, scarcely more than a year when Hugh had decided to remove himself from all responsibilities of wife and wedlock and had purchased a commission in the army. One might say, and Charlotte suspected many indeed did say, that he had been well prepared for war, given the state of their marriage. Even so, he had obviously not been prepared enough, as barely a year later he was dead. The deep, shocking sorrow she'd had at the news was mixed, even now, six long years later, with a fury she was hard-pressed to ignore or understand. Still, it was over and done with, and Isobel wasn't the only one who needed to get on with her own life.

At least one of the four gentlemen here today was an intriguing candidate for helping Charlotte do just that, and all present were those she included in her list of friends. There was Lord Warren, who was devilishly handsome, with far too much free time, money, and charm. Charlotte was probably only immune to him because she'd known him for much of her life and thought of him with the fondness one has for an unrepentant brother. Mr. Addison had become a friend as well in recent years. The man was a brilliant critic of art, in the process of making a rather distinguished name for himself and great fun to debate on almost any subject imaginable. Then there was Mr. Manning. The younger son of an earl, he fancied himself a writer of plays, although one had yet to be produced, or even, to Charlotte's knowledge, finished. Still, he was of clever character, financially sound, from a good family, and he'd been head over heels for Isobel since the moment he'd met her. Not that Isobel had noticed. Not yet.

And last, but certainly not least among their number, was the Earl of Pennington. Marcus Holcroft. Charlotte had met him at a party in the country, and they had continued their acquaintance upon their return to London. He was charming and witty, with a dry way of looking at the world that was most amusing. With every passing day Charlotte found his company more and more enjoyable. Indeed, she had recently admitted, if only to herself, that she might be somewhat taken with him and was fairly certain, given the look in his eyes whenever her gaze would meet his, that he might be taken with her as well. It could even be love, although Charlotte wasn't at all sure she would recognize love. Not real love.

She'd once thought she'd known real love, but with the clarity of years and distance, now wondered if what she'd had with Hugh had been nothing more than a concoction of forbidden lust and high passion stirred and flavored with the impulsiveness of youth and the lure of excitement. The fact that they'd wed at all was only due to the dishonorable circumstances they'd found themselves in. To give Hugh a modicum of credit, no one had known of their liaison and he could easily have escaped any responsibility. But he had insisted on marriage, and that alone had been enough to convince her of love on both their parts, although neither had ever said so aloud. Besides, her head had been too full of stars and romantic dreams about eternal devotion and fate and all sorts of other nonsense to realize that she and Hugh simply did not suit outside of a bedroom or a battlefield.

Hugh Robb had been a dreadful mistake, and all thought of him should be left firmly in the past. She was certainly ready to do so. Why, even the dreams of him that had haunted her nights for years, while not gone entirely, were more and more infrequent.

Lord Pennington, Marcus, could well be the best thing that had ever happened to her. Aside from his obvious charms—money, title, family—he was a very nice man. Beyond that, he had not expected more from her than she'd been willing, or perhaps ready, to provide. Considering the reputation she had carefully cultivated through the years of her widowhood, that was high praise indeed.

She suspected, given the offhand comments he had made and any number of other indications, that he was going to bring up the subject of marriage any day now. She had more or less decided that if he did not, she would. It was indeed past time.

". . . past time, too, if I am to turn myself from acceptably charming and rather delightful into a goddesslike creature that will make ladies green with envy and gentlemen swallow their tongues. Charlotte?"

"Yes?" Charlotte's gaze snapped to Eunice, sitting beside her, and she wondered what morsel of interest she might have missed.

"I asked if you were still planning on attending Lady Harvey's ball this evening?" Eunice's gaze slipped from Charlotte to Marcus and back. A knowing smile curved her lips. "Or do you have other plans?"

"Not at all, Eunice. My intentions for this evening include nothing more than attendance at Lady Harvey's." Charlotte couldn't resist a wicked smile. "At least at the moment."

"Excellent." Eunice laughed, then sobered, leaned closer, and lowered her voice. "If marriage is truly what you want, dearest, he is an excellent choice. If not, well, I think he's an excellent choice for that as well. Furthermore, if you don't want him . . ."

Charlotte laughed. Eunice had been encouraging her for years to be freer with her affections, Eunice herself being an example. She and Isobel were the only two people in the world who knew the true details about Charlotte's own amorous adventures.

"I shall see you tonight then." Eunice got to her feet, the gentlemen rising a bare beat behind her.

"Lady Blackwell, you will allow me to see you home, won't you?" Lord Warren flashed the rakish grin that was reputed to make grown women flutter their fans to dispense the heat.

"I would indeed, but Mr. Addison has already requested that honor." Eunice smiled at Lord Warren in such a way as to make the man feel he was more than likely her favorite escort in the world in spite of having just been rejected.

"Do try to be quicker next time, Warren." Mr. Addison looked altogether too, too smug. He should know better.

"I say, I have an excellent idea," Eunice said brightly. "As I have my carriage, why don't *I* see the two of *you* home?"

Mr. Addison sighed and exchanged a long-suffering look with Lord Warren, who grinned in return. It was not the first time Eunice had gotten the better of these two. She had, on occasion, shared the bed of each of them, and it was a testament to her charms or her skill or simply the joy of her nature that they continued to pursue her with the determination that they did.

"It seems then we are on our own, Lady Hazelwood." Mr. Manning cast Isobel a smile that tried valiantly to be confident but succeeded in merely looking hopeful. "If you would do me the honor—"

"I fear, Mr. Manning, I too have my carriage today. However," Isobel drew a deep breath and met the man's gaze directly, "I find myself in need of transport this evening. If you would be so kind as to escort me to Lady Harvey's I would be most appreciative."

Eunice raised a brow and traded glances with Charlotte. Isobel had never before taken such a step.

Mr. Manning's eyes widened slightly, and he nodded. "I should be delighted. Most delighted. Indeed, I will be most extraord—"

"He will be there," Lord Warren said firmly.

Isobel cast the obviously flustered Manning a brilliant smile, and Charlotte feared the poor man would melt into a small puddle at her feet at any moment. Still, that wouldn't be entirely bad. Not simply because Isobel could well use a man melting at her feet but more because, perhaps, at long last, she might just care about the melting. It was an excellent sign.

The company took its leave amidst a flurry of farewells and promises to seek out one another at tonight's gathering, which threatened, as always, to be a crush of immense proportions. It was one of the first big events of the new season, and everyone who had any sort of presence in society was expected to be there. Marcus lingered after the others, obviously to speak to her in private. That too was a very good sign.

"I was wondering if I might have a word," he started.

"You needn't leave yet," she said at precisely the same time.

They stared at each other, then laughed.

"I was hoping you would ask," he said, with the nicest smile.

"Watching Eunice manipulate Addison and Warren is like watching a fencing match between three people, only one of whom knows how to actually handle a sword, with the other two getting by on enthusiasm alone. It's really quite exhausting." She sank onto the sofa and sighed. "Is it too early for a brandy?"

"Not today," he murmured and strode briskly across the room to the cabinet that housed brandy and other spirits. He had the distinct air of a man in dire need of a brandy. Or courage of some form.

She studied him curiously. "Why, Lord Pennington, if I did not know better, I would think you were nervous."

"Not at all." He poured two glasses and crossed the room to her side. "But the word *terror* strikes a familiar chord."

"Terror?" She laughed. "Why on earth would you be terrified?"

"I have something I wish to ask you." He handed her a glass, his demeanor abruptly serious.

Charlotte stared in surprise. "My dear Marcus, are you about to propose marriage?"

"Good God, no," he blurted and tossed back brandy.

She raised a brow. "Your vehemence is most flattering. If you are not careful, you shall quite turn my head."

"Do forgive me, Charlotte. That was not at all what I intended." He returned to the decanter, refilled his glass, and took a deep swallow. His brows drew together, and he appeared to be considering all manner of options in far too somber a manner. Regardless of her own intentions toward him, she was not at all certain she liked this overly serious air. "To insult you, I mean. Or to propose."

"Ah," she said lightly, "then you must be planning on asking me to share your bed."

He choked on the brandy. "Charlotte!"

"I am sorry." She laughed. "I simply could not resist."

"I would never ask such a thing." Marcus took a sip of his drink. He shook his head solemnly, but there was a distinct twinkle in his eye. "I would consider it more of an invitation than a request."

"And are you issuing such an invitation?"

"I can think of nothing I'd rather do." His gaze met hers, and a lovely shiver rushed up her spine.

She laughed as she always did when situations such as this arose. It usually quite disarmed the gentleman in question. Charlotte wasn't entirely sure why she employed such a tactic right now—instinct perhaps. As she had more or less decided not only to share this particular man's bed but the rest of his life as well, why on earth was she hesitating?

"But we were speaking of marriage."

"Then you do wish to marry me?"

"No." He paused. "At least not yet."

"Not yet?" She rose to her feet. "What do you mean, Marcus? What are you trying to say?"

"Blast it all, Charlotte, I am an extremely cautious man

when it comes to matters of this nature. Matters of, well, the heart, as it were. Some even think me a bit cold."

"I can't imagine such a thing," she said with a teasing smile.

"Nor can I." Mock indignation rang in his voice. "Why, such an impression is no doubt nothing more than a misperception based on the natural reserve of my nature in matter of emotions, a distinct tendency toward sarcasm and a rather dry wit."

"Oh dear, Marcus." She shook her head in a mournful manner. "Dry wit will be your downfall every time."

"Even with you?"

She sipped her drink. "I rather like it."

"Charlotte." He drew a deep breath. "I should like to call on you in a more serious manner than I have thus far with an eye toward . . . that is to say . . ."

"Dear Lord, Marcus." She gasped dramatically and draped the back of her hand across her forehead. "Not marriage?"

He narrowed his eyes. "Apparently, I am not the only one with a dry wit."

She grinned and fluttered her lashes at him. "Do you like it?"

"I'm not sure." He set down his glass, and before she could protest, he stepped to her and pulled her into his arms. "But it should be great fun to find out."

His lips met hers, and for a startled moment she could do nothing more than stand there. Marcus, along with most of London, would have been rather shocked to know just how very long it had been since she'd been kissed. She closed her eyes, slipped her free arm around his neck, and savored the feeling of a masculine body next to hers. It had been a very long time for that, too.

Like the man himself, his kiss was extremely nice. Confident but not at all arrogant, reserved but not overly so, and, dry wit aside, with a distinct promise of passion in the future. While she did want that, of course, her first marriage had been nothing but passion. What she wanted now was something rather different. A quiet, comfortable kind of affection with a man whose nature suited her own. She already liked him, quite a bit really, and had no doubt she would find a certain measure of love with him.

And his kiss told her this was a man whose bed she could easily share.

"Ahem." The unmistakable sound of a throat discreetly cleared emanated from the doorway.

Marcus raised his head and grinned down at her. "I think we are discovered, Mrs. Robb."

"I do so hate it when that happens, Lord Pennington." She smiled, stepped out of his arms, and glanced at her butler, who had tactfully averted his eyes. She appreciated the gesture and wondered idly how devastating it would be to the servant's sensibilities if she were indeed as active in matters such as this as she was reputed to be. "What is it, Willis?"

"You have a caller, ma'am," Willis said with a slight note of disapproval in his voice, whether for the late-afternoon visitor or Charlotte's compromising position, a brandy in one hand and an earl in the other, in the late afternoon no less, she couldn't tell. Willis had only been in her employ for a few years and did seem to disapprove of a great many things. "It's a Lord Tremont."

"Lord Tremont? Your late husband's brother?" Marcus's brows drew together. "I thought he was dead?"

"The older brother, Edmund, is. He died within a year of the news of Hugh's death. This must be his younger brother, Bertram." She set her glass aside and nodded at Willis. "Do show him in."

At once the butler took his leave. Charlotte shook her head. "I can't remember the last time I saw Bertram. He has a tendency to stay in the country. I wonder what brings him to London now and what he wants."

"Something regarding financial matters? A question of inheritance perhaps?"

"No, all that was settled years ago." In truth, while the duration of her marriage had not been overly long, Hugh, or, more than likely, his older brother, had made certain there was a trust in place to provide for her should anything happen to Hugh. Beyond that, she had received a substantial inheritance from her grandmother upon her twenty-first birthday. "Bertram's a pleasant enough sort, although I have really never had more than a passing acquaintance with him. His calling on me now is most curious."

"We shall find out soon enough what he wants." Marcus glanced at the doorway then stepped closer to her in an instinctive gesture of protection. It was very sweet, and she realized, after all these years, that she had at last chosen wisely. She cast him a grateful smile.

"Char?" A deep voice sounded from the doorway.

She turned toward the door. An instant before she saw his face, his voice registered in her mind. And echoed in her soul.

Only one person in the world had ever called her Char.

Her smile faded, her breath caught, and she stared in stunned disbelief.

He was as tall as she remembered, his shoulders as broad, his hair as golden. And even from across the room his blue eyes bored into hers with an intensity that twisted something inside her she thought long dead and buried.

He moved toward her. "Charlotte?"

Without thinking, she stepped toward him. Her vision, the very world itself, narrowed to no more than his face. A rush, a roar sounded in her ears. Stars swam across her eyes. She could barely croak out a single word.

"Hugh?"

"And then, of course, she did what any well-bred woman would do when faced with a dead husband standing in her parlor looking astoundingly well, considering his demise," Marcus said thoughtfully.

"Yes?" Reggie leaned forward in an eager manner.

"Really rather clever of women when you think about it. Gives everyone a moment to catch their breath, as it were. Gather their wits about them and that sort of thing."

"Damn it all, Marcus." Reggie glared. "What did she do?"

Marcus shrugged. "She fainted."

Chapter 2

" And?" Reggie prompted.

"And certainly you can see how my position was decidedly awkward." Marcus swirled the brandy in his glass.

Reggie drew his brow together. "Actually, I'm not entirely sure I can."

"I didn't know what to do. I was not her betrothed, nor was I her, well, lover for want of a better word. My instincts were to rush to her side, yet there was her dead husband, and I rather suspect if I had come back from the dead I would not want some man I had never met touching my wife."

"I can see where that would be awkward," Reggie said slowly. "What did you, and he, do?"

"It doesn't sound at all good in hindsight," Marcus murmured.

"I can't imagine it would."

"Nonetheless we did what anyone would under the circumstances."

"And that is?"

"We introduced ourselves.

"Bloody hell." Hugh Robb, formerly Captain Robb and now, thanks to his resurrection, Lord Tremont, stared at the prone figure of his wife in a crumpled heap on the floor. "She dropped like a stone."

"Not unexpected under the circumstances." A man Hugh had scarcely noticed upon entering the room moved toward Char, then hesitated. "We should probably, or rather, one of us should—"

"Probably." Although Char certainly wasn't going anywhere, and it might well be best first to know exactly who his competition was. Char's companion was annoyingly attractive in a way women would certainly find appealing and looked vaguely familiar as well, but Hugh couldn't place him. Of course it had been more than seven years since he had left London. "And you are?"

"Pennington. The Earl of Pennington." The man—Pennington—stared. "You're Captain Robb, aren't you? Charlotte's husband. Charlotte's *dead* husband."

"Indeed, I am the husband." Hugh narrowed his eyes. "And are you her—"

"No!" Pennington paused. "At least not yet."

"Good." Hugh nodded with a surprising amount of relief.

He bent beside his wife and gathered her into his arms, ignoring the flood of emotion that washed through him at the feel of holding her again.

The last thing he needed was to have Char's affections engaged right now. From what he'd learned since his return to London yesterday, her affections had been engaged by a fair number of men since the report of his death. Not that it mattered. From the moment he'd decided to return home, he had vowed not to consider anything she might have done while believing him dead to be of any importance whatsoever. He had certainly not been a saint and he'd well known he had a living wife. Some of the time anyway. There had been a few years that had simply been lost, but for at least the last two he'd been fully aware of who and what he was. And where he belonged.

He straightened and for a long moment simply stood unmoving, holding her close. Savoring the weight of her in his arms, the heat of her body next to his, the faint floral scent she wore, that had haunted his dreams even when he had not been able to remember her face.

"You might put her down now," Pennington said firmly.

"Of course," Hugh murmured, glancing around the room.

Nothing was as he remembered it. Every piece of furniture had been replaced, the window hangings had been changed, even the paint on the walls was a different hue. As if Char had swept away any evidence of his existence along with the old furnishings. Regardless, this was his house, or rather, their house.

He deposited Char carefully on a sofa and knelt beside her. She was as lovely as he remembered. Errant strands of dark hair escaped their imprisonment on top of her head and tumbled around her face. Her features were regular, with a somewhat delicate quality that belied the nature of her character, but her lips . . .

Ah, her lips. Full and deep in color, as if she had just eaten something rich and red and delicious. He could almost feel the warmth of them against his own, the way they had whispered against his or met and matched his demands with her own.

In repose, she was peaceful and serene, but she'd always

had an air of restlessness about her. A sense of reckless, carefree exuberance they'd both shared. It had drawn them together and led them along the edge of scandal. And they had reveled in it. She'd been only eighteen when they'd wed and he a bare two years older. Neither had known anything of life save fun and excitement and high, heady passion.

Had she changed? He stared at her lovely face. He was certainly not the same man who had stalked out that very door seven long years ago. He had left a selfish, stupid boy and returned as . . . what? A man at long last willing, even eager, to live up to the responsibilities of his life? Dear God, he prayed he had indeed become man enough to do so.

And prayed as well he had not lost his wife in the process.

Her long, lush lashes flickered and her eyes opened, caught sight of him, and widened.

"Char?"

Char's gaze searched his face as if she were trying to determine if he was real or nothing more than a dream. Slowly, she raised her fingers to his face and traced the scar above his right eyebrow. Her hand drifted down his face to rest upon his cheek. Her dark eyes met his, and he read wonder and awe and . . . fury.

She cracked her hand hard across his face.

The sound reverberated in his head and around the room, and he jerked back on his knees. Even Pennington winced.

"You're alive!" She stared in shock and disbelief and struggled to sit up.

"Indeed I am." Hugh rubbed his cheek gingerly. "You do not appear quite as pleased as I thought you'd be."

"You thought I'd be pleased? Pleased? Hah!" She scrambled off the sofa and moved away from him as if to keep a safe distance between them. "How long have you been alive?"

"Nearly nine and twenty years now."

Pennington choked back something that sounded suspiciously like amusement. Char shot him a lethal glance, which Hugh found rather heartening. Divide and conquer was always a good tactic.

"I don't mean that and you know it," she snapped.

"It's a very long story." Hugh searched for the right words. "Some of it is confusing and some rather unpleasant, and," he drew a deep breath, "much, if not all of it, is my fault."

"*That* was never in question." She shook her head. "This is impossible. You simply cannot be here looking so . . . *alive!*" Char turned on her heel and paced. "You must be nothing more than a dream—"

"A good dream?" A hopeful note sounded in Hugh's voice.

"Hardly," she muttered, scarcely paying any heed to him at all, as if she was trying to work out the answer to his sudden reappearance in her life without any help from him. Or from anyone, for that matter. It struck him that she had probably been doing exactly that for seven years. And struck him as well that she might not need him or, indeed, anyone at all.

She halted and addressed Pennington. "Marcus, is there a man standing in this very room looking suspiciously like my husband? My *dead* husband?"

Marcus? She called him by his given name?

Pennington nodded reluctantly. "I'm afraid so, my dear."

My dear?

"Are you very sure?" She gazed up at Pennington with a hopeful look on her face, and Hugh's heart twisted. He couldn't blame her, of course. He'd known his appearance would be a dreadful shock. Still, he had harbored a tiny hope that she would be a little pleased to learn he was still alive. "Is it at all possible that he is merely a ghost? A vengeful spirit come to haunt me?"

Pennington shook his head. "He seems very much alive."

She ignored him. "A specter perhaps, conjured up by nothing more significant than a rather surprising qualm of conscience given my newfound intentions regarding you and I?"

Intentions?

Pennington grinned. "Intentions?"

"Marcus," she snapped, "that is neither here nor there at the moment. I have a dead husband come to life in my parlor, and I need assurances that he is indeed dead and I am simply dreaming!"

"Char." Hugh stepped toward her.

She whirled toward him. "Quiet! You are not here! You do not exist! You are nothing more than the product of an overwrought imagination!" She turned to Pennington, desperation in the very line of her body. "Please tell me he is not here."

"I am sorry, Charlotte." Pennington shrugged in a helpless manner. "He has every appearance of being flesh and blood."

"I *am* flesh and blood, Char." Hugh stepped closer. "Touch me."

Her eyes widened and she stared at him for a moment, then once again smacked her hand across his face.

"Yow!" Hugh clapped his hand to his cheek and glared. "Bloody hell, Char, why did you do that?"

"It did seem a bit excessive," Pennington said under his breath.

Char stared at her reddened palm. "That hurt."

Hugh rubbed his cheek. "Damned right, it hurt. I should think it would have hurt the first time."

"The first time I scarcely felt it," she murmured. Her gaze shifted from her hand to Hugh's face. "You really are alive. Real."

"I daresay there were better ways to prove it," Hugh muttered, then drew a deep breath. He was determined to do whatever was necessary to make his resurrection easier for her. It seemed the very least he could do. Besides, it was the first step toward the resumption of their lives together. A resumption that was obviously going to be even more difficult than he had anticipated. "However, you may slap me again if you need additional proof."

"Thank you but no." She shook her head slowly. "I do appreciate the offer, and I should like to reserve the right to smack you again should I need to do so."

Hugh narrowed his eyes. "As you have now verified the solidity of my presence, there should be no need to do so in the future."

"I suspect there will be every need to do so in the future." Her eyes flashed, and she crossed her arms over her chest. "Where have you been for the past six years? What have you been doing? Why didn't you come home? Failing that, why didn't you let anyone know you were alive?"

Hugh blew a weary breath. "As I said, it is a long story. Complicated and confusing."

"Apparently, we have a great deal of time to sort it all out. I do not expect the full details of six years in six minutes." She set her jaw. "But do feel free to begin at the beginning. *With your death.*"

Hugh glanced pointedly at Pennington. "I would prefer to do this privately."

"I should take my leave." Pennington nodded and started toward the door.

"No." Char moved to block the earl's passage and glared at her husband. "I would prefer that he stay."

"Char, this is none of his concern."

"It is very much his concern," she said sharply.

"It is?" Pennington raised a brow.

"Is it?" Hugh snapped.

"Indeed it is." She cast her husband a smug smile. "He is my fiancé."

"What?" Hugh glared.

"What?" Pennington stared.

Char's gaze met the earl's, and they stared at one another. Blast it all, from this angle Hugh couldn't see the look in her eyes; only the understanding in Pennington's.

Pennington smiled and shrugged in a manner at once resigned and pleased. "As Charlotte said, I am her fiancé."

"And I am her husband." Hugh drew his brows together. "Rather awkward, don't you think?"

"It is exceedingly awkward," Char said. "And due entirely to the fact that you are not dead. So tell us," she sank into a chair and waved at Pennington to do likewise, "why aren't you dead?"

"I was assumed dead, indeed I was sorely injured." Hugh clasped his hands behind his back and absently paced the room. He had gone over this in his head a hundred times, choosing the right words to make her understand. Not at all easy, as he did not entirely understand it himself. "Some of this I have been told, some I have pieced together.

"A horrendous number of men in my regiment were killed at Albuera, and there was a great deal of confusion. Apparently I was listed among the dead and, due to some bureaucratic error, some dreadful twist of fate, misplaced among the wounded. I was identified as a German and ultimately transported to Bavaria."

"Why didn't you say something?" Pennington asked. "Tell them who you were?"

"For one thing, I was unable to." Hugh shrugged. "You must understand, I was not expected to live, and I was rather a mess as well. Those charged with my care and transport had never met me, nor had they met the man I was purported to be. I did not recover for months, nearly a full year, and my mind was, well, to be blunt, addled by all I had been through. I had no true memory of who I was. I found myself on a farm surrounded by people who claimed me as a relative but looked at me as a stranger. Johann Berringer." He shrugged. "That was my name."

"You don't speak German." Suspicion sounded in Char's voice.

"Which made it all the more confusing." Hugh smiled wryly. "Apparently, I looked a great deal like Johann, hair color, eyes, height, that sort of thing. The differences in appearance were attributed to the rigors of my ordeal. Beyond that, Johann had been a mercenary since his youth and had not been home for many years. His family consisted of his younger siblings and their children. They were more than happy to get their brother back.

"I accepted who they said I was. Indeed, as my mind was an empty slate, I had no reason not to accept it. I learned to speak the language and, I must admit, my life was not at all unpleasant." His gaze caught hers. "Except for the dreams."

She swallowed hard. "Dreams?"

"Of places, at first. Spain, of course, then England. London. Tremont Park. And then, finally," his gaze met hers. "Of people."

"Oh?" Her voice was light, as if she did not care.

"They were annoyingly vague as dreams are wont to be. Little more than scarce hints, dim memories of a voice or a laugh. A scent or a touch. Nothing specific. Nothing to indicate they were more than the fevered imaginings of a wounded mind. I never spoke of them to anyone. At the time, I feared I was mad. You see, I had no reason to believe I wasn't who everyone said I was. I think now that my mind could not begin to recover until my body had."

Pennington stared in fascination. And why not? It was indeed a fascinating story. And true for the most part. "When did it all come back to you?"

"It wasn't like that. What I mean to say is it didn't all come back to me at once. There was always the sense that all was not right with my world, that I did not quite belong. I thought it was a restless aspect of my nature. The same thing that had driven me—or rather Johann—to leave his home in the first place. And there were the dreams of course, more vivid and detailed with time. Still, they were no more than dreams, and I paid them no heed. I was Johann Berringer, a farmer, member of a community and large family—"

"With his wife and children no doubt," Char said coolly.

"Johann never married," Hugh said just as coolly. "Not that he didn't have plenty of opportunity." He caught Pennington's gaze. "Women were especially fond of Johann."

Char sniffed in disdain.

Pennington bit back a smile. "Go on then."

Hugh drew a deep breath. "Two years ago—"

"Two years!"

"Do be quiet, Charlotte, and let the man finish," Pennington said firmly, and Hugh's opinion of him notched upward. The earl might be a rival for the affections of his wife, but he was obviously a fair sort. In addition, fiancé or not, his hesitation to go to Char's side in the presence of her presumed dead husband spoke of a highly developed sense of honor. Pennington might prove to be an ally rather than a rival.

"Then," the earl added, "if you wish to place him in his grave for good I shall not attempt to dissuade you."

Or not.

"Very well, Marcus. I admit to a certain morbid curiosity." Charlotte turned her gaze back to Hugh. Challenge sparked in her dark eyes. "You were saying?"

"Nearly two years ago, there were travelers passing through my village speaking English, and I knew what they were saying."

Char rolled her gaze toward the ceiling. "Of course you knew what they were saying."

"You don't understand." Even now the memory of that moment brought a raw edge to Hugh's voice. "I had not heard English since my recovery. It had been years."

Sympathy shone in Pennington's eyes. "Since Albuera."

Hugh nodded. "I had no idea I understood it, let alone spoke it. And I spoke it like a native. It was a revelation of astonishing proportions."

"I can well imagine." Pennington leaned forward eagerly. "What was a German, a former mercenary and now a farmer, doing with the ability to speak English?"

"Exactly."

"Then what?" Impatience colored Char's voice.

Hugh stifled a smile. She was interested in spite of herself. It was a good sign.

"It was very much as if a candle had been lit in a dark room. In the first moments there are a few bare flickers of illumination, then abruptly the shadows are gone." He searched for the right words. "One moment, I was Johann Berringer who led a pleasant and uncomplicated life, and the next I was Captain Hugh Robb, a man of substantial means. The brother of Viscount Tremont and the husband of Charlotte Robb."

Her chin rose slightly, and there was the faintest suggestion of a tremble in her voice. "Why didn't you come home then?"

"Because I remembered, Char. I remembered everything." He wanted to step toward her, but he wasn't sure he should. Wasn't sure even now if he had the right. "I remembered the kind of man I was when I walked out that door after another of our endless fights. Johann Berringer was a good, honest, hardworking man. Hugh Robb was a scoundrel, selfish and irresponsible. Oh, he—or rather I— was a good enough officer, and I think if all this had not happened, I would have been a different man when I returned.

"Still, it had been four years since my 'death,' and I thought, given all that had passed between us, you would be better off as my widow than my wife. I was a disappointment as well to my family, my brother especially. I looked at Hugh Robb from the vantage point of Johann Berringer and I was not proud of the person I had been. I thought it might well be best for everyone if I remained dead. Myself included." He braced himself. This was not an easy confession to make. "The life I was leading of hard work and simple pleasures was not at all the life of rank and privilege I had been born to, yet somehow it suited me. I had been relatively happy until I discovered the truth about myself. I thought I could remain happy as Johann for the rest of my days."

"Why then did you decide to return now?" Pennington asked.

"Because I am indeed a different man," Hugh said simply. "Hopefully, a far better man than when I left. Try as I might, I could not ignore the past and the obligations I had abandoned. I made inquiries and learned Edmund had died and I had forever lost the chance to reconcile with him. I will regret that for the rest of my days. Bert never wanted the title but, because of my absence, had no choice. As for my wife," his gaze met hers, "she had never remarried. She was young and beautiful, and she deserved far better than she had received at my hands."

Char stared at him wide eyed, and he held his breath.

"I should be going," Pennington said abruptly and stood. "There are any number of things the two of you need to discuss. Charlotte?"

She nodded but didn't look at him, her gaze instead focused on Hugh. He'd wondered, before today, if he would still be able to see her thoughts reflected in her eyes. She had always worn her heart in her eyes. Now, he knew. It was most disturbing. Aside from those first few moments, when she'd stared at him with shock and disbelief and anger, her eyes were shuttered, her thoughts private. Even her voice sounded neutral. "It's quite all right, Marcus. I shall see you tonight, then?"

"Tonight?" Hugh said.

"Tonight? Is that wise?" Pennington nodded pointedly at Hugh. "You might well have more pressing matters on your mind tonight."

"Not at all." She rose to her feet but continued to stare at Hugh. "I think it's best to go on as if nothing has happened. We are expected, and there will be talk if either of us does not attend, although it might be best to arrive separately."

"Attend what?" Hugh asked.

"Lady Harvey's ball."

"Until tonight then," Pennington said, his voice faded as if he were already far away.

"Tonight," she murmured.

"Of course, Lady Harvey's, the beginning of the season. How could I have forgotten?" Hugh chuckled. "Has she forgiven us then for that unfortunate incident at our last appearance together at her fete?"

"She forgave *me* years ago."

Hugh chuckled. "But not me?"

"You're dead. Everyone forgives the dead," Char said with an offhand shrug.

"Do you?" An intensity he could not hide underlaid his words.

"I haven't thus far." Her voice was level, even, without discernable emotion. When had she become so good at hiding her feelings?

"I see." He stepped closer to her. "Can you?"

She raised her chin slightly. "I don't know."

Her gaze locked with his. They stared unspeaking for a long, silent moment. At last, she wrenched her gaze away and glanced around the room. "Where did he go?"

"Pennington?" Hugh scanned the room. "Apparently he's left. No doubt so that we may speak in private. We have a lot to discuss."

"Indeed we do, but not right now." The vaguest edge of panic sounded in her voice, and she started toward the door. "I have a great deal to think about. My mind is as muddled at the moment as you claim yours was."

He wasn't entirely sure he wanted her to think. Their marriage might well have been impulsive and ill-advised eight years ago, but he knew now as he had known then, at least in his heart, and, somewhere in the back of his mind, had known always, that she was the only woman for him. They were destined to be together. Fated for each other. Half of the same soul. Above all else, she was what had pulled him home.

He forced a casual note to his voice. "Perhaps we could talk on our way to Lady Harvey's tonight?"

"What?" She swiveled toward him. "Surely you do not plan on attending Lady Harvey's ball?"

"What better place to announce to the world that I am alive and well and ready to resume my place in society as Viscount Tremont."

"Good Lord, I'd forgotten about that. You are Lord Tremont now, and I . . ." She shook her head. "That scarcely matters at the moment. Of course, the world should know that you are alive, but perhaps it would be best not to inform the entire world at the same time. Think of the shock. And Lady Harvey's is so . . . public. Everyone will be there."

"So much the better."

"You can't, you simply can't. It isn't . . ." She thought for a moment. ". . . fair. To Bertram. Yes, of course, that's it. It isn't at all fair to your brother to allow him to find out that you are not dead in this manner."

"Unless he has changed dramatically, occasions like this have never been Bert's idea of a pleasant evening. Indeed, I would venture to say he isn't even in London today."

"Even worse," she said quickly. "If he is in the country, everyone will know of your resurrection and his loss of the title before he does. If you have truly changed—"

"I stopped at Tremont Hall on my way to London. Bert and I had a most enjoyable reunion." He chuckled. "My brother, at least, was pleased to see me alive and well."

She gasped. "I am pleased to see you alive."

He raised a brow.

"I am." A defensive note sounded in her voice. "I never wished you dead."

"Never?"

"Never!" Her eyes narrowed. "Although it was you who left me. If indeed I had wanted you dead, who would have blamed me?"

"Not I." He shrugged. "In truth, though, I went off to the aid of my country. To fight Napoleon. Some might well call my actions noble."

"Your actions, perhaps, but your motives?"

He winced. "An unpleasant fact but true nonetheless." He met her gaze curiously. "You know, for the life of me, I cannot remember what our last argument was about."

"You accused me of flirting with Lord Wexley, and I charged you with bedding his wife," she said without hesitation.

"Ah yes." He paused. "Were you?"

"Yes, but flirting is all I was doing." She studied him for a moment. "And were you sharing Lady Wexley's bed?"

His immediate impulse was to deny it. It was a very long time ago, after all, and scarcely mattered now. Still, he suspected the question was a test of sorts. Of the kind of man he was now, probably. "No." Pity he had to pay the price for the kind of man he had been then. "But that had been my ultimate intention."

"I see." She stared at him for a long moment, then nodded slowly, as if to herself as much as to him. "I am glad that you are not dead, Hugh. However, you can certainly see where it is most awkward. I don't know what to do, nor do I know what to think, and I certainly have no idea how I feel about it all. Or about you."

"You are suffering from shock, I think."

"Shock?" She laughed an odd sort of high-pitched laugh. "I daresay shock is mild compared to what I am feeling."

"Char." He started toward her.

"No! Stay away." She thrust her hand out. "Please, Hugh." She drew a deep breath. "You have had years to comprehend all that has happened to you. I have had but a few minutes. I need time to sort this out, in my head at the very least. And I am far from ready to do that in front of all of London society. Do you understand?"

He nodded. "Completely."

"Thank you." She breathed a sigh of relief, then started. "Are you planning on staying here?"

"It is still my house, Char."

"Yes, I suppose, although I did inherit—" She shook her head. "Obviously that is no longer pertinent. There is indeed a great deal to sort out. Tomorrow, I should think we can begin." She smiled for the first time since his arrival. How could he ever have forgotten that smile? It was all he could do to keep from pulling her into his arms. "My *shock* should have abated somewhat by then."

"Tomorrow then."

She nodded and again started toward the door.

"I should warn you, Char," he called without thinking. "I fully intend to have my life back."

She paused but did not look back. "And what of your wife?"

"My wife is my life. She always has been. It just took me a very long time to realize it."

For a moment she simply stood frozen, then without words swept from the room.

Hugh blew a long breath. This had not gone as well as he had hoped, but it had not been nearly as bad as it could have been. Char had not thrown him out or thrown anything of substance at him, for that matter. Indeed, she had even listened and seemed, as well, to accept his story. Which was something at any rate. As true as it was, it was still a far-fetched tale.

As far-fetched as her engagement to Pennington. It had been obvious that Char's claim as to their betrothal was the first Pennington had heard of it. Still, he had not protested, nor had he looked the least bit dismayed. Just how great an obstacle the earl was remained to be seen. Pennington bore watching, but of all the concerns Hugh had at this point, Char's alleged fiancé was not prime among them.

As for giving her time to sort out her thoughts and feelings about his return, well, he had no intention of that. If she had changed as much as he, if she had indeed become more rational and mature since their days together, she'd probably become cautious as well. It might be years before she agreed to resume their life together, and that would never do. He had lost far too many years with her already. No, he had to strike now.

And Lady Harvey's was the perfect place to start.

Chapter 3

*R*eggie blew a long, low whistle. "I'm not certain which of the three of you deserves my sympathy more."

Marcus shook his head. "Did I mention it was awkward?"

"Yes, but it bears repeating," Reggie said under his breath. "What happened then?"

Pennington raised a brow. "You know as well as I. You were there."

Reggie stared in confusion, then his expression cleared. "Yes, of course. Lady Harvey's ball." He chuckled. "How could I possibly have forgotten?"

Charlotte gazed over the crush of guests at Lady Harvey's and, for the first time today, let her mind dwell on Hugh's unexpected resurrection. It seemed safe to do so now, when she was surrounded by people. It had not seemed so earlier.

She had left him in the parlor, fled from him, if truth be told, like the specter she had originally hoped he was. She had given instructions to Willis to prepare rooms for him, leaving which rooms to the discretion of the butler, but she'd suspected Hugh would request those rooms that had once been his. The rooms that connected through a dressing room to her own. And as Hugh was Lord Tremont, and his former rooms were the largest to be had save hers, she had no doubt Willis would give him the best the house had to offer.

Charlotte glanced at the wide, sweeping stairway that marked the entrance to the ballroom. Even though one climbed a grand stairway from the foyer to the first floor, upon entering the ballroom one found oneself on display at the top of a second, shorter, but no less imposing, stair from which one descended into the ballroom itself. The arrangement was ideal for the announcement of new arrivals and the perusal of said new arrivals by guests already present, even though, on evenings such as this, one could barely hear a name announced over the din of the crowd.

She hadn't for a moment debated whether or not she would be among their number tonight. She certainly couldn't stay home, with him, *alone*, tonight. She simply wasn't ready for that.

Charlotte had practically barricaded herself in her rooms and spent the hours until she could reasonably leave for Lady Harvey's preparing for the evening. She'd stayed in the bath so long that her fingers had wrinkled. She'd tried on and discarded no less than a half dozen gowns even though she had decided on the new, pale green frock days ago. She'd done no end of insignificant things to keep her fingers and her mind busy. All part of an effort to delay facing exactly how life had changed today. It was entirely too much to grasp at one time and remain sane. She needed to take it in one tiny detail at a time. Of course, none of said details was especially tiny.

Hugh was alive. *Alive!* It was still barely comprehensible. This sort of thing simply didn't happen. Once one was a widow one tended to remain a widow until one became a wife again. *But never with the same man!*

She'd spent so long putting her past—their past—behind her. From the moment he'd left, she'd pretended that it hadn't mattered. That she really hadn't cared. She'd told herself that what she had felt for him had been nothing but impulsive, youthful passion. It hadn't been, of course. Eunice and Isobel knew, but no one else so much as suspected. Indeed, who would have ever imagined that she had married Hugh not merely to avoid the shattering of an already questionable reputation but because she was head over heels in love with him and had been from the very moment she'd seen the roguish gleam in his deep blue eyes and the way the corners of his lips curved upward in a wicked, knowing smile. And when he'd taken her in his arms . . . she shivered with the memory.

She'd learned he had bought a commission in the army and was off to Spain to fight the French when it was too late to stop him. Certainly, she might not have stopped him even if she'd had the chance. Charlotte knew full well she had been that foolish and that selfish and that childish in those days.

The report of his death a mere year later had devastated her, but again only her closest friends had known. It had taken her years to accept his death, to understand he would never return to her. Even her parents had not been aware of how great a blow Hugh's loss had been. Charlotte had actually overheard her well-meaning mother commenting on how this might be for the best and Charlotte could start her life anew and, this time, find a far more suitable match who would settle her down.

She hadn't of course and hadn't really looked. Until Marcus, there hadn't been a single man she'd considered a serious candidate for her heart or her bed. Not that anyone save Eunice and Isobel knew that either.

Charlotte had cultivated a mildly scandalous reputation which wasn't really scandalous at all. She was a widow, and widows did not have to abide by the same rules society set for unmarried women. Eunice believed it was well worth enduring a period of mourning for that benefit alone. It had started nearly two years into her widowhood with a gentleman who had been paying her particular attention and had furthermore been involved in a wager as to whether or not he could get her into his bed. She should have been offended, but, given the fast and loose reputation she and Hugh had had before and during their marriage, it was probably to have been expected. The gentleman in question had been a good sort really and had had an attack of conscience and had confessed all to her. As he had been in dire straits financially, Charlotte had suggested they both allow the world to think he had indeed shared her bed. It had been dishonorable, she supposed, but it had served those who had made such a bet right.

From that point on, it had been generally assumed that many, if not all, of the men who paid her court also joined her in her bed. No man wanted it known he had failed where others had succeeded, and each typically said nothing at all, which only increased the speculation, as well as respect for her discretion. After all, no one truly *knew* anything. Charlotte had never protested such gossip and had allowed Eunice, who indeed did make something of a sport out of bedding a variety of gentlemen, to encourage it. Charlotte rather liked her reputation and thought it worked as an odd sort of protection. If she was chaste in her widowhood, she would be a challenge, and efforts to bed her would be unceasing.

What would Hugh think? A heavy weight settled in the bottom of her stomach. He would certainly believe the gossip, and why not? It was exactly what he would have expected from her.

Regardless—without thinking she squared her shoulders—he was the one who had abandoned her, and he could scarce complain now about her actions. His behavior had no doubt been far worse. Women were especially fond of Johann, indeed. Besides, no one, including Charlotte, could reasonably expect Hugh to return. *He was dead!*

Except he wasn't dead. He had returned. She wasn't a widow and certainly didn't feel at all like a wife. In truth, she wasn't entirely sure what she was, or worse, what she wished to be.

She scanned the crowd and spotted Eunice and Isobel heading in her direction. Good. They were the only people in the world she could truly talk to about this. She'd sent Marcus off to fetch refreshment knowing full well that, given the size of the crowd, it would be some time before he returned. He hadn't yet mentioned their engagement, and for that Charlotte was eternally grateful. It was a complication none of them needed and served only to draw poor Marcus deeper into her dilemma. He deserved better. He was a wonderful man and indeed the first man she had really considered any sort of involvement with at all, but he wasn't . . .

The thought brought her up short.

He wasn't Hugh.

"I fully intend to have my life back."

Surely he didn't expect that they could pick up precisely where they had left off? At least she couldn't. He'd been out of her life for seven years, dead for six of them, and nothing was the same.

"My wife is my life. She always has been. It just took me a very long time to realize it."

But Charlotte was not the same woman he had bedded or wed or left behind. Not at all the same person who saw nothing wrong with parties that lasted until dawn, drinking and wagering in excess, and living life with a rapt abandon and complete disregard for propriety or for other people. Nothing like the girl whose blood would quicken when a wicked glint would appear in his eye coupled with his announcement that he had an excellent idea, the inevitable prelude to a new, highly questionable, probably scandalous adventure. She wasn't stuffy by any means; she had simply grown. Age and experience, together with the tragedy of losing the love of her life, had matured her, and she no longer saw the world in the same way.

In spite of his claims, had Hugh truly changed as well?

Perhaps she needed to know that before she could make any sort of decision about him or her or the future or anything at all. Perhaps she needed to know a great deal more before she could begin to sort out the tumult of emotions careening inside her. At the moment, she was still too stunned to understand her own feelings.

She did, however, understand all too well that regardless of what he'd done or what had happened to him or how long he'd been gone, he remained, in the eyes of the law and society, her husband.

Until death and, apparently now, beyond.

"You arrived far too early," Eunice said with an accusing wave of her hand. "You never come to these things until they are well under way. I didn't expect to see you even now. Why, Isobel and I only arrived a few minutes ago and very nearly at the same time." She favored Isobel with a satisfied smirk. "Isobel, of course, on the arm of Mr. Manning."

Isobel smiled a long-suffering smile. "I daresay it is not all that significant."

Eunice gasped. "It is most significant. Indeed, it is monumental. Don't you agree, Charlotte?"

"Monumental," Charlotte murmured. "That's the word I was thinking."

Eunice's brows pulled together, and she studied her friend. "You have the oddest look about you, Charlotte. Is something amiss? You are extraordinarily pale tonight, as if you had seen a ghost or something equally shocking."

"A ghost?" Charlotte choked. "A ghost?"

Eunice and Isobel exchanged glances.

"Whatever is the matter?" Isobel said slowly.

"Something even you would agree is significant." In spite of herself, the strangest-sounding laugh came out of her. Odd, as she certainly didn't feel like laughing. "Truly monumental."

"Stop it this minute." Eunice stared with obvious concern. "What on earth is wrong with you?"

"I have seen a ghost." Charlotte sniffed back yet another laugh. "Hugh's ghost."

"Oh dear," Isobel murmured.

"Not again." Eunice sighed. "I thought you were done with that nonsense."

"It's not nonsense." Charlotte wiped her eyes. "Hugh is back."

"Dead men do not come back," Eunice said firmly.

"Do you think it's because she's considering a serious liaison with Lord Pennington?" Isobel said to Eunice.

"I wouldn't be at all surprised." Eunice sighed. "Guilt, no doubt, although I don't see why. Hugh is dead, after all."

"Dead?" Charlotte couldn't hold back a fresh round of giggles. "Dead?"

"Stop it at once, Charlotte." Eunice laid her hand on her friend's arm. "You needn't feel guilty about—"

"I don't feel the tiniest bit guilty. This has nothing to do with guilt." Charlotte struggled to compose herself. "And I'm not at all sure I can explain. It sounds so ridiculous." This really wasn't the least bit funny even if it had all the basic elements of a farce. "It seems that the report of Hugh's death in Spain six years ago was not entirely accurate, and today, well," she drew a deep breath, "he returned."

"What do you mean, 'he returned'? From the dead?" Isobel's eyes widened. "Resurrection?"

Charlotte shook her head. "Bureaucratic error."

Eunice stared. "That's absurd. Whoever heard of one's husband returning from the dead? It simply isn't done. Think of the scandal."

"Of course, Hugh was never overly concerned with scandal," Isobel murmured.

"Neither is Eunice," Charlotte said pointedly. "I can't believe she's mentioning the possibility now."

"A dead husband coming back to life is of far greater interest than any minor indiscretion I might commit. And it scarcely matters, as I certainly don't believe you." Eunice crossed her arms over her chest. "I think you're simply hysterical over the thought of being unfaithful to a dead man, which is ludicrous anyway as a man forfeits all right to that kind of loyalty when he's dead and buried."

"He isn't buried at all. He's at my house at this very minute." At once it struck Charlotte how very ridiculous her words must sound. One generally did not keep dead husbands around the house. "Or rather I should probably say our house."

"Your champagne, Charlotte," Marcus stepped up behind her. "Good evening, ladies."

"My lord, Charlotte says her husband, her *dead husband*, mind you, has returned from the grave," Eunice said without hesitation. "I think she's gone mad. What do you think? Is she mad?"

Marcus handed Charlotte a glass and cast Eunice a reluctant smile. "To my everlasting regret, she is entirely sane."

Eunice's eyes widened. "I don't believe you. Either of you. It's not possible. It's—"

Marcus's gaze slid to the top of the stair. "I thought you said he wasn't coming."

"Good Lord." Charlotte couldn't quite bring herself to follow Marcus's gaze. She knew all too well what she'd see, and she certainly should have expected it. "I shall have to kill him for this." She took a deep, bracing swallow of her wine. "Permanently this time."

Regardless of what Hugh might have led her to believe, she should have known he would make his first living appearance here, where it would make the greatest impression. It was exactly the sort of thing he would have done. Changed? Hah! Even as she turned toward the stair, she heard his name announced. Perhaps, she prayed, given the noise in the room, no one would notice.

Hugh stood at the top of the stairway, and Charlotte's heart caught.

Isobel gasped.

Eunice sucked in a sharp breath. "Dear God, he is alive."

"Indeed he is." Charlotte huffed and stared at the man who had been, or rather now *was*, her husband.

At once she was struck by the attitude exhibited in his stance. The overt arrogance she remembered was gone, replaced by an air of quiet, even modest, confidence. As if this was a man who knew precisely who and what he was and was furthermore at peace with that knowledge. The thought struck her that it must have been quite horrible for him to have lived for years not really knowing who he was or where he belonged. Believing what he had been told and struggling to communicate in a new language when his dreams, his heart, told him something entirely different.

"Was he always that tall?" Isobel murmured. "Or that blond?"

"Certainly he was that tall, but I do not recall him looking that, well, healthy. Or handsome. And his shoulders were most certainly not that broad." Awe sounded in Eunice's voice. She had always considered herself something of a connoisseur of men's shoulders. "Death obviously agreed with him."

"Not death—farming," Charlotte said. "He was mistakenly identified as a German solider when he was wounded and transported to Bavaria, but his mind was as injured as his body and he didn't know who he was for years."

Eunice snorted, but her gaze never left Hugh. "Do you believe that?"

"Unfortunately." Charlotte blew a long, resigned breath. "I very much fear I do."

"I would," Isobel said staunchly. "If my husband arose from the dead and returned to me, I would believe anything at all."

"Yes, my dear, but your husband was rather a better sort all around than hers," Eunice said firmly and nodded at Charlotte. "What are you going to do?"

Hugh started down the stairs and a gasp sounded from somewhere near Charlotte, just loud enough to draw the attention of those nearby to the man descending the stairs. Within moments, similar gasps, an occasional shocked expletive, and the low murmur of excited voices washed

around the room, and all eyes turned toward the tall, power-
fully built, and, admittedly, rather magnificent god of a man.
So much for her hope that his arrival would go unnoticed.

"At the moment, I am going to go to the side of my," she
grimaced, "*dead husband* and see what can be done to mit-
igate the sure and certain scandal that will arise from his
resurrection." She downed her champagne, thrust the empty
glass at Isobel, and started off. "Beyond that, I have no
idea."

"I'll take him if you don't want him," Eunice said behind her.

"Charlotte, perhaps it would be best . . ." Marcus's voice
trailed after her.

She pushed aside a twinge of guilt. Marcus was a very
nice man and she liked him a great deal. This afternoon she
had fully intended to pursue a life with him. That was impossible now, of course. Fortunately, Marcus had never
mentioned love, and while she was confident they had
shared a certain amount of affection, she was also confident
his heart would not break at her loss. Still, she suspected he
would hurt a bit, and for that she was deeply sorry, but what
could she do?

She had, after all, a very live husband who was, at this
particular moment, approaching Lady Harvey. He claimed
to be a different person than he'd been when he'd left, but
she had no intention of taking him at his word. Who knew
what he might be saying to Lady Harvey.

Charlotte picked up her step. She was certainly not the
same girl who had danced barefoot in the park with him or
frolicked hand in hand in fountains scantily clad or skated
with abandon by his side on the edge of scandal and danger
and excitement. Certainly her morals were mildly questionable, but society forgave that in a widow. No, she'd spent far
too much time and effort living down the wild days of her

youth—their youth—to allow Hugh to destroy it all now simply because he had the nerve to be alive.

Hugh reached Lady Harvey a scant few steps before her, and she braced herself for whatever might come next.

"Good evening, my lady." Hugh lifted the older woman's hand to his lips. "Forgive me for my uninvited presence, but I could not possibly have failed to attend what has always been one of the highlights of the season."

"Aren't you supposed to be dead?" Lady Harvey's eyes narrowed in suspicion. "I thought you were dead. Indeed, everyone," Lady Harvey's gaze slipped to Charlotte and back to Hugh, "thought you were dead."

"My apologies, my lady." Hugh chuckled. "I fear I am very much alive."

Lady Harvey studied him. "Up to no good then?"

"In truth, you see before you a reformed man." Hugh's tone was light, but there was a distinct and rather fetching note of sincerity in his voice.

"It is good to see you here with all of your clothing on at any rate," Lady Harvey's lips pressed together. "Sans horse, I might add."

Hugh winced. "For that, too, I offer my apology, as belated as it is. At the time I thought I was most amusing, but I see now my behavior was inexcusable. Attributable only to a misspent youth combined with the bad influences of unruly companions and excessive drink. War and age have both conspired to show me the error of my ways, and I hope you can find it in your heart to forgive me."

"It seems to me you have a rather impressive number of people to beg forgiveness from." She raised a brow. "Are you starting with me then?"

"No, my lady, I started with my brother," Hugh said smoothly.

"As well you should." Lady Harvey nodded. "And what of your wife?"

"My lady, I—," Charlotte started, but the older woman motioned her to be quiet.

"I have a great deal to make up for in regards to my wife. I intend to spend the rest of my life earning her forgiveness." Hugh's gaze locked with Lady Harvey's for a long moment.

At last she nodded, as if deciding something important. "See that you do."

The lady leaned close to Hugh, said something low in his ear, then straightened and glanced at Charlotte. "I suspect, Lady Tremont, that your husband's presence among us is going to cause quite a sensation. It is exceedingly rare for a deceased gentleman, especially one who was infamous for his pranks, ill-advised behavior, and misguided wagers, to reappear."

"Exceedingly." Charlotte smiled weakly.

"I further suspect there is a fascinating story behind it all." Lady Harvey studied Hugh carefully. "Your mother was a dear friend of mine, and I have watched you grow, generally with a great deal of dismay. There is, in truth, something different about you now, my boy."

He smiled wryly. "One can only hope."

"Indeed." Lady Harvey favored him with a slight smile, nodded dismissively at Charlotte, and turned her attention to another newly arrived guest.

Hugh offered Charlotte his arm, and she hesitated.

"You do realize the eyes of nearly everyone here are on us, don't you?" he said in a low voice.

He was right, of course. They were indeed the center of attention. Even the volume of noise had lessened as each and every person in the grand ballroom strained to overhear the discussion between the new Lady Tremont and her long-dead husband. Given the fact that their battles had been as well known as their antics, the crowd no doubt expected something most entertaining. Especially since most spectators had probably realized by now that they had not arrived at the ball together.

He fixed a pleasant smile on his face. "And while once you did not care about things like gossip or the opinion of others, I very much suspect now you do."

Indeed, she could almost hear the questions and comments and speculation.

Did she know he was alive?

Where has he been all this time?

Will they take up where they left off?

Charlotte cast him a blinding smile, took his arm, and gazed into his eyes in a manner befitting an adoring wife delighted to have her deceased husband returned to her. "Why are you here, you damnable beast of a man?"

He chuckled and led her across the room, acknowledging with a smile and a nod the stares of those they passed, as if he'd last seen them no more than a day or two ago. "I never said I wouldn't come—only that I understood why you didn't want me to come."

She forced a light laugh, as if he had just said something most amusing. "You led me to believe you wouldn't be here. That you understood that I needed time to grasp the fact of your existence and I did not wish to do so in a public manner." She fairly spit the words. "Under the eyes of everyone in the ton."

"Watch yourself, Char," he murmured.

She forced a smile back to her face. "You lulled me into a false sense of well-being. Deliberately, I might add."

"Perhaps. And while I rather like the idea of lulling you into anything, I did not lie to you." He glanced at her, his blue eyes darkening with an unspoken emotion and the oddest sensation of weakness washed through her. At once she was grateful for the support of his arm and extremely annoyed that it was necessary. "I do not intend to ever lie to you again."

"What are your intentions, Hugh?" she said out of the side of her mouth and cast Lady Wentworth a pleasant smile in passing.

"Is everyone still watching us?"

"Everyone who is still alive," she said without thinking.

"Very good." He grinned. "It's nice to see that you have not lost your sense of sarcasm."

"I suspect I will need it. Now then, your intentions?"

"I should very much like to dance with my wife, but, as I have not been in a ballroom like this in many years, I fear I might make something of a fool of myself."

She raised a brow. "That's rather humble of you."

"I am exceedingly humble," he said with a grin that hadn't a shred of humility in it. "And it shall serve me, or rather us, well."

"What do you mean?"

"You and I, Lord and Lady Tremont, are going to greet everyone of significance in society in attendance here tonight personally, beginning with those who were friends of my parents." Determination sounded in his voice. "The Duchess of Roxborough is across the room, and I believe she and my mother were great friends in their youth. We shall begin with her."

"I don't understand—"

"The last memories these people have of me are of an ill-mannered scoundrel. I am not the same man who left here, and I wish for there to be no doubt as to that. I never cared about such things before, but I now want . . ." He set his jaw, but his smile didn't waver. "I want to do this properly. My father died when I was very young, and I know I was always a disappointment to Edmund. It's past time I lived up to the responsibilities that come with my family name and title and position."

She stared in shocked silence. She'd never heard talk of responsibility and propriety from his lips before. Perhaps this was indeed an entirely new man.

He slanted her a determined look. "I meant it when I said I want my life back."

"And your wife," she said under her breath.

"Especially my wife."

Still, as much as she knew she herself had changed too much to return to the life they had once lived, the man she had long ago fallen in love with was rash and impetuous and exciting. If indeed the man now by her side was not the same man she had married, could she love him now?

And in spite of his words, could he love her?

Chapter 4

"*I* am exhausted." Charlotte sank into a sofa in the parlor, leaned her head back, and closed her eyes. Her feet throbbed, there was a persistent ache at the small of her back, and the muscles of her face had frozen into a permanent smile.

Hugh chuckled. "It has been a rather long evening."

"Long?" Charlotte snorted. "Endless."

She heard Willis's low voice at the doorway and Hugh's equally quiet response, but at the moment she was too tired to care what either of them was saying. She heard Hugh walk across the room and the distinct sound of a cabinet opening. She did hope he was fetching brandy. Brandy would be most welcome after tonight.

It had been a remarkable evening in any number of ways. Hugh had been as good as his word and had indeed made it a point to chat with anyone of importance in society, as well as nearly everyone else. Certainly these conversations had not been significant in either length or content, no more than idle pleasantries really, but he had been gracious and apologetic when necessary and not merely charming. He had been charming in a genuine sort of way, as if he had really been delighted to reacquaint himself with Lord Whosit and Lady Whatshername and the Countess of Wherever and the Marquess of Whocouldpossiblyremember. Still, the more she'd watched him through the long hours of the evening, the more she'd realized he had indeed been pleased to see these people again. The very people he'd had no use for in his youth. It had been nothing short of astonishing.

Of course, she had made her peace with society years ago, but upon reflection it had perhaps been easier for her. After all, she'd been the extremely young wife of a man killed fighting for king and country. Couldn't her behavior before and during her marriage be attributed to the influence of her unruly and irreverent husband? She had probably even used that assessment to her own advantage. And why not? This was one situation in which society's view of women as being easily led, less competent, intelligent, and nearly everything else than men actually worked in a lady's favor.

It must have taken rather a lot of courage for Hugh to make his first public appearance tonight. Looking back, she wasn't sure she'd ever seen courage in him before. Oh, certainly he'd been daring and reckless and adventurous, but she saw now, where she hadn't seen before, that bravado was a far cry from courage.

True courage might well be accepting responsibility for one's actions—past, present, and future.

Had she accepted that responsibility?

Charlotte felt Hugh settle on the sofa beside her. "Brandy?"

She smiled to herself and opened her eyes. "What did Lady Harvey say to you?"

He chuckled and handed her a glass. "She said she would deny it if asked, but she too had thought my last appearance at her ball was most amusing."

Charlotte laughed and sipped her brandy. "You were exceptionally charming this evening, you know."

"I know." He grinned. "That was part of my plan."

"The plan to get your life back?"

"And my wife," he said pointedly.

She ignored him. There was no need to deal with his intentions as they pertained to her at the moment. "In terms of taking your rightful place in society as Lord Tremont, I think you made great strides tonight."

"I was charming," he said with a smug smile.

"Genuinely charming." She chose her words with care. "There is much about society that is superficial and shallow. Yet even those who embrace that questionable quality among themselves reject it in others." She studied him curiously. "You really were pleased to be there tonight, weren't you?"

"It doesn't sound at all like me, does it? Given the rebellious ways of my youth, that is." He shook his head, his smile ironic. "But, Char, for the first time in years I felt, I don't know, *right*. As if I belonged, I suppose. Who would ever have imagined such a thing?" His amused gaze met hers. The tiniest hint of what might have been longing flashed through his blue eyes so quickly that she might have been mistaken.

Even so, her heart caught.

She stared into his eyes for a long moment. How had she forgotten that their color was the exact shade of a midsummer sky? Full of warmth and joy and promise now tempered and shaded by war and pain and confusion. She'd lost herself in those eyes years ago, the eyes of a boy really, and now gazed into the eyes of a man, compelling and just as irresistible.

Without warning her weariness vanished, swept away by the electricity that abruptly sizzled in the air between them just as it had years before. And a nearly forgotten sense of yearning surged within her.

"Is it working?" he said softly.

She swallowed hard. "Is what working?"

"My plan." He leaned ever so slightly toward her. His gaze slipped from her eyes to her lips and back.

Without thinking, she leaned ever so slightly toward him. "Everyone did seem—"

"Not that plan." His lips were a scant inch or so from her own.

Dear Lord, she remembered exactly how his mouth had felt against hers. "No?"

Exactly how his hands had felt caressing all those private places no man had touched before or since.

"The plan to get my wife back."

Exactly how his naked body had felt pressed against her own. She shuddered with a desire she thought never to feel again. "Perhaps."

"I shall take that for the moment. In the meantime." His lips brushed against hers and her breath stilled. "What are you going to do about Pennington?"

"Pennington?" Her eyes drifted closed, and she pressed her lips closer to his. He tasted of brandy, warmed by his lips. A myriad of long-forgotten sensation and emotion gripped her.

"Your fiancé?"

Her lips froze against his. "My fiancé?"

"Pennington?"

She opened her eyes. "What does Marcus have to do with this?"

"A great deal, I should think. He does intend to marry you."

"Yes, of course." She jerked away. What could she have been thinking? Or indeed, was she thinking at all? "My fiancé." And what must Hugh think of her? She'd been a scant second away from kissing him, and God knows what would have happened after that, and she was supposed to be engaged to another man. "Marcus."

"I believe that is his name," Hugh said mildly.

She tossed back the rest of her drink and got to her feet. How on earth did he expect her to think about Marcus when he had almost . . . when she had almost . . .

"Well? What are you going to do about him?"

She crossed the room to the liquor cabinet, needing both distance and a moment to pull herself together. She drew a calming breath and turned toward him. "Marcus is a very nice man."

"No doubt."

"I've scarce had a moment to consider what to do about you, let alone what to do about him."

"Come now, Char, you've had"—he glanced at the clock on the mantel—"nearly ten hours now to consider exactly what to do about your husband and your lover."

"He's not—" She caught herself and glared at Hugh. "What Marcus is or is not is none of your business."

"It's very much my business." He sipped his drink thoughtfully. "I am your husband."

"You forfeited that title when you died." Anger surged within her.

"Yes, but as I didn't—"

"Six years, Hugh." Her voice rose. "You've been dead for six years. Only you weren't dead at all. You were simply gone!"

"Yes, but for four of those years I did not know who I was." He calmly got to his feet. "They should not count against me."

"Fine," she snapped, "I will give you those. That still leaves two full years."

"A month or two less to be exact."

"Hugh!"

"Very well, I told you, I thought you would be better off without me. And I thought I was better off as Johann than as Hugh."

"That's terribly selfish of you."

He snorted agreement. "Yes, it was."

She drew her brows together. "You admit it then?"

"Indeed I do. And therein lies the problem."

"What?"

"Johann was a better man than Hugh, at least the old Hugh. Perhaps better only because, as he could not remember his past, he did not have to drag it along with him. He could start life anew with no encumbrances, no strikes against him. Regardless of the reasons for the improvement in my character, the man I had become would not permit the indulgences of the man I once was or the abandonment of his responsibilities. The man I had become had to return home to face whatever awaited him."

"And am I then a responsibility?"

"No," he said simply. "You are my life."

She scoffed. "Fine words, Hugh. Very nice indeed. Have you spent the last year practicing?"

"More or less." He paused. "I don't blame you for being angry. I would have been shocked if you weren't. But I meant what I said tonight about spending the rest of my life earning your forgiveness. And I do not expect it to come easily."

"Good, then you will not be disappointed. I know women who do not speak to their husbands for a month because they fail to come home for a single night."

"Really?" His brows drew together thoughtfully. "By my calculations then, you really should not speak to me—"

"Stop it at once!" She glared at him. "How can you think this is amusing? There is not the least bit of amusement in any of this."

"On the contrary, this is the most amusement I have had in a very long time," he said quietly.

There was something in the tone of his voice, no more than a hint really, of all that he had been through. All that he had seen. Her heart twisted for him, and her anger vanished.

She drew a deep breath. "You have not yet told me of your injuries. I imagine they were quite awful."

"They were." He fell silent for a moment, then blew a long breath, and at once she knew he would never tell her more than that. "But I survived. I have often wondered how." He took a sip of his brandy, as if for fortification. "And, more to the point, why."

"Why?" She studied him. "I don't understand."

"As we both agree, I had not lived my life up till then in a manner that would merit salvation. Indeed, one could accurately say my life before I left here was selfish and purposeless and a waste. There were surely far better men, more admirable, more worthy to live than I. Better sons, brothers . . . husbands.

"I think now I owe it to the men who died on both sides, to Johann Berringer, poor devil, wherever he may be, dead or alive, to now live my life well and honorably. Not to waste this gift, this second chance that I received and they did not.

"And there were so many . . ." His voice was casual, his tone belied by the shadows that flickered in his eyes. "All told, the casualties on both sides at Albuera numbered thirteen thousand men. Thirteen thousand, Char. A betting man would not have wagered on survival at Albuera. Why did I live when so many didn't? Since the moment I remembered who I was, that question has haunted me."

"I had heard it was a terrible battle." *It was where I lost you.* The thought flashed through her mind, and she pushed it aside.

"When I could remember nothing else of my life, I could remember Albuera. The smell of the smoke. The rain, blinding and deadly. The noise." He shook his head. "God, Char, in my worst nightmares I have never heard such noise. The report of the guns and clash of swords, the ring of metal hitting metal. The odd, quiet sound when steel pierces flesh."

Her stomach turned but she didn't want to stop him. She suspected he had not often spoken about what he'd seen and heard and felt. That he now chose to confide in her was both significant and touching.

"And above it all, or under it all, I don't know, were the sounds of the men, of the injured and the dying. The cries and screams and groans. Some, I think now, my own. And blood. Always, always blood in a battle, but at Albuera . . ." A slight, humorless smile curved his lips as though, if he did not smile, he would surely weep. The look in his eyes was remote, as if he were seeing it all again. Or still. "There was a great deal of blood. Everywhere. The stench of it hung in the air. It mixed with the mud on the ground. It was"—his gaze met hers—"hell. By anyone's definition. Right here on earth, although I daresay hell in the afterlife could not be any worse." He shrugged. "It seems, therefore, I now know what to expect upon my demise."

"Don't say such things," she said sharply.

"Does it bother you? The thought of my burning forever in the fires of hell?"

"Of course it bothers me." She turned away from him, as

much to refill her glass as to restore her own composure. She poured the brandy, and her hand trembled.

"Why?" His voice sounded directly behind her. She hadn't heard him approach.

"Because," she forced a light laugh. "Of all the times I suggested you go straight to hell I never imagined you would."

"Char—"

She turned abruptly and found him no more than the distance of the span of her hand away. She gazed up at him. "When you walked out in the midst of that last argument, that stupid, stupid argument—"

"We had fought about far less."

"We had fought about everything." She shook her head. "But if I had known this would be our last, if I had so much as suspected you would have the final word by going off to war, I would have done all in my power to stop you. I would have abandoned all sense of pride and thrown myself in your path if necessary."

"I knew that. Or maybe I simply hoped." He cast her a resigned smile. "I have wondered, in retrospect, if I also knew that the only way to become the man I was always supposed to become was to serve a higher cause than myself."

"You served it with your life, and, in some ways mine as well." She drew a deep breath. "For six years, Hugh, I have blamed myself for your death. If I had not been such a termagant, if I had been a proper wife, the lady I was raised to be—"

"Then you would not have married me in the first place." His smile was wry. "Nor would I probably have paid you any notice whatsoever. Although, even if you had been eminently proper and not had a penchant for illicit adventure," his gaze roamed over her in a hungry manner, "I suspect I always would have taken notice of you."

"Listen to me, Hugh. I felt your death was my fault." Without thinking, she leaned closer, grabbed the lapels of his coat, and gazed up into his eyes. An urgent need to make him understand gripped her. "Not one day has passed of the last six years that I did not feel a measure of guilt and regret and sorrow."

"Sorrow?"

"Of course, sorrow." She shook her head and glared at him. "Blast it all, Hugh, regardless of the tempestuous nature of our relationship, you were the most important thing in my life."

"Was I?" His voice was low, his eyes dark. "How was I to know?"

"How?" She stared in disbelief. "Has it been so long that you do not remember? I shared your bed. I suspect that was an indication. I married you. I—" At once it struck her what he wanted to hear, and she wasn't sure she could say it. She never had before. At least not aloud. Not to him. She released his coat as if it were on fire and tried to step away.

He caught her wrists and held them tight against his chest. "What? You what?"

"I . . ." *I loved you! You ripped my soul out when you left, and when you died, I died too.*

"What, Char? Say it." She could feel his heart thud in his chest.

"There's nothing more to say," she lied.

"I think there's a great deal more to say." His gaze bored into hers.

She wanted to pull away, thought it was for the best but couldn't seem to move. Slowly, he lifted her hand to his lips and kissed the tips of her fingers. She shivered at his touch. He followed suit with her other hand. All the while his gaze never left hers.

She stared into his blue eyes and knew she was lost. As

lost as she'd been the first moment she'd gazed into those summer eyes of his. And neither time nor distance could ever change that. She'd loved him all those years ago and she'd never stopped, not for a moment. He was alive and he was back and she was a heartbeat away from being in his arms. Where she belonged.

She drew a deep breath and surrendered. "You're right. There is something more to say."

"Yes?" He held his breath.

"I have missed you a great deal." She shook her hands free and gently traced the scar over his eyebrow with her fingers. "I have missed the sound of your laughter."

"Char—"

She raised up on her toes and brushed her lips against his. "The feel of your lips against my own."

He shuddered and wrapped his arms tightly around her.

She slipped her hands around to the back of his neck. "The heat of your skin beneath my fingers."

No matter how much had been wrong between them, this had always been right.

"Char." He groaned and crushed his lips to hers.

A wave of indefinable emotion washed over her and held her frozen. Feelings and desires and passions she thought long since dead gripped her with a force so strong it tore at her soul.

Hugh was alive!

And she realized she had not been truly alive herself, not for a single second since she'd been told of his death, not until this very moment when his lips had met hers. Years of hidden sorrow and acting lighthearted and carefree overwhelmed her, and something inside snapped. She tightened her arms around his neck, and a sob broke from her lips.

Hugh raised his head and stared with concern. "Char. Are you all right?"

"Y-e-e-s." Uncontrollable sobs racked her body, and for an endless moment she clung to him. He held her close, and there was nothing in the world more right than being in his arms. "You're . . . you're . . . really . . . ali-i-i-ve."

"Yes I am." A perplexed smile curved his lips. "It might well be considered good news."

"It's . . . it's . . . ," she hiccupped, "very good."

He laughed softly. "I'm glad you think so." Gently he kissed one eyelid, then the next, as if he could kiss her tears away. "I can tell you, I am very glad to be alive."

She sniffed and lifted her face up to his.

He kissed her wet cheeks. "And I'm very, very glad to be here."

She closed her eyes and reveled in the feeling of his lips on her face. It was sweet and caring and extraordinarily nice. "I'm very glad you're here too."

He kissed the corners of her mouth, and her lips opened slightly. He covered her mouth with his and they tasted of one another, tentatively, as if he was afraid she would break and she was afraid he would vanish in yet another dream. He angled his mouth harder over hers and his kiss deepened.

Without warning, all hesitation between them vanished. All reserve shattered. He pulled her tighter to him, the welcome heat of his body searing her own through the layers of clothes between them. His mouth plundered hers and she responded with a greed born of never-forgotten desire.

They moved as if in a dream of frantic hunger and long-denied passion. She barely noticed when he scooped her into his arms and carried her up the stairs. Was scarcely aware of either of them discarding their clothes in a frenzy of need. Hardly noted how they tumbled onto the bed—his bed—together, a tangle of arms and legs and yearning. All she knew, all she wanted was his flesh against hers.

He caressed her back, her buttocks, her breasts. His

hands, roughened by hard work, were everywhere at once, more intoxicating than she remembered, and her body came alive beneath them. She needed his touch and needed as well to touch him. To explore the hard muscles of his shoulders, the flat plane of his stomach. To know he was real and solid and here by her side. She remembered the sheer perfection of his body, the smoothness of his skin. Her fingers now trailed over the lines and ridges and welts of long-past-healed wounds, and she sucked in a short breath in surprise.

"Dear God, Hugh." Her heart ached, and she realized how very much of a miracle his presence here and now really was.

He raised his head, and she wished she could see his eyes in the dark. And more, wished he could see hers. His voice was resigned. "Does it bother you, then? I am sorry, Char, obviously there's nothing I can do." He started to pull away. "If you would rather wait or—"

"Don't be an ass, Hugh. Every scar is a badge of honor of sorts, I think, and I am not the least bit bothered. I am simply shocked by the evidence of how gravely wounded you were and deeply grateful that you are here now. Besides." She drew him back to her. "It has been seven years since we've been together, and I have waited far too long for you. At this particular moment," she nipped at his shoulder, "I'd scarcely care if you've grown two heads and a tail."

For a moment, he didn't move, then he laughed softly against the curve of her neck. "A tail would be interesting."

She laughed with him and with the utter joy of being in his embrace again and with the miracle of it all.

He kissed the hollow of her throat and she arched upward, urging him on. His lips trailed a line of fire and delight between the valley of her breasts. He cupped one breast and took the other in his mouth, and she wondered through a haze of sheer arousal how she could have waited so very long, knowing at once it was because he and he alone could do this to her. And knew as well it was not merely how he caressed her body but how he touched her soul.

She raked her nails lightly down his chest and across his stomach and lower until she reached his member, hard and hot, and she wrapped her hand around it and felt it throb against her hand. He groaned and she stroked him until abruptly he shifted to kneel between her legs. She slipped her hands around his neck and pulled his mouth to hers. He braced himself with one hand and guided himself into her with the other.

Charlotte held her breath, her mind, her body, the very essence of her existence focused on their joining. He was larger than she remembered, and she was tighter than she expected. Still, she was wet with need and more than ready and he slid into her with a slow, measured ease. She'd almost forgotten how remarkable it felt to have him inside her. For a long moment he lay still, and she savored the feel, the fullness of him, the joining of one body to another. Right and good and perfect.

He started to move within her, and she matched her movements to his. He moved faster, and she clutched at him and urged him on. The rhythm of his strokes increased, harder and deeper. Her hips rose up to meet him, welcome him, consume him. With every thrust, urgency built within her, and she felt it build within him. In the tension of his body and the labor of his breathing and the searing heat that enveloped them both. They moved together, in harmony perfect and profound, joined as one. As if they had never been apart. As if they had moved together like this always. Inseparable. Forever.

And when she thought she would well die of the pure pleasure and sweet ache that spread from her body to her soul, release gripped her, and she clutched at his shoulders. Waves of intense delight coursed through her, and she called out his name. As she had in her dreams. As she had in her heart.

Dimly she noted he gasped and shuddered, and warmth filled her. He stilled for a long moment, his body pressed against hers, the thud of his heart beating in rhythm with her own, then he rolled over, shifted his weight, and took her in his arms. They lay together silent, spent, content for now in one another.

"I did not suspect resurrection could be so exciting," he murmured at last.

She smiled. "You have been dead a very long time."

"And I have dreamed of this, of you, nearly as long." He kissed the tip of her nose. "But my dreams fade in comparison."

"Yours?" She snuggled against him. "Or Johann's?"

"Johann needs to find his own wife. And his own dreams." He drew her closer and kissed her, slowly and deliberately, and desire flared again within her.

And why not? It had indeed been a very long time.

After all these lonely years, her dreams too had at last come true. And, judging by the evidence pressing against her, were about to come true again.

Hours later he lay asleep in her arms. She trailed her fingers over the ridges and puckers of his scarred body. They didn't mar the perfection of his skin as much as adorn it. She rather liked them. They spoke of where he had been and who he was now. Of courage and survival and resurrection.

She noted that the anger she had harbored for him had vanished, lost among the sheets and the passion and her own private acknowledgment of what he still meant to her. Besides, he had been through more than any man should have to endure. Certainly, she was not ready to forgive him for the past two years or for leaving in the first place, but the fury that had coupled with sorrow inside her had gone.

Even so, this, she heaved a heartfelt sigh, was a huge mistake. Delightful and absolutely delicious and Lord knew it had been a very long time, but a mistake nonetheless.

There had always been passion between them. Obviously that had not changed. And there wasn't a doubt in her mind that Hugh had. The proof was in his actions and his story.

The old Hugh would never have admitted to regaining his memory two years ago and never would have confessed to debating whether to come home at all. The old Hugh would have swaggered into the house as though he had left it only yesterday. And the old Hugh would never have tried to make amends to all of society for his past misbehavior.

Still, she couldn't just let him back in her life as though nothing whatsoever had happened. Why, she didn't really know this new Hugh Robb—Lord Tremont—at all. He was practically a stranger.

Beyond all else, she had been faithful to him, even if he would never know it. Even if he had been dead. There wasn't a doubt in her mind that Johann hadn't been celibate, nor had the resurrected Hugh gone for two years without a woman in his bed.

Would he tell her the truth about that if she asked?

Possibly. She blew a long breath. And that was really the crux of her dilemma. As much as she had missed him, as much as she had longed to have him back, this new Hugh was damn near perfect. Charlotte was far from perfect, nor had she ever wished for perfection in herself or a husband. Could she live with perfect? And could perfect live with her?

Hugh had been forged by the fires of hell itself and emerged strong and good and a man any woman would be proud to call her own.

No, Hugh had definitely changed.

The question now was, had she?

Chapter 5

"The next morning Charlotte was in an impressive state of turmoil." Marcus blew a long breath and shook his head. "In truth, she was rather horrified by what she saw as a flaw in her own character."

"What do you mean?" Reggie stared in confusion.

"She perceived her actions as an indication that, while she had always thought she had gained a certain measure of wisdom and maturity with the years, perhaps she was wrong. Indeed, she feared she was about to repeat history itself. In one way, she already had. She had fallen into bed with Tremont without so much as a second thought. Precisely as she had done years before."

"Perhaps, but he was her husband and . . ." Reggie narrowed his eyes in suspicion. "How do you know this?"

"You told me to draw my own conclusions."

"Even so, I can't imagine—"

"I know all this because by some odd twist of fate, some curse placed upon my head, no doubt, long before I was born, I became . . ." Marcus searched for the right word. "I'm not entirely sure what I became. An intermediary, I suppose. A third party from whom one could ask assistance, seek advice, share confidences, that sort of thing."

"A friend?" Reggie winced. "I am sorry. Dreadful when a woman you are amorously pursuing wishes for nothing more than friendship."

"Don't remind me," Marcus muttered.

"So you became a confidant to her then?"

"Not just to Charlotte." Marcus took a sip of his brandy and grimaced. "To them both."

"I don't exactly know how to say this." Charlotte paced the parlor, absently wringing her hands and trying to find the right words.

Marcus lounged against the mantel, arms crossed over his chest in that coolly casual way he had. "You're throwing me over for your husband?"

Charlotte stopped in her tracks and stared at him. "That's not at all what I was going to say."

He raised a brow. "You're not throwing me over for your husband then?"

"Well, I suppose I am, but . . ." She drew her brows together and huffed. "It's not like that, Marcus, and you well know it. Obviously I have little choice."

He studied her for a long, thoughtful moment. "Obviously."

She narrowed her gaze. "Why do you say it in that manner?"

"Come now, Charlotte, I knew the moment he walked in the door you were lost to me."

"How could you possibly know that?"

"When a man has been engaged as long as I have, he learns a few things about his intended," he said wryly.

Charlotte winced. "I am sorry about introducing you as my fiancé. It was the first thing that came into my head, as a sort of protection, I suppose."

"That's what I thought."

"I do so appreciate your going along with it, as well as you not bringing it up last night."

"I knew you had other things on your mind and we would sort out our relationship eventually, whatever it might be."

"Thank you." She cast him a weak smile, then drew a deep breath. "I need your help, Marcus."

"I am at your service, of course, but what can I possibly do to help?"

"I need advice, really. I simply don't know what to do." Charlotte resumed her pacing. "Shall I allow Hugh back into my life? Shall we pick up precisely where we left off?"

"I really don't think—"

"Even disregarding the years his mind was muddled, there were two years when he knew full well who he was. Am I expected to forgive him for not returning then?"

"It seems to me—"

"On one hand I should like to forgive him immediately, but that seems as if I am, I don't know, being disloyal to myself in some manner. I daresay he doesn't deserve to be forgiven right away. He has promised to spend the rest of his life earning my forgiveness, and it seems that effort should take more than one day on his part."

"I can certainly see—"

"Beyond that, what if he's truly changed and I, well, haven't? If all he's been through has indeed made him a better person, and I think he's shown every evidence of that thus far, what happens if he learns that I am still the silly, impulsive girl he was when he left?"

"You are scarcely—"

"Honestly, if I had any sense at all, if I had indeed matured, I would . . . I would"—she paused and nodded at him—"I would prefer you to him."

"There is that," he said under his breath.

In spite of herself, she grinned. "You are indeed a very nice man, Marcus."

"Good for me," he muttered.

"And I consider you a true friend."

He rolled his gaze toward the ceiling. "Even better."

"Now then, to go on," she resumed her pacing, "I am terrified that deep down inside myself, I am precisely the same as I was when he left. He makes me feel as I haven't felt in years. As no man has ever made me feel. It's really rather intense and frightening."

Marcus groaned. "Charlotte—"

"Why, I fell into his arms last night the very same way I did eight years ago without regard to the consequences or—"

"Charlotte!" Marcus straightened in obvious alarm.

Her gaze shot to his. "Yes?"

"I don't think this is something I should know."

"Come now, Marcus, we are adults." She cast him her friendliest smile. "And if I cannot talk about this with my fiancé, who can I talk about it with?"

"Your husband?" he snapped.

She waved off the comment. "He's the last person I could talk to about this, and you, of all people, should understand that."

"Very well then, I shall listen if you insist, but it's against my better judgment." He adopted a long-suffering look and heaved a resigned sigh. "Still, wouldn't it be best if you confided in Lady Blackwell or Lady Hazelwood?"

"Best? Judging by their reactions last night, it would be a complete and utter waste of time." Charlotte crossed her arms over her chest. "Eunice would see nothing wrong with sharing Hugh's bed and going our separate ways in all other matters, and Isobel would simply admonish me to be grateful he is not dead." She sighed. "What am I to do, Marcus?"

"Well." He furrowed his brow and thought for a moment. "I suppose it very much depends on what you want to do."

"Oh, that's an enormous help. I have no idea what I want to do. I like the man that he has become. The man I married certainly wasn't at all responsible or thoughtful or honorable, although he was great fun. Still, I have long thought our marriage a disastrous mistake, and now . . ." She drew her brows together. "Perhaps it wasn't such a mistake after all? Or at least it doesn't need to be."

"Then I should think—"

"But I don't think I can be married to a paragon, Marcus."

"I daresay he isn't—"

"Do you know he is even now in the library meeting with his solicitor? About issues pertaining to his army commission and the estate and finances and all else that one has to deal with when one comes back to life unexpectedly, but he's also arranging to send a sizable sum of money to his family, the people he thought were his family that is, in Bavaria. He's become positively noble."

"That does indeed seem—"

"And do you know how I know that?" She grimaced. "I listened outside the door."

"Certainly, I can see—"

"I can't imagine that a paragon, a noble paragon at that, would wish to be married to someone who eavesdrops on private conversations. I too have changed with the years, but I have not become perfect by any means, certainly no one would call me a paragon, and I do rather enjoy a fair amount of irreverent—"

"Charlotte!" Marcus said with a huff. "Do let me get at least one word in."

She widened her eyes in surprise. "Wasn't I?"

"No," he snapped, then pulled a deep breath. "My apologies, Charlotte."

"Certainly," she murmured. "You needn't be huffy about it."

"I have never been in an engagement, feigned or otherwise, to a woman whose husband has returned from the dead. It seems to call for a certain amount of huffiness. Now then." He thought for a moment. "It seems to me there is only one real question to consider here." He studied her carefully, as if he could see the answer to his question on her face. "Do you or do you not still love your husband?"

An ache rose in the back of her throat. "I . . ." She shrugged helplessly. "I have loved him from the moment I met him and I have never stopped."

"Then you really have very little choice." He sighed in resignation. "Take him back into your life and forgive him. However, as your fiancé, good friend, or whatever else I might be, I would be remiss if I did not also advise"—a wicked smile spread across his face—"your requiring him to grovel and indeed work, and work hard, to earn your forgiveness for a long time. A year at the very least."

"I don't know." She shook her head. "What if—"

"Charlotte, my dear." Marcus stepped to her and took her hands in his. "I have never truly been in love before, although, for a moment, I came perilously close."

Her heart caught. "Oh dear Marcus, I am so very sorry."

"No need for apologies. I recognize the inevitability of fate when I see it." A reluctant smile lifted the corners of his mouth. "Regardless of my own lack of experience in such matters, I have been told by experts in the field that love can overcome most obstacles."

"It did not do so when first we wed," Charlotte said slowly. Could love indeed conquer all?

"That was eight long years ago. You were both scarcely

more than spoiled children. Neither of you are the same people you were then. I would wager a great deal it might well be entirely different now."

"Do you really think so?"

"My dear Charlotte." Marcus smiled ruefully. "I would bet my heart on it."

Hugh lounged in the doorway to the library and watched the closed parlor door with narrowed eyes. Pennington was in there with Char, and who knew what they might be saying to one another. Pennington could well be trying to convince her to seek a divorce or run off with him. Only a fool would give her up without a fight, and the earl did not appear to be a fool.

Still, given last night, Char could at this very moment be ending their engagement. Although she could also be throwing herself into Pennington's arms, confessing what had happened last night, *with her husband*, and begging his forgiveness.

God, he hoped not. Their night together had been nothing short of magnificent. The fulfillment of each and every dream he'd had since he'd first left her bed.

Odd, though; given her reputation, she certainly had not made love like a woman with a great deal of experience. There had been a freshness, almost an innocence, in their coupling. Of course, that could be attributed to enthusiasm and emotion. He smiled to himself. And she had most certainly been enthusiastic.

Still—his smile faded—it might well be he was only seeing what he wished to see. The very idea of Char sharing her bed with other men tore at his soul. Not that she hadn't been perfectly within her rights to do so, of course. She had been a widow after all, or at least she'd believed she was. And he had vowed to himself that he would not hold her accountable for anything of an amorous nature that she had engaged in while she, and the rest of the world, had thought she was free to do so. It was proving a difficult promise to keep.

The parlor door opened and Hugh straightened. Pennington bid his farewell to Char, permanently if Hugh was lucky, stepped into the foyer, and started toward the front door.

"Lord Pennington." Hugh pasted a pleasant smile on his face. "Could I have a word with you?"

Pennington cast a longing look at the front door, then nodded in a reluctant manner. "Of course."

Hugh stepped aside, ushered the earl into the library, and waved him to a seat. He quite liked the library. This was the lone room in the house Char had not changed in his absence. Of course, the bookshelves were built into the walls, and aside from a desk and two large, comfortable chairs, there was little to change. And he really hadn't used it much at all in the past save for the occasional smoking of cigars. In truth, as he looked back on it, they'd rarely been at home in those days. Now, he had little desire to be anywhere else.

Hugh settled in the chair behind the desk, noting in the back of his mind how very odd it was for him to be sitting in a position of symbolic authority. And odder still to rather like it.

"Would you care for some refreshment?"

"No, thank you." Pennington shifted uncomfortably in his seat. Good. He should be uncomfortable. He was engaged to another man's wife.

"Cigar then?"

"Not at the moment, but again, thank you." Pennington studied him. "Shall we get on with it?"

"With what?" Hugh smiled pleasantly.

"With whatever it is you wish to talk about. I suspect it is in regards to Charlotte."

"Very well then." Hugh picked up a pen and tapped the end of it thoughtfully on the desk. "I assume you have ended your engagement?"

"Actually, we haven't." Pennington shrugged. "It seems unnecessary to do so as your reappearance makes any betrothal meaningless."

"Of course." As it should be, really. No need to negate something that was already pointless. Still, an official breaking off would be— A thought struck Hugh, and he narrowed his gaze. "She doesn't love you, does she?"

Pennington stared at him for a moment, then chuckled in a dry manner. "No, Tremont, she does not love me. I am fairly certain any affection she feels for me is in the category of," he grimaced, "a friend."

"Ouch." Hugh winced. "Bad luck on your part, old man."

Pennington snorted with disgust.

"Do you think then, and I am asking you as her friend, mind you," Hugh forced a casual note to his voice, "there is anyone she might . . . love?"

Pennington stared in disbelief. "Surely you're not serious."

"Oh, but I am." Hugh leaned back in his chair and debated just how much he should say. The earl was Char's alleged fiancé, but Hugh did think he was a decent sort. In the army, he'd quite prided himself on his ability to assess a man's character, and his instincts now told him that Pennington was the kind of man Hugh too might someday call friend. Hugh drew a deep breath. "I confess, I am at a loss as to what to do. I don't know how she feels. I don't know what she wants."

"You don't?" Pennington said cautiously.

"I don't know anything." Hugh shook his head. "She has changed, Pennington, grown. I left a charming girl and returned to find a lovely woman in her place. She's really rather, I don't know, mysterious now, I would say. At least to me. I used to be able to read her feelings in her eyes, but they have become cool and reserved. Private is the word that comes to mind."

"I thought that perhaps last night she had indicated—"

"There were any number of excellent indications as to her feelings, but were they only of the moment. I have no idea how she feels beyond last night. And given her reputation—" He shook his head. "Not that I blame her for that, of course."

"Nor should you."

"Still, it does bother me. She is my wife, after all."

"She was your widow," Pennington said pointedly.

"I know. Regardless." Without thinking, Hugh tapped the pen a bit harder. "I must admit to a fair amount of jealousy."

"Even though you have not been faithful to her?"

"I expect better of her than I do of myself, she has always been a better person." Hugh paused, then met Pennington's gaze. "However, you should know, before I left I was never actually unfaithful to her, although I admit I might well have been if I hadn't gone."

"I see."

"I wonder now if my leaving might not ultimately have been the best thing for both of us. Certainly not being gone for seven years though, although that was not of my choosing."

"No." Pennington studied him for a long, thoughtful moment. "I wonder . . ."

"What?"

"I will take that cigar now."

"Of course," Hugh murmured. He leaned forward, picked up the cigar box that sat on precisely the same corner of the desk it had always sat on, opened it, and stared. "It's empty."

"It has been seven years. I wouldn't be at all surprised if

Charlotte hadn't thrown out your cigars the very day you left," Pennington said with a grin. "She doesn't like the smell of cigars."

"That will have to change." Hugh caught the earl's gaze and winced. "Or not. If she doesn't like cigars, then there will be no cigars."

"That does it then. A gentleman shouldn't have to give up his cigars." Pennington nodded firmly. "There comes a time in every man's life when he has to decide where his loyalties lie. With a woman he has no possible future with or with his own kind."

"His own kind?"

"Men, Tremont. The masculine gender. We may well rule the world, but we are often outmaneuvered by those known as the fairer sex. A misnomer I believe designed to circumvent our defenses. It's time you knew exactly what you have come home to. Let me see if I can explain."

"Please do."

Pennington chose his words with care. "When it was noted that Charlotte and I were seeing one another, I found myself sought out, in the most casual of ways of course, by one man after another whose name had at one time been linked to hers. Without exception, they attempted to discover if Charlotte and I had . . . well . . . that is," Pennington frowned, "this is exceedingly difficult to say to her husband."

"Shared her bed?" Hugh nodded. "Go on."

Pennington stared at him, then shook his head as if to clear it. "At any rate, I had the distinct impression from each of them, I might add, that their curiosity was spurred by their own, for want of a better word, failure in that area."

"What are you trying to say?"

"I am trying to say that I don't believe your wife has earned the reputation she has. I have also noted whenever there is any mention of her amorous activities, she neither denies nor confirms; rather, she simply smiles in an enigmatic manner. In addition, of her two closest friends—Lady Hazelwood—looks distinctly uneasy during such discussions, while Lady Blackwell appears decidedly smug."

"I don't recall Lady Hazelwood, but I do remember Eunice. Her reaction could well be due to Char's following what I hear is her own impressive example."

"Possibly, but Charlotte's very demeanor tells me otherwise." Pennington leaned toward Hugh in a confidential manner. "We have seen one another for months, yet we have shared nothing more than a kiss. I suspect, for her own reasons, whatever they may be, she rather likes being thought of as . . . busy."

Hugh stared in disbelief. "Do you honestly think that for as long as I've been gone, for seven years, seven very long years . . ." It was nonsense, of course. "Including six when I was believed dead, that Charlotte didn't . . ." No one, not even Char, could possibly . . . "That Charlotte never . . ." No man, at least, but women were unique in and of themselves. "Never?" Although Pennington's theory made rather a lot of sense, given last night. "Not at all?"

"I can't absolutely say never, not at all." Pennington shrugged. "But I suspect never, not at all."

"Never." Hugh shook his head in disbelief. "Seven years. Bloody hell." It was nothing short of amazing. Remarkable. Miraculous. "Do you know what this means?"

"I know what it meant for me," Pennington murmured, then winced. "Sorry."

"She waited for me, Pennington. Even when she thought I was dead, she waited for me."

"I'm not sure she was actually waiting," Pennington said pointedly. "You were dead, after all."

"But she hadn't replaced me. And I had not yet been

home a day when I was back in her bed." Hugh grinned. "This is very, very good."

"Well, it had been seven years for the poor woman," Pennington said under his breath.

"Seven years." Hugh chuckled. "Seven long years. You know what else this means? It means she loves me. It means she has always loved me. There is hope after all. Thank God. I have to admit, I was worried for a—" A thought struck him, and his stomach turned. "Good Lord, Pennington, she's a saint."

"I would scarcely call her a saint."

"I can't be married to a saint. And a saint would detest being married to me."

Pennington snorted. "Not at all. She thinks you're a paragon."

"A paragon? Me?" Panic gripped Hugh, and he got to his feet. "How can she possibly think such a thing?"

Pennington shook his head. "You've changed, remember? Not the same man who left, a better person, living up to your responsibilities and so forth and so on?"

"But I'm scarcely a paragon. She's sure to be disappointed. What am I to do?"

"Why is everyone asking my advice?" Pennington glared and stood. "In this farce we seem to be trapped in, I am . . . I am the second lead. I have lost the girl. I have nothing of any worth left to say. If this were a play, I'd certainly be off stage by now."

"And yet here you are."

"Here I am." Pennington rolled his gaze toward the ceiling.

"And you are her fiancé—"

"No, I'm not. I had hoped at some point, but, no, we have never been officially betrothed."

"Oh, I knew that." In spite of his words, a delightful feeling of relief washed through Hugh. "Given the look on your face when she introduced you as such, I would wager you had never heard of your betrothal before that very moment."

"Something like that."

"But you do care for her, do you not?"

"Well, yes, of course—"

"Then who better to seek advice from than you?" Hugh stepped to Pennington's side and slapped him on the back. "Besides, we share a bond. Men united against women and all that. Loyalties, old man, remember loyalties."

"God help me," Pennington muttered. "How did I get into all this?"

"Char says you're a very nice man," Hugh said in a confidential manner. "Not exactly how I would want to be described by my fiancé, but not a dreadful assessment, I suppose."

"My cross to bear. Let me ask you this, Tremont." Pennington met Hugh's gaze directly. "Do you love her?"

"Of course I love her, I have always loved her. I married her."

"Then it seems to me the two of you can certainly straighten this mess out without me." The earl started toward the door.

"Wait, Pennington." Hugh shook his head. "I have faced horrors too numerous to mention, I have struggled to find my own name, and I have returned to accept my responsibilities. None of which I find as daunting as trying to recapture the affection of my wife. I don't know what to do."

"Damnation, Tremont, I have no idea what you should do either, but, for what it's worth," Pennington's jaw clenched, "here's what I'd do. I'd tell her that I love her. That I have always loved her. Then I would spend the rest of my life making up to her for the years that I lost."

"Yes, but we aren't counting some of those ye—"

"Damnation, man! It scarcely matters. *You* left *her*. *You* started the chain of events that led you both to this point. *You* are the one responsible."

Hugh drew his brows together. "And I fully accept that responsibility."

"As well you should. One last thing, Tremont, Charlotte is a lovely woman, but she is not a saint. Nor does she wish to be. Furthermore, she fears she cannot live with a paragon, nor can a paragon live with her."

"I'm certainly not a paragon."

"Personally, I never suspected otherwise, but the only opinion that counts in all this is Charlotte's."

"So what am I to do?"

"I've given my advice. I have no idea if it's valid or completely ridiculous. You may heed it or not, as you wish." He started toward the door. "I do, however, know where to start." Without warning, Pennington yanked the door open.

Char practically fell into the room.

"Lady Tremont, may I introduce your husband, Lord Tremont? The two of you have a great deal in common. You foolishly wed one another eight years ago, fought for yet another year, and then separated. You have obviously never lost your feelings for him, and I suspect, in spite of all his talk of responsibility and change, you are the true reason why he has returned."

"Does he always get this agitated?" Hugh said under his breath to Char.

"I have never seen him this way before," Char murmured.

"I think you are quite mad, both of you. And I shall be among your company if I do not take my leave at once." Pennington turned to go, then turned back. "By the way," he said in a lofty manner. "The engagement is off." The earl stepped out of the room and snapped the door shut behind him.

Char stared at the closed door. "Did he just throw me over?"

Hugh studied his wife. "Did you hear everything we said?"

"I might have missed something at the very beginning," she murmured.

"Oh?"

"You needn't look at me like that. You were talking about me, after all." She folded her arms over her chest. "I am most certainly not a saint, and the sooner you understand that, the better we shall both be."

"You are more of a saint than you wish people to believe." He paused, then drew a deep breath. "Why did you let everyone think—"

"I rather enjoyed it." She jerked her chin up and met his gaze defiantly. "It was like receiving the prize without having to win the contest. Indeed, I quite liked everyone thinking I was a very merry widow."

"But you weren't."

"Perception is everything, Hugh. Besides." She shrugged. "It also served to discourage amorous intentions. Those who did not share my bed had too much pride to continue their pursuit once they realized they would not receive the favors they thought others had."

"Do you not realize what a dangerous game you played?" It had not dawned on him until this moment how very dangerous it could have been. "It might well have provoked unwanted attentions. There are men who do not take no for an answer under such circumstances."

"I am well aware of that. I am not stupid." Her eyes widened in indignation. "It was not a game. I never teased, nor did I overly encourage anyone. Furthermore, each and every man I allowed to call on me was a well-mannered, honorable gentleman and someone I liked. I was extremely selective."

"You were extremely lucky."

"Perhaps." She lifted a shoulder in a casual shrug. "I do now wonder, though, if I did not choose such gentlemen precisely because they were exceedingly safe."

"You just said—" He narrowed his gaze. "I don't understand."

"Not safe in terms of my person, but rather safe in terms of . . . well . . ." She clasped her hands together and wandered aimlessly around the library, her gaze never leaving his. "My heart."

"Your heart?"

"In spite of their sterling qualities, their handsome faces, their charm—"

He drew his brows together. "They were all charming and handsome, then?"

"Of course, Hugh." She laughed lightly. "You have always appreciated a beautiful woman, I cannot imagine that has changed. Why should I not appreciate an attractive man?"

"Because I don't like you appreciating any man at all," he muttered, more to himself than to her.

"However, you were dead. Now then, to continue, while they were all *quite* charming and *most* amusing and I did like them, I never found one who was especially," she thought for a moment, "exciting. Yes, that's it exactly."

"Exciting," he said slowly.

"Exciting," she said firmly. "In many ways, the men I allowed into my life were virtual paragons of nobility and respectability themselves. Honorable and very safe." She ran her fingers idly along the back of a chair. "I realize now what I did not understand as late as yesterday"—she flashed him a pleasant smile—"before your resurrection, that is, that I am not especially attracted to honorable and safe. To paragons. And I am certainly not suited to be the wife of one." She shook her head. "I am most definitely no saint."

"Char—"

"Yet, just as you have changed, so too have I. I cannot go back to the girl I was, nor can I live with the kind of man you once were." She wrinkled her nose, and his stomach clenched. "It appears I am caught between what once was and what now is. I cannot live with a man whose only concern is the next inappropriate prank or scandalous party or exorbitant wager, nor can I spend the rest of my days with a—"

"I am not a paragon, Char." He stepped toward her. "It's true, I have changed, but in many ways I am the same man I always was."

She shook her head. "You've been through so very much. It's entirely unfair for me to expect that you would not become more serious and somber—"

"I'm not the least bit somber." He forced a wide grin. "See? Can you call a man who smiles like this somber?"

She bit back a smile of her own. "You look absurd."

"I am absurd." At once, his doubts vanished. He knew precisely what to do. What, deep in her heart, she wanted of him. And what he wanted.

Before she could protest, he moved to her and pulled her into his arms. "I am absurdly, ridiculously, passionately in love with my wife. I have been since the very first moment I met her, although I was remiss in that I never told her so."

She caught her breath and stared at him. "Why didn't you?"

"I was a fool. Young, stupid, arrogant."

"Why are you saying this now?"

"Because I'm not nearly the fool I once was. Because I do not want to repeat the mistakes of the past. And because, if I have learned nothing else, I have learned one has no assurances that each moment in life will not be the last. Start over with me, Char. With Pennington's introduction. I have been given a second chance at my life. Let us have a second chance together."

"I don't know, Hugh." She shook her head. "You are not the least bit safe."

"I'm not?" He tried and failed to hide a most satisfied grin.

"Not at all. You never have been." Her expression crumbled, and her gaze met his. For the first time since his return, he could see into her soul. "You make my heart pound and my blood pulse, and when I'm with you, I forget all about anything remotely safe or proper or . . . anything at all. It was like that from the very first moment we met, and, God help me, it is still like that. Apparently, when it comes to you, I have not changed at all. It's most distressing and terribly exciting and too, too wonderful and completely terrifying. I haven't been scared like this in years."

His grin widened. "You haven't?"

"I thought I had grown out of that feeling." A note of desperation sounded in her voice. Or resignation. Or surrender. "Thought in truth, I had grown out of you. I had to do so, of course, as you were dead."

"I am sorry about that," he murmured.

Char stared at him for a long moment. "It's inevitable then, isn't it?"

"What?"

She swallowed hard. "You and I."

"Like the stars in the heavens."

"Still, I don't know . . . I'm not sure . . ." She shuddered and pulled out of his arms.

"Char." He took her hands and gazed into her eyes, her dark, glorious eyes in which she held her heart. "I am scared as well. Eight years ago we met and loved and married and—"

"And it was dreadful and turbulent and foolish."

"Indeed it was. Now, however, we have been given the opportunity to start anew." He drew a deep breath. "I wonder now—no, I believe—that we have that opportunity because we are meant to spend the rest of our days together. That whatever or whoever rules our lives, be it fate or destiny or God above, decreed that we had to spend those years apart first. Perhaps we needed to grow up or know our own hearts or become better people, I don't know. Perhaps it was a penance of sorts. We had to earn this."

"You are the one who earned it. You said it yourself, you have experienced hell." Regret colored her face. "I have experienced noth—"

"Hell of a different sort, I would say." He smoothed her hair away from her face and met her troubled gaze. "You lost a husband and spent six years blaming yourself for his loss. You have earned this as well as I."

Char was silent for a long moment. At last she drew a deep breath. "Should I agree, you do understand such agreement does not mean I have yet forgiven you for your absence?"

"Nor should you. Besides, it would take all the fun out of earning your forgiveness."

She narrowed her eyes. "How do you intend to do that?"

"Precisely?"

"Yes, precisely."

"Well," he thought for a moment, "I suspect I shall grovel on occasion."

She nodded slowly. "On occasion is good."

"Allow you to have your way. Not always, of course, but a great deal of the time." His gaze slipped to the cigar box. It was a very small price to pay. "Whether I like it or not."

A reluctant smile quirked the corners of her lips. "I know I shall like it."

"Surprise you with unexpected and terribly expensive gifts."

"Emeralds are always a good choice."

"And now and again do something outrageous to remind you of our youth."

"Nothing too outrageous," she said quickly. "I don't really want to do any of the absurd, silly, scandalous things we once did just to prove we could. Still, I . . ." She sighed. "I don't know what I want."

At once, the most ridiculous thought struck him. "I have a proposition."

She raised a brow. "Do you indeed?"

"Indeed, I do." He grinned. "I propose that during the daylight hours and when in public we shall be eminently respectable and everything you would expect a paragon and a saint to be."

"And what shall we do at night?"

"Ah, at night," he drew her back into his arms, "at night I shall fill your life with excitement and adventure of a private and personal nature."

She sighed. "This shall not be easy, you know, for either of us."

"We shall have to put a certain amount of effort into it, but we are well up to it." He nuzzled the side of her neck and felt her body sag against his. "Now."

"What if we return to our old habits?" she said weakly. "What if we argue? Do battle the way we used to?"

"We shall have a great deal of fun making up," he said firmly.

"Very well then." She drew a deep breath, pulled away, and looked up at him. "Lord Tremont, it is my very great pleasure to meet you."

"The pleasure, Lady Tremont, is mine." He laughed and met her lips with his.

Hugh held her close, and she clung to him, and he knew without question, without doubt, he was where he was always supposed to be. His life had come full circle and he was back where he started, with the one woman he loved in his arms. And he would never let her go again.

He drew back and grinned down at her. "Now, regarding that proposition, I have an excellent idea."

"Oh no." She shook her head, but a glimmer of delight shone in her eyes. "Not an excellent idea."

"I suggest we go to the roof and make love in the moonlight."

She laughed. "Don't be absurd. It's still morning. There is no moonlight."

He cast her a wicked grin. "Then we shall have to wisely fill our time until night falls."

"It's a very long time until sunset."

"So much the better." He grabbed her hand and started toward the door and the stairs and his rooms or hers. "By the time the moon rises, you shall have conquered all your fears and confessed your undying love for me."

"Undying being the appropriate word," she murmured.

"You love me and I want to hear from your own lips," he said firmly. "You loved me in the beginning and you have never stopped."

"Of course I love you." She pulled up short and studied him suspiciously. "Did Marcus tell you that?"

"No, my darling Charlotte. At long last," he pulled her back into his arms, "I can read it in your eyes."

Epilogue

"Is that it then?" Reggie studied his friend. "The end of it all?"

"My part at any rate." Marcus sipped his brandy thoughtfully. "I suspect it is simply the beginning for them."

"Are they happy, do you think?"

"It's been nearly a month now and I have yet to hear rumors of any discord between them. Indeed, I have run into Lady Blackwell on more than one occasion, and she assures me they are blissful." He chuckled. "She is rather intriguing herself."

Reggie grinned. "Oh?"

"But not for me." Marcus swirled the brandy in his glass and stared at it for a long moment. "I have never come as close to falling in love with any woman as I did with Charlotte."

"At least now we know you can."

Marcus met his old friend's sympathetic gaze. "In many ways she was perfect for me, you know."

"Except that she was already married."

"A minor inconvenience." Marcus waved away the comment. "The trouble with Charlotte wasn't simply that she was married but that she loved her husband once and loved him always."

He heaved a heartfelt sigh. "Dead or alive."

VICTORIA ALEXANDER *was an award-winning television reporter until she discovered fiction was much more fun than real life. The* New York Times *bestselling author lives in Nebraska with her family, a house under constant renovation, and a spoiled bearded collie named Sam.*

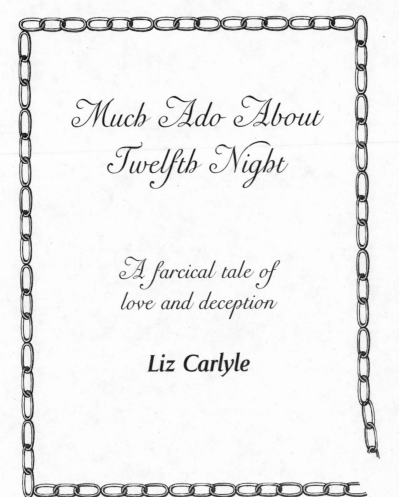

Much Ado About Twelfth Night

A farcical tale of
love and deception

Liz Carlyle

Chapter 1

Two Gentlemen of Wiltshire

*L*ate spring was the height of the season in London, when the clamor of its balls, ridottos, and soirees rose to a frenzied pitch. But just a day's ride west, the Marlborough downs of Wiltshire were always restful and quiet; some would even say deadly, mind-numbingly dull. Sir Oliver Addison *had* said it, on more than one occasion, both drunk and sober, and to anyone who would listen. Just last week, he'd said it to his Grandmama Euphemia.

But was there any mercy to be shown him? No. The Addison dynasty, it was explained to him, was perched on the brink of a crisis. And so Oliver had been packed off to the family pile in Wiltshire. To help. In a manner of speaking.

On this particular May afternoon, Oliver was cooling his heels in his cousin's library, sprawled in an old, worn armchair, which possessed an especially sadistic spring that kept poking him in the arse. But after a week in Wiltshire, more than Oliver's mind had gone numb. So as his cousin, the new Marquess of Rythorpe, kept ripping through the slag heap which constituted the afternoon post—or the afternoon duns, if one preferred perfect honesty—Oliver stared through windows at the rolling downs and tossed back the last of his cousin's armagnac.

Suddenly, it became obvious, even to Oliver, that the mind-numbing silence had given way to a more dangerous sort of hush. In fact, time felt suspended, as if delicately balanced on the tips of the grass, which surged back and forth in the Wiltshire wind like an ocean of green.

Oliver looked around to see that the paper Rythorpe clutched was trembling. And then the marquess roared like an outraged lion, splintering the peace to shards. "Damn and blast such impudence!" he bellowed, stalking toward the hearth as he crushed the paper in one fist.

Yes, the old boy did look rather like a lion, Oliver concluded, watching his cousin hurl the paper onto tomorrow's kindling. It seemed all those years on the Peninsula had taught Rythorpe to move like a big cat, too; calm and languid, but with an unmistakable sense of purpose. His shoulders were broader, his gaze harder, his stride more stealthy than before. His skin had been burnt a very un-English bronze, and his hair was streaked with gold—a little silver, too, courtesy of the *Grand Armee.*

But Oliver wasn't so dull-witted that he didn't know his cousin inside and out, so he was not in the least put off by all Rythorpe's roaring and stalking. Oliver had been watching his cousin wield his silver letter-opener for better than a half hour now, and that had not been the first of his letters to garner a good cursing. But it was the first to land in the fireplace. An intriguing little mystery, that.

"Well!" murmured Oliver from his armchair. "What did that one say, old chap?"

"None of your bloody business," grumbled the marquess, seating himself rigidly behind a quarter-mile of polished mahogany, which was supposed to be a desk. "If it were a death warrant from the king, it would still be the least of my concerns just now."

"Are you sure?" returned Oliver, flipping open his snuff-box. "You went a tad pale."

"Quite sure!" snapped Rythorpe.

Oliver managed to grin as he took his snuff. "Ah, out of the army but two months, and already bitter about your new life?"

"Damn it, I'm here to do my family duty, aren't I?" said the marquess grimly. "But one does not simply walk away from an army post without a backward glance. Military matters kept me on the Continent this last year—and I wish to God they'd kept me another, to tell the truth."

"For pity's sake, Edward, this *is* a marquessate." Oliver let his gaze drift round the library of Sheriden Park, taking in the marble floor covered with once opulent carpets, the deep windows flanked by pier glasses of gilt gold, and the sculpted cherubs, which frolicked with one another across a high, frescoed ceiling.

Rythorpe lifted a pair of unfathomable brown eyes. "And I am just a soldier, Oliver," he said solemnly. "I was not raised to inherit this, nor did I wish it. And now, whilst my regiment is in Belgium getting ready to give Bonaparte his much-deserved coup de grace, I am here, mired up in my brother's swamp of bad debts, and burdened with an estate which is already—"

A stuccoed cherub chose that very instant to lose its life-long grip on the ceiling and explode into shards on the marquess's desk.

"—falling apart?" supplied Oliver amidst the settling dust.

Rythorpe barked with laughter. "Falling apart!" he echoed. "Or *caving in about our heads?* And there's always *teetering on the brink.* Choose any trite expression of ill luck, Oliver, and I daresay it will fit in someplace."

Oliver smiled. "Most men would gladly trade places with you, Edward," he reminded him. "After all, Sheriden Park is the finest estate in Wiltshire, and—"

"Was," interjected Rythorpe. "It *was* very fine indeed until Reggie beggared it with wenching and horse racing. And do not be so sanguine about it all, Oliver. Remember, you are *my* heir. Perhaps I should bolt for Belgium after all. If I meet my Maker on the business end of old Boney's bayonet, then you'll be the damned fool tasked with dragging this brick pile back from its metaphorical brink."

Oliver blanched. "God, I'll need another drink to wash that thought down," he said, stumbling to his feet and heading for the chinoiserie cabinet. Pulling out a decanter of plain brandy, he cocked one brow in Rythorpe's direction. "Ball of fire, cuz?"

Rythorpe glanced at the clock. "Why not?" he muttered, rising to dust the plaster from his coat. "Damn it, Robert Adam must be spinning in his grave."

Thrusting out a glass of brandy, Oliver looked at him blankly. "Robert who?"

"The horrendously expensive architect who spent three months on this plasterwork ceiling," Rythorpe said, taking the proffered glass. "Grandfather had him renovate the whole house a few decades back, much good has it done us. And the state of the house, Oliver, is not the half of it."

Oliver shot him a speaking glance. "Things really are quite bad, then?" he asked quietly. "We've all feared it, you know."

"It is bad. But not beyond hope." Rythorpe paused to drink generously. "Still, I've had to sell my own estate in Suffolk, and Grandfather's sugar plantation. Not to mention the two thousand acres of prime pasture it took to settle Reggie's notes of hand. His tailor, his vintner, and Tattersall's will likely claim a couple of tenant farms. And so you—" Here, the marquess held his glass high and toasted the remaining cherubs. "Yes, you, my fine, fat fellows, must bloody well wait your turn. Ring for someone to sweep up, Oliver."

But Oliver just leaned across the desk. "I overheard the laundry maid complaining to old Bagshaw that there mightn't be enough good linen to make up the guestrooms for Grandmama's birthday party," he whispered. "She made it sound as if old Reggie had sold the very sheets off the beds."

Rythorpe gave a strange half-smile, and for the first time, the fatigue was apparent in his face. "Well, he wore out a few, to be sure," he said. "But he sold only Mama's jewels and a bit of the state silver. We can keep up appearances, Oliver, for some time yet."

"Long enough to get through Grandmama's party?" Oliver murmured dryly. "That *was* her letter you hurled into the hearth, wasn't it, old boy? The scent of Grandmama's rosewater can still make my knackers shrivel."

Finally Rythorpe laughed and fell into his chair. "Have it out then, Oliver, if you must take pleasure in another man's misery."

Grinning, Oliver went to the fireplace and plucked the crumpled ball from the kindling. He returned to his chair, smoothed it across his knee, and read. Then, with a quick glance at the marquess, he reread the postscript.

"Moreover, my dearest Edward," Grandmama Euphemia had scrawled across the bottom in her bold, loopy letters. *"You will be Most Pleased to learn that I will be Bringing with me a quite Dear & Special guest who Begs leave to make you a very Pretty offer which will set to rights an old error in Judgement, and may likely come as No Shock to you, and given your present and Most unfortunate circumstances, My Love, I hardly think you in a position to Refuse her."*

"Good Lord, Grandmama never did know how to punctuate," muttered Oliver. "What's this nonsense about an old error in judgment? What sort of offer can she possibly mean?" Then sudden insight lit his face, quickly shifting to wide-eyed horror. "Good Lord, Edward! Grandmama Euphemia means to marry you off!"

"The devil she will," swore Rythorpe.

This time, Oliver lifted both brows. "Edward, she's already taken it into her head! What choice will you have?"

"What *choice?*" growled Rythorpe. "A vast deal, I should think."

Oliver shook his head. "Oh, no, cuz. You know how it will be. One cannot refuse Grandmama Euphemia anything. She won't allow it."

"What a milksop you sound, Oliver! I can assure you that I am beyond being pushed around by a seventy-five-year-old relic who reeks of rosewater, and whose only weapon is a brass-knobbed walking stick."

At that, Oliver threw back his head and roared with laughter. "Then tell me, dear cousin, how the devil did you get rooked into this birthday party business?"

Rythorpe's expression sobered. "Well, it did seem rather a small thing at first," he admitted. "She wanted me to host a few friends and relatives. Cards, a dinner, perhaps a picnic."

"A picnic!" Oliver practically tittered. "She pinched your earlobe and gave it one of her infamous backhand twists, didn't she, Edward? Did it to me at Almack's last year, trying to make me dance with that spotted, bucktoothed chit of Lord Staley's."

"I met Miss Staley in London last month," said Rythorpe. "I thought her quite lovely."

Oliver laughed. "Edward, ever the gentleman! You've never seen an ugly woman in your life."

Rythorpe smiled faintly. "So did you dance, Oliver?"

"Yes, and you will, too, old boy! Now, who do you think this—let me see now—" He consulted the wrinkled paper. "Yes, who will this *'dear and special guest'* be?"

Rythorpe's face suddenly flushed with color. "I've no notion."

Oliver studied him. "Why, I've never known Edward Addison to tell a bounder," he mused. "But hang me if you ain't lying now."

Abandoning his brandy, Rythorpe turned away and went to the window, his hands clasped tight at the small of his back. "Lady Sophie St. John, then, if you must know," he finally answered. "That's my guess."

"Lady Sophie!" said Oliver. "Why, she's glued to the shelf, Edward! But she's pretty—and plump in the pocket, too, unless her dowry died of old age. Good Lord! Can it be Grandmama has hit upon the answer to your prayers?"

"I don't want Sophie's goddamned money!" snapped the marquess.

"Oh, just *Sophie,* now, is it?"

Rythorpe spun abruptly about, his posture stiff and soldierly. "I have known her, Oliver, all her life. We are cousins. She has, and always will be, Sophie to me. Do not read anything more into it."

Oliver lifted one brow. "In point of fact, Edward, Sophie St. John is no kin to us at all. She is Grandmama Euphemia's grandniece on her third husband's side. I daresay we're closer kin to the butcher's daughter."

Rythorpe sighed. "Well, you'll treat her like a member of this family, Oliver, when she steps down from Grandmama's traveling coach tomorrow," he said. "And she will, you may depend upon it."

"And what of the happy nuptials?" teased Oliver. "May I depend on those?"

"You may not. Not with Sophie St. John. This whole damned house would have to cave in first."

And on that bold challenge, another cherub surrendered, this time striking just half an inch from Rythorpe's toe. Through the cloud of roiling dust, Oliver burst into peals of laughter.

"Oliver," said the marquess when the dust had settled. "Shut the hell up."

Oliver jerked to his feet and snapped a theatrical salute. "Yes, Major Addison, sir."

Chapter 2

A Comedy of Errors, Accidents and Deliberate Prevarication

"Good Lord, Will!" Lady Sophie St. John tossed down her pile of old racing sheets and sprang from her chair. "One cannot wear a lilac waistcoat with blue trousers! Put it back this instant!"

Standing at the foot of his bed, her younger brother lifted his eyes from the trunk he was packing. "Why, this ain't lilac, Soph!" Will stared at her through a shock of unruly hair. "Is it?"

Gently, Sophie took the waistcoat. "Oh, my love, you really are quite color-blind," she murmured, going straight to her brother's wardrobe and pulling out a garment of pale yellow silk. "Sit down, Will, and let me finish."

With a grateful expression, Will hurled himself into Sophie's chair. "Drat old Watson for going down to Brighton at a time like this," he complained. "I never could tell colors. What's a chap to do without his valet?"

Sophie cut him an impatient glance. "It's Watson's first holiday in an age, Will. We promised him."

"I know, I know!" muttered Will. "But I'm nervous as a cat, Soph. What if we can't pull this off? What if our money ain't enough? What if old Staley gets suspicious and buys that horse before we even *get* to Sheriden Park?"

Sophie tugged a wrinkled brown coat from her brother's wardrobe and gave it a little shake. "Then I am sure," she said, scowling at the coat, "that Miss Anna Staley will make you a most charming bride."

"Blister it, Sophie, q-quit saying that!" stuttered Will, coming half out of his chair. "I ain't getting leg-shackled! Especially not to that spotted, bucktoothed Anna Staley. And especially not over some bloody horse."

Sophie tossed Will's coat onto the bed. "Twelfth Night is not *some horse,* Will," she said grimly. "He is the finest piece of bloodstock on three continents. And he is going to be the salvation of Papa's stud farm. In short, Will, that horse is *your* future."

"I'm only four-and-twenty, Soph!" her brother exclaimed. "I'd like to enjoy that future a bit. Why don't *you* get married?"

"I rather doubt I'm Miss Staley's type," she said.

Will crossed to the bed, set one hand firmly on the bedpost, and leaned into her. "Look here, Soph, just cozy up to Major Addison," he suggested with an air of desperation. "He asked you once. And he'll do it again, if you turn him up sweet. Then we'll have that stallion in our pocket for sure."

It was Sophie's turn to blush. "Remember, he is Rythorpe now." Then, in a quiet voice, she added, "And I am not at all sure he'll be pleased to see me again, Will. That is why we must go about this horse-buying business with the utmost delicacy."

"But why shouldn't he want to see you?" asked Will,

sounding affronted. "Everyone likes you, Soph. Besides, it ain't like he really wanted you, is it?"

Sophie's expression softened. "Well, no," she answered. "But I think I may have hurt his pride. Still, that was years ago, wasn't it?"

Just then, a rapid knock sounded. "Hullo, my little darlings!" sang a high, cultivated voice.

Sophie looked up to see her aunt Euphemia framed in the open door, and behind her, their butler, Travers, his expression apologetic. Euphemia wore a lavender turban so lavishly befeathered that it looked as if she'd left a whole flock of denuded peacocks somewhere in east Hampshire. Her avian masterpiece was paired with a carriage dress horizontally striped in gold and puce. Had they actually been blood kin, the mystery of Will's color blindness might have been solved.

Sophie dashed across the room to seize Euphemia's hands. "Oh, Aunt Euphemia, you are early!" She pecked the old lady's plump, well-rouged cheek.

"No, my loves, you are late!" Euphemia said, turning the other cheek to Will. She somehow detached her nest of feathers and sent it sailing onto Will's bed. "I remember that your dear mother could never get anywhere on time," she added. "So I knew you'd wish me to help with the packing."

And with that, she trotted off toward Will's wardrobe and began to whip out coats and trousers as if she dressed a peer of the realm every day of her life. But in truth, Lady Euphemia St. John was thrice widowed, her last husband having passed on a decade earlier. Such misfortune had not, however, discouraged her from clasping her late husband's family to her bosom. And thank God for it.

When Will and Sophie's parents had died some eight years ago, it had been Aunt Euphemia who had wrested control, charmingly but ruthlessly, from their trustees. And following the funeral, it had been Euphemia who had brow-beaten the rest of the family into allowing Sophie and Will to remain at Huntington Park, despite Sophie's having been but seventeen at the time. And more recently, it had been Aunt Euphemia who had supported Sophie's burning desire to rebuild her father's once-famous stud farm.

"Sophie! Sophie, dear, are you listening?"

Sophie looked up to see Euphemia, hands on hips, staring at her.

"Did you pack your emerald green silk? And the olive green riding habit?"

"Oh, yes," answered Sophie vaguely. "Just as you suggested."

"Such a good, sensible girl!" said Euphemia briskly. "Green becomes you, and it was always Edward's favorite color."

"Edward's favorite color?" asked Sophie, confused. "Isn't it just the color of our money which should interest him?"

For an instant, Euphemia hesitated. "Well, Sophie, I think you'd best have a care in dealing with Edward," she finally said. "He can be a rather uncompromising man, and this is a most delicate situation."

"What are you saying, Aunt?"

Euphemia pursed her lips. "Befriend him first, dear girl, before making your offer," she advised. "Be sweet and kind to him. Soften him up. You were once very fond of him, I recall."

Sophie lost her breath for a moment. She'd been more than fond of Edward, and it hurt a little to think of it, even now. But the sad truth was, Edward had never really wanted her. He'd merely done the dutiful thing—probably at Euphemia's urging—in issuing a halfhearted marriage proposal to his newly orphaned almost-cousin. It was just the thing Edward would have done, too.

All through the years, whether it had been a skinned knee, a lost hair ribbon, or, eventually, an obnoxious dance partner who could not quite keep his hands where they belonged, Edward had always been there, quiet, competent, and steadfast, setting things to rights for all of them. It was as if he'd been cast at birth into the role of family caretaker. Sophie had known it and had let him off the hook, cleanly and quickly, as soon as his proposal was spoken.

So Edward had smiled a little sadly and gone off to take care of a regiment instead of a burdensome young wife. And somehow, without even meaning to, Sophie had gone through the rest of her life measuring every man she met against Edward Addison. It had been a disappointing experience.

Sophie shook off her regrets. "Aunt Euphemia, I wish merely to purchase a horse from Lord Rythorpe," she explained for the tenth time. "And yet, when you talked me into this trip last week, you proposed I bat my eyes and tell him how handsome he'd become! You said I should *flirt* with him, when you know perfectly well that I am hopelessly incapable of it—and that Edward could never be taken in by such scheming anyway."

Euphemia gave her a mollifying smile. "Yes, yes, my dear! Quite so!" she agreed. "I was wrong, I daresay, about that flirting business. But what is the harm in—well, in *reacquainting* yourselves? Remember, dear girl, you and Will are in competition with my old friend Lord Staley. He wants that horse as badly as you, and—"

"Did Staley say that?" interjected Will, leaping back into the conversation. "Did you hear it from his lips?"

Again, Euphemia hesitated. "More or less, my dear," she murmured, pausing to neaten Will's neckcloth.

Sophie looked at her suspiciously. "What do you mean, 'more or less'?"

Euphemia smiled enigmatically. "My dear child, there are some things which a woman of experience *knows* will happen long before they *do* happen, if you know what I mean."

Sophie cut her eyes at Euphemia. "I begin to wonder if I do."

"Sophie, Sophie! Just trust me!" Euphemia folded her hands across her puce-striped belly like some plump, affable monk. "If you just do as I say, then I promise you, my dear, that you *will* have your horse."

Will's face burst into sunshine. "Oh, I say, Aunt Euphemia, that's awfully good of you."

"Oh, heavens, look at the time!" Euphemia suddenly cried, bouncing off toward the door. "Travers? Travers!" she called into the passageway. "Is that baggage cart ready or not?"

In fair weather, the vast estate of Sheriden Park lay but a half-day's journey from Hampshire, and this particular day was very fair indeed. Still, the cerulean sky and warm weather did little to calm Sophie's unease. Seated beside Aunt Euphemia, she found her apprehension growing with every passing mile, until their coach was rolling beneath the arched gatehouse and up the rutted carriage drive. And suddenly the stunning sight of Sheriden Park burst into view, snatching Sophie's breath away.

Despite the rumors of ruination, the sprawling brick mansion seemed outwardly unchanged. Row upon row of massive windows glittered in every wing, and already the door was flung wide in greeting. Sophie saw Edward long before they reached the house. He would have been unmistakable, even in a crowded room. But he stood alone on the bottom step like some golden god, his shoulders rigidly back, his eyes hardened against the sun. Sophie's heart leapt into her throat.

A footman hastened forward to put down the steps. "Get out first, Will," instructed Euphemia, prodding at his ankle with her walking stick. "Go round and tell Edward's servants to have a care with my hat boxes. I'll not have any broken feathers, do you hear?"

"Yes, ma'am." Will leapt down.

At once, the new marquess took his hand. "Good afternoon, Weyburn," said Edward, using her brother's title. He gave Will a confident handshake, but, strangely, his eyes remained on Sophie.

Will turned away to greet Sir Oliver Addison. In the carriage door, Sophie froze. Edward was staring up at her, his gaze dark and his jaw hard, as if newly chiseled from stone. Well. He did not look quite the same after all, did he? He seemed taller, broader—and anything but glad to see her.

Behind Sophie, Aunt Euphemia cleared her throat. Snapped back to the present, Sophie gathered her wits in one hand and her skirts in the other, then put one foot gingerly on the top step.

But in that instant, something went badly awry. Her heel seemed to catch on something behind. Sophie pitched perilously forward. On a strangled yelp, she flailed backward. It was no use. Edward leapt forward, catching her. Instead of landing face-first in the gravel, she fell against the hard wall of his chest as his arms bound her solidly to him.

"Oh, dear," said Euphemia in a small, bewildered voice. "Did I drop my stick?"

But Sophie barely heard her. Instead, she was drawing in the scent of Edward and his freshly starched cravat. When he spoke, his breath stirred her hair.

"Good afternoon, Sophie." He sounded blasé, as if he

saved graceless women from breaking their necks every day of the week. "Welcome back to Sheriden Park."

"Oh!" she said stupidly, pushing herself away from his very warm, very solid body. "How mortifying! Th-thank you, my lord." Sophie felt heat flood her face. She still wasn't sure just how she'd managed to trip so awkwardly.

Edward set her back onto her feet, and it was then that Sophie made the foolish mistake of looking up into his eyes. A deep shade of gold rimmed with brown, Edward's eyes had always been his most striking feature.

He held her gaze with a startling intensity. There was an unfathomable emotion simmering inside his eyes. An ageless sort of weariness. Perhaps a hint of a challenge, too. But of what nature? Sophie did not know. She knew only that she could not tear her gaze from his. And in that instant, she was suddenly afraid that nothing had changed.

Then Edward bowed, slipped past her, and the spell was broken.

Everything had changed. *Everything.*

Plastering a smile on her face, Sophie turned to see Oliver coming toward her, his arms thrown wide in greeting. Behind Sophie, Euphemia had begun to scold Edward about the ruts in the carriage drive. Oliver winked and caught both of Sophie's hands.

"Lady Sophie St. John!" he exclaimed. "Survived the trip with Grandmama yet again, eh? I vow you grow more lovely with each passing year!"

"Then she must be utterly breathtaking by now," quipped Will over one shoulder.

Oliver's eyes twinkled as Sophie made a mental note to strangle her brother.

Since Edward was still being lectured by his grandmother—the subject had shifted to his abysmal lack of a good haircut—Oliver began to help organize the unloading.

Soon, a second carriage came rattling up behind them, and Sophie saw Lady Jane, Edward's sister, leaning out the window.

"Hello! Hello!" she cried, waving gleefully. "Edward! Grandmama! And dear Sophie, is that you? Oh, what a wonderful time we're going to have!"

Strangely, at that very moment, Edward's gaze caught Sophie's again. This time, he looked at her across a teetering pile of baggage, and there was no mistaking the wariness that glittered in his gaze.

A wonderful time.

Somehow, Sophie doubted that Jane's prediction was going to hold true.

Chapter 3

As Sophie Likes It

By teatime the following afternoon, Sheriden's drawing room was filled with familiar faces. In addition to Sir Oliver Addison and Lady Jane, there were at least a dozen other guests whom Sophie knew well. Jane was as warm as ever, and Oliver was an incorrigible but charming flirt. And despite the task that lay before her, Sophie was exceedingly glad that she had come. She realized just how much she'd missed this affectionate, boisterous family, which had adopted her into its fold.

As the last of the guests settled in, Sophie passed a lovely hour romping through the gardens with Lady Jane and her three young children. Near the rose garden, they came upon Edward, speaking in hushed tones to a man Jane identified as Sheriden's estate manager. As usual, Edward was standing ramrod straight, his hands clasped behind his back. The men were staring into the distance at a newly furrowed field, and their expressions were grim. Jane shot Sophie a worried look, and as if by mutual agreement, they turned in the opposite direction.

The rumors of ruin, or something frighteningly near it, were soon confirmed. "I daresay you've heard poor Reggie bled us dry," said Jane, looking back over her shoulder at Edward.

Sophie paused to lift a swath of forsythia from their path. "Aunt Euphemia implied something of the sort," she admitted as Jane ducked under it.

Jane stood up, her eyes merry. "Dear Sophie, always so diplomatic," she answered. "But everyone knows it's true, just as they know it is now left to Edward to repair the damage."

On the path ahead, Jane's brood was bent over a tortoise they had discovered. "I feel a little sorry for Edward," Sophie said softly.

Jane's voice sobered. "He has had to sell his own estate, the one Uncle Arthur left him," she admitted. "And the West Indies properties, too. Now he must turn his attention to restoring Sheriden Park and its farms."

Sophie understood. Even at a quick glance, one could see that things were looking a little frayed around the edges. But the new Lord Rythorpe appeared to have matters well in hand. She'd seen plasterers on scaffolds in the library, glaziers knocking out windows in the conservatory, and roofers ripping the slate off the south wing. Oh, it was all done unobtrusively enough, but there was little wonder Edward was liquidating real estate. The shocking thing was, he obviously had no clue just what a valuable commodity stood idly munching away in his stable block, or he'd have sold Twelfth Night already.

But then, Edward had never been a racing man. He had always been more interested in farming and soldiering, and he was nothing at all like his elder brother. A brother who, in a moment of drunken braggadocio, had stupidly paid twice what Twelfth Night was worth just for the amusement of owning a famous racehorse.

"A terrible error in judgment," Aunt Euphemia had called it. And now, Sophie hoped to persuade Edward to sell Twelfth Night at a reasonable price. But in listening to Jane's words, she began to feel a little guilty about what she had come to do.

Jane must have seen her expression. "Oh, do not worry about Sheriden Park, Sophie," she said with breezy confidence. "Now that Edward is home, he will take care of everything. He always does, you know."

It was true, thought Sophie. He always did. And something about that suddenly seemed just a little unfair. Who, Sophie wondered, ever bothered to take care of Edward?

Soon it was time to go in for tea. Other than exchanging a few pleasantries as the guests trickled into the drawing room, Edward avoided Sophie altogether. While Jane poured, he chatted briefly with Will and a few of the other young men, but otherwise hovered in the background, oddly withdrawn from the crowd. Euphemia, of course, was in her element as the guest of honor, and Edward seemed content to let Jane act as his hostess.

The crowd was beginning to thin when Sophie noticed Euphemia crooking her finger in Oliver's direction. He finally saw it and hastened across the room. But he blanched a little, Sophie thought, when Euphemia stabbed one finger at the chair beside her.

For a moment, their heads were bent in conversation. Soon Oliver began to look vaguely uncomfortable. Then he began literally to squirm. Another dressing-down from Grandmama, then. Poor Oliver. His charm always kept him in trouble.

At that moment, someone brushed her elbow. She

glanced up to see Will, whom she'd scarcely spoken to in the whirlwind since their arrival.

"He looks different, don't you think, Soph?" said her brother, his expression grim. "Rythorpe, I mean. All big and dark, with his hair turned bronze. Not sure I would have recognized him."

Sophie watched as Edward settled Jane's youngest on his knee and began to bounce her up and down. The toddler shrieked with joy. Edward tossed back his head and laughed, causing the deeply tanned lines at the corners of his eyes to crinkle.

"No, he is unchanged in the ways which matter," she said quietly. "I would have known him anywhere."

Will shrugged and sipped from his teacup. "I hear Lord Staley broke an axle," he whispered, changing the subject. "He's stuck somewhere on the Bath Road. We should slip out to the stables and have a look at that horse."

Sophie nodded. "I shall say we are going for a walk," she agreed. "Meet me on the west lawn in half an hour."

"Lady Sophie!" interjected a jovial voice. "Weyburn!"

Oliver drew up beside her. He had escaped his grandmother's clutches, then. "Sophie, I find myself desperate to be trounced over a game of piquet," he announced. "Will you oblige me with a hand after tea?"

Sophie set down her cup and saucer with a smile. "How kind you are, Oliver. But I have just promised my brother a walk."

"A walk!" said Oliver, briskly rubbing his hands together. "What a splendid notion! I could do with some bracing country air myself."

"But haven't you been here a sennight already?" asked Will.

"Well, yes," agreed Oliver with a grin. "But I do so love the country. One can never get enough fresh air, can one?"

* * *

Edward dressed for his grandmother's birthday dinner with his usual military precision, putting on a coat of dark blue superfine, and linen so severe it garnered a mild frown from Reggie's valet. And Grandmama was right about one thing. His hair was far too long. Nothing to be done about it now, though. Finished, he looked at himself in the cheval-glass, scarcely recognizing the man who looked back. God, how he wished he could hang up this strange civilian rig and just put on his dusty old regimentals.

As to the valet, he really didn't want him, either. But he'd not the heart to fire the poor devil. One could hardly blame him for Reggie's having been such a well-dressed wastrel.

Behind him, the valet was frowning.

"You disapprove?" asked Edward.

Their eyes met in the mirror. "The coat is a bit ordinary, my lord," he answered honestly, giving the back of Edward's collar a little tuck. "But I think you'll do."

And then, there was no escaping it. Edward had to march down to the gold-and-white salon, a room thrown open only on the grandest of occasions, when all he really wished to do was have a bowl of soup in the parlor and read a good book. Or perhaps drift off in his favorite chair by the fire.

Lord, what a dull fellow he'd become, he thought, as he went down the sweeping turn of the stairs. Or perhaps he'd always been dull? Perhaps it was no wonder Sophie had never wanted him.

Damn. There she was again, popping into his head. *Lady Sophie St. John.* The one person whom, short of outright discourtesy, he meant to avoid for the next several days. And if his grandmother dared broach the subject—which, oddly, she'd thus far shown no hint of doing—then he would simply forbid the topic with his darkest glower. Even

Grandmama Euphemia would not dare to cross swords with him then. Not overtly.

He strode into the salon and saw no sign of the dreaded Sophie. Grandmama Euphemia one could not miss; her wardrobe was not just bright but boldly inimitable as well. So he tucked her plump arm around his own, forced a welcoming smile, then proceeded to do his best to make each guest feel as though the affair would have been ruined by their absence. Once that hour was spent, he took a glass of madeira and retreated into a corner to watch the crowd.

Only a few dear friends and relatives! Grandmama had pleaded. If he counted correctly, he had thirteen cousins, six aunts, four uncles, and a dozen of his grandmother's nearest and dearest, all of whom were squeezed into his grand salon.

It was not the best time for entertaining, what with the house in such a shambles. But what the hell, he'd told himself. Grandmama would turn seventy-five but once, and Reggie's behavior had been no secret. So as a result, all twenty of Sheriden's good bedchambers—the ones with ceilings that didn't leak—were now stuffed nigh to bursting, and the footmen, poor chaps, had been relegated to sleeping in the stables.

Ah, well. So long as he kept everyone from beneath the library's collapsing ceiling, they were all apt to survive this. At least Jane had come to lend moral support, God bless her.

Edward searched the crowd for his sister's face and saw her standing by the hearth with Sophie. Well. It was to be expected, he supposed. The pair had always been inseparable on such occasions.

He wondered, though, how Sophie had slipped into the room without his having noticed. He seemed to notice everything about her. He always had, and the past two days, drat it, had been no exception. Tonight she was wearing a dinner dress in a deep shade of amethyst, the color so dark and so rich it almost matched her eyes.

The gown was not, so far as he could tell, an especially fashionable one, but it flattered her slight, tidy figure. Sophie wore her dark brown hair twisted up in an artful arrangement, which left just a few tendrils free to tease at the back of her neck—which was right where he kept wanting to set his lips. It was a bizarre notion, and it kept assailing him when he least expected it.

Good God, why on earth was the blasted woman not married? It made no sense. Wasn't Sophie considered a great beauty? Most men would have considered her so, he guessed. But the frightening thing was, it almost didn't matter to him *what* she looked like. She was Sophie, and he had the strangest notion that if he'd come home to find her plump, gray-haired, and dressed like a dowd, it wouldn't have stopped that strange, bottomless feeling in his stomach every time he saw her.

But that was not the problem. No, as much as he hated to admit it, whilst he'd been on the Continent, Sophie's youthful promise of beauty had bloomed into the full flower of womanhood, leaving her lovelier at twenty-five than she'd been at seventeen. Damn it.

Suddenly, the mantel clock struck the hour. Jane glanced at it, touched Sophie solicitously on the arm, then hastened from the room. The baby's bedtime, no doubt. And Jane was not one to let servants tuck her wee ones in, a quality he rather liked in his younger sister.

But her departure had left Sophie standing alone by the hearth. No one moved to join her. Sophie glanced about the room as if wondering what to do. And then, somehow, Edward found himself pushing his way through the crowd. He told himself he was merely being a good host. And yet he hated the fact that he was playing into her hands.

Or was he? In that instant, Sophie caught his approach from one corner of her eye, and he thought he saw trepidation sketch across her face. Edward turned away and made a pretense of refilling his wineglass. It was not the first time since her arrival he'd seen that look. It was dashed confusing, too. The come-hither gleam he'd expected to see in her gaze had thus far been absent. No flirtatious smile had yet to curve her mouth. Not so much of a crook of interest had tilted either of her eyebrows in his direction—though she had spent much of the afternoon with Oliver, now that he thought on it.

He was almost disappointed. He had very much looked forward to flinging Sophie's "pretty offer" back into her pretty face. Could it possibly be she was as much a victim of this farce as he? He sipped slowly from his glass, considering it. No. Grandmama's words had been too specific. Sophie realized she'd made an error in judgment by refusing him so bluntly all those years ago.

Now, however, Edward was Lord Rythorpe. And Sophie, for whatever reason, was a spinster. Perhaps she'd hoped he'd make this easier on her. Perhaps she'd hoped he would simply renew his suit, as if her cold refusal all those years ago had not hurt him. But once refused, a gentleman could not do that. Not without some very specific encouragement from the lady. So apparently, Sophie meant to cut to the chase. She meant to go beyond encouragement and boldly make him an offer.

Of course, Edward knew he should have been outraged. But now that the initial shock had passed, was he? No. Surprisingly, his rage had burned down to a mere simmer. In part because he'd been unable to forget how soft and lithe her body had felt against his own when she'd tumbled out of that damned carriage. And tonight, as he approached her, surreptitiously taking in the familiar turn of her cheek, and watching that soft hair tease at the nape of her neck, he wondered if he oughtn't just say yes, and have done with it.

Didn't he need a wife, now more than ever? Didn't Sheriden need an heir? And hadn't the late Countess of Weyburn brought her daughter up to fulfill just such a role? Sophie had been running a vast estate for almost a decade. She would know just how to help him set right this nightmare Reggie had left him. Really, what would it matter if she married him for his title? Weren't a hundred such matches made every season?

But the difference was, those matches were made for duty and convenience, not out of a devotion, which had withstood the test of time.

Devotion?

Edward gave an inward groan. What foolishness! Next he'd be fancying himself still in love with the chit. Fleetingly, he wondered if the strain of inheriting the marquisate was getting to him. Sophie looked at him expectantly as he drew up beside her.

"Good evening, Sophie."

"Good evening, my lord," she said. "I trust you've had a pleasant day?"

"Quite," he agreed. "It has been good to renew old acquaintances."

Sophie's smile deepened. "Yes, I'd not seen your sister Jane in an age," she returned. "Her children are quite shockingly tall, are they not?"

"Yes, yes. Quite tall."

An uncomfortable moment of silence followed, and Edward realized he could think of nothing else to say. It was often thus with him. Men he could command with perfect

clarity, but ladies—especially this one—left him speech-
less. In the last eight awful years, he had thought of a hundred things he'd like to say to Sophie St. John, but where
were those sharp, witty words when one needed them?

"Aunt Euphemia looks well, does she not?" Sophie interjected into the silence.

"Oh, yes. Quite well."

"And Mr. Hastings seems to be enjoying himself im-
mensely."

"Indeed, yes."

The silence became heavier. Sophie's smile shifted to a
look of bemusement. "I think," she said quietly, "that we
are expected to make small talk before dinner, my lord."

Small talk. Edward was not sure he was capable of it. He
was a man of few words, and fewer graces. But he should
try. *Wanted* to try, with Sophie.

"You are not married," he suddenly blurted.

Sophie's brows went up. "I beg your pardon?"

He stumbled awkwardly. "I expected, Sophie, that you
were," he went on. "When I returned from Spain, I mean. I
thought that by now you'd have a gaggle of children and . . .
and a dog."

Her face suddenly lost its color. "Well!" she said a little
breathlessly. "I suppose that qualifies as small talk."

Good God, what had come over him? Edward wished his
drawing room floor would split open and swallow him into
the bowels of hell.

"I daresay I meant to," Sophie went on. "But I just . . .
well, I think I just forgot."

Edward was still wondering where his remark about the
dog had come from. "Forgot what?"

Sophie's color was returning in the form of two bright,
burning spots on her cheeks. "Forgot to get married."

"Oh," he said. "Oh. I see."

Sophie looked at him strangely. "Really, Edward, did Aunt Euphemia never write to you in Spain?"

Not about you, he almost said. Indeed, he'd expressly forbidden it. And for once, his grandmother had listened.

But Sophie was still explaining. "After Mama and Papa died," she was saying, "I became so busy taking care of Will and the estate and so on, that one day, I woke up and realized that—well, that I'd just never got round to it. I was on the shelf, and I rather liked my life that way."

Her even tone took him aback. She did not sound at all like the Sophie he'd known; a girl who'd once laughingly confessed to him that she wanted at least a dozen children—a remark which had given him more hope than it obviously ought to have done.

In truth, he could not remember a time when he *hadn't* wanted to marry Sophie. But she'd been so young, so full of vivacity and promise, that he'd forced himself to wait. He was a full seven years her senior, and even then, he'd understood life and all that was required of him. It had seemed only fair to give Sophie time to grow up. Time, perhaps, to fall at least a little bit in love with him.

Then the unthinkable had happened. Lord and Lady Weyburn had died suddenly, orphaning their children. And in his haste to protect Sophie, to make sure that she and Will did not fear being left alone, he'd rushed in too soon. He'd never been much good with words, and as a result, he'd proposed awkwardly, and a little stiffly. He'd stumbled through his explanations without thinking, without waiting to consider if his devotion was returned.

It had not been returned. Sophie's quick, cold refusal had made that plain.

And now she spoke of marriage as if it were just another chore. Was that what she had thought? Was that why she'd refused him? Had a life with him seemed to Sophie but another duty to be endured? *Well, damn her,* he thought, and let the awful silence simply hang.

Suddenly, salvation arrived in the form of Bagshaw, his butler. "My lord, another of Lord Staley's servants has just come with a message," he said quietly. "I've put him in the library."

Edward turned to Sophie. "I must go," he said, more harshly than he'd intended. "I shall see you at dinner."

"Yes," she murmured. "Yes, of course."

But then, at the last possible instant, she touched his arm. Surprised, Edward jerked to a halt and turned to face her. "My lord," she said very quietly. "May I ask, have I given offence in any way?"

"Edward," he corrected. "No, of course you have not."

"Yet you seem so . . . so different."

Somehow, he had regained his usual composure. "I am different, Sophie," he said quietly. "War does that to people, I fear."

But Sophie just shook her head. "Not like that," she whispered. "You seem angry, Edward. Angry at *me.*"

Something inside him gave way at that, and he laid his hand over hers on his coat sleeve. "I am not angry," he said, and in that moment, he meant it. "I fear I've not been much in society these last eight years. The army has dulled my manners. Pray forgive me."

"Yes, of course." Sophie withdrew her hand.

Edward gave a stiff bow and walked away.

Sophie watched him go, his shoulders back, his posture rigid and perfect as he made his way toward the door. She was mortified to feel a strange, hot pressure welling up behind her eyes. Her breath was beginning to hitch. A sense of loss, sharp and unexpected, assailed her. Then Sophie gave up all pretense of composure. She hastened up the stairs, threw herself across her bed, and cried as if she were seventeen again. And the worst part of it was, she wasn't sure why. Or perhaps she was.

Oh, God. Perhaps she was.

In the last eight years, there had not been one day in which she had not thought of him, and of what had almost been. Not one night in which she hadn't prayed for his safe return from war. Never had her eyes scanned the newspapers without looking first for any news of his regiment. And never once had any other man turned her head.

It was not an obsession that she felt for him. No, no, not that. It was something far more subtle, and far more enduring. Something that seemed almost a part of her, as essential and undeniable as her heart or her brain.

Was it possible she was just being fanciful? Certainly that was what she would pray for tonight. For whatever Edward had once felt for her—call it fondness, sympathy, or a sense of familial obligation—he clearly did not feel it now. She was going to have to accustom herself to that fact. She was going to have to give up her almost-dream all over again.

Chapter 4

Love's Labor Takes a Troubling Turn

*I*n the grand state dining room of Sheriden Park, the dining table seemed to stretch into infinity, laid as it was with almost forty place settings of crystal and silver, and all of it glittering richly beneath the candlelight. Despite the light, the laughter, and the grandeur, Sophie did not enjoy her meal, though no one observing her would have guessed.

Her discomfort began as the guests were taking their chairs, when Aunt Euphemia decided to rearrange the seating. "Oliver!" she said imperiously. "Go round and switch chairs with Mr. Hastings. I wish most particularly to sit by him. Ladies in their dotage must be indulged, you know."

It was a shocking breach of etiquette. But few guests heard, and no one who did dared reproach Euphemia. His face pink, Oliver leapt from the chair beside his grandmother and moved further down, an action that put him on Sophie's right. For an instant, all eyes were on them. Then Edward, who had been conferring with Bagshaw over the wine, turned back to the table. If he'd overheard, he gave no sign.

Oliver looked at Sophie apologetically. "Dotage, my arse," he grumbled under his breath. "Sorry, Soph."

Sophie felt her own cheeks grow warm. "Really, Oliver! What can she be thinking?"

Oliver shrugged lamely. "She and old Hastings have been quarreling all afternoon," he answered, motioning the footman to fill his glass. "Tory politics, of course, so she cannot bear him to get the last word."

Sophie was not sure she believed him.

"Anyway," Oliver cheerfully added, "it's his loss and my gain, Sophie. I wanted to thank you for the walk through the stables."

"Will and I enjoyed it," she lied.

Oliver's smile deepened. "Say, old Reggie had a taste for pricey horseflesh, didn't he?" he remarked, taking up his fork. "Did you notice that fine black stallion as we strolled past? My God, what a horse!"

Luckily, Edward chose that moment to raise a toast to his grandmother, throwing Oliver off any further discussion of Twelfth Night. But he then proceeded to spend the rest of the meal monopolizing her to the point she was scarcely able to converse with those around her. In fact, Oliver had been dogging her steps almost since her arrival. And while there was nothing overtly inappropriate in his manner, he seemed to persist in leaning very near, and dropping compliments rather too lavishly.

It was all very confusing. In Sophie's short life, she'd fended off more than a few fortune hunters, and one quickly came to recognize their telling look of desperation. Oliver simply didn't have it. So why was he flirting? Was he just bored?

In any case, Sophie could handle Oliver. Somewhat reassured, she smiled and tried to keep her mind on Oliver's inane flattery, and her eyes off the Marquess of Rythorpe— the one man she was not at all sure she could handle.

By the time dinner ended, Edward could feel the blood pounding in his temples. His hand was wrapped so tightly around the stem of his glass that it was a miracle it hadn't snapped, and he thought his face might well crack from smiling. Eventually, however, the ladies withdrew and port was brought in, leaving Edward to champ at the bit until the last drop was drained.

Finally, the gentlemen rose to rejoin the ladies, filing from the room in a cloud of smoke, bonhomie, and back-slapping. Unwisely, Oliver lingered behind. Edward laid a firm hand on his arm.

"A private word before you go, Cousin," said Edward quietly. It was not a request.

Oliver was instantly on guard. "Yes?"

Edward set one hand against the doorframe. "Just what are your intentions toward Lady Sophie?" he asked in a dead-calm voice.

Oliver's eyes widened. "*My* intentions?"

"You have been paying a marked amount of attention to her," Edward gritted, his grip on the doorframe tightening. "I hope, Oliver, you know how that looks. I hope you are not trifling with her."

Oliver burst into laughter. "Good Lord, Edward, I'm not trifling!" he retorted. "I'm flirting! And it doesn't *look* like anything at all, because no one save you has noticed. Besides, Sophie is dashed pretty, so we—"

Edward had Oliver slammed up against the wall before he realized his intention. "There is no *we* in this conversation, Oliver," he growled, his hand fisting in his cousin's lapel. "Take your boredom back to London. She is no light-skirt to be used for your amusement."

"Well, she's no green girl just up from the country!" Oliver returned. "Sophie knows how the world works, Edward. Besides, who named you guardian angel? Two days ago, you dreaded the very sight of her."

"The young lady is a guest in my home." His voice was so cold he barely recognized it. "She is to be treated with respect, or you will deal with me. Stop staring down her bodice, Oliver. And stop breathing down her neck."

"Or what?" snarled Oliver. "I'll have to offer for her, and get you off Grandmama's hook?"

Edward felt as though the air had been crushed from his chest. "Yes," he managed to answer. "Yes, Oliver, you might just have to do that."

Oliver's eyes went wider still. "Look here, Edward, you are ruining my new coat," he protested. "Let it go, old fellow, and just admit the truth."

Edward had not realized he still gripped Oliver's lapel. "And what truth would that be?"

"That this tiff is more about you than me," he answered, brushing violently at the wrinkles in his coat. "Did it ever occur to you, Edward, to simply yank that ramrod out of your arse, stop trying to do the right thing, and just go do what you damned well please?"

Edward felt something inside him snap. "If I did what I pleased at this moment, Oliver, you wouldn't draw the breath of life ever again."

Even Oliver, it seemed, had his limits. "Then name your bloody second if you're so bent on a fight, old fellow!"

"Go to the devil, Oliver."

And on that bit of advice, the marquess shoved his cousin from his path and followed his guests down the corridor.

After forcing his temper to calm, Edward stalked back toward the white-and-gold salon. He wanted to throttle Oliver, but he had the uneasy feeling that his cousin was half-right about something. Just what, he wasn't sure. Certainly he didn't want to *shoot* Oliver. Lord, things were getting out of hand! Exasperated, he shoved his hands through his hair and went inside.

In the salon, Jane was already serving coffee. Edward took a cup and retreated to a corner, where his uncles seemed to be arguing the merits of breeding pointers versus setters. They were single-minded fellows, requiring nothing more of him than an occasional grunt of agreement. This afforded him ample opportunity to look about the room for Sophie—to make sure Oliver was not annoying her, of course.

Oliver had not come in at all, which suited Edward's present mood. Sophie was on the sofa beside his grandmother, who had dressed for dinner in about six different shades of pink and red. Sophie, however, was looking startlingly elegant in a dark green gown set off by a strand of milky pearls. Her hair was swept high on her head, baring her neck, and Edward found himself suddenly glad that Sophie had shunned the current ladies' fashion of chopping off one's hair.

And then he remembered Oliver's accusation, and he cursed beneath his breath.

"Quite right, my boy!" remarked one of his uncles, apparently misinterpreting his expletive as some sort of concurrence. "There, Harry! You have it from the artillerist himself. A fowling gun of that bore would be worse than useless for grouse!"

"Fred, you're a damned fool!" swore Harry. "Afraid a wounded grouse might turn on you? Why, that blunderbuss of yours would make pâté of the poor devil."

The argument droned on. Edward drifted away, keeping one eye on Sophie. For an instant, she lifted her gaze to glance about the room. Once, she caught his eyes, colored

faintly, and looked away. And suddenly it dawned on Edward that while he'd not been wrong about Oliver's behav-
ing badly, he had not done so well himself.

He was the host, for pity's sake. And he had shown no
warmth and even less welcome to Sophie. On two occasions, he'd been deliberately short with her. On a third, he'd
pried into her personal life. His manners seemed to be going the way of his conversational skills. No wonder Sophie
found Oliver entertaining. She had spent the better part of
two days with him. Perhaps she no longer wished to make
Edward any sort of offer at all. Perhaps this time, he had
genuinely hurt her. That would not do. Sophie was a part of
his family. He was going to have to apologize.

Sophie had risen and strolled toward the French windows, which opened onto the terraced lawns. It was a warm
night, with a breeze strong enough to stir the heavy velvet
draperies, which were drawn half open. Sophie stood there
for a long time, simply watching the room and sipping at her
coffee. It was almost as if she were waiting for something.

Then, for an instant, a footman distracted him with a
question about the coffee. When Edward turned back, he
barely caught the flash of green silk slipping between the
velvet panels and into the night.

Sophie had gone outside?

Edward considered it but a moment before excusing himself. It was the perfect opportunity, he told himself, to make
that apology. To be alone with Sophie, away from prying
eyes. Perhaps if they were alone, she would even go ahead
and make her offer. Of course he meant to say no. Still, he
reasoned, it would be best for both of them to just get it
over with. And on the heels of that thought, Edward found
himself wondering if Sophie still looked lovely in the
moonlight.

He reached the draperies and slipped silently through.

But he'd gone only a few feet into the gloom when his heart almost stopped. A decidedly masculine voice was carrying on the breeze from the shadows. Sophie was meeting someone? Good Lord.

A gentleman would have turned back, or perhaps announced his presence with a tactful cough. But for once in his life, Edward did not do the gentlemanly thing. Instead, he slid into the shadows like a blade through butter, melting soundlessly into its depths. He was good at it, and he did not have far to go. At the end of the terrace, a man sat sprawled across the wrought-iron bench that overlooked Sheriden's west lawn. Edward could see Sophie's bare shoulders reflect the moonlight as she floated through the night toward him.

Damn Oliver's eyes! He was taking his flirtation just a tad too far. This time, Edward meant to throttle him. But it would not do to make a scene just now. Instead, he would stay near. Just in case Sophie needed him.

But she didn't look as if she needed anyone. She moved with perfect confidence as she gathered her skirts and sat down. Edward crept closer. At once, he realized it was not Oliver whom she'd joined. Relief flooded through him when he recognized her brother's voice.

It was a short-lived emotion.

"You're still confident you can get him, Sophie?" Will's words were soft, but unmistakable. "What will it take?"

"Money, Will." Sophie's voice was grim. "Pots of it. But everyone has his price. I just have to figure out what Edward's is without insulting him."

Too bloody late, thought Edward. But a strange sense of mortification was stealing over him. Sophie was awfully damned confident he'd marry her, wasn't she?

In the darkness, he heard Will chuckle. "Well, I'm deuced glad it's your job, Soph, and not mine," he whispered. "Old Rythorpe looks a bit fierce to me."

"I think it's just that he's under a vast deal of pressure," she answered. "Don't worry, Will. I'll manage Edward."

Her brother hesitated. "Perhaps you ought to be careful, Soph."

Sophie shrugged. And then, the conversation took a very strange turn. "He really is quite fine looking, isn't he?" Sophie said, her tone warming a little.

In the moonlight, Edward could see Will open his hands expansively. "I'd say so, but you're the better judge," he said. "You are still pleased at the prospect of having him, Sophie?"

Sophie laughed lightly. "Oh, I think I'll be well satisfied."

Edward felt frozen in place, appalled. *Well satisfied—? Good God! Had she no shame?*

Then Sophie dropped her voice to a whisper. "To tell you the truth, Will, I still get a little shivery just looking at him."

Will snorted. "Lud, Soph! You sound sixteen again."

Sophie elbowed him sharply in the ribs. "And to imagine I'd almost forgotten what he looked like! Did you notice those long, strong legs? That glorious mane?"

"But a tad ragged," countered Will. "He could certainly be better groomed. And I didn't much care for his coat. Very ordinary, I thought."

Ordinary! That puppy thought his coat was ordinary? The damned nerve! But the words had a familiar ring.

"He's been a little neglected, I fear." Sophie dropped her voice. "But the truth is, Will, his looks don't much matter to me anymore. It's the pedigree I'm after."

"Well, I know that, Soph!" her brother answered. "But looks don't hurt."

"Oh, Will!" Sophie laughed. "With his bloodlines, you could just throw a feed sack over that shaggy mane and make good use of the parts that matter."

Will gave a groan of disgust. Edward felt his blood run cold. He forgot to breathe. Good God Almighty! Was this what was said of him these days? That the Marquess of Rythorpe was in such dire straits, he'd sell his own cock to the highest bidder?

"Sophie, you're beginning to sound vulgar," he heard Will say.

Vulgar? She'd surpassed vulgar eons ago. The moment she'd fallen out of her carriage and into his arms.

"I'm simply stating the facts, Will," Sophie countered. "He's a tad long in the tooth now to be of much use for anything else. But I'd be a fool to overlook his lineage. Just imagine the possibilities!"

No, thought Edward grimly. *Not in a million years.*

But he *was* imagining it, and it disgusted him. Suddenly, he itched to turn Sophie St. John over his knee and wear the hide off her backside with his bare hand. How dare she speak so crudely of him? Or anyone else, come to that? She wasn't supposed to sound like those jaded women of the *ton* who'd had far too much experience in other men's beds. She was his little Sophie. Or so he'd thought.

Edward suppressed a bitter laugh. Good Lord, in his heart, he'd come home hoping she was still sweet and seventeen, hadn't he? What a damned fool he was. *Sophie knows how the world works,* Oliver had said. Well, apparently, she did. But she obviously didn't know that Grandmama Euphemia had already tipped her hand.

Yes, now that his *bloodlines* were of use to her—now that he was the Marquess of Rythorpe instead of some obscure army officer—it seemed she might condescend to share his bed. No, it was worse, even, than that. She thought she could buy him. Well, by damn, he'd sooner burn in hell.

Suddenly, Will rose and stretched his arms wide. "Well, Soph," he said on a huge yawn. "I'm for bed. You coming?"

Disappointed and disgusted, Edward turned and walked quietly back toward the French window.

"I think I'll stroll along the terrace and take the air," came Sophie's distant answer. Her voice sounded oddly wistful.

From the shadows, Edward watched Will stride across the flagstones, through the open window, and back into the salon. In the distance, he could hear the heels of Sophie's slippers as she paced back and forth along the terrace edge.

His rage was melting away now, leaving only a familiar, ice-cold fury. He wondered what Sophie was thinking as she walked. And on his next breath, he found himself wondering if she was cold. The breeze had grown stiffer, the air more chill. Sophie wore only her green silk gown and a gossamer shawl about her shoulders.

And he was a fool to give a damn. What should it matter to him if she were standing out here stark naked, dripping wet, and hacking with consumption? But it did matter. It still mattered. Perhaps it always would, and that angered him even further.

Just then, the sound of Sophie's footsteps grew more distinct. *Christ!* Was she coming straight toward him?

Edward slid behind one of the stone pillars that supported the balustrade above. He wondered if she would see him. Probably not. But he could see her, a faint shadow floating nearer in the gloom. He must remain perfectly quiet, he told himself. Perfectly motionless.

And then, without even meaning to, Edward cleared his throat and stepped squarely in front of Sophie.

The Marquess of Rythorpe was the last person Sophie expected to see as she made her way toward the salon. But when the broad, immutable shape slid from the shadows to block her path, she knew instinctively that it was he. Her every nerve ending tingled with awareness.

He propped one shoulder against the pillar, looking far more indolent than usual. Fleetingly, she wondered if he'd had too much to drink at dinner. "Good evening, Sophie." His voice was a low rumble in the dark. "Shouldn't you be inside with the other guests?"

"Good evening, Edward." Her voice sounded suddenly breathless. "I was just enjoying the night air."

He stepped unmistakably closer. "Some say the night air can be dangerous," he murmured. "Besides, it is not at all the thing for young ladies to be roaming about alone in the dark. Or have customs changed whilst I was abroad?"

Sophie did not back away as she should have done. "Will was with me."

"Was he?"

Sophie could feel Edward's eyes burning into hers. He sounded not at all himself. Could he have overheard her conversation with Will? No, their voices had been soft. And surely they would have heard his approach.

"Thank you for your concern," she said quietly. "I feel perfectly safe here at Sheriden."

"Do you?"

"Indeed, yes," she muttered, moving as if to go around him. "Pardon me, I wish to go in now."

But he had no intention of allowing her to pass. She sensed it. His broad shoulders blocked out the light from the window. She could feel his gaze rake over her, even in the dark. When he set his hands on her bare shoulders, she knew she should turn away.

But she did not. "My lord?" she said, looking up at him uncertainly.

"*Edward,*" he corrected, the word a low growl. Then his mouth came down hard over hers.

Sophie tried to gasp, but his grip on her was unassailable, his mouth hot and urgent as it moved on hers. Somehow, she jerked her head away, but he forced her face back into his and kissed her again.

Alarm seized her. She tried to protest, but Edward's mouth opened over hers, capturing the sound. His tongue slid deep inside her, an intimacy that shocked her. In response, her stomach bottomed out, and her knees went weak. A traitorous warmth went spiraling through her body. The sharp, heated scent of soap and male sweat filled her nostrils. The dark shadow of his beard raked across her skin; a heady, exhilarating sensation.

She must have made a sound of pleasure. In response, Edward gave a little growl of satisfaction somewhere deep in his chest and settled one hand against the small of her back, drawing her hips to his. Suddenly, Sophie realized she was not fighting it. Fighting *him*. She was not shoving against his chest, or kneeing him between the legs as she ought to have done.

Instead, she was kissing him back, her face turned up into his, greedily drawing his tongue into her mouth and sliding her own sinuously against it. She could feel his breath, hot and hard on her face. She could feel the swell of his erection against her belly as the heat of his hand burned into her spine. Could feel herself melting. Melting against him, into him, her body molding hungrily to his as she slid into a languorous, sensual stupor.

But her awakening was rude and cold.

As quickly as he'd begun it, Edward jerked his mouth from hers and stepped back, his heels clicking firmly on the flagstones. His hands had fallen to his sides. The warmth and scent of him were gone, leaving Sophie to feel suddenly cold and deeply ashamed.

"And that, my dear Sophie," he murmured, "is why young ladies should not venture into the dark alone."

Then the Marquess of Rythorpe slid back into the shadows from whence he'd come, leaving Sophie standing alone in the dark, more shaken and confused than she'd ever been before.

Chapter 5

Measure for Measure and Tit for Tat

*J*t was just after breakfast two days later when Oliver went sneaking through the house in search of his cousin. Edward had been looking daggers at him lately, and it was time, Oliver had decided, that he started dealing from both sides of his pack. Time to load the dice. Hedge his bets. Teasing his cousin was all well and good, Oliver supposed, but a chap could ill afford to make Edward truly angry. And truly angry was just what the old boy had looked for the last couple of days.

"In the stables," said Reggie's valet with a disdainful sniff when Oliver poked his head into Edward's bedchamber.

So Oliver went sneaking back down the stairs again, keeping a watchful eye out for his grandmother, whom he definitely wished to avoid. It was easy enough to find his cousin. The old boy was standing half-naked in the rearmost foaling stall, his broad shoulders glistening with sweat. When they had been little more than boys, and Gentleman Jackson the latest rage amongst fashionable young bloods, the stall had served as their makeshift boxing ring.

For a few moments, Oliver stood aside, silently watching as Edward pounded at their old punching bag, or what was left of it. Apparently the stableboys had picked up where he and Edward had left off, for the leather was worn and cracked. Each of his cousin's perfectly timed punches landed hard, yet not with the healthy thud of brute force on leather, but with a flatter, more brittle sound. Near the top, a seam had split, and a tuft of cotton batting was sprouting forth. It wasn't even a real bag, just something they'd had the village saddler gin up.

Edward had been at it, Oliver guessed, for a while now. Despite the cool spring morning, the sweat was already forming rivulets down his back and biceps. Very large biceps, Oliver noted, for he made a habit of self-preservation. Christ, did they make artillery units eat lead shot for breakfast and tote their own cannon?

Perhaps he should take Edward's advice and stop following Sophie around like some besotted pup. He was spending every possible moment at her side. Oliver definitely did not want to make an outright enemy of Edward, but he couldn't resist the temptation to prod the old boy just a bit. Besides, he'd made his deal with the devil.

Oliver watched his cousin give the bag an artful series of left-right jabs, then delicately cleared his throat.

Edward spun around, and with the back of one hand, raked a sweaty lock of hair off his forehead. "You, is it?" he said, looking vaguely disoriented. "I did not hear you come in."

Oliver smiled. "You have not lost your rhythm, cuz," he answered. "You still have better timing than one sees at what passes for a high-stakes mill these days."

Edward dropped his hands, looking a little sheepish. "I had to get out of the bloody house," he admitted. "That pack of females I'm harboring means to run me mad, I think."

"A *pack?*" Oliver strolled a little closer, since he didn't seem to be Edward's next target. "How many women make up a pack, old boy?"

Edward made a sound of disgust and grabbed an old feed sack he'd tossed across the box wall. "On her good days, Grandmama alone can constitute one," he grumbled, beginning to wipe himself down. "She-wolves, all of them, I begin to think."

Oliver propped one shoulder casually on the doorframe. "And Sophie St. John?" he said quietly. "Do you include her in that category?"

Despite the shadows, he could see Edward's eyes narrow. "Damn you, Oliver, don't taunt me this morning," he warned, tossing aside the sack. "I've already had to deal with another of Reggie's spurned bill collectors, not to mention a collapsing granary roof, two orphaned lambs, and a fresh bout of Grandmama's meddling. But I'm not so tired I can't yet whip the impudence out of you."

Oliver held up both hands, palms out. "Pax, Edward," he swiftly answered. "A bad subject, I confess."

"Good." Edward strode from the box stall and down the passageway toward the huge water trough, which was filled each morning. Oliver sauntered along behind, watching as Edward doused his head in, all the way up to the shoulders. He came up sputtering, then leaned over it to sluice water off his chest and arms.

"It has been a most interesting house party so far," Oliver casually remarked as Edward snatched his shirt from a peg by the trough. "I look forward to this afternoon's picnic. Grandmama has already chosen her sunbonnet. It is especially breathtaking."

Edward dragged the linen over his head. "If by that you mean the very sight of it makes one gasp, I can believe it."

Oliver laughed, and turned the subject. "Tell me, cuz, what do you make of the charming Miss Staley?"

"Who?" he asked.

"Lord Staley's chit," said Oliver. "Young Weyburn might trip on his tongue whilst gawking, if he's not more careful."

Edward barked with laughter. "Oh, yes, the spotted, bucktoothed girl who turned up at breakfast yesterday," he answered. "Poor child. Such a handicap."

Oliver grinned at the sarcasm. Admittedly, he deserved it. Somehow, the homely Miss Staley had metamorphosed into a breathtaking beauty—just in time for her second London season, too. Bloody convenient, that.

"Ah, well," said Oliver equably. "She's still not as pretty as Sophie, is she? Now there, cuz, is a *real* woman."

His cousin began stabbing in his shirttails with short, violent motions. "Just what is it, Oliver, that you wish to say?" asked Edward. "Spit it out, and be done with it, for God's sake."

Oliver shrugged. "I was just thinking about Sophie, that's all."

"Thinking?" Suddenly, Edward ripped off his shirt again and hung it back up. "What the devil is there to think about?"

Oliver eyed him carefully. "What are you doing?"

But Edward was already striding back into the depths of the stable again. "I thought I was finished pummeling at inanimate objects," he growled. "I was wrong. Keep your distance, Oliver."

Doggedly—and bloody bravely—Oliver followed anyway. "We were speaking of Sophie," he called into the shadows.

"Fine," Edward said, disappearing into the foaling stall.

"Speak, by all means, if you've something intelligent to say."

Oliver slowed his pace. "Why is it, do you reckon, she never married?"

There was a long, pregnant pause. "Who?"

"Sophie."

Oliver could hear Edward curse beneath his breath. "I have no idea," he finally answered as he began to jab at the leather bag again.

Oliver leaned against the door and peered in. "But she's dashed pretty—"

With another hard blow to the bag, Edward cut him off. "I believe, Oliver, that we've established that."

"Yes, well, and that's why it makes no sense," Oliver pressed, wincing a little at Edward's rapid one-two punch, followed by a muzzler that could have crushed a chap's molars. "Do you reckon she's wearing the willow for someone?" he bravely ventured. "Maybe had her heart broken by some fellow she fancied in her youth?"

"I do not think," said Edward, giving the bag another swift series of blows, "that women are truly capable of having their hearts broken." The bag was swinging wildly now, the chain overhead shrieking in protest.

"Oh," said Oliver. "Well, I daresay you've had a vast deal of experience with the opposite sex, then? Because, you know, I was not aware of that shortcoming."

"Oliver," said Edward, dropping his fists and pinning him with his glare.

Oliver leaned solicitously into the stall. "Yes, cuz?"

"Shut the hell up."

Oliver smiled and closed his mouth. His duty done, he swept his cousin an elegant bow and departed the stables with rather more haste than he'd come.

* * *

"Sophie? Sophie, my dear, may I give you my arm?"

Roused from an absentminded study of her luncheon, Sophie looked up to see Oliver standing over her picnic blanket. Silhouetted against the afternoon sun, he was extending his hand down to her, his expression expectant.

"Forgive me, Oliver." Sophie set aside her plate. "What did you say?"

Oliver grinned down at her. "We're hiking to the top of Silbury Hill," he repeated. "Grandmama Euphemia said you particularly wished to go."

Sophie frowned. "I never said so."

Oliver shrugged. "Well, come on anyway! The view is grand. I'll even tell you the legend of the hill when we reach the top."

"Why not?" For the last two days, Sophie had desperately needed someone to distract her from her thoughts. Oliver's companionship had been much welcome. She stood and brushed the crumbs from her skirts. "Who else is going up the mound?"

"Everyone under thirty." Oliver pointed at the trail of young people making their way along the path toward the rounded hillock in the distance.

Just then, one of Sheriden's footmen swooped down on Sophie's plate, which was still laden with food. "Good Lord, Soph," said Oliver. "You scarcely ate a bite."

Sophie smiled weakly. She hadn't been able to eat her breakfast, either. "I shan't faint, Oliver, and force you to carry me back down, if that's what you fear."

Oliver laughed. "Hurry up, then! Your brother set off five minutes ago with Miss Staley on his arm. From the look of it, you'd best go chaperone."

Lord Staley and his daughter had finally arrived yesterday morning just as breakfast was ending. Over coffee, the baron had seemed singularly uninterested in discussing

anything to do with horseracing, even though Sophie had
twice turned the conversation in that direction. And despite
his earlier protests, Will had seemed instantly captivated by
the vivacious Anna Staley. Oliver had simply sat staring
over his coffee at the girl, occasionally allowing his mouth
to fall open.

"Miss Staley is quite lovely, is she not?" murmured Sophie as they set off after the others. "I was a bit taken aback,
for I'd heard that she was, well, a bit *plain*."

"Plain!" muttered Oliver. "The mind boggles, does it
not?"

Sophie blushed a little. "Well, someone said she had
spots and buckteeth," she admitted. "But if she had spots,
they've vanished. And while her teeth are very large and
white, they certainly don't stick out. Indeed, her smile is
radiant."

"Ugly ducklings do sometimes turn into swans, don't
they?" remarked Oliver a little morosely. "And I hear that
little cygnet has twenty thousand in the funds."

Sophie pulled a sad face. "Poor Oliver! Has Will stolen a
march on you?"

Oliver's smile returned. "Ah, by no means, my dear!" he
said, tucking her arm around his. "I could not be better
pleased by my choice of a walking companion."

"You are going up to the top of the mound, Oliver?"
asked a deep, quiet voice behind them.

Sophie froze on the path but did not turn around. She had
not heard Edward's approach. The man moved like some
sort of ghost. She should know, for she'd spent all day trying to avoid him. Worse, Edward's steely eyes had started to
ice over when their gazes met.

Oliver, as usual, seemed oblivious to the strain. "As
you've noticed, I'm seeing Sophie safely up," he said.
"Everyone else has gone on ahead." With that, Oliver

stepped off the path, as if making way for Edward to join the others.

After a moment's hesitation, the marquess gave them both a curt nod and strode past. But to Sophie's consternation, he did not move very far ahead of them.

It was a steep climb up the mound. By the time they reached the top, Sophie was gasping for breath. On the flat summit, Edward's guests were milling about, taking in the view, their hands shielding their eyes from the sun. Along the mound's edge, the shrieking children were pushing and pulling one another over in some haphazard version of King of the Hill.

Sophie watched Edward move through the crowd, and frustration bit at her again. She was still enraged about what had happened two nights past. Did Edward think her fast? Was that why he had kissed her so crudely? Absently, she touched her fingers to one corner of her mouth, remembering how frightening—and how thrilling—it had been to be kissed so intimately.

Sophie had bragged to Will that she was not afraid of Edward, but she was no longer sure that was so. Each night, she'd tossed and turned in her bed, burning with shame, remembering the feel of his mouth on hers. She had wanted him. Wanted *more*. And each morning, in the bright light of day, her hurt and anger sprang forth anew. She was hurt that Edward believed he could use her so cruelly. And hurt because he had made her wonder if she really knew him at all.

But her anger was turned inward. Because, despite his behavior, she still cared for Edward. No, it was worse than that. She still loved him; had always loved him. She knew it for certain now. And she still had this girlish, almost desperate need to find honor in him. Yes, she wished, as much as ever, to believe that Edward Addison was some sort of knight in shining armor, a truth that only made her angrier still.

It was a vicious circle of the worst sort. Lord, she would not dare ask Edward to sell Twelfth Night to her now, and she had no idea how she was going to explain that to Will.

Just then, one of Jane's brood went rolling off into a thatch of briars below. Jane screamed. Edward dashed over the edge to catch him.

Sophie watched, still a little breathless, then forced her attention back to Oliver. "Oh, my!" she complained. "I may have to roll back down, too. How far did we climb?"

"One hundred thirty feet, pretty much straight up," said Oliver as he peered over the edge. "My God, Sophie, come look! You can still spot Grandmama's orange and purple bonnet all the way up here."

"I can't walk that far." Sophie plopped down on a big rock. "Perhaps I shall swoon after all."

"Then I shall catch you, my dear," Oliver declared.

"If she is unwell," gritted the deep, quiet voice behind them, "then for pity's sake, summon the footmen to haul her back down again."

Sophie gave a little scream at the sound. "Good Lord, Edward!" she snapped. "Will you please quit creeping up on people?"

Edward looked at her very strangely. "I was not aware, Sophie, that I was *creeping up* on anyone. Have I given that impression?"

"Not thirty seconds ago, you were over there," she argued, pointing at the opposite edge. "Now you are here. What do you call it?"

Edward's brows arched. "Attending to my guests?"

Sophie could feel the heat flooding her face. Even Oliver looked uncomfortable. "I beg your pardon," she stammered, looking away. "You startled me, that is all. Oliver, I believe you were about to tell me the legend of Silbury?"

Oliver swallowed hard. "Indeed, yes," he agreed. "It is not a true hill at all, but the burial mound of an ancient king."

"Is it? How marvelous." Sophie refused to look at Edward. "Which king?"

Oliver looked uncertain. "King Sil, I believe," he answered. "Hence its name, *Sil*-bury."

"How clever you are Oliver!" said Edward dryly.

Shifting on the rock, Sophie turned her back fully to Edward. "And is there any romance attached to it, Oliver? Did the king perhaps die of a broken heart? Or saving his fair lady?"

"Driven to suicide by her, more likely," muttered Edward. "Poor devil."

Oliver cut an uncertain look at the marquess. "No, there isn't any romance so far as I know," he demurred. "I think old Sil just keeled over and turned up his toes. But it is said he was buried on a horse of solid gold, so a few chaps have tried digging him up over the years."

"How exciting." Sophie smiled brightly at Oliver. "Treasure beneath our very feet!"

Behind her, Edward snorted scornfully. "There's no treasure, nor anything romantic to it," he corrected, stepping fully into view. "It is just a pile of dirt, Sophie. In fact, it's generally believed the thing is Satan's handiwork."

"Satan's handiwork?" Sophie's tone was scornful.

Edward ignored the warning and continued. "They say the devil flew up from hell with a sack of scorched earth, meaning to drown the good citizens of Marlborough with it," he went on. "But the Avebury priests tricked him into dropping it here. That, and not some sort of sentimental drivel, is just as apt a tale of its origin."

Sophie looked up at him, her eyes narrowed against the sun. "Edward Addison, I have long known there wasn't a quixotic bone in your body," she said in a hard, quiet voice. "And I accept that you are not, and never will be, romantic. But must you continually insist upon souring life's sweeter moments for the rest of us?"

Edward's face went tight with suppressed emotion. "Oliver, I believe Jane needs help managing the children," he said after a moment had passed. "May I prevail upon you?"

Oliver looked back and forth between them, his expression wary. "I daresay I ought to go," he finally answered. Then he vanished into the throng, leaving an uneasy silence in his wake.

Sophie stood at once. "Excuse me, my lord. I wish to take in the view from the very edge of the precipice."

Edward caught her by the arm. "Oh, don't tempt me, Sophie!"

She wheeled on him then. "Just what is your problem, Edward?"

"Do you wish to go with Oliver?" he demanded, holding her gaze quite ruthlessly. "If that's what you meant, Sophie, just say so."

"If that was what I meant, trust me, I *would* say so," she snapped. "You may recall, my lord, that I have never been especially shy."

An almost self-deprecating smile tugged at his mouth. "You certainly were not shy last time we were alone together."

Sophie tossed an anxious glance over one shoulder. "You are the worst sort of cad, Edward, to bring that up whilst we're in public," she whispered.

"But we are never alone. You have been avoiding me for days now."

"And do you blame me?" She jerked at last from his

grasp. "I would to God I'd backhanded you through the face when I had the chance."

"But you didn't," he said softly. "Why?"

"Because I am a fool, I suppose." Her voice hitched on the last syllable.

His voice softened. "Look, Sophie, let's not quarrel—"

"We aren't," she answered. "Because I'm leaving now."

"Wait, Sophie." Edward shoved his hands through his hair, a boyish habit he'd thought he'd broken long ago. "Look here, I— I just wanted to say . . . well, to say I'm sorry."

"For what?" she hissed. "For assaulting me? For sticking your tongue down my throat? Or for just being rude in general?"

"I—I don't know. All of it, I daresay."

Edward watched her quietly for a moment. For a woman who'd spoken so boldly of bedding him, there was a vast deal of anger and apprehension in Sophie's eyes. Good God, did she want to marry him or not? He was going slowly insane trying to figure her out.

That night on the terrace, he'd given her the perfect excuse. He realized it now. If she'd wanted a noose round his ballocks, all she'd needed to do was go back inside the salon and squeeze out a tear in front of Grandmama. With her just-kissed lips and tumbling hair, she would have been more than credible. And he would have been forced to do the honorable thing.

But Sophie hadn't chosen to do that. Instead, she'd chosen to avoid him, lavishing her attention instead on Oliver and every other gentleman from twelve to eighty. Last night, there had been dancing after dinner. Sophie had danced with two of Edward's uncles, her brother, and Oliver—not once, but twice. Then she'd refused Edward's invitation by saying she was too tired.

Of course, as civility dictated, having refused him, she did not dance again. This, despite the fact that Edward knew Sophie loved dancing above all things. Well, perhaps all things save horses. Sophie had always been horse-mad.

Something in his brain clicked. Perhaps he was on to something there. Perhaps he could invite Sophie to ride with him, then make a proper apology? Reggie had left a stable full of prime horseflesh. Several fine mares. And there was that big black racehorse to be got rid of. Perhaps he should just offer her a choice? A gift by way of an apology?

Suddenly, the soft swish of muslin drew him back to the present. Edward looked up to see that Sophie was stalking away. He started after her, catching her gently by the shoulder. She wheeled on him, her eyes cold. "Take your hand off me, Edward," she said. "I wish to leave."

Sophie moved to do precisely that, but in her haste, her shawl slipped off one shoulder. She heard Edward draw in his breath, sharp and sudden. She glanced back and saw the blood draining from his face, his eyes fixed on her arm.

He touched her on the shoulder, gently turning her fully toward him. "That mark," he said hollowly. "That bruise on your arm, Sophie. Is it . . . did I . . . leave that?"

"No." She told the lie smoothly, instinctively.

His hand, warm and strong, slid down her upper arm. His thumb fit the bruise perfectly. "Good God." His voice was barely audible. "Your skin is so white. And that mark is so . . . so *appalling*. Sophie, you should have backhanded me. You should have."

"Perhaps." She shook her head slowly. "I don't know. But the mark is nothing, wherever it came from."

He let her go then, and she relaxed a little. It would not

do, she realized, to continue squabbling with Edward. There was nothing to be gained, and much to be lost. Besides, everyone on the mound was now looking at them. And so Sophie walked away, but her spine was as stiff as a poker, her chin another notch higher.

Chapter 6

A Midsummer Night's Folly

One more day, thought Sophie as she dressed the following evening for her aunt's birthday ball. While her maid smoothed the yellow silk ball gown over her undergarments, Sophie studied herself in the mirror, trying to mimic Edward's hard-hearted glower.

She drew her lips into a thin, hard line. No, that was not quite right. She narrowed her eyes to wicked little slits. Yes, there! Perfect. Let him approach her tonight, and she would look at him just as he looked at her. And by this time tomorrow, with any luck at all, she'd be halfway to Hampshire, which was as far away from Edward Addison as she could practically get. All she had to do was survive the ball, then tomorrow's breakfast.

With her dress smoothed into place, her hair piled high on her head, and her mother's pearls round her neck, Sophie went downstairs half an hour early. She hoped to steal a moment alone with her brother to break the bad news about Twelfth Night. Alas, it was not to be. As he had been doing since her arrival, Will was dogging Anna Staley's every step. Tonight he was in the billiard room with Oliver and Anna, where they were all playing under the watchful eye of her doting father.

Sophie lingered just long enough to see that Will and Oliver had not a prayer of beating Anna and her papa, then left the pair to suffer their whipping in private. Along her way, she passed by the white-and-gold salon, which opened onto one end of the ballroom. Under Jane's supervision, Bagshaw and the footmen were folding back the massive oak doors to connect the rooms.

"Oh, thank heavens, Sophie!" cried Jane. "Do come in and help us! Where must we put these trays? Have we enough champagne glasses?"

Grateful for the distraction, Sophie went in. She would seek Will out during the ball, she resolved, and break the bad news. They would be going home empty-handed.

It was almost midnight before Edward finished his obligatory dancing. He had opened the first set with his grandmother, this last one with his sister, and in between had danced with every female who was either married, arthritic, or senile. The young, spry widows and the virginal debs he avoided like the pox. He had enough trouble, he had decided, with just one eligible young lady. And he certainly had no wish to fire up the rumor mill as the young Earl of Weyburn had recently been doing with Miss Anna Staley.

The orchestra was tuning up for the final set when Edward spotted Romeo himself. Will St. John was standing by one of the marble columns, which Jane had surrounded with a frothy arrangement of plants and palm trees. Will's eyes were frantically searching the crowd. He was looking, no doubt, for his tart-tongued sister.

It was wrong, of course, but Edward burned to know why. The pair seemed to share some truly fascinating conversations. It was a simple matter to excuse himself from his last partner and circle round the ballroom until he was standing on the opposite side of the palms. Mere seconds later, Sophie came striding in their direction.

Ha! thought Edward. She was nothing if not predictable.

"Will!" she frantically hissed. "We have to talk."

"Aw, Soph!" Her brother's voice was sharp. "Let it wait!"

Through the forest of green, Edward could see Sophie's gloved hands wringing at the ends of her shawl. "Look, Will, I cannot go through with this." Her voice was oddly tight. "I don't want to explain why. But we must just think of something else, do you hear?"

"Lord, Soph!" he said. "Can we worry about this later? After the dancing?" Will's head kept moving, as if he still studied the crowd.

"Will, this is important!"

"I know! I know!"

"Then meet me on the terrace." Sophie sounded impatient. "I shall slip out."

"But I really want to dance with Anna once more," Will said.

But he was speaking to his sister's back. Through the palm fronds, Edward watched the sway of Sophie's hips beneath her yellow ball gown as she walked purposefully across the ballroom with swift, neat steps.

He liked that about her, he suddenly realized. Unlike most ladies of his acquaintance, Sophie always looked as if she were going someplace important, or doing something that really mattered. And she usually was. Sophie had never been a fribble. She was pretty, but not in a showy sort of way. Her clothes were always more classic than fashionable, her long, dark hair always simply dressed. Whatever the occasion, Sophie managed to look both pretty and . . . and what? *Competent.*

What a strange word. Still, it had leapt at once to his mind. Sophie was all those things. Capable. Beautiful. Classic. She was not the sort of woman a man married so that he might hang her off his arm like a pretty ornament. She was the sort of woman a man wanted in his corner when he was tired and worn. Just the kind of woman you could use when your luck was out, and you needed a warm embrace, some sage advice, or a good swift kick in the hindquarters.

And he had wanted her for those very things; indeed, he had thought of her and wished for her at least once in every one of those godforsaken days he'd spent on the Continent. In his heart, he'd wanted her every day since he'd returned to England, too. And it was in that instant that Edward suddenly realized the great cruelty his grandmother had unwittingly done him. *She had given him hope.*

Hope for something that was looking less and less likely with every passing day. He watched a little sadly as Sophie waded into the crowd and vanished. The truth was, Sophie had nothing to say to him. She did not want him. There was no offer. Had he not overheard her conversation with Will, Edward would have bet good money that she'd never had any such intention. Indeed, he'd been wracking his brain lately, trying to see if he'd somehow misinterpreted what little she *had* said.

Suddenly, a movement on the fringe of the crowd caught his eye, and he saw that the rector and his three daughters were making ready to leave. Good heavens, he had a duty to attend to, and here he was, lurking about behind the potted plants like some sort of escaped bedlamite.

Cursing under his breath—he seemed to be doing a lot of that lately—Edward circled back around the ballroom and saw his neighbors safely to their carriage. That done, he returned to the ballroom just in time to see young Will vanish through the doors that opened onto the gardens.

Well! Fortuitous timing indeed. Unlike his evening in the dark with Sophie, tonight the weather was quite sultry, and lanterns had been hung outside to welcome those who wished to take fresh air. He hesitated but a moment before following Will out. There was nothing wrong in doing so, Edward reasoned. If anyone needed a breath of fresh air, it was he.

But once outside, he saw no one. The sting of disappointment forced him to admit the truth: that what he'd really wished was to bump into Sophie. Still, he was sure that somewhere in the depths of the garden, she was having her little tête-à-tête with her brother. And sooner or later, she would have to make her way back in this direction. With that vague sense of purpose, Edward ambled slowly along the main path, turning neither left nor right.

His journey was a short one. Near the rose garden gate, he saw Sophie's brother, and the sight stopped him dead in his tracks. If Edward looked like a bedlamite, Will looked like a moonstruck dolt. The young man knelt in a patch of damp grass, a pink rosebud tucked behind one ear, his face turned plaintively upward. Curious, Edward circled round the gate, and realized at once that trouble was afoot. Before him, Miss Anna Staley clung awkwardly to a lamppost. Her other hand was clutched tightly in Will's.

Oh, dear Lord.

Will's gaze was ardent. "Please, please, Miss Staley! I swear it will be my life's ambition to make you happy!"

Edward picked up his pace. "Good God, Weyburn, get up, man!"

Two sets of ingenuous blue eyes turned to him. Miss Staley gasped, almost losing her grip on the lamppost. Poor

Will tried to stand, but his toe caught in Miss Staley's hem. A dreadful ripping sound tore through the night.

"Lord, tonight only wanted this!" muttered Edward. "What are the two of you about here?"

"I came out for air!" said Anna defensively.

"I thought she was my sister!" claimed Will.

"You came sneaking out here to propose marriage to your sister?" snapped Edward.

"Oh, no, sir!" Will shook his head. "I was supposed to meet her, see? Saw her yellow skirts slip through the curtains, and thought I was following her. Turned out to be Anna, though. Then I got distracted."

"But Miss Staley is wearing green," objected Edward. "Good Lord, is Sophie out here, too?"

Will's face had turned pink. "Green? Are you sure?"

"It certainly is not yellow," said Anna peevishly. "No one of consequence is wearing yellow this year."

"Well, hang me!" muttered Will. "Dashed colors all look alike."

Anna looked hurt. Will was scratching his head. Edward's brain was about to explode. "See here, the both of you," he said, settling a firm hand on Will's shoulder. "Get back inside this instant. Weyburn, you have all but compromised Miss Staley's virtue by being alone in the dark with her."

"Well, then I shall have to marry her," said Will rather too cheerfully.

"We have already discussed this," hissed Anna.

"And you made me no answer," responded Will.

"Lord Weyburn, I barely know you!" said Anna with a sniff. "But as I said, you may ask my papa's permission to court me, and we shall see if you prove worthy of my affections." With that, she turned and flounced away, eighteen inches of ruched lace hem trailing in her wake.

"Lord, I think my heart is broken," muttered Will, his eyes baleful as he watched her go.

"Yes, well, it only gets worse with age," snapped Edward. "Now, where, Weyburn, is your sister?"

Will looked at him blankly. "No idea," he answered. "What d'you want with her anyway?"

What did he want with her?

A bloody good question, that. What was he doing out here? What had he meant to say to Sophie if he found her? And what good would it do? She had made her opinion of him plain yesterday. He *crept up* on people. When, of course, he wasn't busy assaulting them, or just being rude in general. And then there was his most damning sin of all: He was *not romantic.*

Edward *was* romantic. He was, but he couldn't seem to show it. The right words just wouldn't come out of his mouth, whereas fellows like Oliver were always glib and charming. Even this pup Weyburn was having better luck with women, and he was wearing a damned rosebud.

No, there was no point in pressing Sophie any further. If she had refused to marry him eight years ago when they'd actually *liked* one another, she certainly wouldn't have him now. Perhaps Grandmama had been mistaken all along.

Somewhere in the midst of his musings Edward had abandoned Will in the dark. He now found himself standing on the threshold of his own ballroom, staring through the door like some starving street urchin who'd pressed his nose to a sweet-shop window. Beneath his glowing chandeliers, a dozen couples twirled to the tune of the last dance, their movements light and carefree. Anna was already dancing with Oliver. Everyone looked happy. Everyone looked as if they *belonged.*

He wasn't sure he did. But he pushed back through the draperies and went in anyway. At once, a footman advanced on him with a tray of champagne. Edward waved him off and went straight to the brandy decanter in the back of the room. It was time for a serious drink.

Unfortunately, it was there that his grandmother cornered him. One could not miss the row upon row of red lace, which trimmed her white satin gown, her hat, and even her gloves. She looked like a short, purposeful barber's pole bearing down on him.

Edward considered drinking straight from the decanter.

"Such a lovely, lovely affair, my dear!" chirped Euphemia, laying her hand on his coat sleeve and causing him to slop out half a glass. "I cannot think when I have enjoyed myself so much!"

"I am glad, Grandmama." He shoved the stopper back in with a harsh scrape.

"Are you enjoying yourself, my boy?"

"Lord, yes!" Edward lifted his glass and drank generously, his eyes searching the crowd. "Damned near delirious."

"Edward!" she chastised. Then she cast him one of her sly, sidelong glances. "Are you looking for Sophie?"

"No," he lied.

Euphemia hesitated. "You two have not been seen much in one another's company," she remarked. "Sophie has not, I take it, made you that offer I spoke of?"

"She has not." Edward set his brandy glass down on the table rather violently. "And with all due respect, Grandmama, I pray you will not mention Sophie's name to me ever again."

"Oh, dear, a quarrel!" said Euphemia fretfully. "You know what she meant to ask, then? And you have no interest?"

"None whatsoever," he lied again.

Euphemia cut him another odd look. "Then you will not, I take it, have any objection to Oliver's stepping in with an offer?"

Edward gritted his teeth. "By all means, Grandmama!" he snapped. "Tell old Oliver to jump in with both feet if he's so bloody determined."

"Oh, he is determined!" clucked Euphemia, reaching up to neaten the folds of Edward's cravat. "The dear boy has quite shocked me with all his thinking and planning. In fact, his interest has only grown since he took that walk through the stables with Will and Sophie."

A walk through the stables? Edward couldn't think what point his grandmother was trying to make. Perhaps she was up to some sort of trickery. Or perhaps she was just talking nonsense. Obviously, it wouldn't have been the first time.

"There!" she said with a satisfied little pat. "I have you almost straightened out now, Edward."

"Pardon me, ma'am," he said with an abrupt bow. "I see that Bagshaw is looking for me."

He left his grandmother still clucking in his wake.

But he could not leave his thoughts behind quite as easily. They dogged his every step as he saw the last of the evening's visitors out the door. They tormented him over coffee with his houseguests in the drawing room. Then they followed him up the stairs and into his bedchamber, causing him to kick off his shoes, rip off his coats and cravat, and send all of it hurling against the dressing room door—which sent Reggie's fainthearted valet scurrying off like a scalded chicken.

By God, he'd managed this badly! A gentleman, once refused, did not renew his suit without invitation. But he had had a lucky break. Sophie had come here meaning to ask him to marry her—or at the very least, to hint that *he* should ask *her* again—which was precisely what he'd wanted for the last eight years.

And what had he done? Bludgeoned her at every turn. Bollixed his life up completely. Blown his last chance. And now Oliver was going to step into what should have been *his* place! The worst of it was, he knew Sophie did not love Oliver. He could have borne it, he supposed, if she'd really cared for the old boy.

Oh, she liked Oliver well enough. And she obviously enjoyed his company—which was, he supposed, rather more than could be said for him. But there was no love between them. And if she was willing to wed a man she didn't love, why must it be Oliver?

In a fitful temper, he began to pace the worn Axminster carpet as he listened to the sounds of the rambling old house being put to bed for the night. But the sounds brought him neither peace nor comfort. For the next hour, he paused only to refresh his brandy. But he was not drunk. Oh, no, not yet.

And then, just as the clock struck half past two, something inside him seemed to snap. Perhaps it was the strain he'd been under these last few months. Or perhaps it was his having drunk far more than he was used to. Or the fact that this was absolutely his last chance. But in that instant, Edward decided to take matters into his own hands. He decided to demand some answers. Indeed, he should have done so years ago.

Resolved, he set down his glass, threw open his door, and marched straight down the hall to Sophie's room. And he knew precisely which one it was, too.

Chapter 7

Edward James His Shrew

At first, there was no answer to his knock. But he could hear the rustling of bedsheets. The mental image of Sophie sliding from between them almost caused him to forget his purpose. He listened as her soft footfalls approached the door.

"Will?" she hissed from the other side.

He knocked again. The door opened to reveal Sophie clutching a candlestick, her bare feet peeping from her nightdress, her dark hair fanning over one shoulder like a silken waterfall as she peered out into the passageway.

He'd expected her to be flustered, but Sophie merely glowered up at him. "You!" she hissed. "Go away, you fool!"

"They say it takes one to know one," said Edward, shouldering his way past her. "And I begin to suspect it's true."

Her heart in her throat, Sophie hastily shoved the door shut. That, no doubt, was a grave error. But the sight of Edward, standing in the corridor in his shirtsleeves, his face a mask of anguish, had stunned her. Had he lost his senses? What on earth was he thinking?

Certainly, she knew what the result would be if they were caught together. She steadied one hand on the doorknob. "Look, Edward," she warned. "You are going to cause serious trouble for us both. The kind of trouble you cannot possibly want."

"Sophie, you have no notion what I want," he answered. "I wonder if you ever have."

Sophie shook her head. "Please just leave. Go back to your room."

Edward paced deeper into the room. He paused, then picked up a half-empty scent bottle, which sat upon her night table. "This is my house now," he said, pulling out the stopper and drawing Sophie's familiar fragrance deep into his lungs. "And I am not leaving until we talk, Sophie."

"Talk? About what? Edward, it is two o'clock in the morning."

Edward turned his back to her and stared into the shadows for a long moment. "About us, Sophie," he said, his voice grim. "Don't you owe me that much, for old time's sake?"

For an instant, Sophie closed her eyes, trying to suppress the hope in her heart. "Edward, there is no *us*."

He wheeled around and pinned her gaze with golden eyes, as if he were staring through her, into her soul. "Yes, and whose fault is that, Sophie?" he challenged. "Is it mine? *Is* it? If it is, then tell me, by God, what I did wrong."

Sophie did not know what to say. This was not the Edward she knew. Surely he did not think . . . he did not mean . . .

No, that made no sense. He must have had too much to drink. "Edward, you're going to have a sore head on the morrow, I fear," she warned, putting down her candle. She grabbed his arm and tried to drag him toward the door. "Get out, and go to bed at once."

He shook her off and put the bottle down. "I'm not drunk, damn it," he argued. "And I'm bloody sick and tired of going to bed alone. I want to talk to you, Sophie. I want to know why you refused me all those years ago. And I want to know why you came back to Sheriden again."

"Why I came here?" Sophie couldn't believe her ears. Or her eyes. Edward looked . . . hurt. Badly so. Could it be he still cared? He *did*. Yes, at least a little. Her heart began to race. "Edward, I came because Aunt Euphemia insisted," she said, softening her voice. "I did not mean to cause trouble between us. I'm sorry we've got off on such a bad footing. In truth, I am quite . . . well, *fond* of you."

"Fond," Edward echoed. "You are *fond* of me." His shoulders fell, and he looked away. "What a damning compliment that is, Sophie! And now you mean to marry Oliver, do you?"

"Marry *Oliver?*"

Edward heard the incredulity in her voice. He swallowed hard, forcing down his pride. He wanted her, he realized. He wanted her so much that Sophie's reason for coming here no longer mattered. "Oliver is a good man, Sophie," he managed to whisper. "It would be unchivalrous of me to say otherwise. But he is not the man for you. He will never treat you as well as . . . as you deserve."

Sophie's warm fingers slid around his chin, forcing his face back to hers. "Edward, please be honest with me. Just how much have you had to drink? I need to know."

"Not enough," he growled, jerking from her grasp. "Are you going to marry Oliver or not, Sophie? I think you'd best tell me. I am, you know, the head of this family now."

Sophie smiled faintly at that. "You always have been, Edward, so far as I could tell," she returned. "But I am not about to marry a rogue like Oliver. Besides, he's half-besotted with Miss Staley—which is no bad match, you know, for *she* might be willful enough to reform him. Personally, I haven't the forbearance."

Edward felt deeply confused. "But . . . but Grandmama said—"

"Yes, well, heaven only knows what Euphemia might say," finished Sophie, gently taking his arm. She tried to propel him toward the door again, but in her heart, a little spark of hope was just about to burst into full flame. Still, this was a matter best deferred until morning, when everyone was rested and sober. She put her hand on the doorknob.

"I'm not leaving, Sophie," he warned. "I'm serious about this."

In the gloom, she looked up at him. "Edward, please go. Get some sleep. Forget about Oliver. Really, I begin to think Euphemia's touched in the upper stories. I have no intention of marrying anyone. Especially not a man of Oliver's ilk."

Edward jerked to a halt. "What ilk, then?" he asked stubbornly.

"I beg your pardon?"

He set his hands firmly on her shoulders, heating her skin through her thin muslin nightdress. "You didn't want me, either, Sophie," he said. "You turned me down flat, and now you won't even tell me why. So what sort of—of *ilk* would you marry?"

Sophie couldn't hold his gaze. "I'm not sure that is any of your business, Edward."

In response, Edward's hands tightened, and it was then that Sophie realized he looked suddenly—and rather frighteningly—sober. He jerked her hard against him, snapping her head back.

"Sophie," he said, staring down into her eyes. "I have decided to make it my business." And then his mouth came down on hers.

She tried halfheartedly to push him away, but his lips molded stubbornly over hers in a kiss of pure desperation. Sophie never had a chance to protest, wasn't even sure she wished to. His grip was unassailable; his hands heavy and warm as they slid down her body, stroking and circling, pressing them fully against one another. He tempted her as he had that night on the terrace, with his lips and his tongue, coaxing her into a kiss that went deeper and deeper, then utterly drowned her in its hunger.

It was as if Edward possessed her, as if he seduced the very breath from her lungs, leaving her trembling against his chest. His mouth moved hotly over hers, his lips soft yet certain, his breath warm and sweet with brandy. In the dimly lit room, everything lost focus, then spun away, until there was nothing but the two of them, alone in the night.

With a soft sound of pleasure in her throat, Sophie molded herself to his body, wordlessly pleading for more. Her knees were weak, and a warm, dangerous sensation was melting through her. Her pulse was an urgent tempo in her brain, and vaguely, she thought of the bed just behind them, and of what they could do there.

That thought, at least, finally shook her. She tried to pull away, but Edward wouldn't let her go. Instead, he just kissed her again, melting her good intentions into another sizzling puddle, leaving Sophie teetering on the brink of something that felt earth-shattering.

Perhaps he wasn't much with words, but Edward certainly had his hands in all the right places. And apparently, he was telepathic, too. "Yes, Sophie," he rasped, his mouth against hers. "Yes, let me. *Please* let me."

She knew what he was asking, and she knew she should

have been frightened. Yet she wasn't. She tried to answer him, tried to say *yes, yes!* quite loudly and distinctly. But as if he feared her words, he took her mouth again, his fingers sliding into her hair to capture her head and hold her still against him. This time, he drew her tongue deep into the warmth of his mouth, gently sucking it until the pulsing rhythm left her panting.

She knew vaguely that he shouldn't be here; that they were both about to be snared in an awful trap of their own making. His mouth left hers and slid down her throat, his lips open against her flesh, searing it.

"Edward," she finally whispered. "Maybe we should stop?"

His arm came fully around her, binding her hard against him. "I can't," he said into her hair. "Ah, Sophie, I can't. Tell me I don't have to."

Sophie tossed what was left of her innocence to the wind. "All right," she whispered faintly. "You don't have to."

He kissed her again, harder and more swiftly, then pushed her a little roughly onto the bed. For one heartbeat, he stood, staring down at her, his face a mask of torment. "Sophie," he rasped. "You understand this?"

She nodded and rose onto her knees. He stepped closer and untied the ribbon at her throat, and then those below. Sophie felt the cool air breeze across her breasts as her nightdress fell slowly open. Her gaze held Edward's as he lifted his trembling hands and dragged the garment off her shoulders. She was touched to see his eyes go soft in the candlelight.

"Ah, God, Sophie," he whispered, reaching out to brush his fingers under the swell of her left breast. "You have always been so beautiful."

Surprisingly, Sophie was not embarrassed by the caress. It

seemed almost natural to be naked beneath his eyes. He was just Edward. Her Edward. And she had always wanted him.

He wanted her, too, it seemed. Even the most naïve of virgins couldn't have missed the strain of his breeches over his groin. His shirt was already open at the throat, the sleeves shoved up to the elbows to reveal tautly muscled forearms corded with tendons and sprinkled with fine, dark hair.

Methodically, Edward ripped his shirttails free, dragged off his shirt, and flung it onto the floor. Sophie lost her breath. He certainly wasn't the young man she'd watched go away to war. Now Edward had a man's body, wide and solid, hardened with muscle. A grim-looking scar sliced over one collarbone, and dark hair dusted his chest and trailed seductively downward, disappearing beneath the waist of his breeches.

Ever the gentleman, Edward turned his back to shuck off what was left of his clothing. Breeches and drawers slithered down his hips, and instantly, Sophie's mouth went dry. *Oh, sweet heaven.* She'd always had an eye for a well-muscled thoroughbred, and there was no doubt about it: Edward had the beautifully sculpted backside of a champion.

And then, he was on the bed, covering her body with the warmth and weight of his own. Acting on instinct, Sophie drew her knees up, cradling him. Their gazes met, and in the candlelight, Edward looked suddenly shy. "Oh, Sophie," he whispered. "I am sadly out of practice at this. I will try, my love, not to hurt you."

Something caught in her throat at that. "You could never hurt me," she answered.

He kissed her then, his mouth opening over hers, his touch so sweet, so wonderfully gentle and plaintive, that Sophie feared she might die of the emotions that flooded forth. *Oh, it has been so long,* she wanted to sigh. And yet, she had never been with Edward—or with anyone—so intimately. In her heart, though, it felt as if their bodies were newly reunited; so sweetly familiar to one another that loving him with both her body and her soul could not possibly be wrong.

He shifted to one side then and shocked her by brushing kisses down her throat, and lower still. Her breasts felt warm and tight, her body throbbed. Edward kissed his way back up her breastbone and took one nipple into his mouth, drawing on it gently with his lips. Sophie gasped with pleasure.

"You like that?" he rasped, and Sophie could only nod. He drew his tongue around and around her nipple. "I will never do anything you don't want," he said, his lips brushing lightly over the hard, aching tip.

"Oh, I want," she confessed, her voice weak but certain.

And then he moved again, sliding down the length of her body, placing the weight of one arm across her belly. She cried out when his fingers slid between her legs, and in response, he stroked deeper. She was wet, she realized. Audibly so. Edward approved, she thought, for he made a strange sound deep in his throat and gently eased her legs apart. He knelt between her knees, held her flesh wide with one hand, and touched her lightly with his tongue.

Her reaction was instantaneous and uncontrollable. Her hips bucked hard off the bed, and she cried out, the sound thready and uncertain.

"Easy, Sophie, easy," he whispered, as if she were a shy, unschooled filly. With his free arm, he pressed her down again. "Draw up your knees, love. Open yourself for me."

Somehow, she did it, staring up into the shadowy bedhangings, one hand fisting in her bedsheets. He pushed her knees wide, his warm heavy hand sliding up her inner thigh. Then he set one hand on her mound, opening her wider still, then touched her most private place with the hot tip of his tongue.

"Stop!" she moaned. "Oh, Edward, oh . . . I want . . . I want . . ."

He understood. "Mmm, you want this, yes?" he murmured, stroking his tongue deeper. "Say it, Sophie."

She tried to nod. "Yes, yes, *that.*"

He stroked her again, then drew one finger through her flesh where his tongue had been. Sophie felt raw lust shudder through her. In response, Edward slid one finger inside her, and she sucked in her breath on a gasp.

"So tight, Sophie," he whispered, his voice both pleased and a little anxious.

In the darkened room, she listened to him work her body, first one finger, then another. Her shivers seemed uncontrollable. Her hips fought to rise, but the weight of his arm forced her down, pressing her hips into the mattress. Then he buried his tongue deep in her body, licking and teasing, until she began to drown in the sensation. Until her breath came hard and fast, and her mind began to splinter. And strangely, all she could think of as her world blew apart and her body melted was that she had said no to Edward, and missed eight whole years of *this.*

"Sophie, Sophie." Edward's lips brushed her throat again. "Open your legs, love."

She looked up to see Edward kneeling over her, his body sheened with the sweat of his restraint. His eyes, pleased and knowing, held hers in thrall. Between them, his erection rose up, thick and insistent. He took her hand and guided it to touch him. "God, I have to be inside you," he whispered, easing her hand down his flesh and closing his eyes. "Put me inside you, Sophie. Show me, my love, that you want that, too."

She *did* want it. But she was a little afraid. He sensed it, perhaps, and moved over her with infinite gentleness. She loved that; loved the feel of him pressing her into the softness of the bed. Loved the feel of her thighs being urged wide by his body. The scent and heat of their lovemaking surrounded them as she did as he'd asked, taking the hard, velvet length of his erection and guiding it to the joining of her thighs.

Her slick, warm folds enveloped him, and then Edward made a raw, feral sound, thrusting himself a little inside. Sophie felt instantly invaded. Stretched almost beyond bearing. A bead of perspiration fell from Edward's forehead, landing between her breasts. "Ah, God, Sophie!" he groaned, shoving himself in another inch. "I can't . . . can't . . ."

Closing her eyes, Sophie lifted her hips and urged herself against him. Edward slid deep on an awful groan, his breath exploding on a triumphant cry. Sophie felt a moment of pain and panic, then a wonderful warmth filled her. "Now make love to me, Edward," she whispered.

He laughed, a sharp, almost sardonic sound. "Lord, Sophie, I've waited about a dozen years to hear you say that," he managed. "Could you say it again, please?"

"Edward," she said very softly. "Would you please make love to me?"

He bent his head and kissed her hard on the mouth, then slowly, he began to move inside her with a fluid, sinuous rhythm. "Sophie, I want to make you burn for me," he rasped. "Even if it's just one night, I want you to ache for me as I have ached for you all these years."

Beneath him, she lifted her hips to meet his thrusts. "I do," she whispered. "I burn for you." And she did, she realized. She always had. Now, after all the pleasure he'd given her, she still trembled and yearned. There was more, she sensed. More and more that Edward could give her.

As he rode her body, his breath sawed in and out of his lungs. Her yearning deepened, spread through her belly, warm, molten lust. She let her head fall back against the mattress as she slid deeper into the carnal abyss. It was too much. Too much. *Not enough.*

"More," she heard herself beg. "Oh, God, Edward, more."

"Say that you are mine, Sophie." His lips were pressed to her ear. "Say it. *Promise* it."

"I do," she panted, dragging her hips harder against his. "I am. I promise."

He braced his powerful forearms on either side of her, holding her gaze as he filled her with long, sweet strokes. The sound of their lovemaking was soft as the darkness. Restlessly, Sophie's hands began to roam over his body, skimming and stroking over hard, taut flesh. Over and over, Edward glided into Sophie, until their breath came swift and hot, until they quickened to one another. She clung to him for strength. And at last, the pleasure roiled up in waves, washing over them, and dragging them down together.

Chapter 8

All's Well That Ends ...
as Well as Euphemia Planned It

*E*dward awoke to the sound of a late spring rain spatter-ing lightly on Sophie's window. The fire was long dead, leaving the room cool, but not quite dark. He stirred to full awareness, wondering at the time. Beside him, Sophie had curled herself into a kittenish ball, and he had wrapped his body protectively about hers.

He buried his face in the soft, fragrant hair at the nape of her neck and felt guilty. Guilty and happy and terrified, all at the same time. And satisfied, too. Oh, God, like never before.

Careful not to disturb her slumber, he slid from the bed and padded naked across the room. Pulling back the drap-ery with one finger, he stared through the rain-streaked win-dow and into the stableblock far beyond. A faint light shone in the uppermost dormers. The grooms and footmen were stirring, then. Damnation. Any time now, the chambermaid might pop in to build up Sophie's fire. And breakfast was to be served early, for all the guests were leaving this morning.

He couldn't put it off. He had to wake her. But what would she say when her mind was no longer clouded with desire? Desperation and jealousy could only carry a man so far. Edward felt a little sick considering the possibilities. Reluctantly, he returned to the bed and gently shook her. "Sophie," he whispered. "Sophie, it's near dawn. I'd best be going."

That woke her. She rolled up onto one elbow, and even in the gloom, he could feel her eyes searching his face. "Edward?"

He settled one hip onto the bed and laid his hand lightly on her knee. "Sophie," he said quietly. "What we did last night . . . God, I hope you do not regret it."

She sat fully upright. He could feel a strange wariness radiating from her. "I did it willingly, Edward, if that is what you meant. Do *you* regret it?"

He shook his head. "Oh, I regret it," he whispered fervently. "I mean, not that I didn't want—oh, hell, Sophie! I'm trying to say that, well, I just cannot think what came over me—"

Swiftly, she cut him off. "You were drunk."

He laughed a little bitterly. "I wish I had been." He paused and drew a steadying breath. What he really wished was that he could just make love to her again. It was so much easier than saying things with words. "Sophie, we have to talk. You know that, don't you?"

Hesitantly, she nodded. "Yes, I suppose."

He settled his hands on her shoulders, as if bracing her for bad news. "Sophie, you cannot get married now," he said grimly. "To anyone but me, I mean. You know that, don't you? That we have to wed now?"

He heard her sharp intake of breath. "Edward, I told you last night I didn't mean to marry anyone," she said coldly. "So don't worry that you've been trapped into marriage."

"Oh, God, Sophie, that's not it!" He said the words gently as he settled his hand over her cheek. "Sophie, I know you came here hoping to—to somehow persuade me to marry you. I am not perfectly sure how you meant to do it. But I know you only settled on Oliver after I was rude and spiteful toward you."

Her gasp pierced the gloom. "I beg your pardon?" she said, her whole body going rigid. "I came here hoping to *what*—?"

Warily, he jerked back his hand. "To make me an—well, an *offer*? Or to somehow rekindle things between us? But Oliver stepped in, and tried to charm you. Then I took that option from you—even if you didn't want him, it little matters—because I barged in here last night and—and did what I did. The two of us, together, I mean, doing it. Together. And that was wrong. And of course, I'm sorry. Sorry for doing it. I-I regret it, but it seems we are stuck with each other now, so we might as well try—"

Abruptly, Sophie clapped a hand over his mouth. "In five words or less," she snapped. "Now, I came here meaning to *what*—?"

Edward's brows went up. "To persuade me to marry you?" he said between her fingers.

Sophie removed her hand. "Why, Edward Addison, you arrogant swine!" she snapped. "I never set my cap—or *anything else*—at you! Why, it would be a cold day in hell before I'd even consider it!"

"Whatever you say, Sophie," he said grimly, rising and beginning to poke about for his clothes. "But you *are* going to marry me this time."

"Oh, am I?"

A deaf man couldn't have missed the challenge in her voice, but Edward was busy hunting up his drawers, so he blundered on. "Yes, you are," he said, shoving his foot through the first leg.

Sophie leapt from the bed, planted five fingertips in his chest, and gave him a little shove. "The devil I will!"

His drawers half on, Edward was forced to hop backward for balance. "Sophie," he said sternly. "I am getting a little tired of this game we seem to keep playing over this marriage business. I am not the same fellow I was eight years ago. This time, by God, I am not *asking,* I am *telling.*"

"Telling?" she echoed incredulously. "*You* are telling? As in *ordering?*"

Finally he got both legs in his drawers and hitched them up over his hips. "Ordering you, yes," he snapped, fastening the ties rather too vigorously. "Because, frankly, Sophie, once we get out of bed, there seems to be no way of pleasing you! I proposed marriage to you eight years ago, and damned politely, too. And all it got me was my heart flung back in my face."

He bent down to seize his breeches, but Sophie was too fast for him. "Oh, your heart, was it?" she sneered, thrusting them behind her back.

Edward snapped his fingers. "Give me my damned breeches, you shrew."

Sophie narrowed her eyes and scrambled onto the bed. "Just hold on a minute, Lord-High-And-Mighty!" she retorted. "I remember your offer eight years ago with perfect clarity—and if *any* part of your anatomy was involved in that lame, lukewarm, sorry excuse for a marriage proposal, then your time would be better spent droning on about the bloody Corn Laws in the House of Lords, because, Edward Addison, you are just plain unroman—*oopmh!*"

He tackled her hard, coming down on her like a sack of meal. Sophie landed sideways beneath him, still carping, the hand clutching his breeches twisted up awkwardly behind her back. He was half-afraid they were going to need a bonesetter for the arm, but at that moment, it seemed wisest to just kiss her senseless and shut her up. He kissed her hard, too, with no pretty preamble and very little tenderness. Still, it seemed to work. Sophie's hand went limp, the breeches slid from her grasp, and her eyes rolled back in her head.

"There, damn it," he said, some fifteen minutes later. They were both panting like they'd just run the course at Epsom. "Now, I love you, Sophie St. John. Will you stop tossing my heart around and marry me? Or not?"

Something in her eyes seemed to melt. "You . . . love me?" she whispered, struggling to sit up. "Really? You've fallen totally, completely in love with *me?*"

He looked at her dumbly. "No, I did not *fall* into anything, Sophie," he answered, watching her rub the feeling back into her arm. "I have loved you for at least half your life. That is generally why a man proposes to a woman, is it not?"

"Well, no, I think it rarely is," she mused, her brows in a fretful knot. "Actually, Edward, I can scarce fathom any of this. I mean, you have never mentioned one word to me about lo—"

And then, he was kissing her again. "How about I just show you, Sophie?" he murmured against her mouth. "I think there'll be less potential for trouble that way."

Sophie laughed and slid one hand down to untie his drawers again. "Oh, well said, Rythorpe!"

It was a good, long while before he finished with her this time. But finally, on a contented groan, Sophie sat back on his thighs—somehow, she'd got on top of him, a trend he rather feared might continue throughout the whole of his marriage. He was still trying to think of what he was going to say to the morning's chambermaid, when Sophie looked down at him, her glowing, grateful expression still in place, and opened her mouth to speak.

"No, don't say another word!" he said preemptively. "Not until you've answered me, Sophie. In five words or less. Can you love me? Will you marry me? Because if you will, I swear I will do whatever it takes to make you happy. I'll care for you in sickness and in health, for richer and poorer, and endow you with all my worldly possessions—you know, the whole bargain, just as the parson lays it out in church."

Sophie looked at him, and he was shocked to see her wink. "*All* your worldly possessions?"

Edward frowned. "Absolutely."

Sophie's smile warmed. "But what if I want just one?"

"Just one?" Edward felt like he was missing something. "Anything, Sophie. For God's sake, if you'll marry me, just name it."

"Oh, Edward, I love you madly." Sophie clutched her hands before her like a schoolgirl. "Yes, yes, I will marry you! And I want but one thing from you. I want Twelfth Night."

Edward prayed to God he was going deaf. "Twelfth *what—?*"

Sophie threw back her head and laughed. "Twelfth Night!" she echoed. "That Irish thoroughbred Reggie bought at Newmarket? He's out in your stables, and I want him for Will—you know, to breed him with our mares? We mean to use him to rebuild the St. John racing legacy." She waited for a heartbeat. "So, anyway, my scheme is out now, isn't it? That's what I came here after. Will and I have been plotting and plotting how to get him."

Oh, God. He was not going deaf. "You mean you came here to make me an offer?" he mumbled a little sickly. "For a *horse?*"

Sophie bit her lip and nodded.

Edward struggled to sit up. "So—it's the *pedigree you were after?* You admired *his long, strong legs?* And you just wanted to use his . . . his *parts? For breeding?* Is that right?"

Sophie looked at him a little strangely. "Well, it sounds a little vulgar when you put it that way, my love, but yes," she admitted. "Aunt Euphemia has always said Reggie made a dreadful error in judgment in buying him, for he paid twice what the horse was worth."

Oh, Christ! Could it be true? Sophie, Will, Euphemia—they'd all been talking about Reggie's damned horse?

He swallowed hard. "An error in judgment, eh?" he croaked. "Is that what she calls it?"

Sophie nodded. "Why, yes, and she told me if Will and I bought him, we'd only be setting things to rights," she said. "Now—may I have him? For the sake of the St. John racing dynasty?"

Edward wanted to crawl under the bed. He could feel his face turning three shades of red. And his tongue—good God, his tongue was going numb. "Sophie," he managed to choke. "If you will just get dressed, and go with me downstairs to breakfast, and tell Grandmama Euphemia point-blank that we are getting married as soon as a special license can be had, then you may have anything it is humanly and legally within my power to give you."

Cheerfully, Sophie bounced off the bed. "Oh, Edward, I will!" she said. "And I can't wait to see the shock on Aunt Euphemia's face! She'll never in a million years expect this. Now, what shall I wear?"

But then he kissed her again, and so they were a little late going down to breakfast. So late, in fact, that almost all the other guests had gone back upstairs to pack. Edward peeked into the breakfast parlor a little sheepishly, to see that only Lord Staley and his daughter remained at the table with his grandmother. By the sideboard, Will and Oliver were looking daggers at one another over the chafing dishes. Damn. No good news there.

Half-afraid that gossip was already spreading through the

servants' ranks, Edward dragged Sophie in by the hand and sharply cleared his throat. "Good morning, everyone," he said as five pairs of eyes turned on him. "I trust you all slept well?"

Oliver looked Edward up and down suspiciously. Will followed suit. Lord Staley jerked to his feet. "Quite well!" he boomed. "Never better! Come, Lady Sophie, and have a seat by me."

Sophie smiled, looking suddenly shy. Edward nodded at them all. "Oliver? Will?" he murmured. "Would you please sit down by Grandmama? Sophie and I have something we'd like to share with you all."

Oliver cut him a strange glance. "Why, I'll just bet you do!" he remarked under his breath.

"Ooh," squealed Anna Staley, her eyes fastened on their joined hands. "This sounds—dare I say it?—a little racy!"

Edward bowed his head in her direction. "Not at all, Miss Staley," he corrected. "Indeed, it is the most revered of occasions, for Lady Sophie has just made me the happiest man on earth. Grandmama, I hope you will remain here at Sheriden for the wedding?"

But Euphemia was already nodding, causing the bright blue and yellow ribbons in her hair to bounce cheerfully up and down. "A special license, right away!" she said, as if the whole thing was her idea.

"Just so." Edward smiled tightly. "As soon as it can be arranged."

Will, who had been grinning from ear to ear, broke into applause. "Well done, old girl!" he crowed. "My heartiest felicitations! Now, sis, don't let me down! Have you asked for Twelfth Night as a wedding gift?"

Sophie looked bashfully up at her betrothed. "Will," she said with an air of relief, "that horse is as good as promised to me!"

Lord Staley cleared his throat, cut a strange glance at Anna, and said, "Well, I should hope not, my dear!"

Will turned at once in the baron's direction. "I beg your pardon?"

But Lord Staley was still looking at Sophie. "I'm sorry, my dear girl, but Edward already sold Twelfth Night." The baron looked very pleased with himself. "I bought him, you see. For Anna."

"For Anna?" exclaimed Will, Oliver, and Sophie in unison.

Oliver threw down his napkin in disgust. "My God, I cannot believe this!" He glowered across the table at Euphemia. "Grandmama, how could you let this happen to me?"

"To you!" exclaimed Will, looking back and forth between Oliver and Euphemia. "What business is it of yours, I should like to know? Aunt Euphemia, you swore to Sophie if she would but follow your instructions, you'd make certain *she* would have Twelfth Night from Edward!"

Oliver shoved away his plate in disgust. "And she promised me that if I would but cozy up to Sophie and make old Edward turn green, she'd see he accepted my offer for Twelfth Night!"

Lord Staley grinned. "Euphemia, you sly dog! You've known for weeks that I was coming here with every intention of buying that horse!"

"Oh, dear God," groaned Edward, tightening his grip on what he hoped was still his bride-to-be.

Euphemia just shrugged and stared down at her empty plate. "Why, what can I say, my dears?" she answered in a small, pitiful voice. "I am, after all, seventy-five years old. One begins to forget things."

"What utter balderdash!" complained Oliver bitterly. "You've never forgotten a thing in your life! And you let me risk life and limb for nothing! He bloody near killed me over her!" He stabbed his finger in Sophie's direction.

Furiously blushing, Sophie looked at Oliver. "I don't understand. What on earth do *you* want with a racehorse?"

Oliver shoved his hands into his pockets. "Setting up my own stables," he muttered. "Bought a place near Epsom. Have some fine bloodstock already."

"Good Lord!" Will rolled his eyes. "You cannot possibly be serious!"

Oliver took obvious umbrage at that. "No, no, don't all of you look at me that way! I know I'm thought a fribble and a flirt, but for once, I was deadly serious. And I still am, by God." With that, he eyed Will narrowly over the tablecloth.

Sophie pressed her fingers to her temples. "But wait!" she exclaimed. "Wait! Edward, this morning after we made—after we had—oh, *bother!* Edward, you swore I could have any and all of your worldly possessions if I would just agree to marry you."

Lord Staley roared with laughter. "My dear, everyone knows Rythorpe is too honorable to tell a lie!" he said rather too cheerfully. "I blindsided him with a wad of cash yesterday right after breakfast. He did not own that horse this morning."

Will shoved back his chair with a scrape. "Blister it, Sophie, I told you to get a move on!" he hissed. "I told you this might happen!"

Edward turned to his wife-to-be and lifted both her hands to his lips. "Forgive me, my dear," he said softly. "I never meant you to hear it like this. I just wanted you so desperately, I did not know how to tell you the horse was gone. May I give you everything else I possess by way of compensation?"

Sophie smiled and shrugged. "Oh, what does it matter?"

"That's right, by Jove!" said Lord Staley. "Spilt milk, and all that! Especially since old Twelfth Night is already Anna's. Part of her dowry, y'see."

"Her dowry?" exclaimed Will and Oliver at once.

Staley stood, patted both hands on his ample belly, and looked about the table. "Like Euphemia there, I'm getting on in years. I'd rather be dandling grandchildren on my knee, so I'm selling out."

"Selling out?" said Oliver keenly. "All of it?"

Staley shrugged. "Well, my ten best fillies I'm keeping for Anna. I mean to marry her off to a chap with a respect for fine horseflesh."

Miss Staley preened. "Oh, indeed!" she said breathlessly. "Papa says that Twelfth Night and my fillies will make a fine start to a new racing dynasty."

Just then, Bagshaw poked his head in. "Carriage for Lord Staley?"

Beaming, Anna rose and took her father's arm. They thanked Edward profusely for his hospitality, congratulated Sophie on her good fortune, then waved their way from the dining room. But the door had no more thumped shut when Will and Oliver threw down their napkins and bolted from the room.

"The devil!" said Edward, staring after them. "Where are they off to in such a rush?"

"To London, if they're any kin of mine," chirped Euphemia, tipping the coffeepot to refill her cup. "After all, Miss Staley has another half a season left. Almost anything could happen. Sometimes it only takes a day or two, you know. More coffee, anyone?"

But Edward did not hear her. "Sophie, my love, will you still have me?"

"Don't be silly, Edward," said Euphemia, putting down the coffeepot. "Of course she will."

"Of course I will," said Sophie, capturing both his hands in hers. "Oh, Edward, I love you to distraction."

Edward kissed her lightly on the nose. "Thank God!" he

said. "And by the way, my love, if Will fails in his mission to London, all is not lost. Old Twelfth Night passed a very busy spring here at Sheriden."

Sophie furrowed her brow. "Why, whatever do you mean?"

Edward placed his lips very near her ear. "I have six very pretty, very pregnant fillies in my stable, darling," he whispered, circling an arm about her still-slender waist. "And soon, perhaps, another a little closer to home."

LIZ CARLYLE *lives in North Carolina with her romance-hero husband and three very fine felines. In her spare time, she supports various animal rescue organizations. Please visit her online at* www. lizcarlyle.com, *or write to her at* lizcarlyle@aol.com.

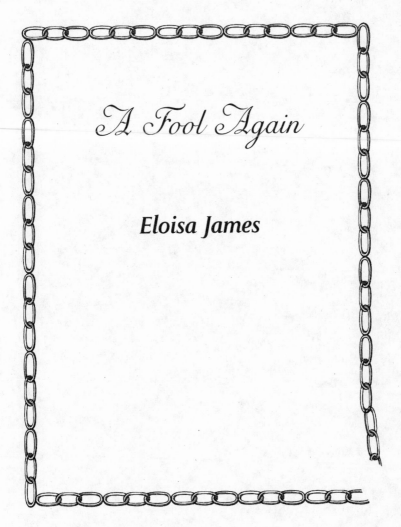

A Fool Again

Eloisa James

Chapter 1

The Funeral Baked Meats

A well-bred lady never ogles a man from behind her black veil, especially during her husband's burial. But Lady Genevieve Mulcaster had acknowledged her failings in ladylike deportment around the time she eloped to Gretna Green with a bridegroom whom she'd met three hours earlier, and so she watched Lucius Felton with rapt attention throughout Reverend Pooley's praise of her deceased husband—a man (said Mr. Pooley) who rose before his servants and even for religious haste, went unbuttoned to morning prayer. Felton looked slightly bored. There was something about his heavy-lidded eyes that made Genevieve feel thirsty, and the way he stood, almost insolently elegant in his black coat, made her feel weak in the knees. His shoulders had to be twice as large as her husband's had been.

Recalled to her surroundings by that disloyal thought, Genevieve murmured a fervent if brief prayer that Heaven would be just as her husband imagined it. Because if Erasmus didn't encounter the rigorous system of prizes and punishments he anticipated, he would likely be discomfited, if not sent to sizzle his toes. Genevieve had long ago realized that Erasmus wouldn't hesitate to rob a bishop if an amenable vicar could be persuaded to bless the undertaking. She threw in an extra prayer for St. Peter, in the event that Erasmus was disappointed.

Then she peeked at Felton again. His hair slid sleekly back from his forehead, giving him an air of sophistication and command that Genevieve had never achieved. How could she, wearing clothes with all the elegance of a dishcloth? The vicar launched into a final prayer for Erasmus's soul. Genevieve stared down at her prayer book. It was hard to believe that she had lost *another* husband. Not that she'd actually gotten as far as marrying Tobias Darby. They'd only been engaged, if one could even call it that, for the six or seven hours they'd spent on the road to Gretna Green before being overtaken by her enraged father. She'd never seen Tobias again; within a fortnight she'd been married to Erasmus Mulcaster. So eloping with Tobias had been the first and only reckless action of Genevieve's life. In retrospect, it would be comforting to blame champagne, but the truth was yet more foolish: she'd been smitten by an untamed boy and his beautiful eyes. For that she'd thrown over the precepts of a lifetime and run laughing from her father's house into a carriage headed for Gretna Green.

Memories tumbled through her head: the way Tobias had looked at her when they'd climbed into the carriage, the way she'd found herself flat on the seat within a few seconds of the coachman geeing up the horses, the way his hands had run up her leg while she'd faintly—oh so faintly—objected. 'Twas an altogether different proposition when Erasmus had stiffly climbed into the marital bed. Poor Erasmus. He hadn't married until sixty-eight, considering women unnecessarily extravagant, and then he couldn't seem to manage the connubial act. Whereas Tobias—she wrenched her mind away. Even *she,* unladylike though she was, couldn't desecrate Erasmus's funeral with that sort of memory.

She opened her eyes to the breathy condolences of Lord Bubble. "I am distressed beyond words, my lady, to witness your grief at Lord Mulcaster's passing," he said, standing far too close to her. Bubble was a jovial, white-haired gentleman who used to gently deplore Erasmus's business dealings, even as he profited wildly from them. Genevieve found him as practiced a hypocrite as her late husband, although slightly more concerned for appearances.

"I trust you will return to Mulcaster House for some refreshments, Lord Bubble?" Since no one from the parish other than Erasmus's two partners, his lawyer, and herself had attended the funeral, they could have a veritable feast of seed cakes.

Bubble nodded, heaving a dolorous sigh. "Few men as praiseworthy as Erasmus have lived in our time. We must condole each other on this lamentable occasion."

A sardonic gleam in Felton's eye suggested that *he* didn't consider Erasmus's death the stuff of tragedy. But then, Genevieve had studied Felton surreptitiously for the past six months, and he often looked sardonic. At the moment he was also looking faintly amused. Surely he hadn't guessed that she had an affection for him? Genevieve felt herself growing pink. Had she peered at him once too often? Think like a *widow,* she admonished herself, climbing into the crape-hung carriage.

"May I give you another handkerchief, my lady?" her maid asked as Genevieve seated herself. Eliza had strict notions about the tears a widow should shed during her husband's funeral.

But Erasmus Mulcaster had long since burned out any affection that his wife might have scrambled together, although not by cruelty, nor by neglect. Erasmus was unfailingly attentive in the two hours he allotted to his wife daily. It was the grueling, grinding boredom of being near Erasmus, of being part of Erasmus's life, that had withered Genevieve's affection. Six long years of watching Erasmus count his spoons every night, for he didn't trust his own butler. Years of turning and re-turning garments because Erasmus considered women's clothing to be an unnecessary expenditure. He had even dictated, from his deathbed, the refreshments to be served at his funeral: an orange pudding, an almond pudding and two light seed cakes. "Two will be more than enough, if you order them cut very slim," Erasmus had noted, raising his head from the pillow to make sure that Genevieve understood. He was certainly right about *that,* Genevieve acknowledged when they reached Mulcaster House and everyone, including the vicar, refused a piece of cake.

There was general relief when Mr. Leeke, Erasmus's lawyer, suggested that they retire to the library for a reading of the will. The room was hung in limp, green drapery, and there weren't very many books, as Erasmus didn't hold with reading. He didn't like any activity that hadn't a clear monetary goal as reward. Genevieve loathed the room, with all its memories of weeping clients and household prayer sessions. Bubble ushered her to a seat for the reading of Erasmus's will with a solicitous attention that made Genevieve's skin crawl. What on earth had got into the man? He had to be sixty, if he were a day, and yet he was acting with the skittish enthusiasm of an adolescent hoping for a kiss.

Felton sat in a chair across from Genevieve and Bubble, his pale hair gleaming in the afternoon sunshine. Mr. Leeke cleared his throat two or three times before he began. "Lord Mulcaster's will is somewhat out of the ordinary," he announced. "I shall just mention, as I always do before reading a will, that even such a document, when issued by my firm, would be extremely difficult to overturn. Lord Mulcaster was indubitably of sound mind when he established the herein conditions."

Once, when Felton had come to dinner, their eyes had met across the table and he'd smiled at her in such a way that Genevieve had felt, well, *beautiful.* Sometimes she feared that her looks had moldered away like the green draperies lining the casements throughout the house (Erasmus had obtained an excellent price and done every window in the same color). But even though she was all of twenty-four, she wasn't precisely ancient. Felton had to be in his thirties. Surely he wished to marry? Yet if Felton wanted to marry, why hadn't he done so? He was extraordinarily handsome, with hair the color of wheat and eyes of indigo blue. And since he was very, very rich (even richer than Erasmus), he'd been the target of matchmaking mamas for years, from what Genevieve could glean from gossip columns.

"Lady Mulcaster!" Leeke was saying. "This section of the will appertains to you. Well, in fact, to you *and* these gentlemen. I know this is a most difficult and distressing time for you, but I must beg the indulgence of your attention."

Genevieve nodded and clasped her hands in her lap.

"The provision for your future, Lady Mulcaster, is unusual but by no means illegal," Leeke stated, looking rather uneasily at the papers he held.

Genevieve straightened. What on earth had Erasmus done?

"I consider it an excellent arrangement," Bubble put in. "Lord Mulcaster discussed it with me at length, and we

agreed that it was a laudable way to ensure Lady Mulcaster's best interests. A widow so young and beautiful has
need of mature advisement," he said with an arch look at
Genevieve.

Felton's face wore its usual expression of impassive still-
ness. "Since Lady Mulcaster and I appear to have been ex-
cluded from that discussion, why don't you proceed,
Leeke?" he drawled.

"To summarize, then," Leeke said. "The will specifies
that if Lady Mulcaster marries either of Lord Mulcaster's
partners within two years of his death, she will receive his
full estate. In the event that Lady Mulcaster either does not
marry, or marries another person, Lord Mulcaster's estate
will go to the Church of England, with the devout request
that a Mulcaster Chapel be dedicated in St. Paul's Cathe-
dral. Lady Mulcaster will receive only her jointure. Which,"
he said, looking at Genevieve, "is regrettably small."

Genevieve knew that. After all, she was another one of
Erasmus's bargains: He'd taken her for nothing, because
she was ruined. Her father had snatched her back from a
fate worse than death, a Gretna Green marriage, only to find
that she had dallied with her husband-to-be in the coach.
And when Tobias Darby hadn't renewed his protestations
of inebriated love but had taken himself off to foreign parts,
Erasmus had taken her secondhand. Would Felton mind that
she was a widow? Thirdhand, as it were? Presumably he
could marry any beautiful young woman in London. She refused to look up, in case she met his eyes.

There was utter silence in the room. The only thing
Genevieve could hear was faint barking from the courtyard.
Erasmus's spaniel must have treed a squirrel again. Embarrassment started to burn in her cheeks. Neither man seemed
to be eager to propose marriage, even given the sweetener

of Erasmus's bequest. She would have thought that Bubble, at least, would lunge at the estate. "I receive no jointure for two years?" she finally croaked, examining the darn on her left glove.

"No. Mr. Felton and Lord Bubble will establish an allowance for your maintenance and support during the period."

A surge of rage at her dead husband flushed Genevieve's cheeks more than did her embarrassment. Erasmus was a tight-fisted old devil. But you already knew that, she reminded herself. It seemed she must find a husband within two years or risk destitution.

"I wish to live in London during that period," Genevieve stated, looking at Leeke.

The lawyer had a puce-colored face and a habit of avoiding all unpleasant subjects, which had undoubtedly kept his nerves in order while serving Erasmus. "I should have nothing to do with that decision," he replied promptly. "As I said, your allowance will be entirely the responsibility of these two estimable gentlemen."

There was silence again. It seemed that she had to take matters into her own hands. Genevieve straightened in such a way as to enhance her chest and deliberately reached up to pull back her veil. Wearing black showed her tawny hair to its best advantage. Then she turned to Lord Bubble. She didn't even need to speak. He exploded into a wilderness of comments about his utter delight at the idea of her hand in marriage, how highly he thought of Erasmus, how exquisitely beautiful she was, how much his (grown) children would love to welcome her as a mother. Genevieve waited, unspeaking, until he wound down like a tired clock, and then she turned, just as deliberately, to Felton.

He had his fingers templed—long, beautiful fingers that made her stomach quake at the very sight of them. "I share

Bubble's enthusiasm," he said, in a dry tone singularly lacking in enthusiasm. She waited, but all he added was, "Naturally."

"Of course, no such ceremony could take place until the end of Lady Mulcaster's mourning period," Leeke put in. "Lord Mulcaster thought that two years was an adequate period."

Two years of mourning! Erasmus had high expectations for himself, Genevieve thought sourly. Even the most devout suggested only a year in black.

"So I need not accept one of these two gentlemen's enthusiastic proposals at this moment?" she asked Leeke, with just the faintest stress on *enthusiastic*.

"Precisely so, my lady."

"In that case, gentlemen, I should like an allowance sufficient to establish myself in London during the years of my mourning."

Leeke cleared his throat. "As it happens, Lord Mulcaster called in a loan just last month and the gentleman in question relinquished a town house in St. James's Square. His lordship hadn't time to sell the establishment before his untimely death."

St. James's Square! Hurrah! Genevieve nodded with widowlike dignity. "That will be acceptable."

"A modest allowance and use of the town house should be more than adequate for the needs of a widow," Bubble noted, "especially one in the mourning period."

Genevieve widened her eyes and bit her lip. "The very first thing I desire in a husband is a generous nature akin to that of my dear, loving Erasmus," she said gently. Bubble undoubtedly knew that any mention of Erasmus's generosity was a jest: Was there another lady within forty miles who was wearing a dress made five years ago and turned twice?

Yet Bubble wasn't a complete fool. "You are absolutely correct, my *dear* Lady Mulcaster," he gushed. "Naturally Felton and I wish you to have a generous allowance, such as Lord Mulcaster would have established for you."

"The town house will need a full staff," she noted. Erasmus may have insisted on maintaining only one maid, but she remembered how a house was supposed to be run, and it was supposed to be *clean.* "And I should like a barouche to be driven in, and a curricle to drive myself. I intend to drive in the park." Avid reading of the gossip pages had convinced Genevieve that Hyde Park was one of the Seven Wonders of the World.

"As long as I am allowed to choose your horseflesh," Felton said unexpectedly.

She swept him a glance to find that his eyes were gleaming with something very like a spark of admiration. "That would be most kind of you, Mr. Felton," Genevieve said. She reached up and pulled her veil over her face again. The subject was closed.

Chapter 2

Lemony Genevieve

One year later

"There's been no public announcement," Neville Charlton told his companion, Lady Perwinkle. "I know she's seen with him a great deal, and there are rumors about her husband's will, but she's not formally betrothed. It would have appeared in the *Times*."

Carola looked up from the tiny garment she was embroidering and shook her head. "While I hate to disappoint you, I do believe that Genevieve is going to marry Felton. I've seen the way she looks at him and, more to the point, she talks of him incessantly."

Neville was an extravagantly handsome young man with fashionably wind-strewn curls and the blue eyes of a dandified cupid. "I must stop her!" he cried melodramatically. "Felton is a loathsome man. His dealings in the City are most suspect."

"I don't agree." Carola was trying to decide whether she

could fit another rosebud onto the sleeve. Perhaps if she left off the leaves? "I think he's very attractive, even if he does have a slightly snakelike manner."

"Snake-like!" Neville cried. "Snakelike! You want to pair a glorious bit of womanhood like Genevieve Mulcaster with a *snake!*" He dramatically tore at his hair, although Carola noticed that he didn't disorder his locks over much. "She is the most luscious woman I've seen in years. She deserves better than a snake. She deserves me!"

"The most luscious, hmmm? Careful I don't take that as an insult, you wretch!"

"You're lovely as well, darling, although you are so unfashionably infatuated with your husband."

"She's not *that* beautiful," Carola pointed out. "Priscilla Blythe has far more regular features."

"It's not a matter of her features," Neville said impatiently. "Although how you can say that someone with eyes like hers, a mouth like a goddess, hair like—"

Carola burst out laughing. "A woman with eyes, a mouth and hair. Goodness, Neville, your standards have fallen rather low!"

"Her eyes are the most unusual shade of gray-green that I've ever seen," Neville said, ignoring Carola's foolery. "And she always looks as if she's about to laugh. How she managed to stay so amusing, given her marriage to Mulcaster, I don't know. I last saw the man four years ago and he was already missing a quantity of teeth."

"I do know what you mean," Carola conceded. "Genevieve is great fun. We had tea yesterday and laughed for an hour."

"Did she mention me?" Neville asked instantly.

"No," Carola said, finishing the rosebud.

"Perhaps she doesn't know that you and I are close friends."

"I don't think she would be interested." The flower looked odd, but she couldn't bear the tedium of ripping out stitches. Besides, the baby wouldn't care, would she? If her baby was a she.

"No other woman in the *ton* has hair as beautiful as Lady Mulcaster's."

"Genevieve loathes her hair," Carola said. "So if you're going to compliment her, Neville, you might want to avoid the whole issue. She thinks it looks striped, like a cat."

"It is like trapped sunshine . . . gold strands mixed with threads of starlight," Neville said dreamily.

"Oh pooh, Neville. Sunshine indeed! I expect Genevieve puts lemon on her hair at night."

"A lemon bright goddess!"

"You're hopeless!" Carola snorted. "But I did hear something of interest this morning." He wasn't paying attention. "Neville!"

"Do you think that lemony rhymes with Genevieve?" he asked, scribbling on a scrap of paper he had taken from his waistcoat.

"Absolutely not," Carola said. "But do listen, Neville: Lady Dorset-Herne told me this morning that Tobias Darby has returned to London!"

"Darby? Don't you mean *Simon* Darby? Of course he's in London. I saw him and his wife in the Rotten Row just the other day."

"No, Simon's brother Tobias," Carola explained. "Tobias ran off with Genevieve Mulcaster, oh, years ago. Her father caught them on the way to Gretna Green and she was married off to Lord Mulcaster, but the truth leaked, of course. At any rate, Tobias and his twin brother left England when Genevieve married, and now he's come back! Isn't that romantic?"

"What's romantic about it?" Neville said, narrowing his

eyes. "Do you think the man is going to attempt to win her hand for the second time?"

"I wouldn't be surprised. Lady Dorset-Herne said that he's tremendously wealthy now. And why else would he return, just when Genevieve is out of her blacks?"

Neville looked glum. "The last thing I need is another rival when Felton has got himself so snugly established. Are you and Perwinkle coming to the opening at Covent Garden tonight?"

"I believe so," Carola replied. It was difficult to know whether her husband, Tuppy, was free to accompany her or whether he would run off to attend a lecture about fish. "We have a subscription."

"As have I," Neville said. "But Lady Mulcaster has committed herself to that deuced Felton."

"Then you must come into our box," Carola said instantly. "Perhaps Tobias Darby will attend the play, and we shall have a fine view!"

"If I can't sit with Genevieve," Neville said morosely, "I certainly am not interested in watching Felton insinuate himself further into her good graces, let alone Darby."

"If you accompany me to the theater," Carola said coaxingly, "I promise I'll give a dinner and invite Genevieve. What's more, I'll praise you to the skies at tea tomorrow."

Neville frowned at her. "In all truth?"

Carola nodded. "Word of honor." There had to be some way she could sneak in a word about Neville in between Genevieve's babblings about Lucius Felton.

By eight o'clock that evening, Genevieve Mulcaster was virtually the only person in London unaware of the fact that Mr. Tobias Darby had returned from India rich as a nabob and was presumably planning to hustle her off to Gretna Green. Not that she would have paid much attention.

Genevieve had plans of her own for the evening, involving an annoyingly elusive Lucius Felton. Lord Bubble had withdrawn his application for her hand after suffering a most unfortunate attack that necessitated his staying in bed for at least six hours of every day; Genevieve accepted that fact with equanimity, as she never thought to marry the man. But Felton's disclination to propose marriage was far more disturbing.

At first, she had thought his gentlemanly behavior was due to her being in full mourning. She had waited six months fairly patiently. Then, when he still acted like a vicar, she had hoped it was due to her half mourning. Those six months had passed with rather less patience. But now she had been out of blacks for an entire week, and Felton continued to greet her as placidly as if he were a distant uncle. He was nothing if not attentive, sending bunches of violets and never failing to inquire what she would like to do of an evening. One couldn't have had a more attentive nephew.

And yet . . . and yet. He had never kissed her. Not once. Honesty made Genevieve admit that he often seemed more amused by her than struck with desire. She sat down at her dressing table and stared in the mirror. All sorts of gentlemen were exhibiting flattering attention; she had just received a poem calling her a lemon bright goddess (an odd phrase, but she appreciated the effort). So why wasn't Felton doing the same? Perhaps the problem was that she looked so tediously *young,* the fault of a snub nose. She simply didn't look like a dashing widow. Nor a Pocket Venus either. That was her ambition, but even the most dashing clothes one could buy weren't effecting a transformation.

"Your very first evening in public out of mourning!" her maid said brightly, popping up at her shoulder. "Would you like to wear the Grecian tunic, madam, or perhaps the lilac robe and petticoat?"

Genevieve gave up trying to arrange her features into a seductive pout. "Do you think I'd look more dramatic if I blackened my eyebrows?" she asked her maid.

Eliza wrinkled her brow. "Odd, more like," she offered. Eliza had no gift for sophistry.

Perhaps Felton never tried to kiss her because she wasn't intriguing. Here she was, a veritable blaze of fashion, and she still looked like herself. It was truly dispiriting.

"Wear the tunic, madam," Eliza urged. "You look a fair treat in it, I promise you that."

The Grecian tunic had just been delivered from the shop of Madame Boderie. It was made of French silk in a dull gold color that gleamed whenever she moved, with a square bosom cut quite low. Best of all, from Genevieve's point of view, was a small train that gave her dignity.

Once the gown was on, she felt slightly cheered. The way her breasts threatened to spill from the bodice was unnerving, but at least she didn't look like a schoolgirl. "I would like to twist the gold beads I bought at the Pantheon Bazaar into my hair, Eliza."

Eliza frowned. She was another of Erasmus's bargains (a lady's maid plucked straight from the dairyroom), and she tended to take fright at the more complicated aspects of her work. "Now how do you think they anchor those beads on the head?" she asked. "I'd hate to find you had strings of beads hanging off you like a jester or some such."

Genevieve sighed. "I don't know."

"Well, I suppose we can try," Eliza allowed. Forty-five minutes later Genevieve had gold beads twined through her hair.

"It looks lovely," Genevieve said, admiring the effect.

Her hair was pulled up in a loose pile behind her head. She rather fancied that the beads made her hair look more uniformly colored. "Thank you, Eliza!"

"Don't waggle your head like that!" Eliza scolded.

"They do feel slightly unstable," Genevieve said, shaking her head. If Felton's kiss—the kiss she was *determined* he should give her—was the least bit energetic, her hair would tumble to her shoulders, beads and all. When Felton kissed her, she would simply keep her neck stiff. It had been so long since she'd been kissed by anyone that she couldn't think of the least objection to that plan.

Chapter 3

The Kiss

*L*ucius Felton was the sort of gentleman whom one never caught smoothing his hair in the hallway mirror. From Genevieve's point of view, the only possible criticism one might have was that he was so formidable, terrifying even, with his heavy-lidded eyes and noncommittal expression. Did he even think she was beautiful? There was no evidence of it. Genevieve swallowed her sherry with reckless abandon and promised herself that Felton would kiss her in the carriage, even if she had to *order* him to do so.

Yet once Genevieve was settled in the carriage, she found herself studying the tips of her golden slippers (slightly pointed toes, which was the very newest fashion) before she could even get the courage to look at Felton. He was wearing a saffron-colored coat tailored with exquisite precision to his body. He looked very, *very* unapproachable. "Are you carrying a new stick?" Genevieve finally asked, desperate to say something.

"Made by Bittlemeir," he said, lifting it briefly for her inspection. Genevieve looked at the stick blankly. What could she say that would lead him to sit next to her? Or was she to launch herself across the space between them, like one of Mr. Congreve's exploding rockets? Likely he would shield himself with the stick, and she would rebound onto the floor.

"I've never noticed that knob before," she burbled. "Why on earth does your seat have a handle below it? Does it open?"

"The seat contains a liquor case," Felton explained.

"Oh, may I see!" Genevieve cried, clasping her hands and hoping that he wasn't repulsed by a girlish display of enthusiasm.

"Certainly." Felton rose with his customary grace, took the cushion from his seat, and removed a mahogany box from the cabinet.

"Do sit next to me," Genevieve said with what she hoped was a seductive smile.

He obeyed her without comment, opening the box to reveal two bottles and two glasses nestled into red velvet. "May I offer you a glass of Canary wine?"

"But of course!" Genevieve said. Now that he was sitting next to her, she was even more terrified. And yet . . . even being close to him made her knees tremble. He was so *perfect*. He hadn't a hair out of place, nor a thing about him that wasn't made of the very finest stuff. He glanced at her sideways, from under thick eyelashes, and Genevieve felt herself blushing.

She took the glass he handed her and drank a sip.

"I am looking forward to Witter's Othello," Felton said idly, tapping his cane on the floor of the carriage. He hadn't poured himself a glass. "I quite enjoyed his performance as Lear, although I doubt that the Covent Garden Theater is the appropriate venue for this play. The boxes are so close together and the audience tends to be, shall we say, inattentive?"

"Felton," Genevieve said. To her horror, her voice trembled a bit.

"Yes, my lady?" he inquired.

The carriage was slowing. If she didn't kiss him now, she'd never find the courage on the way home, and he would undoubtedly be seated on the other side of the carriage. Genevieve dropped her empty glass onto the seat next to her, put her hands on Felton's shoulders, and placed her mouth on his.

There was a dreadful moment when neither of them moved. Then slowly, very slowly, his right hand came up and clasped her neck. He spoke against her mouth: "This *is* a delightful surprise."

Genevieve was frozen in clammy doubt. He didn't sound delightfully surprised: rather the opposite. But then he started kissing her, and his mouth moved so firmly across hers that she almost swooned into his arms.

The carriage jolted to a halt. "Dear me," Felton said, drawing back. "I believe we have arrived at Covent Garden."

Genevieve was trembling. Everything in her was shrieking that he must tell the carriage to continue! Don't stop! Let's . . . let's . . . let's . . . The overwrought idea died in the light of his blue eyes. Men like Felton didn't grapple in carriages. It wasn't as if she were eighteen again, and eloping with Tobias Darby. The moment the carriage door had closed, Tobias had lunged at her like a stalking lion, but he'd been the wild younger son of a neighbor, the man who'd taken her off to Gretna Green after some three hours' conversation. Felton wasn't an unseasoned devil's spawn like Tobias but an urbane, sophisticated gentleman, up to snuff in every sense of the word.

"I believe we should attend the performance," he said mildly, picking up her glass and replacing it in the box.

Genevieve's humiliation was approximately twice as scalding as her desire had been. He'd guessed her thoughts! The footman opened the door. Luckily, Felton hadn't even touched her hair, so her beads were still in place. Of course, two minutes after Tobias had leaped into the carriage, her hair . . . but that was a different story, and years ago.

As they entered the theater and found their way to Felton's box, Genevieve was so busy impressing upon her companion that she was utterly unmoved by their kiss that she didn't notice that their box was receiving an unwonted amount of attention. It wasn't until the first intermission that she realized that virtually every opera glass in the house was trained on them. A quick pat told her that although her hair was precariously pinned, the beads were still in place. Felton sat opposite her, one slender finger absentmindedly tracing the gold leaf adorning the edge of the box, ignoring the sea of interested faces peering at them from boxes to the left and right and even from the pit.

"I gather you were unaware that an old admirer of yours has returned to London?" Felton finally asked, catching Genevieve's bewildered gaze. "His arrival seems to have brought on a violent burst of interest amongst the *ton*. You did not know?" He paused. "I am even more honored by your . . . attentions in my carriage."

"Old admirer?" Genevieve asked. "But I *have* no . . ." Her voice trailed away. For there, just across the theater, in Simon Darby's box, was—was Tobias.

Her Tobias. No! The Tobias who was only briefly hers. Almost her first husband. When they eloped, he was a great, raw-boned stripling, always moving, always restless. The man who met her eyes across the theater was taller and even bigger. His hair was standing in disordered curls all over his head. And his eyes! She recognized that gleam in his eyes.

The reprobate! How dare he greet her so publicly—or, indeed, greet her at *all?*

Genevieve quickly turned her head away. Felton's eyebrow was raised in faint interest. "How very odd it is, when acquaintances return after a long absence," she told him. It was the only comment that came to mind.

"Acquaintances?" Felton asked, the eyebrow shooting even higher.

"Nothing more," Genevieve said, turning her shoulder on him. Really, it was impolite of him to bring up that episode in her past. She was a respectable widow now. She could see out of the corner of her eyes that Tobias was standing up and bowing to Lady Henrietta, his brother's wife, and that meant he was getting ready to leave his box. Knowing Tobias, he would knock on the door of their box in two minutes, with no thought for the scandal of it. She turned to Felton.

"Kiss me, please," she said pleasantly.

He was lounging back in his chair, and he blinked at her like a country yokel.

"Felton," she repeated. "I should like you to kiss me, please."

A mask of impenetrable calm fell over his face like a shroud. "You do realize that such a kiss would signify to the *ton* our intent to marry?" he asked courteously enough. He wasn't going to kiss her. Genevieve felt pink rising in her cheeks along with her temper.

There was a wicked little smile curling Felton's lips. "It seems you are suffering from a bout of nerves. But one must wait for the appropriate time in order to make such a gesture."

She narrowed her eyes. "And when would that be?"

There was a rap at the door and Felton called, "Enter!"

"Well?" she snapped, suddenly furious. They were both despicable men.

"Now," Felton said. He stood up, pulled her to her feet, clasped her face in those long, elegant fingers of his, and kissed her. Straight on the mouth, and in the view of every single important member of the *ton,* including Mr. Tobias Darby, lately returned from India.

Genevieve gasped, and forgot all about the gentleman who had just entered the box. Felton's mouth was cool and strong on hers, and he smelled faintly of an elegant male perfume. She shivered all over and was about to pull him closer when he stepped back.

"Mr. Darby," Felton was saying. "Although we haven't met, it is naturally a pleasure to greet you."

Tobias looked just the same. Apparently devil's spawn didn't change. His hair curled upward with the same untamed freedom as it had when he was a boy. And his eyes were exactly the same: burning with a fierce determination. When she was a girl, she always thought of him as being like the wind that blows over the moors, and he was the same now: bigger, stronger, more vivid than the cultivated gentlemen of the *ton.*

Genevieve edged closer to Felton. "Yes, well," she said, acutely aware of the hundred-some pairs of eyes fixed on their encounter. "I suppose so. Although I would have preferred a less conspicuous encounter, Mr. Darby."

He shrugged. "I meant to visit you tomorrow morning, but here you are. I could hardly pretend not to see you." He grinned at her, and his eyes roamed all over her as freely as any shabster in the street might. "You look exquisite, Genevieve."

Genevieve almost smiled at that. Of course, paying her a

private visit tomorrow would have been the polite, safe thing to do, but Tobias was ever one to take the direct route to whatever he wanted.

"Do take a seat," Felton said, sounding rather amused. "A good part of the audience will be unable to see into our box, and the ensuing agony of curiosity will do them good."

Tobias was much bigger than he used to be. The box suddenly felt almost cramped as he moved toward her. Genevieve stumbled as she sat down.

Tobias Darby looked at the man who'd been kissing his wife—well, Genevieve wasn't *quite* his wife—and resisted the impulse to toss him over the box railing. It wouldn't be politic, as his twin would say. So he bowed instead. "Mr. Felton, it is likewise a pleasure."

Felton waved a hand toward one of the rickety little chairs next to Genevieve. "Do seat yourself," he said in the sort of languid voice that Tobias despised. "We might as well disappoint the crowd further by engaging in a civilized conversation."

"Very kind of you," Tobias replied. To his discomfort, he couldn't quite dismiss Felton as a man-milliner. He had been kissing Genevieve, after all. And there was a ruthlessness in his indifferent eyes. Tobias sat down next to Genevieve. She had pulled her streaked lion's mane of hair up on her head and tried to hide its wildness with frippery little beads. But she was as gloriously untamed as he remembered.

"How is your father?" he asked her. Not that he gave a bean, beyond hoping the old goat had repented for marrying his only daughter to a clutch-fisted old man.

"He died not long after your father, Mr. Darby. I am sorry for your loss." She didn't sound the least bit sorry. "I gather from the fact that you did not return to England that you did not hear of your father's demise until recently?"

As it happened, Tobias had heard of his father's death.

He simply hadn't seen it as an occasion to return home. It wasn't until he heard of the death of Lord Mulcaster that he caught the next available boat.

Genevieve's magnificent eyes were snapping with irritation. "I do believe your father regularly sent out investigators to try to find you," she said pointedly.

"I've been in India," Tobias replied, shrugging off a faint pang of guilt. His father had been a Captain Sharp masquerading as a gentleman; it was absurd to feel guilt for leaving the country after he had been ordered many times to do so.

The theater curtain began to rise, signaling the next installment of Othello's tumultuous marriage. No one in the audience bothered to look toward the red velvet, preferring to watch the Felton box.

"We are attracting rather a lot of attention," Felton pointed out.

Tobias shrugged. "Doesn't bother me."

"But I do believe that Lady Mulcaster is somewhat discomfited," Felton said gently. "I cannot leave the theater, as I am one of Witter's sponsors. Perhaps you would be so kind as to escort Lady Mulcaster to her house, Mr. Darby?"

Genevieve burst out with "No!"

"I'd be more than happy to do so," Tobias said smoothly, cutting off her objection. "Lady Mulcaster?" He rose and held out his arm.

She just stared up at him, that plump lower lip of hers rigid with disapproval. "I don't wish to leave!" she hissed at him.

The faint hum of fascinated polite society watching their box threatened to overwhelm the rolling tones of Othello, who was informing the whole world that he considered his wife unfaithful.

Felton leaned forward. "I greatly dislike the presumption

that *we* are providing more entertainment than Mr. Witter," he noted. "You would do me great service, Lady Mulcaster, if you would accept Mr. Darby's escort."

Genevieve blinked at him. Felton wanted her to go, after what they had shared? After that kiss? Didn't he want to escort her home, to take her in his arms in the warmth and dark of the carriage and— Weren't they betrothed now? Why was he sending her off with another man?

"I will attend you in the morning if I may," Felton said, picking up her hand and kissing it.

Genevieve felt the kiss to the bottom of her toes. She drew away her hand and tried to stop the silly smile that spread over her face. Perhaps Felton was right. She might as well take this uncouth giant out of the playhouse and get it through his thick head that she was uninterested in their further acquaintance. "Very well," she said, putting her hand on Tobias's arm.

Felton smiled at her again, and she detected approval in his eyes. Perhaps an exhibition of nonchalant indifference was the way to Felton's heart? She thought about that as she and Tobias made their way out of the box and down the stairs. Perhaps Felton wished for a wife who would view the world just as he did: with a calm, detached amusement. Whereas she quivered if he put a finger on her arm, stole glances at him constantly, and blushed far more frequently than she could have wished.

Tobias's carriage was enviously luxurious, upholstered in dark blue velvet with silver embroidery. He must have done well in the past seven years, given that he was a younger son whose father had lost their house in a card game. Genevieve eyed him and decided there was no point in raking the man over the coals for his disreputable behavior in the past. After all, it hardly mattered. She was Felton's now. He had kissed her in front of *everyone*.

It was almost amusing, how different Felton and Tobias were. Tobias was the wild boy of Genevieve's youth, and he didn't seem to have changed a bit. He had grown up just down the road, although their families did not visit because her father considered *his* father to be a loose fish. There were rumors about gambling and, increasingly as the twins grew up, rumors about the boys' uncivilized behavior. As a child, Genevieve had lived for the rare glimpses she had of those boys, striding through the village, bursting with life and vivacity. Their father would swear loudly and call them impudent puppies. They would laugh at him and prance away, paying him no mind. It was only years later that she understood the importance of civilized behavior.

"Did you say that you've been in India all these years, Mr. Darby?" she asked, shrugging out of her pelisse and putting it onto the seat beside her. It was remarkably warm. "It must have been a surprise to you to return and find your brother married," she said. "Lady Henrietta is a lovely woman."

"Quite a surprise," he agreed. He truly was good-looking, even with his disordered curls. She was used to Felton's sleek hair. It was a good thing that she was so infatuated with Felton, because otherwise she might relapse directly into Tobias's arms, Genevieve thought with some amusement. The way he was looking at her was a direct opposite to Felton's cool regard.

"Why didn't your brother Giles return to England with you?" she asked.

"He hadn't any reason to."

"And you *did?*" Genevieve said, and then suddenly stopped.

For he was looking at her steadily, and there was something in his eyes. "Yes," he said slowly. "I did."

"Um," Genevieve said, trying to think of another topic of conversation. "So what did you do all these years in India?" she finally asked.

"I made a fortune," he said, still watching her.

"Oh?" Try as she might, she couldn't think what to say to that. "How nice for you."

"I plan to marry," he said in a conversational kind of voice. "Now that I am able to support a wife and children."

"An excellent idea! I can introduce you to some lovely young women." Genevieve suddenly realized what was happening. Tobias had made his fortune, and now he wished to ameliorate for his dreadful behavior seven years ago. He intended to use her to assuage his conscience, but unfortunately she wasn't available. Genevieve had to bite her lip to keep back a smile. "Truly," she added, "I have made a number of friends and I shall introduce you."

"But I already know you," he said softly. Suddenly he was sitting next to her, rather than across from her. "Don't I, Genevieve? Already *know* you, I mean?"

She colored and drew back. "There's no need to be—to be saucy!" she snapped.

"It was a mere statement of fact," he told her, and something in his eyes made a glimmer of shameless memory stir in her mind.

"Lord Felton and I are likely to be married," she said quickly.

"Likely?" Not only was he sitting entirely too close to her but he had started stroking the bare skin of her arm with one finger. "What a very odd way of expressing your betrothal. There *is* a betrothal, isn't there, Genevieve? After all, Felton kissed you before an extremely interested audience. The whole theater, as a matter of fact."

She scowled and then realized exactly what to say. "As

you well know, sir," she said haughtily, "one needn't be formally betrothed in order to *know* each other."

The finger stopped for a second and then continued. "True enough." She couldn't read his eyes. Even with four lamps burning in the carriage, his face was in shadow.

His hand curled around her arm. She shivered instinctively. But when she turned to pull her pelisse over her shoulders, he stopped her.

"Sir!" she protested.

"You didn't call me *'sir'* last time we met." His eyes burned into hers. A lock of hair had fallen over his brow. Goodness, he was handsome. It was nice to think that, if nothing else, she had chosen so well back when she was a mere lass.

She opened her mouth to answer, but he was there. Those hands were lightning quick, for being so large. One tipped up her chin and then his mouth closed on hers before she could even squeak. Tobias kissed with the same boisterous enthusiasm he had seven years before. He invaded her mouth with the impetuous wildness that had led to her—to her—

Down the years of memory, he smelled just the same: a rough, wild, Tobias smell of the outdoors, of a wild boy now a man, of a devil-may-care freedom. His touch brought back memories of all the days she'd walked sedately into the village beside her governess, hoping for a glimpse of the wild Darby twins.

So, just for a moment, and only because of those memories, she kissed him back, let their tongues dance together in a moment's reckless foolishness before she wrenched herself away. "What on earth are you doing?" she gasped, thinking that there really ought to be more indignation in her tone.

"Shall I demonstrate again?" he asked, humor dancing in his eyes.

"What?" she said, her mind foggy. One swift movement later, she found herself in his lap, sitting in the circle of his arms, and he was tasting her again. Her head fell back against his shoulder without a rational protest. And this time, sheltered in the circle of his arms, his mouth moving roughly over hers, her arm clutching tight around his neck, she didn't even remember about indignation. Their tongues tangled to the beat of her heart. He was the one who stopped the kiss, his mouth tracing a smoldering trail over her cheeks.

She just sat there, struck dumb with surprise, while he kissed her ear. What was she doing? What were those shocks dancing up and down her legs, making her breasts feel tender? *What was she doing?*

His mouth was coming back to hers; she could sense it. Could feel the slight edge of tension in his body, the way he curved toward her. She should push him away, warn him, *threaten* him! "Yes," she sighed, winding her fingers into his hair and pulling him closer. His tongue plunged into her mouth as if . . . as if.

There was a faint chiming noise as strings of glass beads cascaded to the floor, set free by strong hands that ran through her hair. His hands were everywhere, touching her neck, brushing down her narrow back, pausing on the swell of her hips. He was touching—his hand was touching—she could hear her own sigh as his hand cupped her breast, and she could hardly miss the hungry sweep of feeling that followed it, the mad urge to strain closer to him.

"Oh God, Genevieve," he said against her mouth, and his voice was rough with desire. She'd heard that note before. "I missed you."

The couch stopped and Genevieve almost tumbled off his lap. "What am I *doing?* Get away from me!" She pushed away so quickly that she almost flew to the other seat. "That must *never*—it was only—it was only due to our past!" she cried. Her hands went to her hair. "Oh no, where are my pins?" The moment her servants saw her hair tumbling down her back, they would know in a flash what had happened, and when they saw she was with Tobias, the gossip would be all over London by the morrow.

"It's all right," Tobias said, handing her three pins from the floor. "This is my house, not yours."

"*Your* house?" Genevieve said, stunned. "Why on earth are we here? That isn't proper! I cannot visit your house unchaperoned. I wish to go home immediately!"

"I have no plans for anything nefarious," Tobias said. "I merely wished to show you the house that I purchased. I bought it only this morning."

"You bought a house this morning," she said, stunned. "I don't wish to see your house, Mr. Darby. How dare you bring me here without even inquiring as to my wishes!"

"I wanted to have a place to bring my wife," he said, watching her. "When I have a wife, that is. You could pin up your hair and then I would bring you directly back to your house. There are no servants here to gossip, as I haven't yet hired a staff."

He was obviously the same disreputable scamp he had been as a boy. Imagine bringing her to his house, for all the world as if she were a doxy who would fall into his arms and then his bed.

"I am no longer fodder for your games, Mr. Darby," Genevieve said sharply. "I am a grown woman and I mean to marry Lucius Felton. So the fact that we shared a kiss is simply due to a bit of nostalgia and nothing more. I will countenance no more of that behavior on your part."

"Absolutely not," he said, with an air of dignified virtue that Genevieve didn't believe for a moment. But she did have to pin up her hair. She could not return home looking like this.

"As long as you understand," she said, giving him a scowl, "that I'm not eighteen any longer. I may have behaved foolishly when I was very young, but now I'm a widow and I know about the world and men of your caliber."

"I can see that," he said promptly.

Genevieve looked out the carriage door. Tobias's groom was holding open the door of the house. It was a beautiful house, tall without being overly narrow, elegant without being overbearing. "I'm not a *loose woman,*" she hissed at Tobias, trying once more to impress the truth upon him. "Just because we once intended to marry doesn't mean that you can take advantage of me!"

"I would never do such a thing, Genevieve."

"I would prefer that you address me as Lady Mulcaster," she announced.

And then she swept ahead of him up the stairs, so she didn't see the way his eyes lingered on her curves. The Grecian tunic was delightful from every angle; the clinging silk left nothing about Lady Mulcaster's curvy little figure to the imagination.

Tobias swallowed and followed her up the stairs. Of course, she wasn't loose, this girl of his. She was just Genevieve. And Genevieve could no more say no to him than she could marry that weasel she'd been kissing. She just didn't understand that yet.

Chapter 4

In Which Genevieve Takes Lessons in Horticulture

"This is lovely!" Genevieve said as she wandered around the dining room. "I've never seen wallpaper in this precise shade. Isn't it apricot?"

"Something like that," Tobias answered. He was following her with an Argand lamp, holding it up so that she could look at the walls, and he could look at her. Her hair was far more lovely than the walls. Apricots and sunflowers, all mixed together with a bit of cream. And her face was just as adorable as he remembered, especially her gray-green eyes. They'd been passionate but naive when she was a girl. Now that passionate interest was tempered by a tantalizing hint of reserve.

"Of course, you need furniture," she continued. "There's a cabinetmaker, George Bullock, in Tenterden Street who has some beautiful pieces."

"I have some furniture following from India, as well as rugs, tea caddies, that sort of thing."

"How wonderful! My friend Carola has a glorious rug from India, all jeweled colors like a cashmere shawl."

"I'm hoping my wife will direct a refurbishing," he said, following her into the ballroom.

"Your wife?" she asked. "But you must acquire some furniture. One doesn't find a wife overnight, you know."

Doesn't one? Tobias thought, watching her sweet round bottom as she leaned over and tugged at the tall windows that lined the ballroom.

"Do these open?" she asked.

"They lead to the garden," he said, moving up next to her and twisting the handle sharply. It swung open into the night, and a rush of perfume came with it.

"What a delicious smell!" Genevieve cried.

"Honeysuckle opens at night." He didn't say that it was the garden that made him buy the house. He missed the lush beauty of Indian flowers.

Genevieve danced out of the doors into the night, and Tobias knew in that instant that she hadn't changed, not a single inch of her. She may have acquired the elegance of a *très-grande dame,* but she still had the exuberance that had sent her into a carriage with him at age eighteen. He would never forget seeing her for the first time. It was at a pestilently tedious party that his father had insisted his three sons attend, because he owed Genevieve's father so much money. Darby Senior had owed everyone within fifty miles of their house substantial sums. "If one of you could marry the chit of the house," his father had told them, "we'd be in the clover."

Tobias had figured that comment was really directed at Simon, his elder brother. Simon was his father's heir, and already more polished and elegant than any gentleman their side of London. Whereas he and Giles were rough-and-tumble lads who scarcely knew their way around the ball-room. They were naught more than younger sons of a hard-ened gambler who always lost. Who would want either of them?

She had. He'd walked into that party prepared to endure twenty minutes of turgid conversation, except there was a girl standing near the piano, and she looked at him. Genevieve was the most beautiful woman he'd ever seen in his life. It took him exactly two seconds to get from the door to her side, and when those greeny-gray eyes smiled at him, he was lost. Her whole face lit up with interest, with pleasure, with *desire*. He might have been young, but he had never been stupid.

Three hours later they were creeping out her father's door with all of his and Giles's money in his pocket. . . . An hour after that they were tooling down the road in a hired coach. . . . Six hours after that, her father caught them. But in between . . .

Well, he'd had years to think about what had happened during those six hours.

It was hard to believe that he'd found Genevieve again. She was standing near a bank of snow-white honeysuckle that hung luminous in the moonlight. Obviously, she wouldn't want to dash off to Gretna Green with him again. She considered herself in love with Felton. And that bastard Felton was apparently so sure of her that he didn't mind sending her home with a rival. But she had kissed *him* in the carriage. She was pretending that episode never happened, but every sinew in his body was assuring him that it had.

"Your hair is still extraordinary," he said, reaching out to touch it. Long curling strands lay down her back, all the shades from brown to gold, as if rocks were spun with gold.

She turned around, a bunch of honeysuckle caught to her face. "This garden is worth the whole house!" she cried, ignoring his compliment. She never had been very interested in flattery, he remembered that.

"Did you know how honeysuckle gets its name?" he asked.

"I don't," she said, eyes alive with interest.

He plucked off one blossom and stepped even closer. "Because the blossoms taste sweet," he said, brushing the frail white petals against her mouth.

She frowned. "Very funny. It's just a flower. No one eats flowers."

He turned the blossom around and showed her the narrow point. "Taste this, Genevieve."

"I wish you would stop addressing me so informally!" she snapped, clearly curious but disliking the intimacy.

Tobias ran the slender point of the flower over the line of her lips. "Taste," he said. His voice was as husky and dark as the gray-blue sky around them.

"I don't nibble on flowers!" she said obstinately, pushing his arm away.

"You do it like this." He put the point of the flower between his lips, and a drop of sweet fluid fell into his mouth. "Here, taste." He put a large hand at the back of all that glorious hair and pulled her toward him. "Taste." His mouth covered hers and then opened, inviting a taste, and she—oh, his Genevieve would never resist such a gift—her tongue slipped into his mouth with a tiny gasp. The sweet of the flower was gone, but the sweet of Genevieve's mouth could keep him exploring all night. The honeysuckle fell between their bodies, crushed between his chest and hers when her hands rose to his hair and pulled him closer.

Desire ran through his veins like thick honey, like the heady smell of crushed flowers. He cupped her face in his and kissed her relentlessly, asking silently, deeply, a question he had no right to ask.

But Genevieve's head was spinning, and she'd stopped thinking again. There was only Tobias and the taste of his mouth, and the feeling of his hands shaping her face, delicately, sweetly, as if she were precious, at the very same time that his mouth ravaged hers. His body was so large and warm: She could feel every ridge of muscle through the silk of her gown, and there were—there were several ridges to enjoy. It was all rather dim, her knowledge of kissing, since it was based on six brief hours, years ago. But it was coming back to her: the hardness of Tobias's body, the way he almost growled in his throat, the way—yes, the way he had scooped her up in his arms, and now he would put her down on the carriage seat. Except there was a soft bank of grass instead, and the smell of flowers, and the irregular song of a bird who'd forgotten to go to bed on time.

She was forgetting something too, but it didn't matter at the moment, not when Tobias was, his hands were, and his leg . . . it felt so good that Genevieve arched up against it, shaking with longing for that feeling she so barely remembered, like a blaze of fire it was.

He was talking, his voice was shaking too. "Sweet," he was saying, "you're so sweet, Genevieve. My Genevieve." He moved his hand over her breast, and the mist slipped over her eyes again, just when she was about to stop him, so she pulled his head down to hers instead. She was burning, an ache spreading from between her legs, a fire that made her bite her lips before she demanded—begged—but he seemed to know. His hand was teasing at her breast, his thumb running over the silk of her bodice, caressing the soft skin just above her neckline. She twisted with an inarticulate protest. He was tormenting her, when all she wanted was that explosion, that passion and burst of light, that—

His hand moved back to her breast again. A yearning moan flew into the night air like music to rival the nightingale.

"Would you like to taste the honeysuckle, Genevieve?" he asked her. His voice was ragged with longing, but steady and controlled. He was brushing a flower across her hot cheek now, trailing its sweetness over her eyes, her lips.

She opened her eyes reluctantly. Opening her eyes meant coming back to herself. Realizing the fact that she had once again played the part of the depraved hussy: What was it about Tobias Darby? Why did *he* inspire her to play such a wanton role?

His eyes were black with longing. Carefully he took a flower and squeezed it against her lips. Her tongue caught the nectar, and then his mouth came swiftly down on hers to share the honeyed drop. "You see," he told her, "one suckles the honey, Genevieve."

"I can't do this, Tobias," she whispered.

"We aren't doing anything," he said to her, thick eyelashes covering his eyes. "We're merely kissing, Genevieve." His hand lay innocently on the side of her breast, not moving, as if he thought she might forget what he had been doing. "I haven't pulled down your bodice, for example."

"I should hope not!" she said, but her voice trailed away as he did just that.

"Oh God, Genevieve, you're even more beautiful than I remembered," he said hoarsely. Her breast was as luminous as the honeysuckles in the moonlight, plump and overflowing his hands, her nipple like a tender bud.

Genevieve was struggling to make herself push him away. To reassert the fact that she was a dignified widow with—with *dignity*. Not the sort of woman who ran away with a man after knowing him three hours, not the sort of woman who could be seduced out in a garden. "You must think I'm nothing more than a light-skirt," she whispered. "Did you come back because you thought that you could simply take me again—wherever you wished?" Her voice cracked.

He froze as if she'd stabbed him in the ribs.

"No!" he said. "No!"

She pulled up her bodice with one swift jerk and in a second she was on her feet and running back to the house, away from that scented garden and its promise of earthly delights. He caught her as she entered the ballroom door "Genevieve!" he said. "*Don't* think such a thing."

But Genevieve had noted the location of a ladies' sitting room off the ballroom, and she snatched up the lamp and darted in that direction. All Tobias could do was lean against the wall in the dark and curse himself. And then, once he could think rationally again, fetch her reticule and offer it to her.

The lady who emerged some twenty minutes later was no hurly-burly girl to be seduced in a corner. She was a lady, hair tamed into a dignified coil at her neck, gown in place as if it had never slipped below its moorings.

"Mr. Darby," she said dryly, "I should like to go home, please."

"Genevieve, you must listen to me." The savage note in his own voice surprised him.

But she put a hand on his arm and smiled, for all the world as if he'd committed some small social solecism such as arriving late to an appointment. "I've given this some thought. I am embarrassed by what just happened."

"But I wish to marry—," Tobias said.

She cut him off. "I expect you do wish to marry me. I have no doubt but that you returned here precisely in the hope of assuaging your guilt over what happened seven years ago, and I honor you for that thought. I seem to be remarkably susceptible to your—your brand of foolery," she said, and for a second a look of panic crossed her face. And then it was replaced by calm confidence. "I think it must be due to our early history. I did agree to marry you once, after all!" She laughed, but there was little humor in it, to Tobias's mind.

He opened his mouth, but she fluttered her hand to stop him from talking. "I just wish to say this, Mr. Darby, and then I believe we should neglect the subject in the future. I honor your intention to marry me, if not the methods by which you hope to attain your goals. Still, those methods were successful last time, so in all fairness, I have to admit that you were perfectly correct in trying them. But I, Mr. Darby, am not interested in marrying you."

Tobias looked down at her and thought about just how fast he could kiss her out of all this nonsense.

"I wish to marry Mr. Felton, you see," she said to him, giving him a dimpled smile. "I may have been overcome by nostalgia on seeing you, but, in fact, I am quite *ridiculously* drawn to Mr. Felton, and I think we shall make a very happy marriage."

Now Tobias didn't feel like grinning anymore. "He looks like a shady customer to me," he barked. "There are rumors about his business dealings in the City."

She raised an eyebrow. "He was my husband's business partner, and if there was one thing that Erasmus understood, it was business." She didn't see any reason to add the fact that Erasmus reveled in shady dealings.

"You cannot marry such a man."

"I beg to differ," Genevieve said with hauteur. "Now, if you would be so kind as to return me to my own house, I would be most grateful. And I shall be certain to keep my eye out for a young lady to refurbish your house."

Tobias pushed himself upright. He could play this game as well as anyone, and it was clear that his little love had made up her mind to be obstinate for the time being.

"May I escort you to the theater tomorrow night?" he asked.

"I am very sorry to say that I have to plead a previous engagement." Any fool could tell from her smile that she was outrageously pleased to have that excuse.

"What is it?" he growled.

"I fail to see why that—"

He put an arm in front of her as she went through the door. "Genevieve?" His voice was just this side of control.

She swung her little nose in the air. "I am attending Lady Rickleshaw's musicale. I'm very much afraid to tell you, Mr. Darby, that it will be a quite exclusive gathering."

Tobias didn't waste any breath with arguing. He could tell, within five minutes of making a public appearance the night before, that London matrons were exquisitely happy with the arrival of a single gentleman of excellent fortune. He didn't anticipate being turned down at any event.

"The next night?" he asked.

"I am engaged," she said airily, climbing into his carriage.

"The next?" he growled.

"Engaged!"

"Genevieve, I shall keep asking you from now until next week. When I was in India, I simply got used to taking what I wanted." The warning in his voice was crystal clear, as was the look in his eyes.

"Well, you will have to learn differently!" Genevieve snapped at him. "I certainly won't be going anywhere in the evening with you again, not after you took the opportunity to drive me to your house in this harum-scarum fashion! I may be a widow, but I still could be ruined by being seen unchaperoned in such a location. You're just as much of a blackguard as you ever were, Tobias Darby! I shall *never* allow you to escort me in the evening."

Tobias hadn't gotten to be a nabob by ignoring possibilities. "An afternoon, then," he said. "Are you engaged tomorrow afternoon, Genevieve?"

"Certainly!" she said.

"And one week from today?"

"I don't wish to be seen with you," she pointed out. "No, I don't wish to *be* with you, Mr. Darby. Spending time in your company will simply encourage you in the mistaken belief that marrying me will compensate for your base behavior of seven years ago."

"Are you so *very* sure of Felton, then?" he asked shrewdly.

She blinked. "Of course I am, although I might point out that your question is characteristically impolite."

"Felton did kiss you in front of the *ton*," Tobias said, nodding.

"Exactly!"

He loathed the way her face lit up when she remembered that lukewarm kiss from her lukewarm suitor. "But then he blithely sent you off with me," Tobias noted.

"Felton has every confidence in me," she said loftily. "And I do believe he didn't understand the depths of perfidity to which you might sink."

"Perhaps he has taken you a bit for granted," Tobias said. "Perhaps it wouldn't be entirely amiss to give Mr. Felton a bit of competition."

"Actually," Genevieve said with a little smirk, "you may not believe this, but I seem to be quite fashionable amongst the London gentlemen. I have no difficulty finding competition for Felton."

"Ah, but I am far greater competition than they are," he said softly. "They are just town bucks, after all, whereas I represent your past. If you wish to encourage Felton into a proposal, Genevieve, you would do well to encourage me at the same time."

"And why would you wish to help me?" she said suspiciously, narrowing her eyes at him.

He tried to school his expression into one of innocence, but she suddenly said, "Oh, I understand! If I am married to such a worthy man as Felton, and you helped in the process, it would assuage your conscience." There was just the smallest note of disappointment in her voice, which Tobias thought very encouraging.

"It is true that I would like to see you happily married," he said. "After all, I feel indirectly responsible for your marriage to Lord Mulcaster."

Genevieve took a deep breath. "Erasmus wasn't so terrible."

"I've heard he was a miser and an extremely ugly man to deal with on the business front," Tobias said, watching her steadily.

"Those things are both true," she admitted.

He touched her face. "I'm sorry, Genevieve. I'm so sorry."

"There's no need to be," she said cheerily, the faint hint of sadness falling from her face. "If I hadn't married Erasmus, I might never have met Felton!" She looked dismayed at the very thought.

Tobias was surprised by the surge of rage that choked him for a moment.

"Yet perhaps you are right," she said a second later. "Felton may well be aware that he has no significant rivals." She blushed a little, and Tobias wondered just what had happened between herself and that elegant lounger. "I shall grant you an afternoon," she said.

He nodded.

"What shall we do?" she asked, looking adorably interested. "Shall we drive in Hyde Park?"

Tobias was sure of one thing. "Absolutely not," he said brusquely. "I took my sister-in-law around the promenade this afternoon"—they'd been looking for Genevieve, although there was no need to mention that—"and a more tedious encounter I have never experienced. Nothing but limp hand wavings at the pace of a snail. I thought the horses might die of boredom before we made the whole circuit."

Genevieve giggled. She was aware, deep down in her soul, that she too had been rather disappointed by the ritualistic drive in Hyde Park. It wasn't nearly as interesting as it appeared in the gossip pages. "What shall we do, then?" she inquired.

"Wait and see," he said.

Chapter 5

Genteel Behavior Is Not Always Called For

"Well, I think it's *so* romantic!" Lady Carola Perwinkle cried.

Genevieve's friend was an enchanting little madam, with her cap of fairy curls and just the smallest evidence of an interesting condition. Genevieve couldn't help smiling at her. "It's not romantic, you silly thing," she said. "What's romantic about Tobias wishing to make amends? His behavior toward me in the past was utterly unscrupulous."

Carola was shaking her head. "You can't mean to say that you don't find it utterly quixotic that Tobias Darby came all the way back from India, just to ask you to marry him! He's waited for you all these years, and now finally you're free," she sighed. "My husband would have just found a trout stream and drowned his sorrows."

"Tobias may have returned to England, but it was only to find that I've fallen in love with someone else," Genevieve pointed out. "Truly, Carola, you make everything sound like a novel."

"I love novels! If this were a novel, Felton and Darby would duel to the death."

But the very thought made Genevieve feel slightly ill. "Luckily, Felton at least is a gentleman and quite restrained in his behavior."

"Well, Tobias Darby doesn't look restrained," Carola argued. "I think he's precisely the kind of man who would be a hero in one of Mrs. Radcliffe's novels."

"Tobias as hero? Never! He's nothing more than the wild boy he always was. He merely hopes to clear his conscience by marrying me."

"A boy? Are you *blind?*" Carola asked, incredulous. "My friend Neville has been desperately in love with you for weeks, even though you likely didn't notice. He almost wept last night when Darby strode into your box. We all saw the way he looked at you. The net result was that Neville tore up the dreadful poem he was composing for you."

"I didn't know that you and Mr. Charlton were friends," Genevieve said. "How long have you been friends and what does your husband think—"

"Don't try to distract me!" Carola scolded. "Which one are you going to take, Genevieve? Felton or Darby? I know who I would marry!"

"Who?"

"Darby, no question about it. Felton is all very well. He has a sinister kind of attractiveness and of course he's quite handsome. But the way Tobias Darby looked at you last night . . . a woman would be a fool to give that up."

"Felton looks at me with a great deal of appreciation," Genevieve said, nettled. "And he did kiss me in front of the entire *ton*. I suppose you saw that as well?"

"Yes, but was that kiss due to your attractiveness or his jealousy?" Carola asked.

Genevieve had considered that very question half the

night. "Jealousy simply indicates the depth of Felton's feelings for me, don't you see?"

"No," Carola said. "I don't. I think the look on Darby's face indicated the depth of his feelings for you."

"I can tell you precisely who I would choose to marry," Genevieve announced. "Felton asked me to marry him this very morning." A tinge of triumph turned her cheeks pink.

"Did you say yes?" Carola asked, with an irritating lack of excitement in her voice.

"Of course I did!"

"Oh, well, in that case, congratulations, darling," she said, hopping up and giving Genevieve a kiss. "Felton's town house is only two streets from mine. So we can ride in the park together every morning!"

But Genevieve heard the tinge of doubt in her voice as clearly as if she'd spoken it out loud. "How did your husband propose to you?" she asked.

"Tuppy?" Carola rolled her eyes. "He stammered. We barely knew each other, and I was truly *horrified* by the whole circumstance. Of course, he had spoken with my father beforehand, and my father had instructed me to accept, so there wasn't much I could do."

"You were horrified? Why? The two of you seem so happy together," Genevieve said, thinking of Carola's tall, rather bashful husband, and the way his eyes lit up when he saw his delicious little wife.

"Well, we are, *now,*" Carola said with a giggle. "But it took quite a few years. At any rate, how did Felton ask you? Did he go on his knees?"

"Of course not," Genevieve said. "Felton would never do anything so ungentlemanly. He merely commented that given his kiss of the previous evening, he rather thought that our intention to marry had been made clear to the *ton,* and that therefore he would send a message to the *Times* directly."

Carola blinked. "That was *it?* He didn't say he loved you, or even ask you if you wished to marry him?"

Genevieve felt herself turning a little pink. "No—that is—I rather think he considered that I had asked *him.* Because I told him to kiss me last night."

"You asked him?" Carola said, stunned.

"Not to marry me," Genevieve said hastily. "Just to kiss me. Last night. And before he did so, he pointed out that such a kiss would indicate our intention to marry."

"So this morning he didn't say that he loved you *at all?*" Carola asked.

Unfortunately, she was echoing just the uneasy question that Genevieve had asked herself repeatedly during the previous night. "He's not the sort of man who expresses himself in hyperboles," she pointed out.

"Yes, but, while asking a woman to marry him—"

"Felton considers propriety very important," Genevieve said firmly, "and I must say that I agree with him. It was due to Tobias's utter lack of civilized behavior that I found myself married to Erasmus Mulcaster for six years, and that wasn't a happy marriage, Carola."

"I know, darling," Carola said. "But are you certain that turning to a man who is quite so rigidly proper as Felton is the answer? After all, Tobias may well have changed in the interim."

"No, he's just the same," Genevieve said dampeningly. "I could tell the moment I saw him last night. Just as wild as he ever was."

"The only man who's ever looked at me the way Tobias Darby looks at you is my husband. And my Tuppy could *never* be considered wild, Genevieve. I would suggest that you may be misinterpreting personal interest for a character trait." She giggled—and there was no lady in London with as wicked a giggle as Lady Carola Perwinkle. "You must keep in mind that one doesn't wish a man to behave in a civilized fashion *at all times,* Genevieve!"

Genevieve colored again. She knew exactly what Carola meant, but she refused to comment on it. "Lucius Felton will always behave in a genteel fashion," she said coolly. "And that is just as I would wish it."

"If you say so," Carola said. The doubt rang clear in her voice. Then she reached over to the table next to her and picked up a small garment. "Look at this, Genevieve. Do you think that I disfigured the sleeve with too many rosebuds?"

Lucius Felton was involved in some suspect dealings, all right. But he was walking just on the right side of the law, although it appeared that Genevieve's dead husband had had no such scruples. From what Tobias could ascertain, Felton was worth a tremendous amount of money, far more, Tobias suspected, than the *ton* imagined. Within five hours of beginning his inquiries, Tobias had gained respect for the man. Felton may be a shade disreputable, but some of his disreputable dealings were clearly brilliant.

One thing Tobias had discovered immediately was that Felton's appearance in Genevieve's life was no accident. He must have seen her somewhere and decided to have her, because Felton had suddenly presented himself to Lord Mulcaster as a partner six months before Mulcaster died, accepting a piddling percentage.

Obviously, Felton was out for bigger prey than Mulcaster's money. He wanted Mulcaster's wife, and money was no object.

Still, Tobias thought he saw one weakness: Felton's stables. Felton was a fanatic with horseflesh, a man who would move mountains to buy a colt he wanted for his stable. It took Tobias four days to buy all five horses in England considered likely to win considerable fame in the next few years.

So Tobias strolled into a dinner party being given by Lady Perwinkle with a sense of well-being, although it quickly dissipated. The first thing he saw after greeting his cheerful little hostess was Felton bending over Genevieve's hand in a display of outrageous gallantry. All that golden-brown hair of hers was precariously tied up with a few flowers; yet somehow a haphazard arrangement that would make any other woman look disheveled made her look more alive. And Lucius Felton saw it. There was a deep, acquisitive sense of possession in Felton's eyes that made Tobias think seriously of murder for the first time in his life.

He walked further into the drawing room and greeted the quite exquisite Miss Priscilla Blythe. Genevieve was playing the piano, and Felton was watching with a sleepy look in his eyes that made Tobias stiffen like a jackal. But he was playing a long game, and so he held his cards, chattering with Priscilla until he was ready to expire from tedium. She seemed to have only one subject of conversation: her small dog, Lance.

There was one interesting moment over port. Lord Perwinkle was chatting with two gentlemen about trout fishing, of which Tobias knew nothing. Lucius Felton was standing by the fireplace, so Tobias strolled over to greet him. He didn't bother with pleasantries: From what he'd discovered in the last few days, Felton's urbane courtesies were all on the surface. "I believe you have something that I want," he remarked. His tone was courteous enough.

Felton raised his head and looked at him. Tobias had seen

adders in Indian marketplaces with kinder eyes. "I never give up my possessions," he said.

Tobias raised an eyebrow. "Under no circumstances?"

"Never. I would recommend that you abandon your efforts, Mr. Darby. The lady in question has no wish to jump ship, you see." He smiled with all the delicate courtesy of a cat playing with a mouse.

But Tobias was no mouse. He smiled as well, and it was a smile honed in the back alleys of Bombay and the marble palaces of Indian rajas. "Shall we leave the lady out of this?" he said softly.

Felton's eyes dropped demurely, and he examined his fingernails. "I simply wished to spare you some trouble," he said. "She is quite, quite attached to me."

"I bought a filly today," Tobias said, watching him. "Prudence, by way of Prunella and Waxy."

Felton looked up again, and there was a good deal more interest in his eyes. "Good choice," he said. "I was looking at that filly myself: hadn't quite made up my mind."

Tobias felt a pulse of rage that the man showed a spark of interest only when it came to horseflesh, not Genevieve, but he quelled the thought. "I have had an interesting few days on that front. I also acquired a beautiful little Hungarian filly, Nyar, by way of Dr. Syntax and Csillog."

"Nyar has some English blood in her," Felton said with commendable indifference, to Tobias's mind. Given that the man was beginning to see the light.

"Minuet as well," Tobias said softly.

"The Euston Stud would never sell Minuet!" Lucius snapped. "She won the Oak Stakes last year."

"Yes, I do believe that Grafton would rather have kept Minuet. But every man has a price, you know." The statement hung in the air. "One further purchase," Tobias said after a moment. "Smolensko."

"Ah. Congratulations are truly in order, Mr. Darby."

Tobias had him now; there was a spark of pure, cold rage at the bottom of those civilized eyes.

"No, no," Tobias said modestly. "I do wonder how the horses will do on the long voyage to India, though. Some horses don't take to being in the hold of a ship for weeks."

"You cannot take those horses to India," Felton stated. "It would be a massacre."

"Of course I can. And I'm negotiating for Whisker as well. You must know of him; I believe he beat both your horses at Epsom Downs last year. Ah, Lord Perwinkle," Tobias said, turning to his host. "I've just been telling Felton that I'm planning to set up stables in India. I've bought a number of horses."

"Good, good," Lord Perwinkle said, smiling his rather charming, absentminded smile. "Shall we join the ladies?"

When they walked into the drawing room, Genevieve was seated at the piano again. Tobias walked directly over to her. Felton was not a man to trail behind a rival; a moment later he was sitting on the couch next to their hostess, looking for all the world as if he had no interest in the corner of the room that held the piano.

Genevieve was examining some sheet music. "I am looking forward to tomorrow afternoon," he said to her.

"I believe it might rain," she noted. "In that event, I shall surely wish to remain in my house."

"I would be enchanted," he said, giving her a wicked grin.

She flushed slightly. "That was *not* an invitation to join me, Mr. Darby!" She stood up and looked as if she might escape, so he moved slightly. To pass him, she would have to touch his shoulder. Sure enough, she stayed where she was. Her gown was all blond lace and slim ribbons, making her look as fragile and exquisite as a narcissus blossom.

"You didn't used to be so enameled," he said. "I remember you in a grass-stained pinafore, with hair falling all over the place and great chubby cheeks."

Genevieve narrowed her eyes. "You never showed any sign of noticing me as a child."

"The memories are coming back to me the way bad dreams do. Could I have imagined a period when your hair had a distinctly blue tinge?"

"Definitely a nightmare," Genevieve said coolly, brushing past his shoulder.

A hand shot out and caught her arm. "You don't remember?" His voice fairly purred with amusement. "My understanding was that you used blackberries to dye your hair."

"You must be thinking of someone else," Genevieve retorted.

But he was staring down at her with those eyes of his, and there was something, a gleam in them, that made a flush rise in her cheeks. "Ah, but I have a remarkable memory," he said.

That slow smile of his ought to be banned! Genevieve seemed to be powerless to look away. He had her hand again and was raising it to his lips. "I seem to remember . . . *everything* about you."

"It was black currants, not blackberries," Genevieve said, and was horrified to find that her voice came out a husky whisper.

"Why would you ever wish to change your hair?" His eyes seemed genuinely puzzled. "It's the most beautiful stuff I've seen in my life. India is full of silks, but I never saw anything to rival this." He touched a curl with one finger.

Genevieve swallowed. It had been a perfectly reasonable attempt to replace her streaked hair with a rippling shade of black. But when Tobias Darby looked at her hair, she couldn't imagine why she'd ever wanted black hair.

"Surely you remember," he said, his voice a mere whisper of sound. "Your hair—in the carriage? I don't seem to be able to forget, no matter how many years pass."

A shiver ran down Genevieve's back. He had been enchanted by her curls, nuzzled them, kissed them, draped her hair over his body and hers, and all the time the carriage had rocked on toward Gretna Green, where he was to make her his wife.

But that had never happened.

She drew herself up and snatched her hand away. "If you will excuse me, Mr. Darby," she said with spurious politeness. "While it is always interesting to discuss childhood memories, I believe my fiancé is waiting for me."

And then she marched over to Felton, her slim back indignant. But Tobias grinned after her. She remembered, all right.

Chapter 6

Bartholomew Fair

*G*enevieve dressed for her afternoon appointment with Tobias Darby full of misgivings. Why on earth was she allowing him to escort her? He was clearly just as wild as he ever was. Honesty compelled her to admit that she had a strange susceptibility to his charms, even given that he wasn't nearly as handsome as Felton, and he had none of Felton's cultured charm. Felton merely had to look at her with a glimmer of approval and Genevieve felt as if he'd given her all her Christmas presents rolled into one smile. Whereas Tobias never looked at her with approval, only with lust. He'd been out of place in the village when they'd been growing up, and now he was desperately out of place in London: too large, too fast-moving, too lustful. Really, it was exhausting even being around him. A woman had to be constantly on her guard, or he would have her flat on her back in the public gardens.

Well, that wasn't going to happen again, Genevieve told herself. She was not *that* type of woman. No, she was Lucius Felton's intended wife. He had asked for her hand in a placid, urbane fashion of which she utterly approved. So why was she wasting her time with Tobias Darby?

Precisely at two o'clock Genevieve traipsed down the stairs, wearing a walking dress of pale, pale blue muslin, trimmed with white lace. It was as demure as it was docile, especially with a matching cloak in blue sarsenet. She carried a lace parasol that came to a sharp point (excellent for warding off men with lascivious intentions). From the tips of her blue slippers to the ribbons plaited into her hair, there was nothing about her that would inspire a man's lust.

So there was no explanation for the slow burn that danced in Tobias's eyes. That darkening shade of blue made her feel uneasy and happy, all at once. He's a blackguard, Genevieve reminded herself. The man is so lascivious that he even ogles ladies whose necklines approach their ears.

"I trust this will be a quite brief outing," she said, walking down the front steps toward his carriage with her parasol opened and pointed in his direction in case he intended to lunge at her. "I must return to dress for the opera. Felton and I are seeing *The White Elephant,* the Earl Godwin's latest composition."

"The composer is an earl, or is Earl his first name?" Tobias inquired.

Genevieve allowed the footman to hand her into the carriage as if she were a fragile piece of china. She was *not* the sort of woman who clambered in by herself. "He is titled," she said languidly, taking out her fan. "The earl is quite famous for his operas."

"Things must have changed in England since I left the country," he said, folding himself into the opposite seat. "I don't recall any peers dabbling in music."

Why did he have to be so *large?* "Where are we going?"

she asked, ladling a generous dollop of boredom into her voice.

"Bartholomew Fair," he said.

Genevieve dropped her air of fashionable boredom. "Bartholomew Fair? But—why on earth? People of our sort don't attend Bartholomew Fair!"

"Why not?"

"Because it's not—it's not for *us,* that's why!"

"Don't be a widgeon. It's Bartholomew day, and anyone with an unscrambled brain in their head is going to the fair."

"Goodness sakes," Genevieve said faintly. "I never heard of such a thing. And what shall we do there, pray?" She fanned herself to hide her agitation. At least no one would recognize them at the fair.

"Eat Bartholomew pig," he said lazily, stretching his legs so that Genevieve had to move over on her seat to avoid touching his ankle. "And gingerbread shaped like people. I, Genevieve, only eat lady gingerbread. And you?"

She narrowed her eyes at him. She had the feeling there was some sort of joke behind his comment. "I have never eaten such a thing in my life!" she told him roundly. "Gingerbread comes in squares."

He laughed. "There are lamentable gaps in your education, love."

"Don't you dare call me *love!*" she cried, incensed.

When Genevieve descended from the carriage she was met by a literal roar of noise: hucksters selling everything from china vases to geese, trumpets and hurdy-gurdies shrilling in the distance, the giddy-go-round squeaking its way in a circle to the music of a breathless man playing a loud pipe. And everywhere she looked there were people: red-coated soldiers escorting comely lasses, apprentices with snub noses and naughty looks, city wives in white aprons carrying baskets of jam, country folk wandering about with their mouths open. She was as dumbstruck as any country provincial herself.

Tobias grinned at her. "Magnificent, isn't it?" he said.

"Oh, it is!" she breathed. "It is! What's that?" she asked, pointing her parasol at a row of sheds, all hung about with brightly colored curtains and decorated with streamers that swirled in the breeze.

"Those are sideshows," Tobias told her, slipping his hand under her arm. "Wire-walkers, acrobats, puppet shows—"

"Let's go see!" Genevieve cried. They made their way through the crowd. "Oh, look! A Mermaid! We must see her! And a Wise Pig: what could be wise about a pig? Flying Boats: we must see those. And a Golden Goose!"

"Mermaid first?"

Genevieve nodded. Tobias gave threepence to a very grimy man at the door, and they entered.

"That was a very shabby mermaid!" Genevieve said indignantly when they exited the back of the shed. "Even I could see that her fins were made of paper! And all that hair. I suspect she was wearing a *wig!*"

"Her breasts were her own," Tobias reassured her.

Genevieve frowned at him. The mermaid's breasts were only partially obscured by her hair, which probably explained why the line in front of her stand was primarily made up of grinning men.

"I should like to see the Living Skeleton now!" she said, turning on her heel after giving Tobias a look. No wonder the so-called mermaid had given him such a come-hither glance.

He bellowed with laughter, but she paid him no mind.

By four hours later, they had done it all. The Living Skeleton turned out to be a man who was quite thin and mournful too, but the Flying Boats truly were miraculous. The Fat Lady was quite fat, although Genevieve thought that Mrs. Pinkler in the village could have given her a run for her money. They saw the Wild Lion, the Wild Boar, and the Unicorn. They watched acrobats throw each other across the floor and ladies in taffeta dance their way across slender wires.

Finally they found themselves in front of the coconut shy, and Tobias handed over five pence for a pyramid of coconuts.

"Your marksmanship is quite good," Genevieve said admiringly, watching the coconuts fly through the air and unerringly strike the mark painted on canvas.

"Nonsense," he said. "Anyone could do it."

"Not I!" Genevieve assured him. "I think it's marvelous!"

"You hit 'em all," the gypsy running the stall said laconically. "Here's yer prize, then."

He handed Genevieve a grimy string that trailed to the ground. "What?" she asked, confused.

The gypsy kicked at something, and there was a pained little squeal. "Out with you!" he growled, and a tiny pink pig shot out from under the stall, jerking the string in Genevieve's hand.

"You can't give us a *pig!*" she gasped.

"Didn't give it. The flash gent here won it. It's yours now." He was obviously enjoying the spectacle of two persnickety swells becoming guardians to a piglet.

"Take it back!" Genevieve said, holding the string out to him. The piglet was rooting around her slippers, and although it seemed to be pink and in good condition, well, everyone knew how much pigs smelled.

The gypsy leered at Tobias. "I'll take back the piggie if yer missus here can hit a mark," he said. "No capsy girlsy can hit a mark."

There was something in his eyes that made Genevieve stiffen. She grabbed a coconut and threw it as hard as she possibly could. Alas, it didn't head straight toward the canvas targets on the back wall. Instead it bounced off a supporting beam with a crack that signaled broken coconut, ricocheted sideways, and hit the gypsy square on the head.

Genevieve took one look at his enraged face, garnished with streams of coconut milk, and ran away dragging the piglet. Tobias was laughing so hard that they only got as far as the next stall, the Scarlet Swan (which they hadn't bothered to see, as Genevieve was quite certain it would be a normal swan with feathers died in beetroot). For a moment she glared at Tobias, but then a giggle escaped from her mouth. The piglet gave a little grunt at her feet, and finally Genevieve started to laugh, and laugh, and laugh.

Tobias braced his arm over her head, against the wall of the Scarlet Swan, and looked down at her. Genevieve's eyes were bright with laughter, and her cheeks were pink. Her hair wasn't in its neat braid anymore, although she didn't seem to have realized it. He couldn't help it: He dropped a kiss on her rosy lips, and then, before she could voice any sort of objection, spun her about and said, "Right! Time to buy gingerbread men!"

Genevieve blinked. He'd kissed her so quickly, not his usual kiss at all. For a moment she'd thought he meant to push her against the wooden walls of the Scarlet Swan (that would be just in his style), but he hadn't.

Not that she cared, naturally.

Dragging the piglet on his string, they went to the part of the Common where the food stalls were.

"A lady *never* eats in public!" Genevieve said, with some horror. "Isn't there a proper eating establishment in these parts?"

Tobias rolled his eyes and bought two mutton pies, a bottle of wine, a couple of tin mugs, and eight gingerbread men (four ladies and four gentlemen).

"I shan't eat such fare," Genevieve observed, although secretly she had to admit that the gingerbread people were quite appealing. Suddenly a drop of rain fell on her nose, and then one hit her arm.

"It's starting to rain," Tobias observed, bundling his purchases under his arm.

"I suppose we had better find your carriage," Genevieve said, feeling unaccountably disappointed. Of course she had to go home. Why, the sky was already darkening. "What time is it?"

"Not late at all," Tobias said. "It only appears to be twilight due to the clouds."

"Which way is the carriage?" Genevieve said rather anxiously. "Do you think this pig might catch a cold?"

Tobias laughed. "I doubt that very much, you silly duck." He dropped another kiss on her head. Then he slipped a hand into her arm and began to draw her through the crowd.

Genevieve walked silently beside him. A big drop of rain splashed down her cheek, and another dampened the sarsenet of her cloak. She was aware that against all her better instincts, she would prefer that he didn't treat her as if she were a small child he'd invited to the fair for a treat. But how would she like to be treated? Ah, that's the rub, she thought to herself. I want— I want— But she wouldn't let herself think about what she wanted, or why her skin seemed to be burning just from the light touch of his hand, or why she kept peeking at him, and thinking that truly, he was very handsome. Very.

A second later, the rain began to splash down with a concentration that suggested they would never make it all the way across the Commons without being soaked to the skin. They weren't walking quickly: It was difficult to keep the piglet from entangling himself in the feet of passersby, especially now that people were running in all directions to escape the rain.

"We'd better go in here," Tobias said, leading Genevieve up the steps to the stall of the Snake Charmer.

"I can't go in there!" Genevieve gasped. "I'm afraid of snakes. And don't snakes eat piglets?"

"We have to get rid of that pig somehow," Tobias suggested, but when he saw that Genevieve drew back in horror, he stuck his head in the curtained entrance, handed the snake charmer a golden guinea, and said, "Make yourself scarce." The snake charmer grinned, bowed, and trotted off into the distance, snake curled around his neck.

"There," Tobias said, pulling back the curtains and tying them open. "We have a splendid view and we're alone." The whole Commons, which had been a veritable mass of brilliant colors and jostling people but an hour or two before, was emptying as quickly as the clouds were scurrying across the formerly blue sky.

"A chair, my lady," Tobias said, pulling forward a dilapidated couch to just inside the entrance. Genevieve gave it a suspicious look, then sank onto it. The sky had turned a pearly-gray color, and darker blue clouds rushed across it as if they, too, were trying to get home before it rained. The queer light made the scene all the more interesting.

Tobias sat down next to her and stretched out his legs. In a moment he had the cork off the bottle of wine and was pouring her some. He handed a glass to her as elegantly as if it were of the finest crystal, instead of a tin mug that he'd acquired with the bottle.

Genevieve had a sip. Perhaps it was the novelty, but the wine had a slightly explosive feeling on her tongue, as if it were champagne gone slightly flat. The piglet snorted and snuffled at her feet again, so Genevieve drew them up on the couch *(a lady never sits in other than a decorous position!)*, glancing sideways at Tobias under her lashes. He had taken out a mutton pie and broken it in half. Without even asking, he handed it to her. It was still warm and smelled tantalizingly good.

Ladies never eat out of doors! Genevieve took a bite. It was so good that she took another. Rain was dashing to the ground now, and the only people still braving the Commons were a group of lads playing a fierce game in which the teams appeared to be named after Queen Mary and Lord Spencer. The boys ran this way and that in wild abandon, shrieking "Come on Spencer," and "Come on Mary," and generally getting as wet as possible.

Tobias pulled her against his shoulder. She heard a little squeal of indignation as he shoved the piglet away from his boots. The only other sound was the faint shrieks of boys and the silver-white rain slanting down and bouncing from the ground.

"I should like to kiss you," Tobias said suddenly.

Genevieve had her head tucked against his shoulder, and she'd been thinking the same thing except, of course, it was only due to nostalgia. Because she was desperately in love with Felton. Yet Felton and all his elegant refinement seemed very far away at the moment. So she turned her face up to his.

Tobias was not one to wait for a second invitation. His head blocked out the rain so fast that Genevieve might have closed her eyes. If ladies didn't eat in public, they definitely didn't—

But she lost the thought. His mouth felt sinfully sweet on hers, a wild sweetness that melted her bones with his very touch.

"Tobias," she breathed, putting her hands into his hair

and pulling him to her. He didn't mind her forwardness: He groaned against her mouth and pulled her onto his lap. Through the thin muslin of her gown she could tell *exactly* how he was feeling. It was there: in the strength of his arms around her, in the barely audible groan that burst from his throat, in the way his mouth wandered away from her lips, tasting her cheek, her eyebrow, her earlobe.

Genevieve was trembling all over. The only thing to be seen through the door was a curtain of silver rain. No one could see them, and they could see no one. It was as if the world had narrowed to Tobias's mouth, slanting hard over hers again and again, those locks of hair sliding past her fingers. Thoughts crept into her head that weren't ladylike— they weren't even within the bounds of ladylike! *Touch me?* No lady would say such a thing. Why did he have his hands on her shoulders when she wanted—she wanted— *No lady wanted such a thing!*

"Tobias," Genevieve heard herself say breathlessly.

But his answer was inarticulate, more like a purr than a word.

She took his hand in hers. He pulled back instantly and looked down at her. His face was in shadow. "Genevieve?" he asked.

She knew with a swift flash of perception that he thought she wanted him to stop kissing her. To venture out into that chilly sheet of rain and fetch the carriage. Without saying a word, just keeping her eyes on his, she brought his hand slowly, slowly to her breast. Her cheeks were burning, but the look in his eyes made *ladylike* seem a foolish, piddling word.

"Ah, Genevieve," he said against her mouth, and his hand was there, shaping her breast. She gasped into his mouth, feeling her nipple strain against his palm, in tandem with the burning weakness between her legs. "You undo me," he said, and his voice was hoarse and yearning.

She barely understood him; her legs had turned to water, and it was all she could do to lie back in his arms and watch the way his eyes moved over her breasts.

He stood up and twitched closed the scarlet curtains, separating the Snake Charmer's hut from the rest of the world, lost as it was in the rain. The light in the shed turned a rosy pink, suffusing a glow over their clothing. He wrenched off his jacket. Then he bent to kiss her neck, and she threw her head back, giving him an arch of creamy skin, a fall of tawny hair, a body straining for his touch.

When she'd put it on, she hadn't thought about the fact that her docile, oh so docile gown was rather easily unfastened. Such thoughts never occurred to ladies.

"You look at me," she said haltingly, "in such a way—"

He raised his head. "As if you were all that I wanted, Genevieve? As if I could bury my head in your breast forever?"

Words choked in her throat.

"As if you were the Holy Grail," he said, and the rasp in his voice couldn't be mistaken. "A cup of sweetness that I traveled hundreds of miles to find. I found you so easily the first time. . . ."

The words drifted dizzily through Genevieve's head. His lips drifted over the curve of her breast and then . . . and then he was suckling her. A little explosion of noise came from her throat and he pulled harder.

"My honeysuckle," he said hoarsely. "Honey sweet Genevieve."

It had been all of seven years ago, and many a bad memory had come in between . . . but Genevieve knew exactly what would happen now. He would come to her. Seven years ago, when Tobias had her on the carriage seat, her clothes vanished. Of course, it hurt back then. But Genevieve didn't even care if it hurt. Let it hurt! Anything that would assuage this burning impatience. She pulled at him.

"Slow," he murmured. But she didn't want slow. She wanted speed and heat, all those things she remembered.

"No!" she said. Then daringly, she pulled up his white shirt. His skin burned under her skin, muscles moving under her fingers in great swaths of power.

"I want you, Genevieve," he said hoarsely. His shirt was gone now and—

"You're so much more beautiful than you were as a boy," she whispered, awed, reaching out with a tentative hand. His skin was golden brown from the Indian sun, a large, powerful man's body. He shivered at the slow sweep of her hand, jumped when her fingers brushed his nipples. Genevieve was beside herself, lost in a wild sweep of exuberance racing through her veins like the rough wine, like the wind in her face when they rode the Flying Boats.

She leaned toward him and rubbed her lips over his flat nipple, tasted him with the tip of her tongue, heard a harsh groan. She laughed softly, triumphing. *She* was the one in charge this time! She was no tender miss anymore, startled into blissful silence by every twitch of his finger. She— She— She—

His hand caressed her leg with a sensual shock that sent her body bucking against his, rational thought flying from her head again. And she would have stopped him—of course she would!—except that he was suckling her, and the sweetness of it, the honey of it, spread through her veins until she couldn't even move her legs. *This* she remembered. The drugging, achy desire that turned her legs to water and her will to nothing, that made her throw away the precepts of a lifetime and dash into a carriage bound for Gretna Green.

His hand was above her garter now, touching her skin, and her skin never felt so soft. It was as if she could feel herself through him, as if his hand were hers, sliding along skin as smooth as that of a baby, slipping between, dropping one finger into—

Genevieve's back arched straight off the couch. His mouth took hers, hard and fast, and his hand was still there, where no one had ever touched her except him. It was all she could do to wrap her arms around his neck as tightly as she could because the tingling was there again, almost frightening, growing and spreading down her legs, making her buck against his fingers. . . . It was better than it had been seven years ago. Worth ruining herself. Worth it all. Even worth Erasmus.

And then, blissfully, it wasn't his hand anymore, but Tobias himself, coming to her with a groan that tore from his throat. She froze.

"Genevieve? Does it hurt?"

It didn't hurt. It was—it was the feeling of him, the odd, wonderful feeling of being part of Tobias. She tasted her own tears.

"Genevieve?" His voice was strained, as if he were clenching his teeth. He didn't move.

So she moved for him: up, up, and the sparks flew clear to her toes. Up again, and again. Then he took over with a groan of pleasure, plunging into her as if he had no control, no borders between his body and hers. Liquid gold ran along her legs like summer lightning, and then she arched against him, shaking and trembling and just managing to say his name before—

Pleasure burst over her head as if she were drowning, pulsed its way to her fingertips. She cried out, buried her face in Tobias's chest, and let the bliss of it pound through her body, a sweet wave of fire that came again and again before it receded.

She didn't even open her eyes afterwards. She was too tired, too weak and too hot. He seemed to know it too. She lay there, feeling the hair sticking to her forehead, and feeling the premonition of tears. He kissed her cheek, her lips, her throat. Then, when she still didn't open her eyes, he began buttoning up her bodice, fumbling a little in an endearing way.

A few seconds later she heard him open the curtains. It sounded as if the rain had lessened, but she wouldn't— she couldn't—open her eyes. That would mean returning to reality, to the truth of the situation. She was ruined *again.*

How could she marry Felton now? Ruined again. Again. Perhaps she would just lie on this dingy couch for all eternity and never return to the fragments of the life she had put together. He came back and picked her up, tucking her against his chest in a manifestly unsuitable position. But after being ruined, it seemed pointless to plead for circumspection.

When he finally spoke, his voice was still rough, with a faint rumble of elation. "Sometime, Genevieve, we're going to have to find a bed together. We could make love slowly, just for a change."

She lay back and let that remark sink into her mind. How much slower could they go? Before he gave up trying altogether, Erasmus had skipped all the parts Tobias began with, and just kept trying to take his—his tool and put it inside her.

A few moments passed. Genevieve could feel her heart slowing from its frantic pace. Tobias was tracing little circles on her shoulder with his fingertip. "I have the oddest feeling that you haven't made love since we made our way to Gretna Green," he said finally.

"Actually, Erasmus . . . ," she said, surprised to hear that her voice was still wispy and almost breathless.

"Was he incapable?"

"He tried," she said, feeling a faint pulse of loyalty. Erasmus had not been a very comfortable husband, but he had been as kind as he'd known how.

"Humph," Tobias said. He was shaping her foot in his palm. "You have lovely, delicate feet, Genevieve," he said presently. "The toes of an English lady, no doubt about that."

"Ladies don't act like this," she said, opening her eyes.

"The lucky ones do," he said, and the vein of amusement in his voice was healing.

"How would you know anything of English ladies? You've lived in India for years."

"Well, actually, I don't," he admitted. "You are the first and only lady I've loved, Genevieve."

"I suppose you met hundreds of Indian princesses, though." She'd read a long description of a visiting Indian raja and his exquisite bride in the *Times*.

"Are you asking me if I maintained a harem?" He started tickling her feet. She curled up her toes in protest.

"Did you?"

"No." Then he added, "Harems are found in other parts of the world, Genevieve, but not in India. I did meet some beautiful women, though. They were ladies, if not born in England."

Genevieve didn't want to discuss it any further. "What time do you think it is?"

"Around eight," he said calmly.

"Eight!" She sat up straight. "Felton came for me at six!"

"You weren't there," Tobias pointed out.

She pulled her foot out of his hand, but he didn't let her up. "You're marrying me now, Genevieve."

Protest flared to her lips and died. Of course she had to marry Tobias. She'd lost her right to marry Felton.

Tobias looked down at her and his heart sank. Obviously Genevieve was having second thoughts, but there were no second thoughts to have. "He doesn't really want you," he said, as gently as he could, trying to explain. "Felton sees you as an acquisition, Genevieve, not as a woman to love."

"Nonsense!" she said, and the stifled note in her voice made him feel panic and then anger.

"He would put you on the mantelpiece to admire," he insisted.

"No, he wouldn't," Genevieve replied, and her voice was so sad that Tobias had to stop himself from shaking her. He set her on her feet and walked to the edge of the door, where he looked over the Commons. Fear had always made Tobias angry.

"Do you know what you would have been if you'd married Felton?" he demanded without turning around. "The same thing you were for six years as Mulcaster's wife. An old man's possession. It sounds as if Mulcaster considered you the next best thing to a china shepherdess, and Felton was going to dust you off and make you exactly the same."

"Felton is *not* an old man! How dare you say such a thing?"

"He acts as if he is," Tobias snarled. "He looks at least forty."

"He is exactly thirty-two," Genevieve informed him.

Tobias turned around and leaned in the doorway, watching her twist her curls into an untidy, glorious knot at her neck. "It must be the way he sleeks back his hair," Tobias said maliciously. "Makes him look as if his hair is going."

"You're jealous!" Genevieve snapped, shooting him an irate look.

"Not of him," Tobias retorted. "I've *had* you, if you remember."

"You unaccountably vulgar—vulgar *cad!*" Genevieve shrieked, suddenly darting toward him and striking him in the chest with her fist.

Tobias looked down at her flailing away at his chest, her hair falling loose from its knot and swirling around her shoulders, and he felt a great well of desire that would never go away. "Genevieve," he said, grabbing her arms so she had to listen to him. She kept flailing against him, her eyes glistening with tears. "I'm sorry."

"What?"

"I'm sorry," he said, and he meant it, with every bit of his heart. "We never should have made love. You had every right to marry Felton."

She stopped, and her eyes were searching his. The pain in those greeny-gray eyes was enough to make him bellow with rage. But he just stood, holding her fragile wrists in his great paws.

"It's not only your fault. I could have stopped you."

The pain in her voice was like another dagger. He couldn't bear it. "He wasn't worthy of you, Genevieve!" The truth of it burst from his chest.

"Don't tell me of his underhanded business dealings," she said wearily, turning from him. He let her go without protest. "I was married to one of the most avaricious men in

all England for six years. I can judge illegalities as well as
the next person. Felton may sometimes walk on the far side
of the letter of the law, but he doesn't engage in truly nefarious practices."

It was true enough. "But he doesn't want you."

Genevieve laughed, and it wasn't a humorous sound. "He
won't now, at any rate."

"I mean it," Tobias said fiercely. It was slowly dawning
on him that he'd made the worst mistake of his life. By taking away Genevieve's ability to choose between him and
Felton, he'd destroyed their marriage. Now she would always pine for that sleek bastard in a corner of her heart. The
horror of it made his voice harsh. "I can show you," he said.

"What do you mean, you can show me?"

She had turned her back to him and was leaning in the
doorway now. The curve of her slender neck, just visible
below the knot of her hair, made him ache with sudden desire. Beyond her the rain was still falling, softer and more
quietly. All the boys had run home, and the huge Commons
was inhabited by nothing but a few birds pecking at crumbs,
heedless of the rain splashing on their beaks.

He didn't touch her. "I can demonstrate to you, clearly
demonstrate, that Felton does not love you as you expect."

"How? By giving me proof that he has a mistress?" she
asked, not bothering to look back at Tobias. "I don't
care."

"What do you mean, you don't care?" he roared, whirling
her about. "You don't mind having a husband with a mistress? And in our marriage? Shall we marry and I sally forth
every Thursday night to spend the evening with a pretty little French minx, and you won't give a damn? Is that what
you're telling me?"

Genevieve narrowed her eyes at him. "If you go off with some pretty French minx, I am quite certain that I can amuse myself!" she retorted.

Tobias opened his mouth to bellow and thought better of it. "You haven't answered my original point, which suggests that you know as well as I do that Felton hasn't the proper feeling for you."

"He has, not that it matters now," Genevieve said steadily. "He simply doesn't express himself in the boisterous manner that you do. He is a *gentleman*."

"We'll see, shall we?" Tobias said.

Genevieve bit her lip. Tobias was obviously enraged, though what he had to be angry about when *she* was the one losing her fiancé, she didn't know.

"I can prove to you that your so-called gentleman doesn't give a fig for you," he said curtly.

"Fine," Genevieve snapped. "Fine! You do that. You can prove it to me this very evening, why don't you?"

"That might be a problem, as Felton expects to spend the evening with you," Tobias said, shrugging on his coat. "Why don't we say tomorrow afternoon, at my hotel?" He looked around the hut. "I very much regret to tell you that our piglet will not be able to attend, as he made good his escape while we were otherwise occupied."

Genevieve looked around the hut. "Oh, no! What will he eat?"

"He's a pig," Tobias said. "He'll find something. Shall we be gone? The rain seems to have lessened."

They tramped across the Commons side by side. The piglet was lost. Genevieve's shoes were ruined. That seemed all one to the fact that her life was ruined. Her elegant, beautiful little shoes were ruined, and her life was ruined, and now she was marrying a big brute instead of her sleek, sophisticated Felton.

Luckily the wind was tossing the oak trees, sprinkling them liberally with rain. And if warm drops mingled with chilly water on Genevieve's face, no one could possibly tell the difference.

Chapter 7

The Betrayal

Naturally, Lucius Felton appeared in response to Tobias's note. Tobias had stowed Genevieve behind a screen, in the corner of his private sitting room at Symon's Hotel. Felton came in, wearing an immaculate gray jacket, fitted in such a way as to make his lean body look as polished as marble. Tobias thought for a moment about smashing his fist into Felton's jaw but bowed and waved him to a chair instead.

Felton took his time, the insolent bastard, strolling around the room and glancing at the furnishings. "I've never liked this heavy Egyptian style," he said. "Thomas Hope has done England a great disservice, to my mind."

Tobias could play this game as well as the next man. He walked over to stand next to Felton and smiled, the smile of an Indian snake charmer. "Genevieve tells me that I should furnish my house with the cabinetry of George Bullock," he remarked. "Do you know of his work?"

"Spectacular pieces," Felton said idly, inspecting a huge

griffin foot that supported the screen behind which Genevieve sat. "Your grandchildren will squabble over who gets your washstand."

Tobias turned briskly to the two seats next to the fire. "Whisker is now in my possession," he said without preamble.

Felton drifted to a seat opposite him and sat down, delicately balancing a mahogony walking stick against his chair. "Ah, what a fortunate man you are," he purred. "Let me see if I have this correct. You are starting your stables with Prudence, Nyar, Minuet, Smolensko, and Whisker? Impressive."

"More than impressive," Tobias said gently. "Those five horses represent the finest racing stock in all England."

"True," Felton admitted.

"I understand you had to shoot a mare at the Brighton Derby," Tobias said, lashing on a bit of false pity. "Silk, from Ormonde and Angelica, am I correct?"

But a glance at Felton's eyes made Tobias close his mouth. That was agony that flashed across the man's face.

"I've had second thoughts about taking the horses to India," Tobias said, watching Felton closely.

"They are unlikely to survive the trip," Felton told him flatly.

"I am thinking of giving them to you."

There was utter silence, broken only by the faint clatter of carriage wheels in the street outside. Tobias waited, willing Genevieve to keep silent in her corner of the room.

"I saw Genevieve Mulcaster for the first time quite accidentally," Felton said, lifting his stick and staring at it as if looking for scratches. "I was investigating a colt in a nearby village. She had to do her own shopping in the village, you know. Mulcaster was too damn cheap to hire enough servants. I saw her, crossing the square."

Tobias could see the picture in his mind. A dusty little English square, and then there was Genevieve, with her laughing face, her magnificent hair, and that glorious, lush little body. It seemed he had made something of a mistake. Perhaps Felton—

But Felton was shrugging. "I love her as much as I'm capable," he said, putting his stick down. "But more and more I am persuaded that I am not capable of the emotion that Genevieve would wish to receive." He looked at Tobias. "Might I point out that her affection for me may prove a problem for you?"

"Or it might not," Tobias said.

"Perhaps you can convince her," Felton said, with a wry twist of his lips.

And Tobias realized with a shock that under different circumstances, he'd quite like the man. Damn him to hell. "I shall do my best," he replied noncommittally. "The horses will be sent to your stud tomorrow."

"Perhaps you'll walk me to the lobby to discuss the matter?"

Tobias was a little surprised, but he closed the door behind them. He walked down the hallway as quickly as he could; if Genevieve was distraught by Felton's betrayal, he wished to comfort her. It couldn't be an easy thing for a woman to hear herself traded for five horses.

Felton stopped when they reached the ornate lobby of Symon's Hotel, with its high, arching ceiling and magnificent Egyptian furniture. He paused for a moment to light a cheroot and then looked at Tobias, shaking back a lock of hair. "You might want to tell Genevieve that she oughtn't to wear perfume on days when she is playing spy," he said.

Tobias stared into his heavy-lidded eyes. "You knew she was there."

Felton blew out smoke. "I want the horses." Then he

looked at Tobias. "Don't fool yourself, Darby. I wanted her as well." His voice was hard. "But"—he blew a cloud—"I believe she'll be happier with you."

Tobias put out his hand. "I wish you well with those horses, Felton."

"They'll have to do, won't they?" And he walked out the door into a blaze of sunshine, a slim figure in gray, swinging a polished cane and walking with a controlled prowl.

Tobias watched him go. Under different circumstances, he would more than just like the fellow. They would indeed be friends.

Then he turned. Genevieve was waiting.

Chapter 8

The Worth of Five Horses

She wasn't crying. She was sitting in the very seat that Felton had deserted, twisting a lock of hair in her fingers. She looked up when he entered the room. To his utter relief, she didn't seem hysterical or heartbroken.

"How are you?" he asked.

"All my life, I've been tossed back and forth between men like a delectable sweet. Why should I feel any different now that I have discovered just how much the sweet is worth in horseflesh?"

Tobias's heart sank. He sat down opposite her.

"I should like to go home now," Genevieve said in a cold little voice. "Unless you would like to take further advantage of your marital rights, or should I call them premarital rights?" She waved her hand toward the closed door leading to Tobias's bedchamber.

"Am I such a bad bargain, then?" he asked. "I told you that Felton didn't have proper feeling for you. But I do have that feeling for you, Genevieve. And you feel for me as well, whether you wish to admit it or not."

She looked at him, and he couldn't read her expression. "I am struck by what excruciatingly bad taste I have," she said conversationally. "First you, and then Felton. Both of you utter muckworms. How could I be so unlucky?"

"Muckworm is a harsh term," Tobias said, controlling his temper with an effort. "I'm sorry if you didn't care for my offering Felton the horses. I wanted you to see what kind of man he was."

"Oh, I'm not talking about that," she said with a sharp little laugh. "I consider your true nature to have been exposed the morning after we eloped, the morning when you did not arrive to ask my hand in marriage."

"Isn't the relevant point that you married another man?"

"*I* had nothing to do with it," Genevieve said with brutal precision. "You took me in a carriage to Gretna Green without having the common sense to evade my father, took my virginity in the carriage, and then failed to stop my ensuing marriage to Lord Mulcaster."

"I apologize for not having the forethought to avoid your father," Tobias said, carefully controlling his voice. "It was the first elopement I had arranged, and I didn't know much about the route."

"You should have asked someone!"

"I believe that I was not thinking rationally at the time."

"You had been drinking!" Genevieve spat. He looked so *innocent,* and yet he was the worst kind of rakeshame.

"All evening," he agreed. "I was jug-bitten."

She was starting to feel shaky. "Otherwise I suppose you would never have thought of such a thing as to elope with me," she said, trying for a dignified tone.

"Likely not," he agreed. He folded his arms over his chest.

"Well, it's nice to have clarified that bit of information," she said bitterly.

"Would you have eloped with me?" he asked.

"I did so, didn't I!" she snapped.

"But you were muzzy as well," he reminded her. "All that champagne . . . I doubt you would have eloped with me had you not been imbibing champagne, Genevieve. We were both inebriated."

"I was not inebriated. I have naught to blame my bird-witted behavior on except youth and stupidity."

"You seem to have embroidered the occasion in your memory, but I have no difficulty remembering that I scarcely knew you from Adam and a few hours later was scrambling down a country lane planning to flee to Gretna Green."

"You knew me! We'd known each other our whole lives." All those days when she'd dressed carefully, spending hours combing her hair and dreaming of the unpredictable, beautiful boy next door, and he would say that he scarcely knew her? "You must be joking!" she cried, more furious than ever. "My father was your parents' nearest neighbor from the time you were eight years old until your father lost his house."

He shrugged. "Of course I know that fact. And I'd seen you occasionally. But I did not know *you,* Genevieve. Not until I met you at that musicale."

Genevieve could even remember the first time she saw him. It was the Whitsuntide Fair, and Tobias was twelve years old. Right in the middle of a play put on by the village children, Mrs. Briglet sprang from her chair with a piercing shriek because he'd tucked a hedgehog into her reticule. Genevieve had worshiped him from the moment she watched him dash from the square, laughing madly as his father howled after him, "Devil's Spawn!" Tobias Darby was the opposite of everything Genevieve had ever known, growing up in her quiet, passionless house, and being raised by an elderly father who was fond of her, although easily tired by her over-boisterous nature, as he called it.

Her rage grew. "What a pretty picture," she said cuttingly. "You meet a young lady at a musicale whom you claim to barely know. You are intoxicated, and she the same. You dash out into the night, hire a carriage, and take off for Gretna Green. You manage to deflower her *twice*—"

"You can't deflower someone twice," he put in. But he wasn't amused.

"You—you take a moonstruck girl and, and take your pleasure twice in a moving vehicle, and then once her father appears, you decide to travel to India, without even bothering to make a formal appeal for her hand. You, sir, are a blackguard! Worse than your father, in fact!"

He was suddenly very white. "How could I have made an appeal for your hand? You married Mulcaster."

"Don't tell me a barefaced lie!" she cried. "If nothing else, you owe me the truth! On second thought," she added bitterly, "why don't we omit the flummery? I quite understand that your conscience has been bothering you. Well, it needn't. I am a respectable widow, thanks to Erasmus having the kindness to marry me after you soiled me. I have a jointure, and no need for a husband."

"But I have need of you, Genevieve. And it wasn't a soiling." He looked straight into her beautiful eyes, choosing his words carefully. "Am I understanding you correctly—"

"Perhaps I might ask the first question," she interrupted. "Perhaps you could explain why you never came for me, after my father intercepted our carriage." Tobias may look as blameless as a buttery cake, but he was precisely what her father had labeled him: a brazen-faced Lothario, who'd taken what he wanted and abandoned her. "My father would have allowed us to marry, given what had occurred between us. Yet you never came." The memories of her father's rage on discovering that she had been wanton enough to lose her virginity in a carriage would never leave her memory.

"By the time I woke up, you were married," he said, his jaw set.

She snorted. "What did you do? Turn into Sleeping Beauty? Erasmus and I were married only after the banns had been read three weeks in a row. And during that time— that time—" But her voice caught, and she refused to show emotion.

Something flashed across his face and he was on his feet. "Three weeks? Did you wait *three weeks* to be married, Genevieve?"

She blinked and looked up at him. "Of course. The banns had to be read, and even if Erasmus had been a generous man—which he wasn't—he wouldn't have taken me if I had been in a delicate condition."

He turned and slammed his fist into the wall next to him. "I had no idea, Genevieve." The anguish in his voice echoed around the room. "Your father's coachman nearly knocked my brains out, if you remember." He swung back to face her, and his face was livid with rage.

"It seems extremely unlikely to me that your recovery took three weeks," she said, standing up and moving so as to put a small table between them.

"I awoke the following afternoon."

"Well," Genevieve said with an edge, "that left you exactly two weeks and six days to remember my existence.

But instead you decided to make a long-anticipated trip to India, ignoring the deflowered girl waiting for you. Or perhaps your excuse is that you were so drunk that the whole evening vanished from your memory?"

"I woke to a message from your father." He walked toward her with the lethal gaze of a Bengal tiger.

Genevieve reached backwards and felt her way around another small table, keeping her eyes on him. Who knew what he might do? "Indeed?" she murmured, edging toward the door. "And what did my father say?"

"Your father informed me that he had long planned your marriage to Erasmus Mulcaster, and that Mulcaster was obtaining a special license to marry you immediately. He said, Genevieve, and I quote: *'By great good fortune, Mulcaster has agreed to marry her immediately even though you debauched her.'* And by the time I woke up, Genevieve, you were married to Mulcaster."

"I was not!" she said shrilly.

"I believed your father."

Genevieve stared at him, forgetting about making her escape. "My father was eminently trustworthy," she said. "Why on earth should I believe you?"

"I can't pull the note out of my pocket." His jaw was set. "It's the truth. What did your father tell *you?*"

"That if you made an offer for my hand he would strongly consider the proposal, even during the time the banns were being read. I waited—" She looked away. "You never came, and then we heard that you were gone."

"Your father was a busy man," Tobias said, looking tired. "He wrote my father as well, and forgave my father's debts to him on the condition that I leave the country and not return for at least ten years. To spare your feelings, should we happen to meet."

Genevieve couldn't think of anything to say. She'd spent seven years thinking that Tobias had simply left the country without giving her a second thought. Seven years of thinking him a degenerate. Seven years of thinking about the importance of finding an honorable, gentlemanly man like Felton. An odd feeling was rising in her chest—could it be joy?

"I didn't know," he said quietly. "I swear to God, Genevieve, I didn't know. I thought you were married off to that old man. There was many a time in the last seven years when I cursed myself for not snatching you away with me, married or not. But I never thought that your father might have lied to me about the special license."

Genevieve leaned against the wall and closed her eyes. Her hands were trembling, so she spread them against the wallpaper and tried to think logically. "Why would my father do such a thing? I know he was enraged with me—"

Tobias was there, standing just before her. His lips brushed over her cheek, and his hands took hers. "Perhaps he thought it was for the best. But I have destroyed it all, haven't I?" he said, and the anguish in his voice caught her heart. "I was stupid enough to believe your father. And I've been just as stupid now, taking you away from Felton. I know how you feel about him. *He* knows how you feel. You heard him!"

"I suppose so," she said, struggling to clarify her thoughts. Felton seemed a million miles away and quite unimportant, given the fact that Tobias was—was *her* Tobias again.

"I haven't been entirely honest with you," he said, taking her shoulders in his large hands. "Felton asked me to walk him to the lobby because he cares for you, Genevieve. He knew you were in the room all the time. He could tell from your perfume that you were behind the screen. But he played it as if he didn't know."

"Why on earth would he do that?" Genevieve said, her eyes flying open.

"I believe he thought that I loved you more than he did. He knew that I'm enthralled to you." And then he took both her hands and brought them to his mouth. "The last time I asked you to marry me, Genevieve, I was jug-bitten and young and incredibly stupid. But I knew I loved you."

A smile was growing in Genevieve's heart, the kind that bloomed and didn't die for years.

He kissed her hands. "I wasn't so stupid. I loved you then, and I love you even more now. Will you, Genevieve? Will you marry me again?"

But Genevieve's heart was so full that she couldn't speak. Her eyes filled with tears, and his hands tightened on hers.

"If you don't wish to, Felton would marry you and— God, I was wrong about this, Genevieve—he wants you. Really wants you. He's just more of a gentleman than I am."

But she didn't want to talk about Felton. She turned her face and captured his mouth, and it was her tongue that caressed his lips, and his mouth that opened to her entreaty, and she who spoke into the sweetness of their kiss. "I don't want a gentleman, Tobias. I want you, my first husband."

He kissed her then, and she melted against him, her heart, her whole body straining to be part of him.

"Are you sure, Genevieve?" he asked hoarsely. "Oh God, I didn't mean to leave you!"

"Yes," she said simply.

But he had to say something important, so he didn't let

her kiss him again. "I know you've become alarmingly elegant, Genevieve, and you play a respectable widow very well—"

"Because I *am* one, except when you're around!" she inserted.

"That's just it," he said, capturing her face in his hands and looking into her eyes. "We're the wild ones, Genevieve. You and me. We belong together. Felton would bore you to tears, and you would drive him to distraction. Our marriage is about passion, Genevieve." He stopped and kissed her, so fiercely and so lovingly that she almost wept. "Your marriage to Felton would be about little more than propriety and genteel behavior."

She had her arms twined around his neck, and she was pressing against him in a way that no proper matron would do. "I love you, Tobias," she said, her eyes glimmering with tears. "I don't want Felton. I want you—it's always been you."

And finally he pulled her close, kissing her ruthlessly until they were both breathing quickly and shaking, and then he said, hoarsely, "This time, we're going to a bed, Genevieve." He swept her up in his arms but she couldn't stop kissing him, even on the way to the bedchamber, so he almost stumbled against a wall and finally had to stop and kiss her so senseless that she couldn't interfere as he walked into the chamber.

There was one thing he had to say. "It's a bed today, Genevieve, but tomorrow—"

She was arching up against him, her gown already around her hips as his hands worked sweet magic. "Tomorrow?" she gasped, trying to pull him down to her.

"Gretna Green tomorrow," he growled at her, ripping her pantalettes. "Again. And we're going all the way to Scotland this time."

She didn't care.

Author of eight award-winning romances, **ELOISA JAMES** *is a* New York Times *bestselling author who lives with her family in New Jersey. Her website is* www.eloisajames.com.

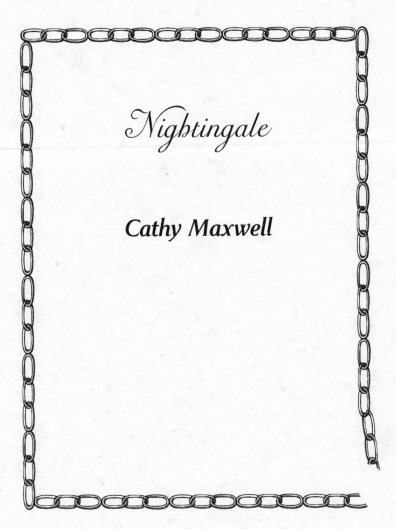

Nightingale

Cathy Maxwell

For Chris Peirson

I value our friendship.

Chapter 1

London

Sir Dane Pendleton sat at his writing desk surrounded by darkness save for the light of a single candle. His pen scratched the surface of the paper as he made out his last will and testament.

This was grim business. He did not plan on dying on the morrow—in fact, he anticipated winning the duel—but Dane was a thorough man. His vast and complicated affairs were in order; however, he had last-minute instructions in case the unthinkable should happen.

Coming to the end of the sheet, he paused. He was done.

He set aside the pen and poured himself a heavy draft of the smoky whiskey he favored. The decanter was already a quarter lower than when he'd started.

All was deadly quiet.

Save for a lone footman who watched the door downstairs, the servants were in bed. At this late hour, the footman was probably asleep, too.

No sound penetrated the study. The rich furnishings and deep carpets, all fruits of his labors, absorbed any noise. Above the mantel, a marble-and-gold clock ticked off the minutes.

Dane let his gaze drift around the room, knowing without seeing where every stick of furniture was located, every vase, every piece of sterling, every book, and the exact cost of each. He'd spent a decade achieving his success and had thought himself if not happy, at least content—until, with a crashing force, he'd been reminded of his past this evening.

Cris Carson, Lord Whiting was a bloody fool.

Only an idiot picked a duel with a man of Dane's reputation. But then Whiting had felt himself the injured party and he'd been dangerously drunk. Dane had attempted to walk away, to disengage Whiting when he'd started reviling him right there in the middle of White's, but the young lord would not let him leave.

Whiting's host, Simmons, had made apologies for his guest, but Whiting had even drowned him out, refusing to listen to all reason. No, the foolish lad had thought he had a reputation to protect, and now it was swords at dawn.

Dane took a deep sip of the whiskey, the bite of the liquor as sharp as his memories—Whiting and his family had never been the injured party. If anything, Dane should have been the one to attack him.

How strange that after all this time, after his many, many successes, including being knighted, there was still that deep emptiness inside him?

And who would have thought a woman could have so much power?

Frowning, he set the heavy crystal glass down and pushed it away.

He'd thought he'd successfully exorcized Jemma Carson from every fiber of his being. He'd thought he'd rid himself of the bitterness—and yet here it was, returned fourfold by her brother's drunken verbal attack.

But then, didn't poets warn that Love wielded a sword sharper than any known to man?

Dane knew it was true, and he had the scars to prove it—*in his back.*

There had been a time when he'd loved Jemma with all he'd had to offer, and it had not been enough. She'd returned his promises, built up his hopes, made him believe they would be together. Then she'd spurned him and married another.

Dane sat very still and slowly released his breath, surprised at how fresh and overwhelming the pain still was.

Of course, there had been other women over the years. He'd kept a string of mistresses, all of them more beautiful than Jemma, all of them vowing love as Jemma had . . . and some may have. After all, he'd paid their bills, kept them in style, and what more was there to love? Women were mercenary creatures at heart. Each and every one of them. They always wanted something. Fortunately, he was a man of means who could indulge their passion for trinkets and petty possessions.

Perhaps I should thank Jemma, Dane mused. If she had accepted his marriage offer all those years ago, he'd probably be a fat, happy clergyman somewhere with a gaggle of children instead of the man of the world he was now. Because of her rejection, he'd left the safe haven of Lancashire and risked all in India. He'd become a man who knew no fear, who'd hardened himself to gentler emotions and knew how to pay blood in blood. A man alone.

Meanwhile, Jemma's life had not been what she'd anticipated. Her husband, the one she'd chosen over Dane, had been titled and wealthy and a fool. He'd had a poor head for wisdom and business. In this day and age, with war in Europe, a man couldn't afford to throw his money out a window. The rumor about Town was that, at his death, Lord Mosby had left his heirs little more than a pittance and his widow destitute.

Dane reached for the decanter, then stopped.

Damn Jemma . . . and damn her stupid, drunken brother. He hadn't let her break him then, and he would not do so now—

A soft rap sounded on the door.

For a second, Dane thought he'd imagined the sound.

The knock sounded again.

"What is it?" he said, his voice harsh. He wanted to be alone. He *needed* to be alone. Tomorrow, he was going to run Whiting through, and then . . . *what?* The word haunted him.

"There is someone here to see you, sir," the footman's voice said from the other side.

At this hour? "Who the bloody hell is it?" Dane demanded. He went ahead and poured himself another whiskey. To the devil with temperance or being a gentleman. Tonight was for exorcisms, although the whiskey didn't seem to be having any effect. He was feeling everything too sharply. He lifted his glass.

"I'm sorry, Sir Dane, I don't have her name," the footman answered. "She refused to tell me or give me her card but asked to see you on the most urgent of business. I let her in because she is obviously a Lady of Quality."

A Lady of Quality? Out and alone at this hour of the night?

Curious, Dane set down the glass without drinking. "Send her up."

There was silence at the door as the footman went to do Dane's bidding. Dane sat, quiet. Who would be coming to see him at this hour? It couldn't be a mistress. He and the last, what was her name? Something French. Always something French . . . although none of them had been French any more than he was. *Danielle*. He had signed Danielle off three months ago and had not had the energy or interest in searching for another.

In fact, for the past year, since he'd returned to London, he had been weighed down by a sense of tedium coupled with a restless irritation over the everyday matters of his life. He'd been going through the motions of living without any clear purpose or desire.

Perhaps he should let Whiting run *him* through?

The idea had appeal. Dane picked up the glass and drained it of the precious amber liquid.

The footman rapped on the door to signal he had returned with this uninvited guest. Dane pushed both the will and his whiskey glass aside before calling out, "Enter."

The door opened slowly, and the footman, dressed in blue-and-gold livery with a powdered wig on his head, stepped into the room. "Sir Dane, your guest."

He moved back. There was a moment's pause, a space of time, three ticks of the clock, and then the woman walked into the room and Dane stopped breathing.

Before him stood Jemma Carson, the widowed Lady Mosby, looking more beautiful than ever.

Chapter 2

*J*emma had never been as frightened in her life as she was now, standing here in front of Dane. She willed herself to take another step forward, but her feet seemed rooted to the ground.

Nor did he invite her in by rising from his chair.

Time stretched out between them, and she realized exactly how long it had been since they had last seen each other.

This was not the Dane Pendleton she remembered . . . but then, she had known he'd changed. He'd hardened, and she could see nothing of the boy she'd once loved with all her being in the man sitting in the candlelight.

He'd always been a big man, but now in the thin candlelight, he appeared taller, more muscular . . . more imposing. The lines of maturity and of experience on his face had erased all boyishness. His hair still had its thick curls, but his temples were turning gray. The strong jaw and firm lips, lips she had once kissed, were still as they had been.

She wondered if the many mistresses he was rumored to keep found him as loving and adoring as she once had. She felt a stab of jealousy, coupled with the bile of regret.

He could have been hers.

Of course, the richness surrounding her was also overwhelming. She'd known Dane had done well for himself. Who in Town had not gossiped about his fortune? A bachelor of such wealth could not pass unnoticed. However, she'd never imagined carpets could be so thick and deep or that gold could be used as an inlaid accent on fine woods.

Even the carefully trained formality of the footman made her nervous. She was in Dane's presence, in his lair, and feeling very much as if she'd come on a foolish—and dangerous—errand.

His hard, glittering gaze held hers. She did not look away. She couldn't.

Dane raised a hand, a signal for the footman to leave.

Now she had no choice. She must either step forward or go running for the front door.

The footman bowed politely to her and made his exit, shutting the door behind him. She and Dane were alone, and she was thankful the servant had taken his candle with him, leaving her in shadowy darkness.

But Dane knew she was there. Sitting in his halo of light, his gaze honed in on her like a hawk sighting his prey.

He'd removed his jacket and wore a vest embroidered in black, red, and gold over a snowy white shirt. Even seated his breeches were so well tailored they seemed molded to his thighs, and his tall, black boots were a tribute to their maker. The knot in his neck cloth was still crisp, as if he had the wherewithal to change to a newly starched one several times a day.

She'd dressed in her best, a cream muslin gown with cap sleeves and edged in white lace. She would have worn it to the opera back in the days when she'd done such things. However, the gown was woefully out of style, and the blue silk Norwich shawl covering her shoulders now seemed out of place and somewhat silly—especially under the intensity of his regard.

Nervous, Jemma hoped he didn't notice how worn her kid slippers were. And she was glad she'd listened to her mother's advice on how to style her hair for this interview. It was so long that she usually braided it and wrapped it into a loose chignon at the nape of her neck. Tonight, however, she'd taken extra care and wore it high on her head in loose curls as if preparing to be presented at Court. Now, she wondered if it hadn't been foolish to waste precious minutes on her appearance. The rumor was Dane preferred blondes—

His deep voice broke the silence between them. "What are you doing here?"

Her throat tightened. She should speak, tell him her business, but she couldn't. She feared his reaction once he knew her purpose—

"Playing the sacrificial lamb again?" he asked.

He knew.

Jemma wet her dry lips. Unable to bear his sharp focus, she shifted her own gaze to the flickering candle flame before saying stiffly, "My brother believes he may have been too hasty this evening."

"Your brother is an idiot."

Generations of pride flared inside her. She met his eye, started to speak—and then stopped. What could she say? Dane was right . . . and tonight's foolhardiness proved it.

"Your point is valid," she answered crisply, "and I may

be an even greater idiot for venturing here this night."

Her honesty was rewarded by the slightest hint of a smile on his lips. She took hope. The man she had once loved would understand why she was here . . . or at least she prayed he did.

She took a step closer to the tight circle of light surrounding Dane and his desk. "Cris was well into his cups this evening. He has had a chance to reflect upon his actions and wishes to retract his harsh words."

Dane smirked. "What? Has he no male companions with enough respect for him to run this errand? Or the courage to come here himself?"

Jemma knew only honesty would do. After all, isn't that what she owed Dane? "In truth, Cris doesn't know I'm here. At this moment he is, uh, sleeping off his excesses of the evening—"

"He's passed out, drunk," Dane corrected quietly, and she heard the unspoken censure.

"His friend Oliver told Mother and I what had happened, and it was decided one of us should discuss the matter with you."

"You mean, your *mother* decided *you* should approach me," he interpreted, "with the hopes I'll spare your wastrel brother's life tomorrow."

Jemma didn't deny his words. Instead, now that her purpose was out in the open, she felt free to take another step forward, sweeping aside all pride. "Please, Dane, you must," she pleaded. "He is all we have. I know he provoked you beyond reason, and if half of what Oliver has told us is correct, you have every right to run him through. But I beg of you, withdraw the challenge. We'll see that his path never crosses yours again. This I promise you."

The touch of desperation in her voice embarrassed her. This was not the first time she'd stepped in for Cris, but it was certainly the most grave, and she knew he would not be grateful. Since their father's death, he had changed.

Dane leaned back in his chair, his hand on his desk, his long, tapered fingers an inch away from the document he must have been studying before her visit had interrupted him. He'd been drinking. The stopper lay beside the decanter and the level was low, his glass empty. A hint of whiskey fumes perfumed the air.

Jemma waited for a response, her heart beating in her throat. His silence was unnerving.

The man she had once loved would not leave her to twist in the wind this way. He'd been generous and always forgiving—but then, she had forfeited all that, hadn't she?

He spoke. "You wish me to call back the challenge?"

She hesitated, then confessed, "I do."

Dane made a soft, self-derisive sound and shook his head. "Will you always be his dupe?"

"He's my brother," she answered tightly.

"More's the pity," he returned without expression, and Jemma knew her fears had been well grounded. If Dane and Cris met, her brother would die.

She spread her hands, her palms open, aware that she was asking much—she was asking for his honor. "Dane, I know I am the last person you would want to please or even help, but I beg of you to withdraw your challenge. I'm the one you are angry at, the one on whom you want vengeance. Do not make Cris pay for my sins."

"You flatter yourself, my lady," Dane said, rising to his feet, his eyes angry glints. "I have no need for revenge. In fact, you did me a favor years ago when you discarded me for something as insignificant and hollow as a title."

The words *No, that wasn't how it was* were on the tip of Jemma's tongue, but she swallowed them back.

Because, in truth, she had chosen another over Dane. She had betrayed their love and the promises that had been between them. Promises that still, after all this time, seemed etched in her soul.

"Please," she said, not knowing what it was she was asking him for. To please understand? To please honor her wishes?

To please forgive her?

Dane shook his head. "You have wasted your time and mine, Lady Mosby. The challenge is not mine to withdraw. Your brother claims to be the offended party. *He* challenged me and I will *not* back down from meeting him. I have no quarrel if he wishes to withdraw, but I will not sacrifice my *honor* and my *reputation* on the likes of him."

"He challenged you?" Jemma repeated, astounded.

"Yes."

"But why—?" she started, then stopped. Why did Cris do anything? She had thought he was growing out of his wild stage. It had been a long time since he'd been rash and foolish, but the possibility was always there, bubbling beneath the veneer of manners. All it took was a little drink. . . .

At her abrupt silence, a muscle tightened in Dane's jaw. In three long strides, he crossed to the door behind her and opened it. "Go home, Jemma. I can't save your brother from himself any more than you can. And I'll be damned before I sacrifice my pride for him."

Or for any of them.

Jemma nodded to herself. He was right . . . and yet, what would become of her family? Cris was the last of their line, a line that stretched all the way back to Normandy, to before the Conqueror. Duty, honor, and obligation to her name had been drummed into her from the cradle. Dane had been her one defiance, and in the end, she had done what had been expected of her.

Just as she would do what she must now.

She'd already suffered through Mosby. She hated the pitying looks she now received because her husband had been unwise. If something happened to Cris on the morrow, what would become of her? She'd surrendered so much of her life already. To let Cris go would be the same as saying her sacrifice had been in vain.

She faced Dane. He stood much closer than she'd thought, his hand on the door handle. A draft from the hall flickered the candlelight, shifting the circle of light. Beyond it, around them, all was dark.

And she knew with a woman's sense that, no matter how harshly he spoke, Dane was not completely immune to her. Nor was she to him.

This was Dane. This was the only man she'd ever loved.

She could shut her eyes and breathe in the scent of him. The years had changed both of them . . . but some things were the same. He wore an expensive sandalwood fragrance that in no way detracted from his masculinity; however, beneath its tones, she could smell the scent of fresh air and promises, of warmth and safety, and of *everything* she'd once thought of as Dane.

For a second, she was tempted to place the palm of her hand on his chest. When they'd been together, she'd done that often because she'd liked to feel his heart beat against the hard muscles of his chest. The years had been good to Dane. She had no doubt he was as strong as he'd been the last time they'd been this close.

And there was something else here, too. Something that

had always been present whenever she'd been near him: Passion. Desire. Hunger.

"Jemma."

The hoarseness in his voice surprised her, and she realized she'd been staring at his shirt front in the area of his heart. She blushed, both embarrassed and confused. "I never meant to hurt you."

There, she'd said it.

Years ago, she'd not had the opportunity. Her father had packed her off to London to marry Mosby posthaste. He'd told her Dane would forget her easily. He'd told her she would forget Dane.

Now she knew her father had lied.

She expected Dane to reject her apology. It was only what she deserved. She could not meet his eye . . . and realized the longer she prolonged leaving, the more difficult it would be for both of them.

Jemma started to take a step back, but then he leaned forward, slightly closing the door and barring her way.

Surprised, she raised her head and found him staring at her lips with an intensity that increased her own pulse. Her breasts grew full, her nipples hard.

He seemed to know exactly what effect he was having on her. Slowly, he raised his gaze to hers. Gone was the glittering hardness, and in its place was a sure intensity that made her knees weak.

Dane smiled, and her toes curled in her shoes, just like they used to when they were younger.

Her toes had never curled for her husband. Ever.

Dear God, what memories this moment brought back! What bright promises had she once shared with this man? They had both been so young and so in love.

And then his smile changed. He became more knowing, more predatory.

More intriguing.

He leaned even closer and in a low voice that hummed through her asked, "Why did you really come here tonight, Jemma?"

Chapter 3

*D*ane wondered what madness he practiced.

He should ring for a servant and have Jemma summarily escorted from his house. He didn't trust himself to do it. Not while he stood so close to her that he could feel the warmth of her skin.

And he had the urge to touch her.

Too clearly, he remembered a lazy summer afternoon when they'd both fallen asleep on a blanket after a picnic. He'd woken first. The others in their party had been exploring some ruins, their shouts far in the distance. The horses had been grazing nearby. He could still recall the exact sound of them moving through the grass and the hum of bees busy chasing buttercups.

He'd turned to see if Jemma was awake and, for the first time, had been struck by an awareness he'd not had before. They'd always been childhood friends; however, he'd just returned from his first year at Cambridge, a confused student without thought of direction or purpose, while still thinking himself a man of the world.

She was seventeen and becoming a woman.

He'd always thought Jemma attractive, but now, lying beside her, he'd suddenly discovered her to be beautiful. Her nose was up tilted and her chin too sharp, and yet the combination of the two gave her face character.

Then, there was her glorious hair. It was the color of mahogany, a rich, vibrant brown with gold and red woven through it in a way only God could master. He'd yearned to touch it, to see if it was as silky as it looked. . . .

He'd clenched his fist and focused on the other things he liked about her—like her laughter. And her dogged determination to see the best in the world no matter how bleak. Certainly, she had her share of troubles. No one could stand her father. He was overbearing and rude, and her mother was the most grasping creature in the county.

Around them, Jemma shone like the rarest jewel. Everyone liked her, and, in spite of the precarious fortunes of her family, she was always included in outings like today.

Furthermore, Jemma had presence. He always knew when she was about. He could sense her. Maybe it was the vital scent of roses that lingered in the air around her, something reminding him of the exotic. Perhaps it was something else . . . something he could not name—yet.

That afternoon, Dane had begun to ache in ways he'd never known before. It had been a need inside him. A hunger.

Almost shyly, he'd given in to impulse and lightly run his finger over the curve of her cheek. Her skin had been downy soft—softer than he could ever have imagined—and unlined by the cares and worries of the world.

She'd wrinkled her nose in her sleep, stretched, and curled toward him while opening her eyes. Smoky eyes.

Sometimes blue, sometimes gray, but always expressive beneath their heavy fringe of black lashes.

Jemma had smiled at him then, pleased he had woken her. . . . and in that moment, *Dane had fallen in love.* The horses, the bees, even the calls of their friends had faded from consciousness. All he'd ever wanted had been centered here, with this woman. The realization had been so sudden and so certain that he'd been surprised he hadn't been struck blind like Paul on the road to Damascus.

A more incredible miracle had been that Jemma had returned his regard. She'd fallen in love with him in spite of his imperfections and doubts. Through her, he'd begun to believe in himself. He could have scaled mountains, fought dragons, found the Holy Grail.

They'd spent the rest of his holiday completely involved in each other. She had encouraged him to follow his calling to the Church. With her love to brace him, he'd found the backbone to inform his father of his vocation, and he'd received his approval. Dane had returned to school a new man, one with goals and the desire to forge a good life for Jemma.

He'd believed she'd shared his hopes and dreams.

He'd been wrong.

Before Michaelmas, she'd married another. A man with a title and wealth. A man twice their ages. A man who'd gained the right to touch her and see her wear her hair down.

Dane had hated that man without ever knowing him.

Rightly, Jemma had refused to see him when he'd stormed Mosby's estate to demand answers. He'd been out of his mind, sick with jealousy and a rage that had frightened even himself.

He'd begun to be the butt of jokes from his comrades. He'd acted the part of a lovesick fool until no one had wanted any part of him. That's when he'd decided to leave. He'd taken a clerk's position with the East India Company and had left for the Orient.

Now, he was discovering that those smoky eyes that had intrigued him in his youth still had the power to beckon him. But this time, he would make the rules of the game.

"What did you *really* want by coming here?" he repeated, angry now by her silence and the flood of memories that reminded him of how vulnerable she'd once made him feel.

"I don't know what you mean," she whispered, her brows coming together in confusion—and yet he knew she was not impassive to him.

The signs were there. The parted lips, the shallow breathing . . . the tightened nipples that pressed against the thin material of her bodice. Had she deliberately dressed to provoke his desire? He wanted to believe so. In this moment, he wanted to believe so *very* much.

He leaned closer, shutting the door. His chest was mere inches away from her breasts, from those tight nipples, and he caught the scent of the soap she'd used. Not something heavy and cloying but light, fresh, and as fragrant as fields on a sunny day.

His reaction was swift, strong, and completely masculine. He wanted her. He'd always wanted her. He was glad the dark shadows could conceal his obvious arousal.

She shifted back but did not move her feet, almost as if she was naïvely oblivious to her effect on him. Otherwise, she could use it to her purpose. And then, she said, "I stated my reason for this call. I asked you to spare my brother."

"At the expense of my honor."

"No," she quickly denied. "I would not do that. I didn't know it had been Cris who had made the challenge."

"Probably because you and your mother never talked to him, did you? You assumed I was the guilty party," he rightly surmised and shook his head. "He's passed out in his cups, isn't he? Dead to the world until his seconds wake him for the duel and as oblivious to his responsibilities to his title and his family as he ever was."

"He's young—" Jemma started.

"He's a drunk," Dane said, "and behaves as drunks often do—saying and doing things they regret once they are sober."

He expected Jemma to challenge him, and that would be good. Her irrational defense of her family in spite of their numerous failings would make him angry. Anger would put distance between them and allow him to send her out the door.

Instead, she said, "Yes, he will wake at dawn and wish he'd not been so foolish as to challenge you."

"Then let him cry off."

Her eyes turned sad. "He won't."

"Then I promise not to kill him. It is the best I can offer. I will not cower."

With a soft cry, Jemma covered her ears with her hands and took three swift steps away, moving toward the circle of light surrounding his desk. For a second, she stood, head bowed. Then, slowly, she lowered her hands, her fists clenched as if strengthening her resolve.

She looked to him, her face half in shadows. "Cris will press."

"He will attempt to kill me," Dane agreed. "He made his intentions very clear this evening, and he is the sort who believes death is honor."

"And you don't?"

Dane didn't answer. He couldn't. The golden candlelight highlighted her full curves and turned her muslin dress into a shadow box that emphasized the indentation of her waist and the flair of her hips. He'd once dreamed of possessively placing his hand there, of pulling her to him and not having to hold back the heat of desire.

He forced himself to concentrate on the conversation. "I was enjoying a game of cards until your brother started taunting me." He added brutally, "His words were molded out of jealousy. He hates the fact that my fortunes have soared while your family's have floundered. When he became completely obnoxious, I said the real pity was that he had squandered a settlement his sister had sold herself for in marriage. He took offense."

She drew in a sharp breath. "As do I."

"Good," Dane replied evenly, almost hating himself for his coolness. "Then the outcome on the morrow will be of no matter to you."

"You are wrong," Jemma responded. Her chin came up. "But then, you have formed your own conclusions about all of us. Everyone in town knows Sir Dane Pendleton takes pride in handling matters in his own way. You could have avoided the confrontation tonight if you had wished, but you didn't."

Dane didn't reply. He couldn't. She was right. He had egged on her insolent brother . . . and maybe for reasons he didn't feel comfortable examining at this moment. Later, once she'd removed herself from him, then, perhaps, he could examine his conscience.

Jemma didn't seem to expect an answer. Instead, she accused, "You have held a grudge against my family for the last ten years and more. So let us have it out between us, Dane. Now, and be done with it."

Her bold willingness to confront the past made him uncomfortable. It was one thing to nurse a grudge, another to flush it out in the open.

Her lips curved into a cynic's smile. "What? Have you nothing to say? When I first arrived you were very free with your opinions of my brother, but let us not mince words, sir.

I'm the one who angered you. And for what? Because I chose to marry another?"

The walls of the room suddenly closed in around Dane. "You . . . *chose?*"

Yes, he'd blamed her, but he'd always assumed her parents had forced her to abandon him. He'd wanted to believe she'd had no choice.

And he hated what he'd just revealed to her.

Worse, she knew.

She pressed her lips together as if swallowing words she feared to say. Her eyes filled with her own pain. "I would not hurt you."

"You haven't." *But she had.*

"I wanted to wait for you . . . to tell you myself."

Dane didn't speak. He feared he would break.

"Lord Mosby was kind. . . ." She didn't continue.

He reached deep inside to the hard resolve that had helped build an empire, the resolve he used as if it were armor.

"Never mind," he answered. "My life has gone on without you."

Jemma nodded, obviously struggling with tears—and *why not?* She'd chosen the wrong man. If she'd married him, he would have moved heaven and earth for her. Instead, she'd chosen the title, and her family was now close to ruin. In her shoes, Dane would cry too.

He opened the door. "I believe we have nothing more to say to each other." The hall was dark. "I'll call for the footman. He shall see you home."

But Jemma didn't move. She stood silhouetted by candlelight. "What is your price?" she asked, her voice tight with pent-up emotion.

"I beg your pardon?" he asked, uncertain if he'd heard her correctly.

"Your price, *Sir* Dane," she reiterated, and now he could

not mistake the anger in her tone. "I've heard you believe everything has a price. They say you are part of the new age, the one that creates its own fortunes. I want to know your price for crying off from the duel with my brother on the morrow."

"There is no price large enough for me to forfeit my honor," he said coolly.

"Really?" she asked. "Nothing?"

"Nothing."

There was a beat of silence, and then she said, "I believe there is something."

"And what is that?" he asked, certain of himself.

"It's what you want, what you've *always* wanted."

Dane smiled grimly. "I have everything I want."

"Do you?" she replied. She dropped the shawl from her shoulders and, reaching up with both arms, pulled the pins from her hair.

It came tumbling down around her shoulders, almost reaching her waist. It was thick and vibrant and shone with a life of its own.

"Here," she said quietly, "this is what I'm offering. My honor for yours. We've an old score to settle. Let us settle it now."

Chapter 4

*J*emma dared to risk all. And yet, what choice did she have?

Or so she told herself.

She stood in front of Dane, her heart pounding so hard against her chest that she was certain he would see her fear. Other than her family and her husband, no one had ever seen her hair down. She expected him to say something, to move, react. Instead, he stood as if turned to stone. Her shadow blocked his expression, and she shifted so the wane candlelight highlighted the hard planes of his face. His mouth had a grim set, and his brows formed an angry vee.

"You would abase yourself for your brother?"

If he'd struck her he'd not have caused more hurt. But then Jemma faced the hard truth. "If you've lived as long as I have with men whose lives are dictated by the bottle, you'd have little pride left. I've learned in this life one does what one must."

Those words caught him off guard, and she felt as if she'd

gotten a bit of her own back. She pressed on before she lost her courage. "Do we have a bargain? My honor for yours?"

Dane leaned back so his expression was once again hidden in the shadows. "I don't know," he said slowly. There was a moment of silence, and then he asked, "Why?"

There was a wealth of understatement in that one word.

"What choice do I have?" It was hard to keep the bitterness from her voice.

Without Cris, she and her mother would be thrown into the streets or, worse, forced to depend on relatives who had nursed numerous grudges against her family. Her father had burned many bridges, and now she and her mother paid the price.

Over the last two years, she'd sold everything she could to keep the estate going. Heirlooms that had been in the Carson family for generations had gone for a song to pay off mounting debts. If her husband had been a better steward of his own money or if his heir and family had been more generous to his young widow, Jemma's circumstances would have been different.

She'd learned not to indulge in "what ifs." Recently, she'd even made discreet inquiries about her finding employment—but no one wanted a governess with a title. Her mother had suggested that she remarry, but Jemma was happier in her own bed.

And then, tonight, her mother had begged her to come to Dane.

He was right. The weak were cunning creatures, and Jemma had no doubt her mother had known matters between them would come to this, to her bartering all she had left to offer. The only question was why had Jemma herself been so naïve? Why did she always trust too much? Or had there been a secret desire on her own part to see him again?

She shoved the idea from her conscience and straightened her shoulders. "Do we have a bargain?" she demanded before she lost her courage.

He slowly circled her.

Jemma forced herself to stand very still while she was inspected as if she were livestock. She clenched her fists at her side, digging her nails into her palms.

Dane stopped behind her. He stood so close that she could feel the heat from his body. He was tall, much taller than Mosby, and yet she knew they would fit together well.

His deep voice said, "There was a time when all I ever wanted was you."

Her knees went weak. She didn't want to be reminded of the choice she should have made. A choice she'd already paid a price for. A dear, dear price.

She brought herself back to reality. "I've heard you treat your mistresses well."

As if offended, he took a step back, and she could breathe easier. "I do," he replied. "But what makes you think I'm willing to pay *your* price?"

There was a harshness in his tone that had nothing to do with anger, and she almost laughed. She knew he wanted her. The tension between them in this room was too strong for there not to be lust. And she realized with brutal honesty that a part of her, the very secret part, wanted him, too. There had been many times with Mosby when she'd shut her eyes and thought of Dane and had wished he had been the one laboring over her—

She broke off the thought.

Jemma had been faithful to her vows. She'd given her husband what she'd owed him and she'd cared for the man in his final sickness, a wasting illness that had lasted years.

But she'd never given him her heart. That, she'd lost years ago to Dane.

Or at least, to the man he had *once* been. He was a hard

CATHY MAXWELL

man now. One who dealt in coin and did no favors for anyone.

In fact, she wasn't certain she *liked* the man he had become.

"You'll pay my price," she said boldly, facing him so they both stood in the tight circle of candlelight, "because you want me. And because if you don't take me this night, there will always be a question in your mind." Just like there was in hers.

His lips curved into reluctant acknowledgment and, yes, a hint of respect. "How far we have both come, hmmmmm, Jemma? Who would have thought?"

"I try not to think about it."

He nodded. He understood.

He picked up the candle. "Well, then, shall we adjourn to a more comfortable room?"

There it was. He had agreed.

Her heart in her throat, she whispered, "Yes," not sounding half as sophisticated as she would have wished.

If he noticed, he didn't say a word, walking instead toward the door. She fell into step behind him as any good concubine would . . . and lost another piece of her soul.

Would her mother care? Would Cris appreciate the lengths she was willing to go for her family?

No.

Dane led her out into the wide corridor. The flickering candlelight cast eerie shadows on the painted wainscoting. It glanced off paintings on the wall. They said Dane collected the Renaissance masters, especially those works of art depicting the Holy Family. She remembered his aspirations at one time of wanting to enter the clergy and to live a life of service.

If he'd let it be known back then that he'd been willing to change his mind and make a fortune for himself, then her father would have had a different opinion of him—and her fate would have been different as well.

Why did regrets always taste like bile?

Dane led her up a wide set of stairs with carpet so thick they didn't make a sound. They walked down a hall lined with doors. It was hard to imagine such a big house for one man, but there seemed to be no presence of life in any of the rooms they passed.

He stopped in front of the door at the end of the hall and opened it. The room was well lit, with a fire burning in the hearth. Jemma caught a glimpse of a man's legs stretched out from an upholstered chair and knew Dane's valet had been waiting for him.

"Stay here," Dane ordered, leaving her in the hall while he entered the room.

The valet sleepily came to his feet. He was a short, thin man, who was rumored to be the best "gentleman's gentleman" in London—or so Jemma had heard.

"Troy, that will be all for this evening," Dane said, dismissing him.

"Very well, sir. Have a good night." The valet started for the door, then stopped abruptly, his foot poised comically in the air, at the sight of Jemma lingering in the hall. Obviously Dane didn't bring women to his room often, a curiously comforting, and embarrassing, thought.

"Good night, Troy," Dane said, reminding the man of his manners.

"Yes, sir, very good, sir," the valet responded, coming back to his senses. He hurried past Jemma, not even pausing to take a candle with him.

"Come in," Dane invited.

Jemma stood where she was, unable to move. She glanced inside the room, both curious and intimidated. This was definitely a man's domain. The hangings and bedspread were of dark blue with gold fringe along the edges. A fire burned in a marble hearth, its glow carried on by wall sconces that cast their light up creamy walls. There was a desk and full-length mirror . . . but the bed dominated the room.

She had never seen such a large, exquisite piece of furniture. Like the desk and the bench before the hearth, it was of the highest style. The headboard went halfway up the wall and boasted carved swirls and flourishes. Elegantly turned walnut columns marked each corner and held up the fringed canopy overheard. Four people could have slept comfortably on the expanse of velvet-covered mattress—although there would be only two tonight.

Jemma quickly averted her gaze, noticing the stack of ledgers on the desk. Beside them was a stone carving of a strong, powerful horse prancing off into the unknown. The desk's chair was turned toward a globe of the world that was the size of a small table. Her impression was that Dane had been working here and had needed to find some reference on its surface for his vast empire.

His world encompassed the farthest reaches of civilization and beyond. He'd seen things and done things she couldn't even imagine.

Whereas she had traveled the same path over and over and over again. Her life was routine and monotonous, while his had been filled with adventure. In fact, her boldness in coming here this evening was the most daring action of her life.

All she had to do was cross the threshold into this room.

Dane watched her, his expression cynical. His eyes said louder than words that he questioned whether or not she'd fulfill their bargain.

In truth, he looked handsome standing there in his dark jacket and blinding white waistcoat and shirt—and a complete contrast to her late husband. Mosby had been chubby and bowlegged. He'd liked food more than Jemma, although he'd done his duty at least once a month. She'd married when she was still seventeen and with only vague notions of the ways between men and women.

Meanwhile, here was Dane, who, in the short year since he had returned from the East, had kept some of the most beautiful women in London. He was the kind of lover women whispered about. They said he'd learned "tricks" in the Orient. . . .

Jemma knew she'd be lying to herself if she pretended she hadn't always wondered what her life would have been like if she'd defied her family and chosen Dane. Still, to take this step—

"Go ahead, Jemma, bolt."

His quiet taunt made her angry.

"I'm no coward," she informed him, pride stiffening her resolve. "I've *never* been a coward." She'd accepted her fate, made her decisions, and built her life the best she could. No, nothing had been perfect, but she had done her duty, and, to this point, her family name and pride had survived.

Nor would she run now.

She walked into the room.

Chapter 5

*D*ane almost dropped his jaw when Jemma walked into his bedroom. She was going to go through with it.

As regal as a princess, she moved right up to the bed and then stopped. Her gaze traveled thoughtfully from the foot to the head. She looked over her shoulder at him, her expressive eyes, with their heavy lashes, shyly seductive, the highlights in her hair red in the candlelight. "Are you ready now or do you—?" She waved a hand.

He forced himself to breathe. "Or do I what?" he managed to croak out, his body reacting to the hundreds of ideas that leaped to his mind. He took a step back.

"I don't know. This is *your* bedroom."

Yes, and the one woman he'd always wanted but could not have was now standing in it, apparently prepared to do whatever he asked.

And the thought scared Dane stiff, in more ways than one!

Here was the one woman who had made him vulnerable. She'd defeated him in a way he didn't like to remember.

Consequently, he'd spent over a decade proving to himself that he didn't need anyone.

He wasn't one to lie even to himself. He'd always known they would meet again. Every coin that he'd earned, every warehouse he'd filled had all been to prove to her she had married the wrong man. There had even been a time, as he'd faced certain death in a Turkish prison, when the one thing that had given him the will to survive had been his need to have her see him as a successful man.

Since his return to London, he'd always been a bit on edge, aware that she walked these same streets, that they traveled in some of the same circles. That at any moment he could turn a corner and she would be there.

But they had not met until tonight.

And never, not even in his *wildest* imaginings, could he have anticipated this turn of events.

Dane didn't quite know what to do. This was not the Jemma he remembered. Gone was the innocence. For both of them.

"Jemma—" he started and stopped, uncertain of what to say. The decent part of him, the *gentleman,* should send her packing.

But there was another, darker, side that wanted her. Desperately. Then maybe his soul would find peace.

She waited, her eyes so wide that they threatened to swallow her face. "You'll have to help me," she said hesitantly. "You must tell me what you want me to do."

What he wanted her to do?

His mind reeled at the possibilities. He wanted to know if she still tasted the same when he kissed her. And there were questions that had plagued him: Were her legs as long as he'd always fantasized they were? And what color were her nipples, dark or pale pink? And he had a need to feel the hair at the juncture of her thighs—

"Come here," he said.

She bowed her head a moment, as if in silent prayer, and then, squaring her shoulders, she moved to him.

Dane might have backed down and sent her packing—except for the squaring of the shoulders. The action pricked his conscience and made him angry. She was not the injured party. He was.

She stopped in front of him.

He said, "Kiss me."

Jemma hesitated, her gaze shifting away from him as if to distance herself from this place and this moment. She drew a deep breath of fortitude.

Dane's temper snapped. "Kissing me is no damn chore," he said tightly, angry at how much he suddenly wanted her kiss. "Or at least, I've not had a complaint."

Her startled gaze swung up to his. "I don't mean to offend—"

"Aye, because we have a bargain," he said derisively, mocking himself more than her.

"I was thinking of how far we both have come—"

"I don't want to be reminded," he interrupted brutally.

"I can't forget," she returned evenly. "I remember it all, Dane. I remember how when we kissed the first time, I placed my hand on your chest like this, over your heart."

He could feel the heat of her palm through the layers of his clothes.

"I liked to feel your heart beat," she said. "I felt it was in time with mine." And then she rose up on tiptoes and placed her lips on his . . . just as she had years ago for their first kiss.

Dane went whirling back in time. He had forgotten nothing. He could even remember the smell of bread baking somewhere in the house. They'd stood in the hallway of her parents' home, where they'd stolen a few moments alone.

He'd recklessly declared his love, forgetting his well-rehearsed speech and blurting out the words. And she had answered in just this way, by placing her hand over his heart and kissing him.

Only now this kiss was different. There were no parents or proprieties to hold him back. No foolish vows of undying devotion. No promises of tomorrow.

But for tonight she was his. All his.

Dane let down his guard. He shoved aside his doubts and let nature take its course. He was a man now, not a foolish boy, and he had a man's desire. A chaste kiss was not what he wanted.

He captured Jemma's hand covering his heart and pulled her closer, bringing his arm around her and fitting their bodies together. Hungrily, he claimed the kiss he'd wanted, the one he'd dreamed of.

She startled and acted ready to pull back. He wouldn't let her. Instead he pressed, demanding her to open to him.

Tentatively, she did, her lips parting slightly—and Dane took full advantage. *Now,* they were kissing. No more of this silly closed-lip nonsense. The force of desire building inside him was almost frightening. He wanted her and tonight he'd have her.

Nor was he afraid to let Jemma know his intent. He was hard and ready. He stroked her tongue with his. She balked as if such a touch was alien to her and attempted to turn her head away. He wouldn't let her, forcing her to accept him, while he cupped her buttocks with one hand and brought her up against his bold, hungry erection.

One moment, there was resistance, and then she melted against him, her breasts against his chest, her thighs pressed to his. He took full advantage, deepening the kiss, burying his hands in her hair, which was even more silky to the touch than he had imagined. Suddenly, the two of them were kissing as if this was the most natural thing in the world to do. She smelled of roses and cinnamon, spicy, exotic, desirable. This was Jemma. *His* Jemma, the one he'd thought he'd lost.

Dane broke off the kiss. Without hesitation, he swept her up in his arms and carried her to the bed. He laid her on the velvet bed cover, her hair spread out around her, and began removing his coat.

Jemma rose on her elbows. Her eyes were smoky dark, her lips already swollen from his kisses.

She looked absolutely delicious. And he knew that right now, her heart raced with the same passionate need as his own.

"Shouldn't we blow out the candles?" she asked.

Dane tossed his coat onto a side chair. "No. I want to see you while we do this."

He could see he'd shocked her. He paused in the act of pulling his shirttail out of his breeches. "What is it, Jemma? Have you never made love by candlelight or during the day?"

She swallowed and shook her head, words apparently failing her.

So, Mosby had been a lousy lover. Good.

Dane leaned over, placing his hands on the mattress on either side of her, his lips so close to hers they could breathe the same air. "There are going to be many things you will do for the first time tonight."

If he'd meant to scare her, he'd done a good job. The color drained from her face. She eased back and glanced around the room as if reminding herself of where she was . . . and why.

Her reluctance rekindled his temper. *Damn her for preying on his conscience.* If he were a gentleman, he'd let her go.

But he couldn't. He wouldn't. They'd come too far. She'd

teased him years ago with empty promises. Well, now it was time to pay the piper. After all, he was a man who'd become accustomed to taking what he wanted.

Dane stood. "It's too late now to cry off, Jemma," he said. Taking the hem of his shirt in hand, he pulled it up over his head.

Chapter 6

*I*t *was* too late. Jemma couldn't have moved if she'd wanted to. All she could do was stare—and not only because, in taking off his shirt, Dane had revealed a muscled, hard body. He was still lean and strong, as he'd been in youth. In contrast to other men she'd seen bare-chested, including her husband and her brother, Dane's muscles had definition, like those of a common laborer.

But what claimed her full attention was the angry scar that ran from an inch above his navel, across his chest, and up to his shoulder. It appeared as if someone had attempted to split him wide open.

Jemma forgot her self-consciousness. The haze of seduction evaporated.

For a moment, she was so shocked she could only stare. Then, tears welling in her eyes, she came to her knees.

Dane tensed, as if he'd forgotten how shocking that angry scar could be. Now, she had reminded him.

He started to take a step back. Jemma reached out to stop

him. "I—" she started, and words failed her. What could she say? She'd been in no way prepared for the sight. Here was something the gossips did not know about.

She placed her hand, palm flat, on the scar where it crossed his heart. He did not flinch. The beat of his pulse was as strong as ever.

Slowly, Jemma ran her hand down, following the scar, and around his torso. She used both arms to embrace him, laying her head against his body. His skin felt warm and vibrant beneath her cheek.

At first, he said and did nothing. Then, gently, his hands came down to her shoulders. "It was a long time ago, Jemma. I rarely notice it."

She looked up at him, her throat tight. "You don't understand."

"Then explain."

For a second, she considered denying his request. She'd learned long ago to keep her true thoughts and feelings to herself. But what did it matter now? She and Dane were practically strangers to each other, strangers who had once shared a youthful, innocent view of the world.

She lightly touched the scar at the point where it started above his navel. It was as he said, he no longer felt the pain . . . but at one time he had, and the memory must still be within him, hidden deep. She knew how it was.

"I had thought you had the perfect life," she confessed. "You left Chipping, traveled the world, and came back wealthy. It all sounds simple . . . but there is more to the story, isn't there? There's always more."

He didn't mistake her meaning. "Do *you* have scars, Jemma?"

She shook her head and smiled. These were her secrets, and, although they were nothing as dramatic as the dangers he must have faced, her scars ran too deep to share. Instead, she realized that tonight she had the opportunity to relive the dream, to be as she'd once been, unscathed by life and full of dreams.

In one fluid motion, Jemma released her hold and stood up on the bed. Her feet sank into the deep mattress as she kicked off first one shoe and then another, pushing them off the side of the bed with her toe. She leaned her head to one side and shook her hair out of the way so she could reach behind and unlace her dress.

Dane followed her every movement with his eyes.

Anticipation and a new awareness of herself as a woman made her bold. She wanted this, more than she'd ever wanted anything in her life. Then, perhaps, she could free herself from regrets and the weight of guilt.

Her dress unlaced, she slid one sleeve and the other down her arms. Her bodice fell down to her hips, leaving her before him in her threadbare chemise.

His gaze went to her breasts, which were right before him. Jemma leaned over and, this time, when she kissed him, she did so in the manner in which he had kissed her.

Their kiss took on immediate heat. His strong arms came around her, lowering her to the bed, and this time, she felt no shyness.

Dane kissed her lips, her chin, her cheeks. When his tongue traced a pattern around her ear, the astonishing sensation threatened to send her straight through the canopy like a shooting star.

His hand on her breast grounded her.

This, at least, was familiar. But his touch was far from the clumsy gropings of her husband. Dane knew what pleased her. She showed her enjoyment by circling his ear with the tip of her tongue.

His reaction was abrupt.

He took the front of her chemise in both hands and ripped it wide open, his face in the crook of her neck, his teeth teasing the sensitive skin. Cold air hit her breasts, but then his hands covered them, warming her in ways she'd never imagined.

His breathing grew heavy. Or was that her own she heard? Deep inside, she could feel everything quickening, tightening, urging.

His lips moved down her throat, and wherever he touched, she grew hot. He pressed her breasts together. They filled his hands.

For a heartbeat, she was embarrassed. Her tight nipples were brown, and she'd always considered them ugly.

Then, he murmured, "Beautiful," and she was.

He covered one breast with his mouth. Jemma felt the pull all the way down to the very core of her. She buried her fingers in his thick hair, and her legs opened to him with a will of their own. He moved to her other breast, giving it the same care and attention, and Jemma could have wept from the pleasure.

This was her Dane. The man she'd once dreamed of marrying . . . and for now, nothing mattered except being here with him like this. She wanted to join with him. *She needed their joining.*

They undressed quickly. Jemma was now glad of the candles lighting the room. They didn't bother getting under the bedclothes but fell on each other gloriously naked. Her lover was a handsome man, but the erection he boasted was something she'd never imagined. Bold, proud, begging to be satisfied.

Her husband had never been like this. The thought startled a laugh from her.

Dane lifted an eyebrow. "What is funny?"

"Nothing," she assured him. "Nothing is funny at all." She punctuated her words by daring to touch him. It was as hard as it looked.

Dane wrapped her hair around one fist, as if he'd stop her if she attempted to escape from him. But she wasn't running away. Her need for him was frightening in its intensity.

She curved her body to meet his, her legs cradling his hips. His hand caressed her hip and down her thigh, encouraging her knees to bend and bring him closer. Not that she needed encouragement. She was hot, moist, ready. She closed her eyes.

He entered her in one smooth thrust.

She gasped aloud and he stopped.

"Jemma? Have I hurt you?"

"No, it feels so good," she said on a sigh, her body adjusting to his size and length. "So right."

"Then open your eyes and look at me," he ordered, and she obeyed.

"Dane," she murmured, and he smiled, the expression tense, as if he had a tight hold on himself. She shifted and took him deeper, and this time, he was the one to gasp—and she couldn't help but laugh, "This is heaven."

"It is," he agreed, and they began moving.

Jemma had never been a participant in making love before. Her husband had never expected it . . . but now, she realized, he'd never taken her to this place. Nor had she wanted him to. How could she, if she'd never known such desire, such passion existed?

Or did it only exist with Dane?

She clasped him tightly, her arms around his neck, her legs holding his hips. She began whispering his name. Her insides coiled tighter and tighter.

He told her she was beautiful, that she was wonderful, that he had missed her—

The force and power of release was overwhelming.

One moment Jemma was of this earth, and in the next, she was beyond, in a place she had never been before.

She cried out her surprise, unmindful of who could hear her, the pinnacle so intense, so vibrant that she'd ceased to exist in every way save this one.

And Dane knew she was there. He buried himself deep within her, and Jemma would have held him there forever if she could.

The life force flowed from him and into her. For one shining, vibrant moment, she was complete. Whole. Sated. Perfect.

Dane's body collapsed on hers. His weight felt good.

"Dear God," he whispered, "dear sweet heavenly God." His fingers were still buried in her hair. He brought his hand to his mouth, raising his lips over it before untangling his fingers. He smoothed her hair over the pillow.

Slowly, Jemma became aware of her surroundings beyond Dane—the fire in the hearth, the flickering candles, the velvety spread beneath her. The air was laden with the scent of sex.

Dane pulled the spread from one side and tossed it over their nakedness. Then, sliding over to her side, he wrapped his arms around her and, like a man, fell asleep.

But Jemma didn't sleep. Her body still hummed with the excitement of newly discovered passion. Ever so slowly, she returned to reality, and with it came regrets.

She had played the devil's game. She would never forget this night. For as long as she lived, she would be haunted by it, because no other man would ever compare to Dane.

In less than one hour, he'd made her feel vital and alive. But now, she had to return to her life as it was. If she didn't, she might be tempted to throw aside all respectability and beg him to keep her. To leave all her responsibilities behind, all the people who counted on her and the allegiance she owed her family . . .

She could give up everything for this one man.

Dane had always had that power over her, and now she understood why her father had fought so hard to keep them apart. In a way, she wasn't certain her father hadn't been right to encourage her to marry another. These emotions she felt for Dane—the lust, desire, hunger—they couldn't be healthy. They were too overwhelming.

Snuggled against him, she ran her hand down his side, feeling his ribs and the bone of his hip. She rubbed her nose against his shoulder, drinking in his scent.

She could stay like this forever. Her fingers touched his now relaxed member. It was still more than what her husband could have boasted, and she smiled before being struck by a wave of sadness.

Tonight had been a magic moment of "what could have beens." But the moment was over. The time had come to leave.

She'd fulfilled her part of the bargain. Cris was safe. She prayed her brother never found out what she'd done to save his life. If he did, Cris was stupid enough to challenge Dane again.

Jemma knew in her woman's soul she could not make love to Dane a second time and escape unscathed. Her heart was involved. She knew that now. The love she had once felt for him had been true. Her father had been wrong.

She'd been wrong.

Hugging him tight, she reveled one last time in the texture of his skin, of being here with him without the barriers of clothing and society. This felt too good. She had to leave.

Carefully, Jemma slipped out of his arms. She took her time about the task so she would not wake him. When she was free, she tucked the bedspread around his body so he wouldn't be cold. She resisted the urge to touch his hair.

Instead, she quietly picked up her dress from where it had been tossed on the floor and shrugged into it. She didn't bother with underclothes. The chemise was ruined. She debated about leaving it behind, then decided it best not to leave any mementos. She kneeled to pick up her shoes, which had been kicked under the bed.

Straightening, she looked up and found herself staring straight into Dane's face. He was furious.

His hand clamped down on her wrist. "Where did you think you were going?" he demanded.

"I thought we were done," Jemma answered, startled by the unbridled fury in his eye. "The bargain's been met."

"We haven't even begun," he said, biting out the words. "Take off your clothes."

Chapter 7

Jemma was leaving him again.

Dane couldn't believe she could do it twice. Had she not felt anything for him, even in the last hour? Or did she think him a bloody fool?

Perhaps he was. He'd trusted her, hadn't he? He'd believed she'd been as emotionally moved as he'd been by what had transpired between them. He'd thought that *this* time things would be different.

Theirs had been no ordinary coupling. The earth had shaken for him. Being inside Jemma, joined with her as one, had been the one thing he'd ever wanted in life. In those too precious moments of fulfillment, he'd been more whole, more alive than ever before—and he'd fallen in love . . . all over again.

Or maybe he'd done that when she'd touched his scar, when she'd acted as if she could feel the pain he'd suffered. In that single moment, everything he'd suffered—the hardships, the deprivations, the fears—had been worth the risk.

Jemma had the power to turn his emotions inside out, emotions he'd denied himself for so long. She brought down all barriers . . . and he could not trust her. She bartered in cold tender.

There was fear in her expressive eyes, and something else, something like disillusionment. Dane didn't care. "Take off your clothes," he repeated.

Her jaw tightened, and the fear disappeared. It was as if she mentally withdrew herself. A wall went up inside her, and it was fascinating to watch. Was this stony creature Jemma? Or was she the woman he'd held in his arms, the woman who'd given herself with such abandon?

"I can't do anything if you hold my wrist," she said, her voice cool.

He released his hold—and she charged for the door.

Furious, Dane bounded out of the bed after her, heedless of his nakedness. He reached the door before she did.

"You would run?" he demanded, blocking her way. *Why didn't she care?*

"We're done," she threw at him. She pushed her hair back out of her eyes. "Let me leave."

A deadly calm fell over Dane. He understood now. Jemma was no better than any whore. Finally, the dream died. She really had come here for no other reason than to convince him to withdraw from the duel—and he almost hated her. Almost as much as he hated himself for having believed.

"I thought you wanted me to cry off from my meeting with your brother," he said, his voice quiet.

Her brows came together in a worried frown. "I've met the bargain."

"No, Jemma. It isn't over until I say it is." He began walking toward her, and he was fully aroused and ready again.

She backed away. "You're angry."

"I am." In the full-length mirror by the desk, he caught a glimpse of their reflections. They could have been actors playing their parts.

Her hip hit the corner of his desk. She started to move aside, but he blocked her path with his arm. She whirled in the other direction. He caught her wrist.

"No, Jemma, no more running," he said and turned her wrist over. He placed a kiss on the delicate skin.

"Dane—"

"Take your dress off." He raised his gaze to meet hers, letting her know he was deadly serious.

Her smoky eyes studied him a moment. She nodded as if realizing she had no choice. Bowing her head, her hair covering her face, she did as he expected.

Dane waited impatiently. Her hair still smelled of the sun and fresh air, but he knew better than to trust his senses anymore.

The dress fell to her feet. She was naked beneath it.

"Look in the mirror, Jemma," he ordered softly.

She hesitated, then slowly turned her head to see the two of them standing together. She was so close to him that the tips of her breasts could brush his chest.

Dane slid his fingers in her hair and pushed it back over her shoulder. Her head tilted back and her eyes fluttered shut, her lips pressed together as if she did not want to be a witness.

Ah, Jemma, he wanted to whisper, but he didn't.

If he was a better man, he would let her go, but he wasn't.

Instead, he leaned past her to push the ledgers aside, clearing a space on his desk. The candles were burning low in their sconces. In the light of the hearth's coal fire, her body appeared to be burnished with gold.

He lifted her buttocks up on the desk, parting her legs with his hips. His sex was so close to hers that he could feel her moist heat. For a moment, he nuzzled her nose, his lips near her ear. "Do you see us?" he asked.

Her eyes opened. She looked toward the glass and nodded, her expression inscrutable.

"Have you ever watched yourself making love?" he asked.

Her lips parted, and he knew he had shocked her.

"You will this time, Jemma," he promised. "You will because I want you to know who it is taking you. I want you to remember."

In the glass, her gaze met his. "Please, Dane, no, not like this." There was a hint of panic in her voice.

"Then how else shall it be, Jemma? What else is there?" He thrust into her.

Her muscles clenched and then accepted him, closing around him and cocooning him to her. But the joy he'd experienced earlier was gone. This was a clinical act, a ritual to exorcise himself from his own demons.

He buried himself to the hilt. Jemma gave a start but didn't say a word . . . not one bloody word. He pulled back and entered her again and again, mechanically going through motions as old as time . . . and it meant nothing.

Too late, Dane glanced at the mirror—and froze. He barely recognized himself because his face was so contorted with anger. His lips were pulled back in a feral anticipation, and his every muscle was tense with rutting lust.

Jemma watched him, her face as pale as death, her teeth clenched tight. This was not the vibrant creature he'd made love to earlier but a woman who was accustomed to being used in this manner by a man. A woman who held her breath and waited for it to be over.

Abruptly he pulled out of her.

For a second, he stood, his breathing heavy as he struggled for control. This was not the man he wanted to be.

Nor was this the way he had ever wanted to treat Jemma. Ever.

Dane took a broken step back and slowly fell to his knees. He bowed his head, wishing he could disappear from the face of the earth. What came over him around her? He prided himself on his control, and yet Jemma had the ability to rip right through him.

He sensed her sitting up, could feel her watch him carefully. He felt little better than an animal.

"Dane? Are you all right?"

The empathy in her voice was almost his undoing. He needed to be alone. *Now.*

"Go home, Jemma." He didn't look at her. He couldn't. He'd proven himself to be a monster.

She slid off the desk and stood over him, her bare toes inches from his knee. He waited for her to leave. She took a step away, then knelt down beside him.

Dane turned away. Didn't she understand what he'd been about to do? What he *had* done?

Her arms came around his shoulders.

He stiffened, but she did not let go. Instead, she rested her head against his. Her hair provided a shelter for both of them. She didn't speak, but hugged him, and he was reminded of a Spanish painting he'd once seen of the Virgin offering solace to a sinner.

Then he felt her tears against his neck—and it was his undoing.

He was a man, one who had faced countless dangers, one who had done what he must to survive . . . and Jemma? She was his one vulnerability.

If she had made a different choice years ago, would he still be this same man? Or another? Perhaps he would have been one who didn't have to be so hard? One who didn't use his pride as a shield to keep himself from feeling or thinking too deeply?

And it was this man, the one he might have been, who let down his guard. Who, in a voice Dane barely recognized as his own, ground out the question that had driven him for years: "Why, Jemma? Why did you choose another over me?"

Chapter 8

*J*emma tightened her arms around Dane. She didn't want to answer this question.

For a second, she let herself drink in the scent of him. She pressed her lips to the crook of his neck, feeling his warmth. Her fingers were sensitive to the texture of his skin . . . and she wished she could stop time, to spend eternity right here in this moment and avoid the dangers of going forward.

He waited, as still as stone. Even his heart seemed to have stopped beating . . . and Jemma knew she could not evade the truth.

She sat cross-legged on the floor, bringing him to sit opposite her. Their knees practically touched, and she placed her hands on his thighs, feeling the strength there. Their nakedness underscored the need for unvarnished honesty.

Dane did not look at her. The candles in another wall sconce burned themselves out, and Jemma feared it was a sign. The lines on his face were hard, bleak with raw emotion.

She'd done this to him. She'd broken him.

The realization of what she had once so carelessly tossed aside overwhelmed her. His love *had* been true. Now, with the experience of life's hard lessons in greed, lust, selfishness, and desire, she understood exactly how rare and fine his love had been. This awareness made her confession all the more difficult. "I married him because I was too young to know any better."

The words sounded trite, even to her own ears.

She wasn't surprised when he pulled back. "No one forced you?" He sounded as if he didn't believe her.

Jemma frowned. "There was pressure from my family . . . and from Alfred," she admitted, referring to her husband by his Christian name. "At the time, he was wealthy—or so we thought—and I would be a Lady. Lady Mosby." The title mocked her.

"But you could have said no?" he questioned.

"I could have," she answered.

He reacted as if she had struck him. She understood. Even though he had spent years blaming her, a part of him, the part that had believed in their love, had rationalized that she'd had no choice. He pushed her hands off his thighs.

His reaction tempted Jemma to throw her arms back around him and swear that her parents had forced her to abandon him. She hated to destroy those last, remaining delusions between them. But she couldn't. She'd already hurt him too deeply.

"I was very, *very* young, Dane," she stressed. "Alfred was worldly and promised a life in London. Remember, my family could not afford a season . . . there were the many advantages to Alfred over you. Especially to a young, naïve girl."

"I thought you loved me."

His words seemed to hang in the air around them.

"I did," she said at last. "But I didn't know what love was. Nor did I have the courage to risk all." She pressed her fingers to her temples and leaned over, wishing she could erase all the past mistakes. But she couldn't. What was done was done. "I wanted to wait until you returned from school for the break before I made my decision, but there was no time. I sent a letter to your school, but I later learned my parents intercepted it."

"Then they were to blame."

Jemma shook her head. "No. The letter was my telling you I had decided to accept Alfred's offer. Dane, you want to believe the decision was not mine. It was." How it hurt to admit her own failings. "I was young and shallow and foolish. The day I married Alfred I knew I was making a mistake, but I lacked the courage to bow out of the marriage. And then you came to Faller Hall—"

She broke off, remembering the pain of Dane's visit. When he'd been informed she was not at home to him, he'd stood outside and called her name until its echo had reverberated through the house.

"Your husband ordered you not to see me," he said tightly.

"Alfred didn't even know who you were," she confessed. "By that time, I was living in my own Purgatory. If I had let you in . . ." She trailed off, unable, even now, to admit she might have run off with him.

"Did you hear me call for you that day?" he asked. "Was that your face in the window?"

She didn't answer.

Dane leaned forward. "I shouted for you until the bailiff arrived and threatened to send for the magistrate."

"Alfred thought you a lunatic."

"I was. I was half mad with grief and anger. If you would only have just seen me—"

She cut him off. "And then what, Dane? I was a married woman. What was done could not be undone. I would only have hurt you more."

"But you *heard* me," he reiterated quietly.

"I heard you," she agreed. "And I refused you."

Silence was his answer.

A knot as hard as stone formed in her chest, making breathing difficult. "I didn't realize what I had in you. Perhaps if I'd known more of the world, had traveled beyond Chipping or had been older or wiser or more beautiful or more ugly—" Her excuses tumbled out of her mouth, until she stopped. She drew a breath and looked him in the eye without apology. "Perhaps then, everything would have been different . . . for both of us." She shook her head. "And I won't apologize anymore for marrying Alfred. I did what I had to do at the time. I had reasons. . . . Looking back, they are still valid. I'm sorry, Dane. I wish I had known my own mind better."

"I would have done anything for you."

"I know," she agreed with a sad smile. "But look at us, Dane. We wouldn't be the people we are now if we hadn't made those choices years ago. We'd probably both still be back in Chipping."

"We would," he answered. "I wanted nothing more than you and a parish with good fishing."

"I abhorred your fishing," she admitted. "You'd spend hours at it. I was jealous. Can you imagine? I was so spoiled and petted, I envied fish." She pushed her hair back over her shoulder. "You are fortunate you didn't marry me, Dane. Back then, I lacked the character to make a good parson's wife. I would have whined and thrown tantrums. You would have been forced to find another career. And, also, my family would have been a great trial. I know their faults and their weaknesses, but they are part of my life."

He did not argue. "My mother told me once she'd feared of what would have happened if we had married."

"Did she know all?" Jemma asked quietly.

"There are few secrets in Chipping."

Jemma nodded. She'd thought as much. "My father didn't trust you because you were the one man who wouldn't get senselessly drunk with him."

"I would rather have spent my evening with you."

"He didn't see it that way. To him, a real man knows when to share a drink." She paused, and then said, "Alfred liked the bottle."

"Are you surprised?"

Jemma shrugged. "In a way. He never seemed to drink as much as my family, and yet the doctor said the overindulgence of spirits took him." As it probably had cut short her father's life too. And her brother was all but lost whether Dane met him or not.

Neither of them spoke for a moment, letting the words they shared sink in. The silence was companionable. The fire was burning down in the hearth. Jemma knew it was time to leave. They had come full circle. They were done.

The harshness was gone from Dane's face. It seemed as if years had fallen away and he resembled again the boy she had once loved.

"Did you ever think of me, Jemma? Over the years?"

"Every day," she admitted. "I suppose when things aren't good, we long for what might have been." She reached out and pressed her fingertips on the point where the scar ended at his shoulder. "I fared better than you." Then, because it was necessary, she added, "I'm sorry."

He drew back, as if her touch burned him. He shook his

head. "You didn't do this. If anything, you kept me alive. I should have died from the wound, but I couldn't. I wouldn't let myself . . . not until I saw you again."

"Why? To prove me wrong?"

Dane leaned back. He stared at her as if her words had struck a nerve. His eyes were sharply focused, his brow frowning as if he didn't like what he saw. "I could have married. I almost did. Several times. There were others."

The surge of jealousy surprised her. Then again, hadn't she felt a jolt of that unflattering emotion every time someone had mentioned the women he kept or the ones who'd set their caps for him? "Why didn't you?" She was proud her voice was steady.

He didn't answer immediately, and she realized he struggled with his own devils. "I told myself it was because you hurt me."

"No woman can be trusted?" she quizzed him tightly.

"Maybe I didn't trust myself."

He came to his feet and took a step toward the hearth, his manner preoccupied, as if he was working out a problem in his mind.

Jemma rose and tossed her heavy mane of hair back over her shoulders, waiting for his verdict and certain she would not like it.

He turned to her. "Perhaps I was making excuses . . . ?" He shook his head. "Everything I own, all that I've collected, every bleeding shilling has all been because of a Chipping lass who rejected me. I wanted to prove my worth and to prove you were wrong."

Jemma didn't know what to say. "I—" Words failed her. She bowed her head and admitted, "Perhaps you are better off now."

"Better than what?" he asked. "Than being the village clergyman I set out to be?" His gaze darkened, the line of his jaw hardening. "I've been many places I didn't want to be, Jemma. Places where I thought God had abandoned me. And there have been times when the faith I had once professed so strongly failed me."

His confession touched her soul. No other man of her acquaintance had this strength of character, this complexity. "*I'm* the only one who failed you," she whispered.

He reached out and ran a hand over her head, pushing her hair back. "No, Jemma. You were right. We had to take our separate paths. We'd not have been good for each other."

Jemma thought her heart would break. She loved him.

But she had done the right thing all those years ago.

She and Dane would not have been good for each other. Her immaturity would have held him back from being the man he could be, the man he *was*.

On one hand, she felt freer than she had in years. On the other, she couldn't wait to escape his presence, find a spot where she could be alone, and have a good, soul-cleansing cry.

Conscious of her nakedness, she moved away from him, pulling her hair down to cover her breasts. "I think the time has come for me to leave." She searched the floor for her dress.

"Jemma—," he started, but she cut him off by holding up her hand. The tightness in her throat was a warning that she'd best escape quickly if she wanted to keep her pride intact.

"Please, Dane, enough." She scooped up her dress and awkwardly hunted for the sleeves. "We've both said enough."

He came up behind her. Her body tingled with awareness. She froze, uncertain. "Please," she pleaded.

"What is it?"

Jemma closed her eyes. How easy it would be to fall back against his chest. But then what? It was too late for them. A declaration of love surrounded by such wealth would sound callow.

"We've come full circle," she said. "We're done."

"Are we?"

Oh, dear God, please help me. "Yes."

He pressed his lips against the nape of her neck.

She dropped her dress. She should tell him to stop. Words died in her throat when he did it again. She struggled for sanity.

"No, Dane," she managed. She took a step forward, but his hands came down on her shoulder, holding her in place. She caught a glimpse of the two of them in the mirror's reflection. He was smiling.

Jemma looked away. "This isn't good," she insisted.

His hand slid down her arm to her waist. He pressed his palm against her abdomen and pulled her back to him. She could feel obvious evidence of his intentions.

Deep muscles clenched. He knew.

"We shouldn't," she said, but her words had lost their insistence.

"We need to."

"We mustn't. Dane, we can't live in the past."

He moved his hips against her. "I was thinking of the present."

But do you love me?

Her question echoed in her mind. What did lie between them?

Dane's hand moved lower. The heat of his touch destroyed all resistance.

"We'll not know if we aren't willing to take the risk," he murmured in her ear.

Her poor heart . . .

There would be a price to pay. There always was. But right now, Jemma didn't care.

She turned in his arms and kissed him fully on the mouth.

Chapter 9

ane's need to make Jemma understand how deeply she had hurt him was gone. *Poof.* Disappeared. Years of anger and resentment no longer weighed him down.

He was free . . . but his attraction to her was still here, and it was stronger than ever.

Perhaps they had been too young to have fallen in love so completely years ago, and yet the tension between them now was as if they had never parted.

Love. The word reverberated in his mind as he kissed her back with all his being. He wanted to be sophisticated, to be wiser. As he slid his palms over her smooth skin, he told himself he must not confuse lust with love. Jemma attracted him as no other woman ever had, but that didn't mean he was falling in love with her again.

Or did it? Did their bodies know something their wary minds refused to consider? Was a second chance possible for the two of them?

Tentatively, her tongue touched his. Dane's blood hit the

boiling point. What man cared whether or not a woman loved him when they were both naked and aroused . . . ?

The time was ripe to teach her new tricks. He hefted her up in his arms. Her long legs circled his waist; her breasts pressed against his chest. Their lips never parted as he walked to the bed.

His one coherent thought as he placed her on the rumpled bedspread was this time, he'd be more cautious. Let her declare herself first. He'd already made a fool of himself once. This time, he would protect his heart—and then she laughed.

He greedily began kissing the line of her neck, tickling her enough to laugh. To laugh! Had he ever thought of laughter and lovemaking? With his mistresses it had been their business to please him, and they'd been very serious about their work. They'd been seductive women who'd known what he liked and done it.

Jemma was merely reacting to the pleasure of his touch.

Dane pulled back. Their bodies were stretched alongside each other. Only two candles still burned, and in their flickering light, her expressive eyes appeared more alive than ever.

She lightly ran her fingers down his whiskered jawline. "You tickled." Her nipples were hard and tight.

"Is that bad?" he whispered, reveling in the warmth of her body against his.

Her mouth silently formed the word *no*. She focused on his lips and reached up to kiss him. Her tongue traced the line of his lower lip, tickling him and making him smile.

It became a game between them. Dane delighted in trying to tickle her with his lips. The sound of her delight was a potent aphrodisiac. He kissed her shoulder, over her collarbone, down to her breasts.

Jemma was no cold lover. She gasped and sighed her pleasure. It urged him on. He gave his attention to her full, beautiful breasts, then kissed his way down the flat expanse of her abdomen, steadily working his way lower.

When he circled her navel with his tongue, she whimpered. He went lower, and lower still until he could have all of her.

The moment his lips touched her intimately, Jemma startled and tried to close her legs. He placed his hand on her waist to let her know this was right and natural. Slowly, she relaxed, and he drank deep.

Her fingers buried themselves in his hair as if to hold on for dear life. Her body curved to him, her legs over his shoulders. She whispered his name. He couldn't help but smile; so sensitive was she to him that she felt the movement and found her release. Her body tensed and arched up off the bed. A sharp cry escaped her, a gasp of discovery.

Dane gave her one last kiss, and she fell back to earth. He rested his head on her stomach, listening to her breath return to normal, inordinately pleased with himself.

Jemma sat halfway up, propping herself up on her elbows, her hair back over her shoulders. "What was that?" she asked.

His chin on his hand on her stomach, he met her astonished gaze and smiled. "Did you like it?"

She released her response on a shivery sigh before adding, "Certainly it is nothing the Church has ever sanctioned."

Her dry response startled a laugh out of him. His own laughter sounded rusty, as if it had not been in use for a long time . . . and it hadn't.

He climbed up to lay beside her on the bed. Jemma turned in the curve of his arms. "And what of you?" she whispered, her fingers tracing the line of his arousal. She kissed him beneath his chin. "What can I do for you?" Her fingers closed around his erection, and now it was Dane's turn to whimper.

He rolled over on his back, bringing Jemma with him. Her eyes widened when she found herself sitting on his abdomen. He didn't want to enter her yet . . . not quite yet.

Her hair created a silky curtain over her breasts. He reached up and caught a shiny strand, measuring its distance down her body.

"I used to wonder how long your hair was," he confessed.

"It's too long for fashion. I should cut it."

"No, you shouldn't," he said quickly.

The stain of a blush colored her cheeks as she admitted, "It's my one vanity."

"And a good one it is. More precious than gold." He slid his hand up her arm to her neck and brought her down to kiss him. She tasted sweet and willing. He bent his knees and entered her in one smooth push.

She tightened around him. Their kiss broke.

"Sit up," he ordered softly.

Jemma did as he asked, impaling herself on him, and he thought he could die from the pleasure of being in her this deep.

"Dane—?" Her voice sounded husky and dark, uncertain.

"Trust me."

She swallowed and then nodded. He felt her movement all the way to the core of her. Using his hips, he thrust up, and knees tightened around him. And again, Dane heard himself laugh with pleasure.

She smiled in agreement, a goddess in her glory. It was on the tip of his tongue to ask if she loved him. He didn't. Instead, he began rhythmically moving. She found following his movements awkward at first. Her hands fluttered as if she wasn't certain what to do with them. He placed them on his chest, one of her palms flat over his heart, and drove himself deeper.

There was part of Jemma that feared such unbridled wantonness. And another part, a newly discovered part, that hedonistically wallowed in it.

The need for release built inside of her, and she wasn't alone. Beneath her, Dane's face reflected a wide range of emotion. There was tenderness and hunger, urgency and desire.

He placed his hands on her waist and showed her how to move the way he liked. His breathing grew heavier. His soft words of praise and encouragement drove her in a way she'd never known before. His pleasure became hers.

Disappointments evaporated. Regrets faded from memory. All that mattered was this moment as together they strove, searching for the same pinnacle. Satisfaction lay within their grasp. Anything was possible. *Anything*.

Dane lunged up from the bed, taking her in his arms. "Jemma," he breathed. "Dear God, *Jemma*." She could feel the force of life leaving him. She threw her arms around his neck, hugging him close, and found her own release.

This time, it was even better than before.

She closed her eyes, her arms around him, and let her body savor every blessed, spiraling sensation. Dane too seemed lost in the intensity of their coupling.

For long, long moments, they held each other—and then he began laughing, quietly at first, and then full-throated, the sound joyful. His jaw was whiskery rough against her skin. "That was good, so damn good."

He took her face in his hands. His sharp eyes studied her, his thumbs lightly rubbing the corners of her mouth. She wondered what he was thinking.

"It's never been like that before," he said.

"No," she agreed. She'd never known how completely involving it could be. But then her woman's intuition told her it was not this way with every man. Only with Dane.

The words *I love you* were on the tip of her tongue, but she held them back.

They would sound trite now. Later, when their passions had cooled, maybe then she would have the courage to speak them.

And maybe he would believe them.

"Ah, Jemma," he said, as if he could read her mind. He put his arms around her waist. They sat facing each other, her legs still around his hips.

"Dane—" she started but stopped, words failing her. Instead, she placed her palm on his chest. His pulse had returned to normal. Gently, she kissed him.

He leaned his head against hers. "I know," he agreed. "I'm frightened, too."

His admission caught her off guard. She raised her gaze to his, but he shook his head. "Tomorrow, Jemma. Tonight, let's not ruin what we have."

His words were like a shot through her heart. She feared they did not bode well—and yet she was afraid to either challenge him or to reveal her own heart.

"Come," he said quietly. "It's time to sleep." He pulled back the bedsheets, and, like a child, she followed his lead and climbed into the bed beside him.

Jemma curled her body to fit his. For an instant, she was tempted to whisper *I love you*. She didn't speak the words aloud . . . or at least she thought she didn't.

Or perhaps it didn't matter that she confessed her heart. Snuggled against the safe haven of his body, she pushed all worries aside. His hand came down around her waist, cuddling her closer, and she fell into deep, exhausted sleep.

* * *

Jemma woke several hours later. The curtains were still drawn tight, and the candles were all burned out. However, she sensed it was morning.

Groggy as she was with the need for sleep, it took a moment for her memory to return, and when it did, she immediately rolled over on the bed to where Dane had been sleeping.

He was gone.

Abruptly, she sat up and looked around the room. "Dane?"

There was no answer. Nor was there a clock where she could look to see what time it was. What was left of the fire smoldered in the grate.

The dress she had worn last night was no longer on the floor by the desk. Her torn undergarments were gone, too.

Outside in the hallway, she heard a woman and a man arguing and knew that was what had woken her.

She raised the sheet up around her to cover her nakedness and pushed back her heavy hair from her face feeling very uncertain—and then she recognized her mother's voice.

The door came open with a bang.

Dane's valet spread himself in the doorway to bar her entrance into the room. "Madame, you will not enter!" he said.

"I most certainly will," came her mother's tart reply. She looked past the valet. "Jemma, call this man off."

Jemma burned with embarrassment from head to toe, but she did not cringe. Instead, she said, "Please, it's all right. Let her come in."

The valet appeared ready to argue but stepped aside. Her mother was wearing her Sunday best bonnet and dress. She gave the man a superior glare and walked into the room.

"Please, shut the door," Jemma said, not wishing anyone to be a witness to a difficult interview.

Her mother complied, her expression smug, and why not? Jemma had no doubt that her mother hadn't anticipated this turn of events. She wrapped herself in her pride.

"So, you did," her mother said. "I had feared the worst."

"The worst? Why, Mother? Was this not what you had expected?"

Her mother nodded, and then her expression of superiority changed to one of deep regret. She raised a distracted hand to her head, pushing her bonnet askew. "I had hoped, but it was all in vain."

"What do you mean?"

"He's duped us both, Jemma. Dane Pendleton met Cris this morning. They are fighting the duel."

Chapter 10

*J*emma had trouble wrapping her mind around her
mother's words. As if from a distance, she heard herself dumbly repeat, "Dane met Cris today?"

"Yes," her mother bit out.

"But he couldn't . . ." Jemma couldn't believe he would.
Not Dane. Not after what had transpired between them last
night.

Then again, what had happened? Had he actually promised to refuse to meet Cris? Or had she been so involved in
her own turbulent emotions that she had failed her brother?

"I suppose now we know you weren't so special to him."
Her mother's sharp sarcasm interrupted her thoughts.

Jemma doubled her hands into fists and squeezed tight. It
was either that or break down completely and behave like a
madwoman. She could have attacked her mother for her
callous words. Or herself, for being so gullible. Again!

When would she learn?

Once more she had been a pawn for her family. Worse,

she had believed Dane cared for her, that he had *some* feeling for her.

With blinding clarity, she realized that all she'd ever wanted in her life was to be loved. First, by her parents. She'd done everything they'd asked to please them—she'd even given up Dane and married Mosby.

And last night, she'd wanted to believe she could reclaim her lost opportunity with Dane, that he could love her again as he had once. Now she knew she couldn't. "He was right to meet Cris. I pray no harm came to my brother."

Her mother could not have been more surprised if Jemma had struck her. "He could kill Cris."

"Cris should learn not to issue challenges when he is in his cups." Jemma looked to her mother. "Could he stand this morning?" Of late, there had been too many mornings when he could not rouse himself until evening.

"His seconds got him up."

"Good. At least he met the challenge like a man." Jemma put her feet over the opposite side of the bed.

Behind her, her mother said in round tones, "I must say you are shocking me! Have you so little feeling for your family?"

Jemma closed her eyes against the burn of tears. With a strength she'd not known before, she rose from the bed, tucking the sheet around her, and faced her mother. "So *little* feeling?" Her voice trembled with the words. "Mother, I have given more than you can imagine." She choked back any other angry words. She had to get out of this house, to plan what they would all do next. Her first concern must be finding out if Cris survived without harm. She had no doubt Dane was safe. He had a clear head. But her poor brother . . .

"Help me find something to wear," Jemma ordered.

Her mother raised her eyebrows but wisely kept her mouth shut. Jemma moved toward the water closet. The separate room had been designed for luxury. The brass-and-wood tub was large enough to accommodate two people, and he had only the most modern conveniences.

"Oh, dear, he *has* done well for himself," her mother said. She was peering into the room over Jemma's shoulder.

Jemma faced her. "Find clothing. The armoire."

"You know, we may be able to salvage something from this," her mother said without moving. "We could accuse him of a breach of promise, or, if necessary, claim rape."

It was an unwise thing to say. The blinders were removed from Jemma's eyes: She now saw her mother as the world did, a grasping woman who wanted everything without offering anything. Her father had been the same way. Of course, with him, Jemma had blamed his drinking . . . but perhaps not. Perhaps they were just greedy people—all of them, herself and Cris included.

But she didn't have to be this way. She could take control of her own destiny. To not be afraid to be alone, and maybe then she could recover her lost dignity.

"I'm done, Mother. I will make no charges and do nothing that will harm him."

Her mother took a step closer. "If you don't, we are ruined. This is an opportunity, Jemma, we can't let it pass."

"How? By destroying my reputation?" Jemma shook her head. "I will not lie. I gave myself to him freely. I loved him, Mother. I was young and naïve, but I loved him." A feeling of overwhelming sadness threatened to engulf her. "Last night, for once, I followed my heart."

"Then continue to follow it." Her mother placed her hands on Jemma's shoulders.

"Are you suggesting I be his mistress?" Jemma asked, shocked.

"If you are discreet, no one will be the wiser," was the complacent reply.

Jemma couldn't speak. She was stunned. Worse, she was tempted. "No." The word rang out in the air.

Her mother's lips pursed as tight as a prune's—but at that moment, the door slowly opened. Dane was standing there. He leaned against the door frame, and she realized he may have been there for quite some time. He wore a bottle green jacket, buff leather breeches, and gleaming top boots. He could not have appeared more handsome.

Her joy in seeing him alive and unharmed was coupled with fear for her brother.

She took a step toward him. "Cris?"

"Is unharmed," he answered.

Jemma could have collapsed with relief.

"He won!" her mother said triumphantly.

"No," Dane answered, walking into the room. "He's more than a bit angry, but I believe when he completely sobers, he will agree with me. His seconds were satisfied with the turn of events, and they will talk sense into him. And now, madame, if you will excuse us, your daughter and I have something," he hesitated slightly before saying, "*important* to discuss."

Jemma's mother jumped right in. "Oh, no, anything you have to say can be said in front of me."

"Mother, leave."

Her mother turned to her. "I can't."

"You must," Jemma answered. "You aren't a part of this," she added softly. Nor would she let her mother interfere any longer.

For a second, she thought the woman would argue. Then, her mother smiled, a sly, secret smile, as if the two of them were conspirators . . . and Jemma wished she could disappear.

"I'll be outside the door," her mother promised, then left the room. Dane closed the door behind him, and they were alone.

Jemma had a hard time meeting his eye. Instead, she focused on the carved stone horse on his desk, and she remembered all too clearly the scene they'd played there. Heat brushed her cheeks. She tucked the edge of the sheet tighter around her chest. It fell down around her bare feet like a skirt with a long train.

Dane walked over to the bed and placed his arm around the footboard canopy post. She couldn't tell what he was thinking, save that he watched her with an intensity that was disconcerting.

She had to break the silence. "I need my clothes."

"My valet is pressing them."

"Thank you." She hated how stiff they sounded with each other, and yet with the dawn of day came common sense. "How did you manage to convince my brother to back off his challenge?"

"I refused to fight him."

Jemma wasn't certain she understood. "It was that simple?"

"Well, I had to have good cause."

"Which was?"

"I would not fight the man who would be my brother-in-law."

For a second, Jemma closed her eyes and let the words roll through her. They filled her with indescribable joy—and heartbreaking sorrow. Distraught, she raised a hand to her head, raking her fingers through her hair, and looked at him, tears in her eyes. "We can't."

Dane appeared to have been holding his breath. He frowned. "Can't what?"

"Marry." Dear God, the word was hard to say, and her heart broke even more.

Straightening, he shook his head. "What game do you play now?" he said, his voice tightening with disbelief. "I heard you last night, Jemma. I heard you say you love me. Why would you refuse me? Why again?"

So, she had spoken aloud. For a second she was tempted to run to him, to throw her arms around him and take back her words. But she couldn't. "I do love you," she answered. "I love you too much to saddle you with the likes of us."

His jaw hardened with determination. "It's you I want."

"But I come with my family. Dane, we would ruin you, and I can't leave them behind." She held up a hand to stave off his protest. "I know. I am protecting Cris . . . but you don't know how it was. When we were children, my brother and I were always there for each other. We protected each other. When Papa was at his worst . . ." She let her voice trail off. She'd never voiced what her life had been like. It had been an unspoken pact between her mother, her brother, and herself.

She continued, "Cris suffers from the same affliction. He's not as angry as Papa was, but it is slowly killing him. I must be there for him. And our debts . . . you can't even imagine."

"I spoke to Cris," Dane said. "I'm doing this right," he explained at her look of surprise. "I asked your brother for your hand. He was, um, worse for wear from last night's drink but reasonably in control of his senses, and we had a meeting of the minds. He knows he must change his ways or answer to me."

"I don't know if he can," she said honestly.

"He's given his word. Jemma, he promised to give up the bottle. Do you believe he will?"

Hope rose inside her. "Cris said that?" she demanded. At Dane's nod, she raised a hand heavenward. This time, she didn't fight back the tears. "I always prayed he would. I thought he *could*. It was just the weight of everything on his shoulders and the disappointments."

"He and I still need to have some discussion about his future, but I was impressed. Years ago, when you and I were together, I liked Cris. He was a good lad and, by all accounts, took his studies seriously in school. Today, I saw remnants of the person he had once been, and I'm willing to put trust in that man. As to the debts," Dane said, walking half the distance to her and stopping, "I believe I can afford you all now. Your mother will be put on a strict allowance, but I should be able to manage you."

The contradictory emotions of elation and alarm filled her. "Oh, Dane . . ." She crossed her arms against her chest. "You could do so much *better* than me."

He pretended surprise. "You are *that* extravagant?"

She shook her head, not knowing whether to laugh or cry. He offered her so much, and she deserved none of it. "No, I've learned how to squeeze a shilling over the last years," she admitted before adding with a touch of pride, "and I've grown up quite a bit."

"We both have." He dropped his hands to his side, his expression serious. "The only question I have, Jemma, is did you mean those words when you whispered you loved me last night?"

Suddenly, she realized how vulnerable he was, how defenseless they both were to being hurt again.

Jemma took her courage in her hands and said, "Yes." There, she'd done it. She had declared herself. "What of you, Dane?" she dared to ask. "Can you forgive me? Can you love me?"

"Jemma, I never stopped loving you."

She flew to him then. Ran right to him and threw her arms around him, the sheet falling between them. They kissed, but this one was different than all the rest. This kiss was full of the promise of the future.

"Then you'll have me?" he asked when they finally broke for breath.

"With all my heart," she answered.

And so she did. Sir Dane Pendleton and Jemma, Lady Mosby married three weeks later on the first of May . . . and no couple ever appeared happier . . . or so much in love.

CATHY MAXWELL *spends hours in front of her computer pondering the question, Why do people fall in love?–which remains for her the great mystery of life and the secret to happiness. She lives in beautiful Virginia.*

If Women Ruled the World . . .

Everyone knows that if women
ruled the world, it would be a better place!
And everyone also knows that in romance,
women do rule . . .
making the hero a better man.

Now read ahead to discover
how the heroines of the
Avon Romance Superleaders—
as created by Jacquie D'Alessandro,
Stephanie Bond, Samantha James, and,
as an added treat, the four stellar authors
of Avon's newest anthology collection—
tenderly, but most definitely, take matters
and men into their own hands . . .

If Women Ruled the World...
Sex would definitely be better

In Jacquie D'Alessandro's *Love and the Single Heiress* we discover what happens when a young woman anonymously—and scandalously—publishes her thoughts on love, marriage, and a woman's place in Regency society. Needless to say, the men are flummoxed . . . and one *particular* man is intrigued.

Today's Modern Woman should know that a gentleman hoping to entice her will employ one of two methods: either a straightforward, direct approach, or a more subtle, gentle wooing. Sadly, as with most matters, few gentlemen consider which method the lady might actually prefer—until it's too late.

A Ladies' Guide to the Pursuit of
Personal Happiness and Intimate Fulfillment

Tonight he would begin his subtle, gentle wooing.

Andrew Stanton stood in a shadowed corner of Lord Ravensly's elegant drawing room, feeling very much the way he imagined a soldier on the brink of battle might feel—anxious, focused, and very much praying for a hopeful outcome.

His gaze skimmed restlessly over the formally attired guests. Lavishly gowned and bejeweled ladies swirled around the dance floor in the arms of their perfectly turned-out escorts to the lilting strains of the string trio. But none of the waltzing ladies was the one he sought. Where was Lady Catherine?

His efforts to seek out Lady Catherine this evening had already been interrupted three times by people with whom he had no desire to speak. He feared one more such interruption would cause him to grind his teeth down to stubs.

Again he scanned the room, and his jaw tightened. Blast. After being forced to wait for what felt like an eternity finally to court her, why couldn't Lady Catherine— albeit unknowingly—at least soothe his anxiety by showing herself?

He reached up and tugged at his carefully tied cravat. "Damned uncomfortable neckwear," he muttered. Whoever had invented the constraining blight on fashion should be tossed in the Thames.

He drew a deep breath and forced himself to focus on the positive. His frustrating failure to locate Lady Catherine in the crowd *had* afforded him the opportunity to converse with numerous investors who had already committed funds to Andrew and Philip's museum venture. Lords Avenbury and Ferrymouth were eager to know how things were progressing, as were Lords Markingworth, Whitly, and Carweather, all of whom had invested funds. Mrs. Warrenfield appeared anxious to invest a healthy amount, as did Lord Kingsly. Lord Borthrasher who'd already made a sizable investment, seemed interested in investing more. After speaking with them, Andrew had also made some discreet inquiries regarding the matter he'd recently been commissioned to look into.

But with the business talk now completed, he'd retreated to this quiet corner to gather his thoughts, much as he did before preparing for a pugilistic bout at Gentleman Jackson's Emporium. His gaze continued to pan over the guests, halting abruptly when he caught sight of Lady Catherine, exiting from behind an Oriental silk screen near the French doors.

He stilled at the sight of her bronze gown. Every time he'd seen her during the past year, her widow's weeds had engulfed her like a dark, heavy rain cloud. Now officially out of mourning, she resembled a golden bronze sun setting over the Nile, gilding the landscape with slanting rays of warmth.

She paused to exchange a few words with a gentleman, and Andrew's avid gaze noted the way the vivid material of her gown contrasted with her pale shoulders and complemented her shiny chestnut curls gathered into a Grecian knot. The becoming coiffure left the vulnerable curve of her nape bare . . .

He blew out a long breath and raked his free hand through his hair. How many times had he imagined skimming his fingers, his mouth, over that soft, silky skin? More than he cared to admit. She was all things lovely and good. A perfect lady. Indeed, she was perfect in every way.

He knew damn well he wasn't good enough for her.

If Women Ruled the World...
Office relationships would be a whole lot easier

In Stephanie Bond's *Whole Lotta Trouble* three young editors are bound together when the smary creep they all dated is discovered . . . dead. Who could have done it? And, more important, how do they all get out of being the prime suspects?

Felicia Redmon dropped into her desk chair and sorted through her phone messages. Suze Dannon. Phil Dannon. Suze again, then Phil again. She sighed—the Dannons were determined to drive her and each other completely mad. Her bestselling husband-and-wife team had separated under nasty circumstances, but had agreed to finish one last book together. Unfortunately, Felicia soon found herself in the middle of not only their editorial squabbles, but also their personal disagreements. Playing referee was wearing her nerves thin, but sometimes an editor has to go beyond the call of duty to make sure the book gets in on time. Still, she was afraid that if the Dannons didn't soon find a way to put aside their differences, the hostile couple, known for their sensual murder mysteries, were going to wind up killing each other.

There was a message from her doctor's office—an appointment reminder, no doubt—and one from Tallie, who probably wanted to firm plans for getting together at their regular hangout. And Jerry Key had called. Her heart jerked a little, just like every time she heard the bastard's name.

She should have known better than to get involved with a man with whom she would also have to do business, but literary agent Jerry Key had a way of making a woman forget little things . . . like consequences. He was probably calling on behalf of the Dannons, who were his clients. And whatever was wrong would definitely be her fault.

Might as well get it over with, she decided, and dialed Jerry's number—by memory, how pathetic.

"Jerry Key's office, this is Lori."

Felicia cringed at Lori's nasally tone. "Hi, Lori. This is Felicia Redmon at Omega Publishing, returning Jerry's call."

"Hold, please."

Felicia cursed herself for her accelerated pulse. A year was long enough to get over someone, especially someone as smarmy as Jerry had turned out to be.

The phone clicked. "Felicia," he said, his tongue rolling the last two vowels. "How are you?"

She pursed her mouth. "What's up, Jerry?"

"What, you don't have time for small talk anymore?"

Remembering the impending auction of one of his clients' books that she'd be participating in, Felicia bit her tongue. "Sorry, it's been a long day. How've you been?"

"Never better," he said smoothly. "Except when we were together."

She closed her eyes. "Jerry, don't."

"Funny, I believe that's the first time you've ever said 'don't.' "

Her tongue tingled with raw words, but she reminded herself that she was to blame for the predicament she'd gotten herself into. The bottom line was that Jerry Key represented enough big-name authors—some of them tied to Omega Publishing—that she had to play nice, no matter how much it killed her.

"Jerry, I'm late for a meeting, so I really can't chat. What did you need?"

He sighed dramatically. "Sweetheart, we have a problem. The Dannons are upset."

"Both of them?"

"Suze in particular. She said that you're siding with Phil on all the manuscript changes."

"Phil is the plotter, Suze is the writer; it's always been that way. Suze never had a problem with Phil's changes before."

"Suze said he's changing things just for the sake of changing them, to make more work for her."

"Have you spoken with Phil?" Felicia asked.

"Yes, and I believe his exact words were 'You bet your ass I am.' "

She rolled her eyes. "Jerry, the last time I checked, you represented both Suze *and* Phil."

"Yes, but editorial disputes are your responsibility, Felicia, and I rely on you to be fair."

She frowned. "I *am* fair."

"Then you need to be firm. Being assertive isn't your strong suit."

Anger bolted through her. "That's not true." She only had a problem being assertive with Jerry—he had a way of making her feel defensive and defenseless at the same time. "Don't turn this around, Jerry—you know that the Dannons are both hypersensitive right now."

"Which is why, Felicia, it would behoove both of us if the Dannons find a way to patch things up and forget about this divorce nonsense."

"And you're telling me this because?"

"Because I think you should find a way to make this project more enjoyable, to make them realize how good they are together."

She summoned strength. "Jerry, I'm not a marriage counselor."

"But you're a woman."

A small part of her was flattered he remembered, but she managed to inject a bite into her tone. "What does *that* mean?"

"It means that . . . you know, you're all wrapped up in the fantasy of marital bliss. If I tried to talk to the Dannons about staying together, they'd know I was bullshitting them for the sake of money."

"Isn't that what I'd be doing?" she asked.

"No, you actually believe in all that happily-ever-after crap."

Felicia set her jaw—it wasn't enough that the man had broken her heart, but he had to reduce her hopes for the future to the lyrics of a bad love song.

Much Ado About Twelfth Night
by Liz Carlyle

*I*n fair weather, the vast estate of Sheriden Park lay but a half day's journey from Hampshire, and this particular day was very fair indeed. Still, the cerulean sky and warm weather did little to calm Sophie's unease. Seated beside Aunt Euphemia, she found her apprehension grew with every passing mile, until their coach was rolling beneath the arched gatehouse and up the rutted carriage drive. And suddenly the stunning sight of Sheriden Park burst into view, snatching Sophie's breath away.

Despite the rumors of ruination, the sprawling brick mansion seemed outwardly unchanged. Row upon row of massive windows glittered in every wing, and already the door was flung wide in greeting. Sophie saw Edward long before they reached the house. He would have been unmistakable, even in a crowded room. But he stood alone on the bottom step like some golden god, his shoulders rigidly back, his eyes hardened against the sun. Sophie's heart leaped into her throat.

A footman hastened forward to put down the steps. "Get out first, Will," instructed Euphemia, prodding at his ankle with her walking stick. "Go 'round and tell Edward's servants to have a care with my hat boxes. I'll not have any broken feathers, do you hear?"

"Yes, ma'am." Will leaped down.

At once, the new marquess took his hand. "Good afternoon, Weyburn," said Edward, using her brother's title. He gave Will a confident handshake, but strangely, his eyes remained on Sophie.

Will turned away to greet Sir Oliver Addison. In the carriage door, Sophie froze. Edward was staring up at her, his gaze dark, and his jaw hard, as if newly chiseled from stone. Well, he did not look quite the same after all, did he? He seemed taller, broader—and anything but glad to see her.

A Fool Again
by Eloisa James

A well-bred lady never ogles a man from behind her black veil, especially during her husband's burial. But Lady Genevieve Mulcaster had acknowledged her failings in ladylike deportment around the time she eloped to Gretna Green with a bridegroom whom she'd met three hours earlier, and so she watched Lucius Felton with rapt attention throughout Reverend Pooley's praise of her deceased husband—a man (said Mr. Pooley) who rose before his servants and even for religious haste went unbuttoned to morning prayer. Felton looked slightly bored. There was something about his heavy-lidded eyes that made Genevieve feel thirsty, and the way he stood, almost insolently elegant in his black coat, made her feel weak in the knees. His shoulders had to be twice as large as her husband's had been.

Recalled to her surroundings by that disloyal thought, Genevieve murmured a fervent, if brief, prayer that heaven would be just as her husband imagined it. Because if Erasmus didn't encounter the rigorous system of prizes and punishments he anticipated, he would likely be discomfited, if not sent to sizzle his toes. Genevieve had long ago realized that Erasmus wouldn't hesitate to rob a bishop if an amenable vicar could be persuaded to bless the undertaking. She threw in an extra prayer for St. Peter, in the event that Erasmus was disappointed.

Then she peeked at Felton again. His hair slid sleekly back from his forehead, giving him an air of sophistication and command that Genevieve had never achieved. How could she, wearing clothes with all the elegance of a dishcloth? The vicar launched into a final prayer for Erasmus's soul. Genevieve stared down at her prayer book. It was hard to believe that she had lost *another* husband. Not that she actually got as far as marrying Tobias Darby. They were only engaged, if one could even call it that, for the six or seven hours they spent on the road to Gretna Green before being overtaken by her enraged father. She never saw Tobias again; within a fortnight she was married to Erasmus Mulcaster. So eloping with Tobias was the first and only reckless action of Genevieve's life. In retrospect, it would be comforting to blame champagne, but the truth was yet more foolish: She'd been smitten by an untamed boy and his beautiful eyes. For that she'd thrown over the precepts of a lifetime and run laughing from her father's house into a carriage headed for Gretna Green.

Memories tumbled through her head: the way Tobias looked at her when they climbed into the carriage, the way she found herself flat on the seat within a few seconds of the coachman geeing up the horses, the way his hands ran up her leg while she faintly—oh so faintly—objected. 'Twas an altogether different proposition when Erasmus stiffly climbed into the marital bed. Poor Erasmus. He didn't marry until sixty-eight, considering women unnecessarily extravagant, and then he couldn't seem to manage the connubial act. Whereas Tobias—she wrenched her mind away. Even *she*, unladylike though she was, couldn't desecrate Erasmus's funeral with that sort of memory.

She opened her eyes to the breathy condolences of Lord Bubble. "I am distressed beyond words, my lady, to witness your grief at Lord Mulcaster's passing," he said, standing far too close to her. Bubble was a jovial, white-haired gentleman who used to gently deplore Erasmus's business dealings, even as he profited wildly from them. Genevieve found him as practiced a hypocrite as her late husband, although slightly more concerned for appearances.

"I trust you will return to Mulcaster House for some refreshments, Lord Bubble?" Since no one from the parish other than Erasmus's two partners, his lawyer, and herself had attended the funeral, they could have a veritable feast of seed cakes.

Bubble nodded, heaving a dolorous sigh. "Few men as praiseworthy as Erasmus have lived in our time. We must condole each other on this lamentable occasion."

A sardonic gleam in Felton's eyes suggested that *he* didn't consider Erasmus's death the stuff of tragedy. But then, Genevieve had studied Felton surreptitiously for the past six months, and he often looked sardonic. At the moment he was also looking faintly amused. Surely he hadn't guessed that she had an affection for him? Genevieve felt herself growing pink. Had she peered at him once too often? *Think like a widow*, she admonished herself, climbing into the crape-hung carriage.

Nightingale
by Cathy Maxwell

A soft rap sounded on the door.

"What is it?" he said, his voice harsh. He wanted to be alone. He *needed* to be alone. Tomorrow, he was going to run Whiting through, and then . . . *what?* The word haunted him.

"There is someone here to see you, sir," the footman's voice said from the other side.

At this hour? "Who the bloody hell is it?" Dane demanded. He went ahead and poured himself another whiskey. To the devil with temperance or being a gentleman. Tonight was for exorcisms, although the whiskey didn't seem to be having any effect. He was feeling everything too sharply. He lifted his glass.

"I'm sorry, Sir Dane, I don't have her name," the footman answered. "She refused to tell me or give me her card but asked to see you on the most urgent of business. I let her in because she is obviously a Lady of Quality."

A Lady of Quality? Out and alone at this hour of the night?

Curious, Dane set down the glass without drinking. "Send her up."

There was silence at the door as the footman went to do Dane's bidding. Dane sat quiet. Who would be coming to see him at this hour? It couldn't be a mistress. He had the last—what was her name? Something French. Always something French . . . although none of them had been French any more than he was. *Danielle*. He had signed Danielle off three months ago and had not had the energy or interest in searching for another.

In fact, for the past year, since he'd returned to London, he had been weighed down by a sense of tedium coupled with a restless irritation over the everyday matters of his life. He'd been going through the motions of living without any clear purpose or desire.

Perhaps he should let Whiting run *him* through?

The idea had appeal. Dane picked up the glass and drained it of the precious amber liquid.

The footman rapped on the door to signal he had returned with this uninvited guest. Dane pushed both the will and his whiskey glass aside before calling out, "Enter."

The door opened slowly and the footman, dressed in blue and gold livery with a powdered wig on his head, stepped into the room. "Sir Dane, your guest."

He moved back. There was a moment's pause, a space of time, three ticks of the clock, and then the woman walked into the room—and Dane stopped breathing.

Before him stood Jemma Carson, the widowed Lady Mosby, looking more beautiful than ever.

The Trouble With Charlotte
by Victoria Alexander

"*B*loody hell." Hugh Robb, formerly Captain Robb and now, thanks to his resurrection, Lord Tremont, stared at the figure of his wife in a crumpled heap on the floor. "She dropped like a stone."

"Not unexpected under the circumstances." A man Hugh had scarcely noticed upon entering the room moved toward Char, then hesitated. "We should probably, or rather, one of us should—"

"Probably." Although Char certainly wasn't going anywhere and it might well be best first to know exactly who his competition was. "And you are?"

"Pennington. The Earl of Pennington." The man— Pennington—stared. "You're Captain Robb, aren't you? Charlotte's husband. Charlotte's *dead* husband."

"Indeed, I am the husband." Hugh narrowed his eyes. "And are you her—"

"No!" Pennington paused. "At least not yet."

"Good." Hugh nodded with a surprising amount of relief.

He bent beside his wife and gathered her into his arms, ignoring the flood of emotion that washed through him at the feel of holding her again. The last thing he needed was to have Char's affections engaged right now. Not that it mattered. From the moment he'd decided to return home, he had vowed not to consider anything she might have done while believing him dead to be of any importance whatsoever.

"You might put her down now," Pennington said firmly.

"Of course," Hugh murmured.

He deposited Char carefully on a sofa and knelt beside her. In repose, she was peaceful and serene but she'd al-

ways had an air of restlessness about her. It had drawn
them together and led them along the edge of scandal.
And they had reveled in it. She'd been only eighteen
when they'd wed and he a bare two years older. Neither
had known anything of life save fun and excitement and
high, heady passion.

Had she changed? He was certainly not the same man
who had stalked out that very door seven long years ago.
He had left a selfish, stupid boy and returned as . . . what?
A man at long last willing, even eager, to live up to the responsibilities of his life? Dear God, he prayed he had indeed become man enough to do so. And prayed as well he
had not lost his wife in the process.

Her long, lush lashes flickered and her eyes opened,
caught sight of him, and widened.

"Char?"

Char's gaze searched his face as if she were trying to
determine if he was real or nothing more than a dream.
Slowly, she raised her hand to his face and rested it upon
his cheek. Her dark eyes met his and he read wonder and
awe and . . . fury.

She cracked her hand hard across his face.

The sound reverberated in his head and around the
room, and he jerked back on his knees. Even Pennington
winced.

"You're alive!" She stared in shock and disbelief and
struggled to sit up.

"Indeed I am." Hugh rubbed his cheek gingerly. "You
do not appear quite as pleased as I thought you'd be."

"You thought I'd be pleased? Pleased? Hah!" She
scrambled off the sofa and moved away from him as if to
keep a safe distance between them. "How—"

"It's a very long story." Hugh searched for the right
words. "Some of it is confusing and some rather unpleas-

ant and"—he drew a deep breath—"much, if not all of it, is my fault."

"*That* was never in question." She shook her head. "This is impossible. You simply cannot be here looking so . . . *alive!*" Char turned on her heel and paced. "You must be nothing more than a dream—"

"A good dream?" A hopeful note sounded in Hugh's voice.

"Hardly," she muttered. "Marcus, is there a man standing in this very room looking suspiciously like my husband? My *dead* husband?"

Pennington nodded reluctantly. "I'm afraid so, Charlotte."

"I am flesh and blood, Char." Hugh stepped closer. "Touch me."

She stared at him for a moment, then once again smacked her hand across his face.

"Yow!" Hugh clapped his hand to his cheek and glared. "Bloody hell, Char, why did you do that?"

Char stared at her reddened palm. "That hurt."

Hugh rubbed his cheek. "Damned right, it hurt."

"The first time I scarcely felt it," she murmured. Her gaze shifted from her hand to Hugh's face. "You really are alive. Real."

"I daresay there were better ways to prove it," Hugh muttered, then drew a deep breath. "However, you may slap me again if you need additional proof."

"Thank you, but no." She shook her head slowly. "I do appreciate the offer and I should like to reserve the right to smack you again should I need to do so."

If Women Ruled the World...

There'd be a whole lot less gambling.
And houses would be cleaner too.

In Samantha James's *A Perfect Groom* we discover what happens when a young man believes he can seduce anyone . . . and puts his money where his ego is. But when he's given the challenge of enticing the one known as "The Unattainable" he knows he's in big trouble . . .

A pleasant haze had begun to surround Justin, for he was well into his third glass of port. Nonetheless, his smile was rather tight. "Don't bother baiting me, Gideon," he said amicably.

Gideon gestured toward the group still gathered around the betting book. "Then why aren't you leading the way?"

Justin was abruptly irritated. "She sounds positively ghastly, for one. For another, no doubt she's a paragon of virtue—"

"Ah, without question! Did I not mention she's the daughter of a vicar?"

Justin's mind stirred. A vicar's daughter . . . hair the color of flame. Once again, it put him in mind of . . . but no. He dismissed the notion immediately. That could never be.

"I am many things, but I am not a ravisher of innocent females." He leveled on Gideon his most condescending stare, the one that had set many a man to quailing in his boots.

On Gideon, it had no such effect. Instead he erupted into laughter. "Forgive me, but I know in truth you are a ravisher of *all* things female."

"I detest redheads," Justin pronounced flatly. "And I have a distinct aversion to virgins."

"What, do you mean to say you've never had a virgin?"

"I don't believe I have," Justin countered smoothly. "You know my tastes run to sophisticates—in particular, pale, delicate blondes."

"Do you doubt your abilities? A woman such as The Unattainable shall require a gentle wooing. Just think, a virgin, to make and mold as you please." Gideon gave an exaggerated sigh. "Or perhaps, old man, you are afraid your much-touted charm is waning?"

Justin merely offered a faint smile. They both knew otherwise.

Gideon leaned forward. "I can see you require more persuasion. No doubt to you Bentley's three thousand is a paltry sum. So what say we make this more interesting?"

Justin's eyes narrowed. "What do you have in mind?"

Gideon's gaze never left his. "I propose we double the stakes, a wager between the two of us. A private wager between friends, if you will." He smiled. "I've often wondered . . . what woman can resist the man touted as the handsomest in all England? Does she exist? Six thousand pounds says she does. Six thousand pounds says that woman is The Unattainable."

Justin said nothing. To cold-bloodedly seduce a virgin, to callously make her fall in love with him so that he could . . .

God. That he could even consider it spoke to his character—or lack thereof. Indeed, it only proved what he'd always known . . .

He was beyond redemption.

He was wicked, and despite Sebastian's protestations otherwise, he knew he'd never change.

"Six thousand pounds," Gideon added very deliberately. "And worth every penny, I'll warrant. But there's one condition."

"And what is that?"

"She must be yours within the month."

A smile dallied about Justin's lips. "And what proof shall you require?"

Gideon chucked. "Oh, I daresay I shall know when and if the chit falls for you."

He was drunk, Justin decided hazily, perhaps as drunk as that fool Bentley, or he wouldn't even give the idea a second thought.

But he was a man who could resist neither a dare nor a challenge—and Gideon knew it.

There had been many women in his life, Justin reflected blackly. Having reached the age of nine-and-twenty, thus far no woman had ever captured his interest for more than a matter of weeks. He was like his mother in that regard. In all truth, what was one more?

And if everything that had been said about The Unattainable was true . . . If nothing else, it might prove an amusing dalliance.

He met Gideon's keen stare. "You're aware," he murmured, "that I rarely make a wager unless I stand to win."

"What a boast! And yet I think perhaps it will be *you* paying me. Remember, you've the rest of the horde to fend off." Gideon gestured to Brentwood and McElroy.

Justin pushed back his chair and got to his feet. "Something tells me," he drawled with a lazy smile, "that you know where this beacon of beauty can be found."

Gideon's eyes gleamed. "I believe that would be the Farthingale ball."